PRAISE FOR

NYXIA

"A high-octane thriller. . . . *Nyxia* grabs you from
the first line and never lets go." —Marie Lu,
#1 *New York Times* bestselling author

"Brilliant concept meets stellar execution
in this fast-paced deep-space adventure. I was
hooked from page one." —Victoria Schwab,
#1 *New York Times* bestselling author

"We've got our Katniss and Tris and Ender
and Thomas and all the other teens that kick a lot
of ass in pursuit of a goal . . . and now we have
Emmett." —Nic Stone, *New York Times*
bestselling author of *Dear Martin*

"Impossible to forget. Impossible to put
down. This wonderfully diverse epic is an utterly
thrilling binge-worthy treat." —Jay Coles,
author of *Tyler Johnson Was Here*

"*The 100* meets *Illuminae* in this
high-octane sci-fi thriller." —*Bustle*

"Fans of the Hunger Games and the Maze Runner
series will enjoy this series opener." —*SLJ*

"Both curious and suspicious at every turn, [Emmett] is an ideal narrator, and a sequel can't come soon enough." —*The Bulletin*

"Emmett's self-deprecation, wit, and ability to see the good in others will keep readers riveted and eager for the next volume in this planned trilogy." —*PW*

"Nyxia seems to have a mind of its own, but its mystery will carry over into the sequel, which cannot come soon enough." —*VOYA*

"An engrossing premise that explodes to life in Reintgen's imaginative debut. Highly recommended!" —Jason M. Hough, *New York Times* bestselling author of the Dire Earth Cycle

"Sleek, fast, and action-packed, this is a thrilling new take on space adventure. I got to the end and instantly wanted more." —Stefan Bachmann, author of the internationally acclaimed *The Peculiar*

"With a vivid cast of characters, relentless pacing, and layers of mystery, Reintgen hits all the right buttons to craft an addictive page-turner." —Fonda Lee, author of *Zeroboxer* and *Exo*

NYXIA

SCOTT REINTGEN

EMBER

Text copyright © 2017 by Scott Reintgen
Cover art copyright © 2017 by Heiko Klug

All rights reserved. Published in the United States by Ember, an imprint of Random House Children's Books, a division of Penguin Random House LLC, New York. Originally published in hardcover in the United States by Crown Books for Young Readers, New York, in 2017.

Ember and the E colophon are registered trademarks of Penguin Random House LLC.

Visit us on the Web! GetUnderlined.com

Educators and librarians, for a variety of teaching tools, visit us at RHTeachersLibrarians.com

The Library of Congress has cataloged the hardcover edition of this work as follows:
Names: Reintgen, Scott, author.
Title: Nyxia / Scott Reintgen.
Description: First edition. | New York: Crown, [2017]
Summary: Emmett accepts an interstellar space contract but learns en route that to win the promised fortune he and nine other recruits face a brutal competition, putting their very humanity at risk.
Identifiers: LCCN 2016038590 | ISBN 978-0-399-55679-1 (hc) | ISBN 978-0-399-55680-7 (glb) | ISBN 978-0-399-55681-4 (ebook)
Subjects: CYAC: Conduct of life—Fiction. | Competition (Psychology)—Fiction. | Interplanetary voyages—Fiction. | Science fiction.
Classification: LCC PZ7.1.R4554 Nyx 2017 | DDC [Fic]—dc23

ISBN 978-0-399-55682-1 (pbk.)

Printed in the United States of America
10 9 8 7 6 5 4 3 2
First Ember Edition 2018

Random House Children's Books supports the First Amendment and celebrates the right to read.

For my wife, Katie.

I hope all the sequels we write have your smile.

PART I

BROKEN THINGS

DAY 1, 8:47 A.M.
Aboard *Genesis 11*

"You all know why you're here."

There are ten of us at the table. We all nod like we even have a clue.

Eight of the richest men and women in the world stand at the opposite end of the conference room. Last night, I used PJ's phone to look them up. Babel Communications. Swallowed Google back in 2036. Some blogger says they're NASA's dark little shadow and have been for decades. Whatever they do, they look good doing it. Each of them wears the same charcoal suit. It looks like someone threaded smoke into formal wear. The overheads dance off all the polished shoulders and shoes.

But the lights and the room and the world are bending forward to hear the man who's speaking: Marcus Defoe. He's black, but not like me. I've spent half my life feeling like an absence, a moonless night. I can't imagine this guy going anywhere without turning heads. Everything about him whispers *king*. It's in the set of his shoulders and the sound of his voice and the quiet power of his walk. He glides toward us, and a series of warning signs flash through my head. One glance is enough to know he's the most dangerous man in the room.

Leaning back, I pull one of my earbuds out. My music was playing low-key but the Asian kid next to me keeps looking over like it's the loudest thing he's ever heard. Tough luck. I leave the volume up just to grind at him. When Babel recruited me, they said all of this was a game. I like playing games, but I like *winning* games even more. The stiff next to me shakes his head in annoyance, and I already feel like I'm up a few points on him.

The earpiece bleeds half beats and old-soul voices. People at school think I like early hip-hop 'cause it's vintage, but the truth is I could never afford the new stuff. When my neighbor glances over for the thousandth time, I nod and smile like we're going to be best friends.

"You were chosen to be at the forefront of the most serious space exploration known to mankind. The results of your mission will change the outlook for our species." Defoe goes on to talk about humanity, manifest destiny, and final frontiers. His head is shaved and perfectly round. His smile is blinding. His eyes are so stunningly blue that the girls at school would call them the color of boom. Babel's king has a single imperfection: His right hand is withered, like a giant took its sweet time breaking each and every bone. It's the kind of injury you're not supposed to look at, but always do. "The reward for your efforts will be beyond your imagination. A trust fund has already been established for each of you. A check for fifty thousand dollars will be put into your account every month for the rest of your lives."

Everyone at the table perks up. Straighter shoulders, wider eyes, less fidgeting. We all react to the numbers because we all must be dead-dancin' broke. Except one kid.

He looks bored. King Solomon just tossed us the keys to the kingdom, and he's hiding yawns? I take a closer look. He's white. I fact-check the table and realize he's the only white boy here. American? Maybe. Could be European. He's sporting a plain three-button shirt. He drums his fingers distractedly on the table, and I spot a tag under one armpit. So the shirt's a recent purchase. His hair looks deliberately imperfect, like he wanted to seem more down-to-earth. When he glances my way, I set both eyes back on Defoe again.

"Beyond monetary stability, we are also offering our medical plans for your families. They now have free access to health care, counseling, surgery, and the *most* advanced treatments for cancer and other terminal diseases. Those services come without a price tag, and they're offered in perpetuity."

I don't know what *perpetuity* means, but some of the kids around the table are nodding wisely. Two of them flinched at the word *cancer*. One's a girl with blond hair, blue eyes, and enough makeup to place in a pageant. I spy a strand of pink-dyed hair tucked behind one ear. The other kid is really tan with bright brown eyes. Middle Eastern's my guess. I wonder if their parents have cancer. I wonder if that's how Babel roped them into this monkey-in-space routine. I wonder if they noticed me flinch right around the same time they did.

It's hard to hear the words that follow, because an image of Moms has snagged my attention. Those bird-thin wrists circled by medical bracelets. We spent enough time in the ICU that the hospital started feeling like a prison. Only difference is that some diseases don't grant parole.

". . . we offer stock options with our company, internal connections with any business in the world, and an opportunity to put your name in the history of the human race. Desmond is passing out a gag order. If you're still interested, just sign on the dotted line."

One of the lesser suits makes the rounds. He sets hot-off-the-presses forms in front of each of us. I can't stop staring at the massive gold watch on his wrist. In less-promising circumstances, I'd whoops my way out of my chair, slip it off his wrist, and stranger my way out of the room before he knew which way was west. But life is good, so I carefully skim a paragraph with words like *privatization* and *extrajudicial.* On my left, the Asian kid considers a strange gathering of symbols. The girl on my right's reading something that looks a little beyond the reach of my high school Spanish. I almost laugh, thinking we're the politically correct version of the *Justice Squad.* But if Babel's looking for heroes, they picked the wrong guy.

I sign on the dotted line and try to look like I didn't just win the lottery.

The suits whisper million-dollar secrets. Defoe prowls a casual, predatory circle to make sure we're all being good little boys and girls. I hit next on my shuffle and a nice unfiltered beat drops. Two voices duet their way to a bare-bones chorus. They trade lyrics until it feels like I'm back in the concrete jungle, ciphering and laughing with the Most Excellent Brothers.

I miss the boys already, especially PJ. Our neighbor-hood's pretty full of dead ends, though, and Babel's offering a way out. I don't know what their offer means to the other kids around the table, but to me it means Moms getting her name at the top of the transplant lists. It means Pops not working night shifts. It means three meals a day and more than one pair of jeans.

To me, this is everything.

One of the girls is the last to sign. As PJ would say, she's more than cute. Taller than me, with her hair buzzed. She's so slender her collarbones have collarbones. Her dark skin makes the woven cords bunched around one wrist look like the bright feathers of a bird. Metal coins dangle and dance from the bracelet, catching the light before scattering it. The thing looks ancient, some kind of African charm. We all watch as she makes an edit to her form. Defoe considers it. His smile is all teeth. He nods and she signs and we're set.

"Very good. Now, as we describe your mission, you are welcome to leave at any point, but the gag order you've signed is something that we are deathly serious about."

Defoe pauses to emphasize his choice of adverb. *Deathly.* Snitches are nothing new, nor the consequences for being one. But a quick glance shows that not all the kids around the table can see the writing on the wall. Translation: Walk-ing away isn't an option.

He continues: "If you speak about this to anyone, you

will find your hands tied legally for the rest of your life. Is that understood?"

Everyone nods. For the first time, I realize Defoe's whole speech has been in English. Definitely my preference, but how are the other kids understanding him? Do they all speak English too? A second glance around the room has me feeling certain they've flown this crew in from every corner of the world. Maybe they've got English-speaking schools in most places these days, but the idea feels like a stretch.

A black glass screen glides up behind Defoe. The other suits scatter, and digital imaging flickers to life. The crazy part is I don't hear a thing. No cooling fans, no grinding gears, no swishing panels. A seventy-inch screen loads images with flawless resolution.

Defoe is flashing teeth again. The other suits look giddy. They've been waiting to reveal this. To us.

"Babel Communications discovered a habitable planet sixty-three years ago." An Earth lookalike appears behind him. "Eden. Our relationship with the planet has been a determined one. We thought life on Eden was possible. Now we know with certainty. The planet does sustain human life." The screen displays distances, star navigation, and planetary readouts. It's all gibberish to me. "Even with our vast technological advancements, the original journey to Eden took twenty-seven years."

Defoe lets that sink in. Twenty-seven years. We all do the math, and we all look a little pissed off as we solve for x. None of us signed up to grow old in space. I know I didn't.

"Of course, that journey now takes us less than a year."

We all let out held breath. Less than a year. Defoe's clearly having fun with us. The suits flash their thousand-dollar smiles at his clever joke. I start to understand who they are, how they see us. I file it away under *A* for *Anger*.

"The Tower Space Station is already orbiting Eden. We will rendezvous there before sending you to the surface. The planet is populated by a species called the Adamites."

Habitable planets. Aliens. Right. Our generation watched the Mars landings. We've seen NASA's recruiting posters all over our high schools. But there's never been a whisper of other life-forms. It's hard to imagine that a secret this big could spend three decades in the dark. As far as I knew, three decades ago we were puddle-jumping around the moon. Babel's asking us to bridge a gap between the history books and their revelations that feels impossible.

We watch as the screen divides into a series of images. We see humanoids in a vast, primitive landscape. They're shorter and stockier than your average human. Their eyes look wider and fuller. Defoe smiles triumphantly, but I've seen way better Photo Factories online.

"Naturally, we've had a few encounters with the species."

Defoe presses an invisible button, and a video wide-screens. We have a zoomed-out shot of mostly military types, some scientists. They're sporting high-tech gear, including *KillCall*-style assault rifles. We watch the negotiations go wrong. Very wrong. Shadows stretch and obscure the so-called Adamites. Shots are fired, but in the chaos and smoke every soldier ends up dead or dismembered. The Adamites spare only one of the interlopers. A girl, maybe seven or eight.

Defoe hits pause. "Jacquelyn Requin. She was born on the first flight to Eden. Our satellites indicate she's still alive. Why? The Adamites revere children and young people. They kept her alive because she represents something lost to them. Currently, the youngest member in their society is twenty-one years old. While they are a long-lived species, it appears they are unable to reproduce now. As such, they adore and treasure children. It is that adoration that has provided us the opportunity for this endeavor."

He reaches in his pocket and pulls out a marble. It's pitch-black, shades darker than the thumb and forefinger he has it pinched between.

"Meet nyxia."

With a quick manipulation, the substance stretches. Defoe's hands dance. After a moment, he holds it up. A black-bladed dagger. He allows us all a good look at the knife, flips his grip, and throws it at a target to his right. It buries itself up to the hilt. Not a bad trick, but he's not done. With another hand motion, he draws the substance back across the room into his palm. He holds the marble up for us to see. Not a bad trick at all.

"Babel Communications has found a number of ways to use the substance. It has secretly become the most valuable resource in the world. Our mission is to harvest as much of this material as possible. Can anyone guess where one might find vast deposits of nyxia?"

Eden, we all think. All right, Defoe, you have our attention. A touch from his thumb replaces the video with a digitally scanned map of the planet. We see areas marked in red. Black dots nest along ridges and next to river basins in unpredictable patterns. Defoe explains.

"Each black dot represents an underground mine of nyxia. Speaking logistically, each of those black dots is worth somewhere in the realm of fifty billion dollars."

My disgruntled neighbor lets out a whistle. We finally agree on something: that's a boatload of money. And there are a lot of dots. I haven't forgotten the dead space marines, though, or their amputated limbs.

A brown-eyed boy to my right calls out a question in another language.

Defoe nods. "The red areas indicate locations that the Adamites have established as off-limits to us. No one from Babel Communications has set foot in any of those regions."

As expansive as the black dots are, they're overshadowed by the red areas. In fact, there's a single circle of accessible land at the lower end of the map, and I don't see a black dot for several kilometers. Defoe asks the billion-dollar question for us:

"So, how do we retrieve nyxia from mines protected by a species with superior technology and an aggressive approach to border disputes?"

Exactly, I think. How can we help? And why risk our lives to do it?

Defoe answers his own question cryptically. "Truly, I say to you, unless you turn and become like children, you will never enter the kingdom of heaven."

The girl with all the makeup adds her southern accent to the conversation. "That's from the Bible, isn't it?"

Defoe nods. "Yes, it is. Your age will protect you. Our journey will give us ample opportunity to train you in safely extracting nyxia from the mines you enter. We will set quotas for each of you. Meeting those quotas will gain you the monetary rewards promised earlier."

The Asian kid next to me objects. Defoe listens patiently before replying.

"Longwei has asked about the risks. He's worried about being killed and not receiving his reward. Not only do we have a confirmed occurrence where they demonstrated a clear precedent for protection of young people, but two months ago we made an agreement with the Adamites. Those of you that set foot on Eden will be permitted to come and go wherever you like. You will be their welcome guests."

"So we just collect this nyxia stuff?" the southern girl asks.

"Precisely, Jasmine. The more the merrier." A quick glance at his partners shows they have one more reveal. Defoe straightens his already-straight shoulders. "You may have noticed that there are ten of you here. At Babel Communications, we find competition to be valuable. Iron sharpens iron and all that. There are ten of you, but we will only be taking eight to Eden."

Real fear is always quiet. All of a sudden, we're statues. Not a breath, except from the white kid. He cracks a knuckle and reclines in his chair. He's not like us. I don't know how I know, but I do. The rest of the group waits for Defoe to say he's just kidding, but of course he's not. A heavyset Asian kid at the end of the table makes a snarky comment. Whatever the joke is, Defoe doesn't find it funny.

"Katsu wants to know what will happen to the other two," Defoe explains. "Our yearlong flight will be a competition of sorts. Every test you perform will be measured. Every task we set you to will be analyzed. From the moment we enter space, you will be under a microscope. Rankings will be posted throughout the ship. Only eight of you will be permitted to travel to Eden upon arrival. Those eight will receive the beneficial packages we've discussed."

More silence. Hearts are breaking.

"The other two will still receive a smaller monetary sum. The average salary for a Babel Communications employee is right around one hundred and fifty thousand dollars. You'll be paid for two years of service and sent back to your home. The other benefits won't be available to you."

In my neighborhood, that kind of consolation prize would be more than enough. I'm sure it's better money than anyone at this table could have imagined before today. But we already know there's something better. We already know there's a promise of riches that stretches on forever. The table's full of greedy faces. Babel's curveball is working.

Competition. Supply and demand. Cage-style.

"Shall we begin?" Defoe asks.

His question echoes and echoes and echoes.

DAY 1, 9:13 A.M.

Aboard *Genesis 11*

A Babel employee leads me to one of the ship's comfort pods and tells me to enjoy the view. The docking bay is chaos. Layered glass mutes everything. It's like watching a silent movie without the subtitles. This launch has probably been on tap for a decade, but the worker ants always have more to do. Techies with glowing headsets scan crates, bark commands, and watch the heavies wheel them out of sight. I sigh, shuffle through songs, and wait.

The door behind me looks like a model blast door straight from the set of one of those remade Star Wars movies. The floor tiles are temperature controlled. Plush cushions grow out of every corner like mushrooms. They call it a comfort pod, but I'm a nervous wreck. Dimmed lighting, lavender walls, and a help-yourself espresso machine. The whole spread just makes me feel more out of place.

The player's scramble lands on a reggae infusion my cousin Taylor produced last year. PJ and the Most Excellent Brothers worship Taylor because they think he rubs shoulders with the rise-and-grind rappers of our generation. Really, though, he's defaulting on loans and working night shifts with my pops. That's the way things go in Detroit. I think of my family, my boys, everyone. Where I come from, low expectations are generational.

So I have to wonder, why me? No easy answers there.

The numbers are clear enough:

Eight out of ten.

Fifty thousand dollars a month. Forever.

I watch the worker bees and breathe deep breaths until the blast door hisses open. I wasn't sure who Babel Communications would fly in to say goodbye, but I should have known. Moms has never been on a plane. And the doctors don't like her traveling long distances anyway. So it's Pops who takes two steps into the room. He's wearing a leather jacket and worn jeans. He has on the newsboy cap that he knows I love. He doesn't smile, because he's already crying.

He offers his hand like I've graduated college or joined the army or something. When we shake, his hand swallows mine whole. We sit down together, and he doesn't bother to wipe the tears away from his bloodshot eyes. Babel recruited me just a month ago. It's crazy how fast all of this has happened, how little time we have left.

"Mr. Defoe told us it'd be three years." His voice is a stalled engine. "Emmett, I know it's a great opportunity. Lord knows I never saw any scholarship money. But are you sure?" He looks around at the strange seats and the glowing tiles. "Does it feel right?"

He asks the question I've been jammed on all morning. What's the fine print? Who's the wizard behind the curtain? Babel has its secrets, but so do I, so do all of us.

"I can't say no, Pops."

"You can always say no."

"They're offering fifty thousand dollars—"

He cuts me off. "Money's money, Emmett. I could've had us sitting pretty if I earned a living doing the wrong things. Does it *feel* right?"

"A month, Pops. Fifty thousand a month." I avoid his eyes, pretending to watch the workers. I know how much he makes every year. I know how small it is compared to what they're offering me. I know life isn't fair. "Forever. Free health care too. You can take Moms tomorrow. Free treatment at any clinic in Detroit. I've seen the bills, Pops. I've seen how long that transplant list is. Babel's the kind of company that will get her to the top of the list. They're the kind of people who pull the strings we can't reach. I know we need this. She needs it."

He ignores all of that. "I asked you a question."

I sigh, but his eyes drill me to the wall. *Does it feel right?*

"I really don't know," I say. "It's hard to tell the difference between rich and wrong."

I'm pretty sure that's a lyric, but it's exactly how I feel. Babel Communications strikes a strange chord, but every billionaire strikes a strange chord. They live in different worlds, move in different crowds, and breathe different air. It's always been that way and it always will be.

Pops looks out at the worker bees. "Never seen anything like it."

"Me neither."

We watch a guy almost get speared by a forklift.

"You scared?" he asks.

"Yeah."

"Just means you're smart."

"Yeah."

"If they ask you to do something that isn't right, what you say?"

"No."

"If they push you to the very edge, what you do?"

"Fly."

"What's your name?"

He used to ask me all this before football games. It's a tradition, a reminder.

"Emmett Ethan Atwater," I say.

"What's Ethan mean?"

"Steady."

"What's Emmett mean?"

"Hard worker."

"What's Atwater mean?"

I hitch. "You never told me that. . . ."

He smiles. "I don't know either."

The fact that he can tell a joke right now unties a thousand knots in my stomach.

"So, they're going to set you up nice, huh?"

"Not just me. You and Moms too." I look away again. "I want it bad, Pops."

"Want it for you first. When you're up there." He looks at the ceiling like it's not there, like the galaxies are spread out in their infinity. "Want it for yourself. I work hard, but you deserve so much more than we've been able to give you. Take what's yours first. Got that?"

I feel weak all of a sudden. A set of bones without a heart.

"They're only going to take eight of us down to Eden."

He nods like he expected there to be a twist. "Out of how many?"

"Ten."

"Pretty good odds."

Oxygen seems hard to come by. The words scratch their way out.

"What if I don't win?"

"What if you do?" he asks.

A second later he's up on his feet. He's not crying now.

"You get in there and fight, Emmett. Be worthy. Not in their eyes, but in yours. Break the rules you need to, but never forget who you are and where you come from. When they knock you down, and they will, don't you quit on me."

I shake my head in promise.

"Ever," he punctuates.

We hug. After, we sit and watch the cargo bay until all the crates are packed. My father holds out a brass key, and my heart stops. I've only ever seen it in a glass case in my parents' bedroom. It's ancient. Scratched all over and about as big as my palm. I turn it over and over and think about all the Atwaters who have held this key. He doesn't bother to explain why he's giving it to me, because I already know. *Break the chains,* the key cries. *Take what is yours.*

DAY 1, 9:33 A.M.

Aboard *Genesis 11*

And just like that, I'm leaving Earth behind.

Not forever, but this isn't the same as boarding a bus for summer camp. It feels wrong, having to abandon Moms just to make sure she gets the treatment she needs. I won't get to be there for her through the hardest stages of treatment, but leaving her and Pops means she has a chance of beating the odds. I have to believe that both of them will be here when I get back, alive and well and on their way to rich and retired. It still feels like something's slipped through my fingers as one of the techies leads me through the ship.

It's massive. Space tunnels lead through a technological stomach. I try to memorize our route, but we go up three levels, down two corridors, and through way too many doors for me to pull it off. A snare drum is wreaking havoc in my headphones, so I miss the first round of instructions.

"What?" I ask, spinning the volume down.

"Your room, Mr. Atwater."

The techie punches digits and swipes a card, and the

door gasps open. For a second I forget we're on a spaceship. The floors are carpeted, the couches are leather, and the library is stacked. Past the living room I spot two doors and figure they're bed and bath. The techie is punching another code into the data pad. Everything about the place is robotic blue and sleek.

"Do I get one of those cards?" I ask. "In Detroit we still use keys."

"Your suits are coded to your room."

"I get a suit?"

He nods. "And a gun."

"Really?"

"No."

For the first time, the guy has a face. He actually made a joke. Something about that makes him more than another piston in Babel's finely tuned engines. He's all sharp angles, light skin, and dark eyes. He looks like someone's uncle. Smiling, I offer him dap. He glances down the hallway, smiles to himself, and bumps my fist.

"What's your name?" I ask.

"Donovan Vandemeer."

"That's not American, is it?"

Mr. Vandemeer shakes his head. "Dutch."

"Oh, I love Denmark."

Vandemeer tilts his head, correction on his lips. Then he figures out I'm kidding.

"Very good, Mr. Atwater."

It's clear that Vandemeer needs to be elsewhere. I see his data pad blinking with a new assignment, and even though he's standing stock-still, I can sense which direction he wants to start walking. The well-oiled cogs of *Genesis 11* are waiting on me. It feels kind of good.

"How long do I have to get ready? Before the launch."

Vandemeer's smile widens. "The launch is happening as we speak, Mr. Atwater."

I grin at that. I've seen one too many *Makers of Mars* movies to believe him. The launches in that series were always filled with chaos and sweat. Vandemeer just smiles as I start across the room. "Of course, my mistake. I got it from here, Vandemeer."

"Your bedroom is the door on the left."

Nodding, I call back over one shoulder, "And the bathroom's on the right?"

Before Vandemeer can respond, the door opens. An Asian girl exits the room on the right. She's wearing a sleek gunmetal jumpsuit. It's hip-hugging leather with ribbed padding around the vital organs. A black metallic mask runs across her jawline. Above it, her eyes are dark and her hair is clipped into a neat ponytail by a plastic strawberry. She walks past, and my soft-spoken hello goes unheard. She waves at Vandemeer and vanishes down the hallway.

I catch the Dutchman grinning and ask, "What's she doing in here?"

"She lives in one room. You live in the other."

"But . . ." I gesture uselessly. "She's a girl!"

Vandemeer smiles. "My knowledge of America is sparse. Are there no girls there?"

"Yeah, but that's different. We don't . . . they don't . . . We have our own bathrooms, right?"

For some reason, the idea of using the same bathroom

as her terrifies me. What if she thinks I smell? What if she smells? What if I forget to lock the door?

"Separate rooms, separate bathrooms. You simply share a common area."

"Right," I say. It's still weird. "Do I have to talk to her?"

"It would be polite," Vandemeer points out.

"Is she American?"

"I believe she's Japanese."

"Right, Japanese. How am I supposed to learn Japanese?"

"You might have noticed the apparatus she was wearing. The mask."

I nod. "It looked like something out of a comic book."

Vandemeer laughs. "It's a nyxian language converter. You'll find one in your room." His data pad vibrates, and the playful smile vanishes. "Any other questions, Mr. Atwater?"

"She's pretty," I accidentally say out loud.

Vandemeer laughs again and departs. The blast door hisses shut and I'm all alone.

DAY 1, 10:30 A.M.
Aboard *Genesis 11*

After I'm all suited up, I check myself out in the space mirror.

I look like straight fire. The suit makes me seem way more muscular than I am. It tugs my stomach in and broadens my shoulders. The padding suggests a six-pack, which I don't have. Aside from the lack of a gun, the suit has me feeling like a galactic James Bond.

Too bad there's only been one black James Bond, and he was a much lighter-skinned brother than me. I take a step closer to the mirror. Every day I look more and more like Pops. Moms always jokes that the only thing she gave me is elbows. I have his nose, his brown eyes, and his round cheeks. I even have the faintest trace of his mustache along my upper lip. It hits me that he never taught me to shave. Babel's schedule has me turning eighteen before I'm back on Earth. One more thing I'll have to figure out for myself.

To the left of my reflection, numbers appear like a

medical readout. Body temperature, blood pressure, heart and breathing rate. I eye them for a second, but I don't have a clue if they're good or bad. I pick up the last piece of my arsenal: the nyxian language converter. I'm totally lost. The thing doesn't have hooks or clips or anything I can use to fasten it to my face. If this is the first test from Babel, the Japanese girl's already lapping me.

I put it up to my mouth, just to see how it's supposed to fit, and the thing snarls to life. I freak as the metal clamps to my skin and the leather padding slaps down against my jaw. It stops just short of my ears, fully attached and a surprisingly perfect fit. I release the front of the mask and it stays like a magic trick. I check my reflection again.

Badass. That's the only word for it. I look like a strange demigod from the future. My eyes are huge and menacing above metallic black. Throw in the gunmetal suit and I feel ready for whatever Babel has planned for us. I duck out of the room, take two steps into the corridor, and realize I have no clue where I am. *Genesis 11*, I remember, is huge.

I follow the walkway, passing clear walls that expose intricate wiring beneath. Through another blast door, I find a new hallway that leads into a broad, open space with rattling metal boardwalks and crisscrossing staircases. All of them lead down. I lean over the railing and see a handful of other challengers hanging out on the lowest level. That's how I already think of them. Challengers. Every one of them wants what is mine.

I pretend to admire the alien lighting overhead as I formulate strategies. Fact-check:

1. There are four girls.
2. There are six boys.
3. I live with the Japanese girl.
4. From what I can tell, this is a global effort.
   Kumbaya and cooperation.
5. But only eight of us get chosen. So it's about
   competition too.
6. Babel is rich. Really rich.

There are a lot of ways to play it. I can keep my mouth shut and my ears open. I'll learn a lot but might get pegged as a spy. Or I can pick out the strongest competitors and try to ride coattails. Maybe form an alliance or two. Problem is I have no idea what our competition will be like.

Before I can decide, someone taps my arm, and I almost freak over the railing. I remember the kid from the meeting. One of the two who flinched at the word *cancer*. Maybe he's here for the same reasons I am. Maybe he's got someone like Moms at home, someone who needs all the help Babel's contract can give them. He looks Middle Eastern. His eyes are a galaxy of browns. Different shades pieced together in an intricate puzzle. The skin above and below his mask is deeply tanned. Even the bulky converter can't hide the kid's smile.

"Hello," he says hesitantly. He pairs the word with a polite wave, like he's worried the device isn't going to work. "My name"—he pokes himself in the chest—"is Bilal."

I give him a head nod and hold out my hand. "Emmett."

We shake. He looks over the railing. "Whoa, big drop. The ship is huge, yeah?"

"Definitely. We don't have anything like this in Detroit," I say, eyeing the drop.

"This is where you're from? Detroit?"

He's doing the get-to-know-you thing adults do, but I'm not sure if I'm game yet. So I shrug and turn the question back at him. "What about you? Where you from?"

"Palestine." That draws a blank, so he tries again. "The West Bank."

Seeing my confusion, he adds, "Bible lands."

I'm not all that familiar with my Lord and Savior, but I nod like I know exactly what he means now. Not sure what else to talk about, I say, "You sound good in English."

He lets out a delighted laugh. With a tug and a click, the mask unmolds into his palm. He smiles wide and speaks in his own brand of Arabic. I can barely separate one word from another. With another quick manipulation, the mask snaps back onto his face.

"You sound very good in Arabic," he says.

"It's kind of cool."

Bilal mimes being cold. "In my room too. Maybe that's just how space is."

I laugh. "No, like good. *Cool* means 'good.' "

Bilal looks at me awkwardly. "You like it cold?"

"Never mind," I say. I gesture down below us. "Should we join them?"

Bilal looks down, takes a deep breath, and nods. We start walking, and I notice that his hands are shaking. It's kind of nice to see that someone's more nervous than I am. We make the loud, rattling descent together. Four flights down, we arrive in a room that looks partly like a cafeteria and partly like a gymnasium. Bilal's pointing at everything excitedly, but my eyes are locked on the seated challengers. Five of them wait in the brightly lit cafeteria. The masks make them look like a band of misfit superheroes. One, the heavyset Asian kid who's as tall as me, stands up and surprises Bilal with a massive hug.

"My name is Katsu," he says. "I'm from Japan."

I offer a hand before he can get me in his big mitts. As we shake, he does that little trick where one finger scratches your palm. I pull away, and he laughs loud enough to shake the floors.

"That's it. The best trick in Japan. My toolbox is empty now. What's your name?"

"I'm Emmett. From Detroit. This is Bilal . . . he's from the Bible lands."

Bilal laughs. "Palestine. The West Bank."

Katsu points in random directions. "In space there are no directions! So now you're just from Bank. Everyone!" he shouts loudly. "If you need money, go to Bilal!"

We laugh and nod our greetings at the others. It's strange to have our language barriers removed so easily. I don't know much about the Bible, but I do remember the story of Babel. I always thought it was weird. God scatters the people and gives them different languages. Babel Communications has gathered the peoples of Earth and reversed it. There's something sacred to our easy, borderless conversation. Either something sacred or something forbidden.

Across the table, the blond girl with the southern accent

sweeps her pink-dyed lock of hair behind an ear and waves at us like a pageant queen. I remember Defoe calling her Jasmine.

"Detroit? I know Detroit! My name's Jasmine, but y'all can call me Jazzy. I'm from Memphis, Tennessee. In the States."

Next to her, the African girl waves at us. She's still wearing the colorful beaded bracelet around her wrist. A handful of silver dime-sized coins dance as she reaches out to shake my hand. Her eyes are dark pools in an even darker face. I have to make her say her name twice to get it right. The syllables sound like the start of a song.

"Azima," she says. "Ah-zee-mah. I am from Kenya."

The last two sit at the end of the table, ignoring us and ignoring each other. Katsu pounds on the table with his meaty fists until both look up. "Friends! Make friends! Don't be pisspots!"

One is the white kid I watched in the first meeting. In his jumpsuit he looks like any of us. His hair looks neater now, and he's got a face you'd find in the portraits decorating a mansion hallway. His eyes are pale green, his complexion pale stone. He offers his hand to us like it's a business card. "Jaime," he says. "I'm from Switzerland."

Katsu laughs. "How painfully neutral!"

The kid shrugs and studies his fingernails. Across from him is the Asian kid I annoyed in the first meeting. He takes us all in, finds us boring, and closes his eyes. I have to admit that he looks pretty cool. His head is completely shaved except for a patch of bangs he sweeps to the left. I remember Defoe calling him Longwei. I wonder where he comes from; I wonder what his strategy is. We all take seats, and Katsu starts telling a long, winding joke about a priest, a zombie, and a cactus that walk into a bar. He forgets the punch line, though, laughs riotously, and points at a handful of other challengers descending the stairs.

My Japanese roommate flutters forward and taps Bilal politely on the shoulder. He looks up in confusion until it's clear she wants him to move over a seat. He slides over and she sits down next to me, like we always sit together or something. In a weird way, she reminds me of PJ. We never had a moment where we decided to be friends. He just sat down next to me in school and decided it was the place he wanted to be. She doesn't say a word, but it's clear she's taking everything in, eyes bright and knowing. I kind of like her already.

The other two take seats at opposite ends of the table. I recognize the girl from the first meeting. As she crosses the room, I can't help noticing a tattoo on the back of her neck. A dark etching of the number eight, or maybe an inverted infinity symbol, wearing a slanted crown on its round head. She offers the table a wave and introduces herself as Isadora.

"From Brazil," she says. "The best country in the world."

Katsu rolls his eyes at that. We all turn our attention toward the other kid. He has dark skin and light-brown hair. His face pinches to thin lips, and the way he holds his shoulders makes it look like he's bracing for impact. Almost like he's waiting for one of us to throw a punch. He says his name is Roathy. We all wait for him to say where he's from, but he picks at a callus on his palm and ignores us.

My Japanese roommate blinks to life, realizing the rest of us are there, and introduces herself as Kaya. When we're all seated and pushing into awkward-silence territory, Defoe enters through a damn magician's door I didn't even notice. His bald head shines in the fluorescence as he offers us that predatory smile.

"Our intrepid crew, welcome. Did you know that you are officially the youngest crew to ever enter space? Already setting records."

The wall behind him parts like a movie curtain. The black panels slide away and reveal . . . Earth. Everyone's caught off guard by the surprise. I thought Vandemeer was kidding. There was no countdown, no Houston, nothing. We're *in* space. I can see oceans, atmospheres, everything. But where's the lack of gravity you always have in movies? Shouldn't we be floating around and laughing as our pocket change drifts to the corners of the ship? Defoe waits for us to fully appreciate the situation before smiling again.

"Welcome to the final frontier." He sweeps out his good hand in a magnificent and dramatic gesture. "Allow me to introduce you to Commander Crocker."

From the shadows on our right, a real astronaut marches out. He's in a bulky, movie-costume kind of suit. He doesn't look as sleek as we do, but all the bells and whistles look professional enough. His face is neatly shaved and his hair is cut high and tight. The only similarity between us and him is the nyxian language converter suctioned to his jaw. I'm surprised when he speaks with a deep southern drawl.

"Welcome to the end of the world, minions. I'm Commander Crocker, but you can call me Crock. I'll be your flight operations commander. If all goes well, you won't see my pretty face until we reach the Tower Space Station."

The marble-sized view of Earth is replaced by holoscreen images. We all eye an architectural layout of the ship. Crock uses a meter stick to indicate grayed areas on the diagram.

"This is where we perform our no-gravity operations. My crew has a heck of a time making sure this ship does all the things a ship ought to do. The best way you can help us keep everyone safe is by not adventuring out where you're not supposed to."

I glance sidelong at Kaya. Crock's using a language converter, but is his southern slang really translating? My new friend looks like she's tracking, but who knows? I jump a little at the idea of friends. Kaya and Bilal seem nice enough. Even Katsu's kind of fun. But this is a competition, plain and simple. Points first and friends second. That has to be my mentality if I want to come home with the gold.

"This black outline indicates the nyxia-sealed corridors. Everything inside that perimeter is available to you," Crock explains. "Just a few reminders. You're in space. People experience changes in space. Report anything unusual to your medics. If you have repetitive nightmares, if you have stomach cramps, if you feel sad at night. Anything. We have an amazing staff, but they can't help you if you're not willing to talk. Any questions?"

Azima raises a hand. "In the movies, there's no gravity in space. Everyone knows this. Why aren't we floating around?" She frowns a little. "I wanted to float around."

Crock smiles. "You know how the Trojans stole away Helen and the whole Greek fleet went after her? Well, Helen ain't nearly as pretty as nyxia. How did we cut our trip by twenty-something years? Nyxia-enhanced fuel. How do we enclose sections of the ship and maintain gravity? Nyxian sealants and filters. How do you poop in space? Nyxia."

That gets a laugh from everyone except Jazzy, who just looks disgusted.

"Actually, we had that last one figured out a while ago. But the magic word is *nyxia*. Babel put the majority of their initial mining deposits back into the space program. Inside this section of the ship, it's not even going to feel like space. Nyxia's helping seal this environment. As a result, your bodies won't even experience the usual effects. My crew and I will be a little taller by the time we get to the Tower Space Station, but you all will be too busy competing to deal with any of that. Honestly, this ship, the station, and Babel's ground operations on Earth are all about one hundred years more advanced than what you're used to using. All thanks to the new black gold."

And we're the only ones who can get more of it, I realize. Which means we have a little weight to throw around. Babel might have recruited us because we're young, but they're hiding that power beneath the competition. I file the thought away under *P* for *Power.*

Without us, they get no more nyxia. Without us, this entire operation is a waste. But that power's meaningless if we're not in the top eight. Clever cats, these Babel folks. Once the eight victors are decided, though, some of that power will shift back into our hands.

"Any other questions?" Crock asks.

Roathy—his sharp eyes narrowed—throws up a hand.

"What if one of us dies?"

The room tightens. Even Commander Crocker pales a little.

"Well, we have policies in place, but the history of space exploration has very few casualties. Babel's records are immaculate, so I wouldn't worry about that."

Roathy nods, but I can see the distrust in his eyes. Crock moves quickly onto a new subject. I should listen to what he's saying, but my eyes drift back to Roathy. He's wound up so tight. His eyes are so knife-sharp that I can imagine them cutting through everything he sees, digging down beneath the bright outer layers. It takes me about thirty seconds to figure out what's so weird about him. He's seeing the world like I see it. The brighter the colors, the more likely something dark is hiding underneath. We both want the truth more than the show.

When I glance back up, Crock is retreating into the bowels of the ship and Defoe has retaken his place.

"My name, as all of you know, is Marcus Defoe. I am in charge of making sure that you arrive prepared for operations. Our competition is designed to be a system of merit. We want the best of the best to go down to Eden and work for us. You already know the rewards we've arranged for being one of the best. My job is to hone the skills and impart the knowledge you'll need before you go to the Adamites' home planet. This process will be very difficult."

He snaps his fingers and Babel assistants ghost into the room. Their padded footsteps are the only sound. I notice that Vandemeer is one of them. I nod at him and he smiles back. The workers place a black ring in front of each of us.

They're plain and undecorated. Like curious kids, we pluck the rings up and start examining them. Mine's cold to the touch. I can feel something too. Something *pulling* at me as I turn it over in my palm. The substance feels active, frenetic with energy. It wants something. I slide it onto a ring finger, and I'm not surprised it fits perfectly. Babel seems like the kind of company that gets the details right.

"You'll learn to use nyxia through a series of different tasks," Defoe explains. "The first of which will begin right now."

Another shock ripples across the table. Already? We didn't even know we were in space two minutes ago. Bilal glances over at Kaya and me. His hands are still trembling nervously, but he whispers, "Good luck, yeah?"

"You too," I reply. And I mean it. I'm glad we bumped into each other. He's a nice kid.

A nice kid who I still want to beat. Have to beat. When this is all over, Bilal will go back to Palestine and I'll go back to Detroit, and I want to do it as a winner, as one of the eight who succeeded. I look away, hoping he won't be in the bottom two, but hoping even more that I can beat him. Defoe holds up the dagger he threw this morning, an eternity ago. Light shivers down its length.

"One of the most crucial functions of your training will be the creative manipulation of nyxia. We want you to be able to use the resource you're mining for us. It takes concentration." With a flick, the dagger shrinks down to the size of a perfectly round stone. Defoe holds it up for all of us to see. "Step one: transform your ring into a stone. You may begin."

I scramble to get the ring off my finger. The whole group is drawn into concentrated silence. That connection I felt earlier kicks back to life. I do my best to hold on to that link, and I imagine a stone. The thought physically leaves my brain. For a second I stare blankly at my hands. What was I trying to do? And then the thought appears in the surface of the pitch-black metal. My ring shudders in my palm and molds itself into a marble. I smile in relief and look around the table. Most of the others have completed the task too.

Only Bilal and the Brazilian girl, Isadora, haven't. My first instinct is to help Bilal, but I don't know *how* I would help him, and I don't know *why* I would help him. If this is a test, let him struggle. The thought's a cold one, and I shiver a little as the screen behind Defoe produces an image. A pair of leather driving gloves.

"Step two: manipulate your substance into this pair of gloves."

This one's harder. My first thought trembles into the stone before I've settled the color of the picture into my brain. It leaves half formed, and I'm holding gloves that are missing a few fingers. I'm amazed at how soft they feel, how like real gloves they look. I stare at the image, focus, and summon the thought again. Just like before, it slips from my brain and leaves me half lost. Then the nyxia reacts and I have my gloves.

On the walls around us, scores appear.

I'm seventh. The thought makes my hands sweat. Only Bilal, Jazzy, and Isadora are below me. Longwei, the stubborn Asian kid with the front sweep, has the highest point total. By a long shot too. Babel's message is loud and clear: winning matters. Defoe eyes the results, and the whole room waits as Isadora continues attempting to make her gloves. She's sweating, and I feel for her, but I'm just glad it's not me. Bilal's eighth. He gives me a nervous look.

"It will get better, yeah?" he whispers. I shoot him a quick nod, but I'm too focused to give him anything more than that. I don't have time to pat backs *and* press pedals.

Defoe touches a button and the image disappears.

"Lastly, I need you to produce a flower with a purple stem and ten petals."

I wait for him to hold up an image, but instead he crosses the room and starts sorting through papers. No guiding image this time, then. I try to picture the strange flower, but I get distracted when Longwei's name goes bold on the scoreboard. A bunch of points get added into his total. I glance across the table and see him tucking the flower into his suit pocket. His eyes narrow in a satisfied smile. He knows we'd all like to see what his looks like to make our own transformation easier. I force myself to concentrate.

Purple stem, purple stem. Ten petals, ten petals.

My nyxian gloves merge and shrink into a lavender stem. The petals, though, are missing. A few more names go bold on the scoreboard, and I'm sweating as I form another thought and release it. The flower appears, but I have too many petals. Panicking, I try it again. And fail again.

By the time I've created the right flower, seven others have already finished. Including Bilal. I've defeated only Isadora and Roathy. If they did cuts today, I would have avoided walking away empty-handed by exactly 4.3 seconds. I stare at my inept purple flower and try not to have a panic attack. Slow and steady wins the race. This is just one event. Just one.

Defoe turns to us when the scores solidify. "As we progress, I will ask you to make bigger and more complex images and items. You're welcome to consult each other for advice on successful manipulation, but I wouldn't want to trade secrets if I knew something everyone else didn't. Please transform your substance back into a ring and follow me."

I glance up to see that Longwei is already sliding his over his finger. My roommate, Kaya, and Azima follow shortly after. The top five form up ranks as the stragglers, including me, stumble after them. I try to keep my chin up, but I feel like I'm lagging behind already. What makes them so much better at it? How is Longwei so unnaturally fast?

For the next three hours, Defoe takes us through a host of other random tasks. Each of us swims for ten minutes in a turbine tank that simulates gale-force winds. Katsu makes a joke about whales, and the attendants have to pull him out just one minute into swimming. He lies on the floor with his hands on his stomach and laughs. Defoe doesn't look amused.

I'm not the fastest swimmer in the group, but I manage a top three that pushes me more safely up the scoreboard. After drying off, we spend an hour in an actual classroom learning about Eden's plant life and some indigenous species. We're surprised by a quiz at the end, which I fail. I was listening, but the names got jumbled in my head. I beat myself up over the mistake. Every point matters, every single point.

Longwei aces the quiz and keeps his distance at the top of the scoreboard. Luckily, Roathy scores worse than me, and his numbers continue to sink with each new task. Our eyes always drift to the scoreboards. It's addicting, to see where we stand, to see what we could have improved upon. Only Longwei never looks, because where else would he be except for first place?

Every now and again, Defoe pauses and asks us to manipulate our nyxian rings into some new form. I get better as we go along, but so does everyone else. Bilal, especially, is improving, and I can't help noticing his name climbing into the spots where mine should be. At one point, he remarks on his progress. I pretend not to hear him.

We perform simulated evasion exercises, as well as a set of situational tests designed to help us understand the way Adamites think.

When we finally break for lunch, my eyes drag down the scoreboard:

1.	LONGWEI	7,324	points
2.	JAIME	4,874	points
3.	AZIMA	4,454	points
4.	KAYA	4,200	points
5.	KATSU	4,124	points
6.	BILAL	4,100	points
7.	EMMETT	3,843	points
8.	JASMINE	3,650	points
9.	ROATHY	3,324	points
10.	ISADORA	2,980	points

All the thrill from earlier today has vanished. We're tired from swimming and running and thinking. Tired from seeing other names above us on the leaderboard and from trying to make small talk in between tasks. Defoe and some of the techies watch from a corner of the cafeteria as we slump into our seats and stare at our plates. I know they're happy. Competition is afoot. Their warriors are being crafted and hardened. *Iron sharpens iron,* Defoe said. He was right. At the end of this, I'll be harder and sharper and colder than I could have ever imagined. I take another bite and remember that it's worth it. The sweat and the competition and the suffering. All I have to do is win Babel's game and I'll go home a king.

"Afternoon activities will be group-oriented."

I glance around and it's clear I'm not the only one unhappy about group activities. We just spent all morning fighting tooth and nail with each other for spots. People above me on the scoreboard? Not my friends. People below? Doubt they're excited to ball out with me either. Defoe ignores the tension and groups us at random. I mentally groan when I see Longwei sorted onto the other team. So far, he's been unbeatable. Whatever the next competition is, his team will definitely have an edge.

Defoe leads us down two flights and through a double-wide blast door. The room is empty except for a mesh barrier that divides it in half. It almost looks like a tennis net, except that it cuts across the length of the space rather than the width. On either side of the hip-high barrier, the empty room stretches thirty meters long, twenty meters wide, and twenty meters high. The ceiling, floor, and walls are all nyxian black. Defoe sends my team to one side and Longwei's team to the other. I scrunch my toes and test the floors with my weight. It's a slightly bouncy material, but not so soft that you lose your balance. Maybe some kind of rubber?

Even though we don't have Longwei, our team isn't half bad. Jaime, Azima, and Kaya are all right behind him in the standings. Isadora, though, is in last place. I eye her like she's deadweight until I realize Jaime and Azima are eyeing me the same way.

They think I'm one of the weak links. I'll have to change that. Soon.

We wait for Defoe as he strides past the mesh net to the side of the room opposite the entryway. He swipes at his data pad, and clockwork mechanisms rumble to life. The floor begins to vibrate as Defoe takes his place on an elevated platform. As always, he's smiling his hunter's smile.

"We call this the Rabbit Room."

He gestures to the walls on either side of him. The black spaces flicker, and identical images of a forest materialize on either side of the net, each with brilliant, lifelike color. It reminds me of the Neverland Simulators, but the digital imagery is a thousand times more realistic. Like looking through a portal into another world. I'm pretty sure the technology in the room is worth more than my neighborhood.

Defoe continues his instructions. "If you make contact with the back wall, you're out of the competition. The team with the most people standing at the end of the exercise wins."

Without another word, Defoe slashes his data pad and the floors literally start to move. Both teams are borne slowly toward the back wall. On the distant screen, an unseen runner begins through the trees. We're the runners, I realize. On a gigantic treadmill.

Jaime's the first to wake us up. "Come on!" he shouts.

At a jog, he moves away from the back of the room. Longwei's team is already to the middle of their side. I can hear them talking strategy as our group follows Jaime forward.

"Let's get as close to the screen as possible."

Jaime doesn't just sound like a captain; he looks like one too. Something about his assumed leadership annoys me, but I don't have a better plan, so I fall in with him and Kaya. The others join us, and when we're close enough to touch the screen, we slow to an arm-pumping speed walk. The forest is so vivid that I feel like I could break through dimensions and be there.

After just a few minutes, the speed increases. I'm already breathing hard, and so is the rest of our team. The path twists, and our first obstacle appears. A massive tree trunk splits the road in two. We keep jogging side by side, waiting for the invisible runner to pick a direction.

Which is why none of us expects the tree to appear. One second, empty air. The next, a full-sized trunk materializes onto the treadmill and *levels* Azima. The crunching sound echoes, and her fall clips Kaya's legs. The two of them are carried back with the tree trunk, which is rooted absurdly into the floor of our treadmill.

I consider going back for them before Isadora shouts, "Watch out!"

Together we duck a low-hanging branch that's just swept to life. Jaime does the same before shifting over to close the gap between us. As the path levels out, I look back to see Kaya trying to pull Azima to her feet. She's too dazed to move, though. Just before they pancake into the back wall, Kaya rolls to one side and sprints away.

Our side of the room pulses. A brief flash of white along the walls and floors and then the speed of the treadmill increases. We're going faster than the other group now. The punishment is clear. Lose a teammate and your odds decrease.

And now the obstacles are coming faster too. A rockslide crashes down from the left, and the three of us swing to the far right. Kaya's nearly caught up with us when some kind of animal thrashes through the trees. I catch sight of fangs and claws and roll instinctively as it leaps to life. The creature's lunge misses me, but it snags Jaime by a shoulder. I watch him go down, hear him cry out, and then Kaya's cry follows his. I look back to see that the beast is gone, but both Jaime and Kaya are tangled together. Before they can recover, the treadmill ferries them to the back wall.

I curse as our side pulses twice and the treadmill goes faster, faster, faster.

We're basically sprinting now. Isadora's holding her side. Seeing her pain reminds me of mine. The stitch in my stomach sharpens, so I shout, "Keep going!"

Side by side, we press through the thickening forest. A massive crash sounds on our right, and I hear shouts from the other team. Their walls pulse with successive lights. I can't risk looking over to check the numbers. Isadora and I keep moving.

Ahead, a stream crosses the forest path. I'm wondering

if we'll have to leap over it when our runner decides to go straight through. A brief flash of the floor is highlighted blue, and my feet slap down right into the colored strip. The ground snags like quicksand. The sudden change clips my footing, and I hit the treadmill hard, nailing my shoulder on the fall. Isadora screams, and we both whip back toward the entrance.

I make it to my feet. Isadora doesn't.

The light pulses again and I'm alone. A quick glance shows Longwei, Bilal, and Jazzy are still up and running. It's a surprise to see Jazzy running at the head of their tight knot, but a second of watching her form is answer enough. She's composed, running like she's halfway through a normal cross-country race. Longwei and Bilal follow her lead through each obstacle.

I pump my arms and manage to get back to the center of our side of the room. The forest clears, and I see a series of twisting ravines ahead. The road dips a little, and my stomach takes a nosedive. Cliffs and canyons wait. The first is a snaking fissure that divides the path in two. I watch the unseen runner approach the edge and leap.

You've got to be kidding.

A red gap appears on the treadmill. I barely leap it as the ravine continues and the path presses through treacherous terrain. A massive canyon cuts in on the right side, and I run on tiptoes with my shoulder scraping the far left wall. The pace is increasing, and my only reward is seeing Bilal miss a jump and get eliminated. Then two jumps come back to back, and the second catches my ankle funny. I feel it almost twist. The stumble leaves me on the wrong side of the canyon. I see the road ahead of me shrinking, ending. In desperation, I put all my momentum into a diagonal leap.

And short it. The red ground shoots a bolt of energy up through my feet. My legs go numb and I whip helplessly back to where my team is waiting, all still gasping for air. The treadmill rolls me into the wall, and the entire room goes silent. The screens blank as Longwei and Jazzy collapse. Sweat pours down our faces and all of the pain pushes its way past the adrenaline. It's something awful.

Defoe prowls over to us. "We will visit the Rabbit Room often. These teams are permanent. The map you run will vary, but you can still discuss strategies if you want to succeed. The dynamics of the game will change as we progress in your training. Today is just a glimpse of the pace we will set for you. Get your rest. In the Bible, the Sabbath comes every seven days. Here at Babel, we break every tenth."

The rest of the group stumbles to their feet. Jaime actually reaches out a hand to help me up and says, "Solid running, Emmett. We'll get them next time."

A part of me wants to tell him we're not friends, that as long as he's above me on the scoreboard, he's my enemy. But thankfully, that part is really tired. I take the offered hand.

"Thanks."

We all weave drunkenly back up the steps and into the wider halls of the cafeteria. I catch sight of the scoreboard and my jaw drops. I finished third in that exercise. Only two other competitors survived the obstacles better than I did. I was expecting to jump a few people on the scoreboard. Instead, I've fallen a few spots:

1.	LONGWEI	9,324	points
2.	KATSU	6,124	points
3.	BILAL	6,100	points
4.	JAIME	5,874	points
5.	JASMINE	5,650	points
6.	AZIMA	5,454	points
7.	ROATHY	5,324	points
8.	KAYA	5,200	points
9.	EMMETT	4,843	points
10.	ISADORA	3,980	points

The others have stopped beside me. We're all eyeing the new standings and trying to figure out how they scored the Rabbit Room. Longwei and Isadora are the only ones who find themselves in the same position. I point to the scoreboard as Defoe passes us.

"I don't get it. I finished third."

Defoe pauses, an eyebrow raised. "Actually, you finished second."

"Jazzy and Longwei were still going," I say. "If they're the only ones that beat me, why'd I drop in the standings?"

"You were on a team. Your team finished second."

Anger bubbles to life, the hot kind that boils up a throat. I *hate* tricks and fine print.

"That's not my fault."

"It's a team effort," Defoe replies. "First place receives two thousand points. Second place receives one thousand points. Next time, I suggest you do everything in your power to make sure your team wins."

"That's not fair."

That makes Defoe smile. He squares his shoulders and adjusts the perfect knot of his perfect tie. Every gesture and movement is a reminder that here, in this world, he's the king.

"I was wondering when we would first hear that word. *Fair.* Dismiss your idea of *fair* here and now. Our rules are our rules. There will be injuries and accidents and mistakes in this competition. You will be sent to the med unit at some point. You may even send others to the med unit. But never forget that this is *our* competition. We say what is fair and what isn't."

With that, he slinks off down a corridor. I glance around at the others, but no one else really looks pissed off. I'm amazed how quickly they're willing to fall in line. Defoe's absence draws the other Babel workers back into the room. My fists are still balled and my face is drenched in sweat. Vandemeer offers me a towel and a wrapped dinner sandwich, but I'm too angry to eat, too disgusted to do anything more than wipe away the soil and sweat.

At the end of the first day, I'm in ninth place. The stunning fact that I might *not* win is slowly sinking in. I think about arriving back in Detroit and having to tell my parents they didn't win the lottery. The consolation package Babel offered would still help, but I'd spend the rest of my life working the same jobs my pops did and grinding out paychecks, wondering what it would have been like if only I'd won.

Bilal's crossing the room, trying to get my attention, so I wrap the towel around my neck and make my way toward the stairs. Kindness is the last thing I need right now. Three flights up, down a lonely corridor, and into my room. I'm not in the mood to talk, not to Bilal, who's ahead of me and safely in third place, not to anyone. I strip off the suit and the nyxian mask and my ring too. In just underwear, I crawl under the covers and try to pretend I'm at home. But the covers are too soft and the bed's too soft and the scent of Moms's herbal tea isn't hanging in the air. This isn't home. Until reality came crashing down, it was just my ticket to make home a better place. But I can't even get that part right.

It's pushing into night. Pops has a shift starting soon. I imagine him, looking just like me but wider and grayer and more ragged. He's wearing that blue work uniform with his name slapped on the front of it: JEREMIAH. When he thinks no one's watching, his shoulders always slump. The weight of years, of never being able to rise. It's not his fault, but that kind of weight's been passed down in my family for generations.

I learned our history in parables, stories of warning. My great-grandfather's restaurant got railroaded by a new interstate project. The government took the land out of his clenched fists and gave him just enough money to try and fail in a neighboring county. My own gramps gave up his scholarship to Michigan after his mom died. He could have been All-American, but he got a factory job and looked after his brothers and sisters instead. In every branch of our family tree, someone's brushed shoulders with real freedom. But there's always a catch in life. There's always been some fine print that snatched dreams just before they were real enough to hold in our hands.

Sighing, I pull the covers down, get back up, and cro
the room. The brass key that Pops gave me hangs from a
metallic peg. I swipe it from the wall and turn it over and
over in my hands, feeling the wear of centuries. I know the
story that goes with this key. My ancestors escaped north as
slaves. A locksmith up near Detroit took the measure of my
great-great-great-grandmother's chains and made her a key.
It was passed down as a symbol to every Atwater as a reminder that we weren't always free to do what we wanted.
Many of the men and women who have held this key still
weren't free, not really.

Pops? He's not a slave, but he's not truly free either.
Life's left him grinding for every single dime. Most days he
looks like he's halfway through a race he'll never finish. He
and Moms never had the chance to go to college. I have a
few cousins who have, but for the most part, my family is
stuck in the same grind of centuries past. I turn the key in
my hands and realize I can write my own story. Not about
lost dreams, but about a future bright as any golden shore.

It's just one day, I remind myself. My fight is one of decades and generations. One bad day won't stop me from
rising up. I won't quit, not today, not ever.

It's tempting to go to sleep. Instead, I cross the room to
my desk and palm the nyxian ring sitting on the desk. I
write down a list of items that I want to create and start
working. Each new image comes faster; each manipulation
has fewer mistakes than the one before it. I go at it until I
feel like I'm seeing double. I go at it until I know that tomorrow will be better.

DAY 2, 8:38 A.M.

Aboard Genesis 11

My dreams are black holes. In the first one, the black hole devours me atom by atom and leaves me in the nothing of the universe. In the second one, I'm the black hole. Towering and dark, I destroy the other contestants one by one. Their screams have no sound. I'm not sure which dream is scarier, the destroyed or the destroyer. As I stare at the ceiling, I realize that Babel's competition will make me one or the other. There's no middle ground on *Genesis 11.*

I know I should take a shower to freshen up, but it's all I can do to crawl into my suit and stumble over to my desk. My muscles are bunched and aching, but I can't afford to be sore. Not when I need to be great. Before I leave, I manipulate my nyxian ring into a black rubber band. Yesterday, I lost precious seconds tugging the ring off a stubborn finger. But now I know that every second counts. So I slide the rubber band over my right wrist and test it. It comes on and off a lot faster than the ring did. Pops always said it's the little things that win championships. I can dig that.

I exit my bedroom and I'm surprised to find Kaya waiting for me. She's sitting on the nearest couch and waves as I come into view. Her hair is done up into pigtails that look oddly childish compared to the fierce-looking nyxian mask along her jaw.

"Good morning," she says. "I have a proposition for you."

I raise an eyebrow. "Does it involve breakfast?"

"An alliance," she replies. "You and me."

The request splits my brain in seven different directions. She wants to team with *me*? What if it's a trap? What if the competition evolves? And why make an alliance so early? I don't think it's the worst idea in the world, but we've literally marked off one day on the calendar. I expected alliances and relationships to form, but making a move this early feels risky. I did watch Kaya compete yesterday. She'd be a huge help, but I'm not sure what I can offer her. And I can't forget my dreams either. All the black holes. Destroy or be destroyed. Can an alliance really survive what Babel's planning for us? What if the final spot comes down to me or her?

"Tell me why."

She nods. "I'm strategic, a strong problem solver. That's my specialty. Finding solutions. If you struggle in a certain event, we can come up with strategies together."

"I meant why me? I saw you work. I know you'd be a good person to team up with, Kaya, but why would you want to team up with me? I'm in ninth place."

She nods again. "Not for long. I heard you up late last night. Practicing, right? I can tell you're a competitor. Babel's going to change the game. There will be other tasks.

I'll help you with your weaknesses; you help me with mine. That's the way an alliance works."

"How do I know you won't team up with someone else?"

"You're the logical choice," she answers. "Think about it. We live together. Outside those doors it's going to be endless competition. We'll be fighting for each point. Don't you want just one place on the ship that isn't like that? If we team up, it'll feel like we're coming back every day to a safe place. I want to feel like I'm coming home."

I can't help nodding. It all makes so much sense. "Me too."

She lifts up a pinky and holds it out. "I swear that, as long as we're not competing directly against each other, I'll help you in the competition. We're in this together."

I wrap my pinky around hers and repeat the words. She surprises me by letting out a huge sigh of relief. I didn't realize how worried she was that I might reject the offer.

"Let's get started," she says. "I have a strategy for the Rabbit Room."

I smile. "Want to explain on our way down to breakfast? I'm starving."

Kaya nods, and we walk through the retracting door. Our hallway is empty; the stairwells too. It looks like everyone is already at breakfast.

"Do you know the story about the tortoise and the hare?" she asks.

"Yeah," I say, thinking back to elementary school. "The turtle wins 'cause the hare's cocky. He takes a nap during the race or something."

"It's a stupid story," Kaya says seriously. "Very stupid. If I was the rabbit, I would have lapped the turtle over and over. Smart and fast is better than slow and steady. But I think I noticed a way for the turtle to win yesterday."

"In the Rabbit Room?"

Kaya nods as we start down the stairs. "The obstacles disappear as they reach the back wall. I noticed it yesterday when I tried to help Azima. About two or three feet from the back wall, they just vanish. We should drop back to the very edge of the treadmill next time. We can protect ourselves there, like a turtle."

I shrug. "Sounds good to me."

I'm liking our alliance already. We join the others at breakfast. Most of their plates are empty and most of them look tired, like they were dreaming of black holes too. I snag a hearty-looking croissant and some fruit. Not exactly Detroit fare, but everything tastes delicious here. Bilal gestures to the seat next to him and I sit down. He offers a polite good morning, but he looks exhausted. The only cheerful one is Katsu.

"Emmett," he calls. "Watch this. It's amazing."

I lean forward. A pair of dark wings stretches. It's little, but Katsu has transformed his nyxia into some kind of shadow bird. I watch it peck at his plate and smile.

"Pretty cool," I say.

"Not even the best part," Katsu replies. "Bring the king his sausage!"

We all watch as the shadow bird flaps over to the buffet. After rooting around, it clutches a sausage link in its talons and flutters back. Katsu laughs so loud the table shakes.

"I am the king!" he shouts, taking a bite out of the sausage. "The king of the world!"

A few of us laugh. Farther down the table, Longwei scowls at the noise, like laughter should be a punishable offense. Jaime's sitting closer to the rest of us today. He still leaves a few seats between us and him, but it's a start.

"Kings only bring trouble," says Azima. I can't help staring at the silver charms on her wrist. It's easier than meeting her eye. She has a way of looking at people with enough intensity to pin them to a wall. "Queens are more proper rulers. Everyone knows this."

Katsu laughs. With surprising quickness, he snatches the bird on his shoulder and manipulates it into a crown. God, he's fast. I'm not the only one who brushed up on his skills last night. He tilts the black metal onto his wide head and folds his arms regally.

"But every queen needs a king," he says.

"King?" Roathy's voice cuts the laughter in two. He examines Katsu with those knowing eyes and shakes his head disdainfully. "I don't see any kings or queens here."

"Thanks, Camp Stupid," Katsu snaps back. "We were just joking."

Roathy doesn't flinch at the insult. He just keeps staring at Katsu, and I know he's seeing past the jokes, through the cheerful play. He's looking at a layer that's deeper and darker.

"Look around you, big man. What's the one thing that connects all of us?"

Katsu doesn't answer. Everyone glances around, like the solution's supposed to be written on the walls somewhere.

They might not have figured it out, but I know exactly what it is: we're all dead-dancin' broke. That's the connection. Babel has unlimited resources. It's not hard to imagine them screening each of us: weighing, measuring, selecting. They needed a way to manipulate us. Poverty just makes their golden ticket look even brighter.

"We're poor," Roathy says without a trace of shame. "They picked us because we're poor. We can be kings and queens, sure, but only if we bow first."

No one denies it. A few people look down at their plates. A few jaws clench. Jaime keeps chewing on a piece of bacon, unconcerned. The casual display lights me up.

"Except for you," I say before I can stop myself.

Jaime looks over. "What?"

"Roathy's right," I say. "We're all poor except for you."

Jaime shrugs like I've got him all wrong. "I don't know what you're talking about."

"Then tell us, Mr. Switzerland—what do your parents do?"

It shouldn't matter, but it does. This competition is everything. If we're going neck and neck with each other at the end of this and some posh son of some posh executive snatches my lottery ticket, I'm going to be pissed. Jaime's smooth under the fire of my question, but I notice how corpse-still his hands are as he explains, like he can't tell the lie *and* act normal at the same time.

"They were farmers, but we lost our farm last year. So screw you, Emmett."

"What'd they farm?" I ask.

Jaime shakes his head, a motion that buys him an extra

second to remember whatever lie he's supposed to tell. I recognize it because I'm one of the *best* at that stalling tactic.

"Dairy. We made mountain cheese."

"I bet you did," I snap back.

We're both standing now, and I'm breathing hard through my nostrils. I don't know why it makes me so mad, but I *know* that he's not one of us. He's something else. He doesn't want it like we do; he's here for some other reason. The fact that he could be the one to take what's mine drives through me like a knife. We're staring death at each other as Defoe arrives. When he sees the two of us sizing each other up, he doesn't smile his normal smile.

"Is there a problem, gentlemen?"

My jaw tightens. I shake my head, eyes locked on Jaime. "No, sir. No problem at all."

I file the morning under *A* for *Anger*. Luckily, the quiet rage I feel because of Jaime's lie helps me focus during the first tasks. We warm up with nyxia manipulations. The hours of practice I did the night before has me flying through each new image. Defoe has us make a spoon, a hilt, and a book with empty pages and a blue cover. I trail only Longwei, Katsu, and Azima through each task.

"Lastly," Defoe says, holding up a glass of water. "Transform your nyxia into water."

Thought, blink, transformation. It happens that fast and I'm holding a clear cup in my right hand, but the water's not there. I perform the process again, but the water's still missing. My eyes dart to Longwei. It's a surprise to see his name not going bold on the scoreboard. He's transforming his nyxia again and again, but like me he can't fill it up with what he needs.

Defoe's smiling, waiting.

"You can't turn it into water," I say.

Defoe's smile widens as my name goes bold on the scoreboard. Somehow the answer heaps a thousand points onto my score. I watch my name slide up into fifth place.

"Very good, Emmett. Nyxia cannot be manipulated into water, food, or truly organic creations," Defoe explains. "So when you're down on Eden, you'll have to use your nyxian resources to gather food and water. You make a pot to boil water in, a spear to hunt with, but you can't simply summon a buffet"—he holds the cup up and takes a dramatic sip—"or even a glass of water."

Rule one noted, we all follow Defoe over to the training area and go through the same process as the day before. A classroom session categorizes the types of mushroom that exist in Eden. Kaya deliberately takes the seat next to me. She catches my eye before manipulating her nyxia into a notebook and pen. She gestures for me to do the same.

Nodding, I copy her manipulation. It takes a few attempts to get it right, but as the videocast rolls on, I start scribbling down everything. Defoe will probably make us put our notes away at the end, but writing everything down gives the words a better foothold in my brain. I've barely finished cataloging all the poisonous colors and shapes when the presentation ends and Defoe passes out data pads to quiz us. He eyes my notes, gives an affirming nod, and moves on.

The quiz is a piece. I still manage to miss a question, but I do a lot better than most of the room. Longwei and Jaime both ace it. I can't help but think Jaime does well because he's gone to better schools or grown up with a massive library in his house. A small, frightened part of me wonders if he's telling the truth, if he really is the son of down-and-out farmers. I've had people jump to the wrong conclusions about me before, so I know how deep a mistaken identity can dig under a person's skin.

I whisper my thanks to Kaya as we head to the next task. Our alliance is already cashing out. On the scoreboard, I've moved into fourth place.

1.	LONGWEI	11,350	points
2.	KATSU	9,124	points
3.	JAIME	8,200	points
4.	EMMETT	7,850	points
5.	AZIMA	7,750	points
6.	KAYA	7,400	points
7.	BILAL	7,300	points
8.	JASMINE	7,050	points
9.	ROATHY	6,324	points
10.	ISADORA	5,080	points

Yesterday I dropped into ninth place and I felt like the world was ending. Sliding up the leaderboard feels great, but I have to remember there's no such thing as safe. The points of each day add up. Today's a good day, but tomorrow I could fail a task and slide four spots.

It's all one big grind.

* * *

One by one, the others slide into the massive tank that Babel has carved into the floor. The simulated winds thrash the water violently, and the challengers swim like they're riding tsunamis to shore. As Katsu flails helplessly in the stormy waters, I manipulate my nyxian band into swimming goggles. I ball them up and hide them behind my back while Defoe calls Jazzy forward.

When he calls my name, I pull the strap of my manipulated goggles around the back of my head. The plastic suctions around my eyes and I'm in my own bubbled world. I slip into the tank and start swimming. Already I can feel the difference. Yesterday I swam through the thrashing waves blindly. It wasn't horrible, but a few times I drifted to the sides of the pool and slowed my progress trying to readjust. Seeing makes a world of difference. I pound through strokes and know I'm outpacing myself, outpacing the others.

Ten minutes later, the waves die down and I climb doggedly out of the pool. Kaya's the only one swimming after me. She manipulates her own goggles, and just like that we're a team, my strengths added to hers. When the results are tallied up, my name ticks past Jaime and Katsu on the scoreboard. Second place.

Instinctually, I glance over at Longwei. He's still breathing hard from his own swim. He locks eyes with me and nods once. Challenge accepted, I think. The thought has me smiling as we head to the Rabbit Room. Longwei doesn't know that I have an ace up my sleeve. Kaya huddles us together on the tread floor. Jaime refuses to look at me, but he does listen as Kaya gives the group the same explanation she gave me that morning.

"So if we stay on the very back of the treadmill," she says, "none of the obstacles will even reach us. You just have to be careful with your footing, all right?"

"I don't like it," Jaime says. "One slipup and there's no recovery."

"But all we have to do is run," Kaya replies calmly. "No dodging or jumping. When the treadmill picks up speed, we can move forward to give ourselves more room. I thought we could hold at the back until we arrive at the ravines."

Jaime opens his mouth to complain, but Azima cuts him off. "I remember the tree disappearing. This is a good strategy, everyone knows this, but what if the other team sees what we're doing and copies us?"

Kaya nods. "We'll only have the advantage today. We could start off at the middle of the treadmill and drop back when the first obstacle comes."

Azima nods. "Clever girl. Let's win today. I came here to win."

Jaime flashes a look of annoyance, and it's not hard to see why. Yesterday we followed him. Today we're following Kaya. There are no points on the scoreboard for being a leader, but I'd bet Babel's paying attention to everything. After a frustrated pause, Jaime nods his agreement and we all take our positions. The other team's formed a tight line with Jazzy at the front. They stagger the formation slightly so that one fall won't send them all stumbling back. Defoe holds up a hand for attention.

"Same rules as yesterday. Lose a player and your speed increases. Good luck."

The tread floor kicks to life. Our invisible runner begins through a familiar forest, and the only noises are light breathing and steady footsteps. The pace continues for a few minutes before we see a series of fallen trees up ahead. At Kaya's signal, we slow down. No one from the other team notices as we drop back to the last few feet of the treadmill and pick up our pace. Defoe sees it, though, and his eyes narrow curiously.

The downed trees materialize before us: a complicated stagger of branches, which the other team zigzags through. Longwei's shouting out commands, and they look like well-trained ducklings. Our team holds its position at the back end of the treadmill. Panic rises in my chest as the trees get closer and closer and then *vanish*. Kaya flashes a satisfied smile and we all hold our pace. Jaime was right: there isn't much room for mistakes. About a half meter behind us and a half meter ahead. But Kaya's plan is definitely working.

In the distance, two wolflike creatures leap to life. The other team swings to the right and I see a flash of black shadows. Their nyxian rings form up like little shields. Both wolves graze along the side of their compact formation but are fended off easily enough. I watch as our wolves snarl their way into nothing. Kaya actually lets out a laugh this time. Across the netting, Jazzy drops back to put a hand on Katsu's back. He's a lot bigger than the rest of them, and the pace is already too fast for him.

We keep running. A massive landslide trembles to life,

and Katsu can't avoid it. Jazzy ducks around him, but his flailing hand snags her suit, and they both rush to the back wall. The room pulses twice, and now the remaining three are moving faster, and faster, and faster.

Ahead, the forest road is dipping, and I spy the series of canyons we ran through the day before. I can't believe how much more energy I have this time around. We haven't lost anyone at all, and our pace is still at a comfortable jog. Bilal, Roathy, and Longwei are sprinting.

"Kaya," I call out. "Time to move forward?"

She's spotted the canyon. "Take the lead, Emmett. Stay out of the red, everyone."

My strides lengthen. The canyons are twisting and full of little crevices. I swing off to the left, and my group follows behind me like a snake. The other team is stumbling their way through leaps already, and I do my best to stay focused on our progress instead of theirs. We're leaping our first big canyon when the lights flash to our right and the treadmill comes to a stop. All five of our teammates are still standing. Even Jaime is all smiles, like this morning is ancient history.

"Congratulations," Defoe says. "Expect adjustments to the course tomorrow."

Translation: *The glitch will get fixed, but we like that you took advantage of it.* I file this under *W* for *Winning* and walk over to give Kaya a one-armed hug. The rest of the group crowds around, and her smile's so wide that even the nyxian mask can't hide it. I'm not sure why, but this feeling is so much better than winning the individual competitions. I like giving Kaya the props she deserves, and I like winning, together. I ask her to go ahead and give us a new strategy and she launches in excitedly. It's only as we head back to our rooms at the end of the day that I realize the real significance of our win: it has me in first place.

I remind myself there's still a long way to go, but as I fall asleep that night, there's a smile on my face. For the first time, I feel like I belong here, like I actually deserve to go to Eden. I know that when I wake up in the morning, I won't just be content with the top eight.

I want to win.

DAY 7, 8:38 A.M.

Aboard *Genesis 11*

1.	EMMETT	38,900	points
2.	LONGWEI	36,750	points
3.	AZIMA	29,900	points
4.	BILAL	29,300	points
5.	KAYA	28,450	points
6.	KATSU	27,400	points
7.	JAIME	26,200	points
8.	JASMINE	22,050	points
9.	ISADORA	22,080	points
10.	ROATHY	21,324	points

Babel's competition isn't a sprint.

It's a marathon in which we're occasionally asked to walk on water. Already I can tell that seventh days will be the hardest. Deep into a week of work, but not close enough to taste the Sabbath to come. It will be the day that frays at our forced friendships and formed alliances. People will get hurt on seventh days, lose their minds on seventh days.

So far the only breaks we've gotten are for the behavioral simulations. Sometimes they're more exhausting than the Rabbit Room. But every day that passes is a reminder, a testament.

I'm good enough. To finish in the top eight, to win. Kaya preaches perspective during our daily rendezvous, but I know I'm a legitimate threat because of Longwei. He spends half his time glaring at me. We've started trading the lead back and forth. I don't back down when he looks at me. I won't back down, not from him or from anyone else.

On the seventh day, Babel creates warriors.

Defoe leads us down an unfamiliar corridor and to a room that's a massive, padded pit. It looks like one of those indoor trampoline places. The room has three or four different levels, cushioned walls, and a rack of black-tipped weapons on either side of the doorway. Different-sized swords and cruel-looking maces. I even see a set of throwing stars.

Something twists in my gut. After seeing the Adamites shred through a fully weaponized marine unit, I should have known we'd be trained in some kind of combat. I should have known that the only possible practice would be against each other. Kaya and I exchange a meaningful glance. I'm not sure who will be teaching who in this competition. She's small, but a person doesn't have to be big if the knife's sharp enough.

Defoe's data pad lights up. We all watch the distant screen blink to life. A *Combat Kings* version of Bilal and Azima appears on it. The digital faces of their avatars gaze out at us. I have to squint, but I can make out a health bar above their heads and vitals listed.

"The weapons will feel real. We've designed them with their genuine weight and balance. However, they're coated with a nyxian oil of our own invention. They cannot actually cut or touch other physical objects." Defoe hefts a hand-held ax. He approaches the nearest outcropping of square blocks and swings. The air shimmers, and the blade blinks right through the padding.

Jazzy says what we're all thinking. "That's *amazing*."

Defoe sets the ax back. "The damage you do to your opponent will be reflected in the video display. There are winners and losers to this game. Sever a limb and your opponent will lose the use of it. Knick an artery and they'll bleed out. Strike a killing blow, and you win. Understood?"

We're all nodding. They're really going to have us fight each other. I glance over at Jaime. It wouldn't surprise me if we get matched against each other. That's how it always happens in movies. You get put against the one person you wanted to fight earlier. And they crush you.

Azima and Bilal step forward.

"Choose your weapons wisely," Defoe instructs.

Azima goes straight for a body-length spear. She gives it a few testing thrusts before climbing down into the center of the arena. But Bilal looks lost. I doubt the kind-natured kid has ever fought *anyone*. He walks up and down the rows of weapons, eyeing them like snakes. Eventually he grabs a short sword. He holds it awkwardly as he descends into the pit. They turn to face each other. On the screen, their avatars do the same. Even though the two of them are standing still in real life, the avatars crouch into fighting stances.

"You may begin," Defoe calls.

Our fights lack movie drama. Real fights don't last for minutes. Real fights are ended in seconds. Bilal holds up his sword and stumbles away as Azima's spear lashes forward. He's still in the middle of his backpedal when a second strike catches his thigh. On the screen, blood spurts from his wound, and I see his health bar light up. Bilal tries to bull-rush forward, but Azima ducks to the right and lunges upward. Her spear drives through his neck, and the Bilal on the digital screen collapses in a bloody mess.

For the first time, I don't like how realistic the images look.

"Next," Defoe calls.

Bilal shakes Azima's hand and compliments how fast she is. I notice Defoe frowning. He wants bone-deep competition, but Bilal's too honorable for that. Katsu and Longwei appear on the screen next. Katsu goes straight for a massive, wicked-looking ax. Longwei picks a glinting sword with an engraved hilt. They face off in the center of the square, and Defoe releases them.

I'm expecting Longwei to be as good at this as he is at everything else, and he starts out that way. They trade a few awkward blows, and Longwei slices a cut along the side of Katsu's calf. His avatar winces, but when Longwei goes in for a second strike, Katsu's backhand sends him flying. For the first time in the fight, Katsu's size advantage is obvious. A massive swing from his ax jars the sword out of Longwei's hands. Katsu's barrel of a chest flexes as he brings it swinging around again. Longwei tries to dive to one side, but he's too slow. The ax buries itself in his thigh, and his avatar withers overhead. The real Longwei is on the floor, scrambling for his sword, when Katsu finishes him.

"I am the king!" he shouts again. Everyone but Longwei laughs.

Kaya and Jaime go next. Instead of facing him hand to hand, Kaya uses one of the trampolines to get to the upper levels. It takes two seconds to see that she spent her time on the sidelines planning out a strategy for the fight. She maneuvers through the obstacles and leads Jaime into a beautiful trap. He chases and chases until she buries a throwing star right in his forehead. Looks like we'll be learning from each other. Jaime starts to complain that it wasn't a fair fight, but Defoe ignores him and summons the next combatants.

Jazzy and Isadora. My eyes lock on Roathy. He'll be my first opponent. He's a lot smaller than me, but I expect him to fight and scrape. Everything about him says he's a scrappy kind of kid. My guess is he'll be reckless, undisciplined. The natural counter is to fight defensively and wait for an opening.

My eyes turn back to the fight below. Jazzy takes a second to tie her blond hair up in a ponytail. Isadora kneels opposite her. I watch as she traces the tattoo on the back of her neck with a thumb before lifting a pair of daggers and setting her feet.

After what we've seen in the Rabbit Room, I half expect Jazzy to have the upper hand, but her athleticism doesn't translate into combat. She lunges twice before Isadora lands two violent jabs with her knife. Isadora's been quiet so far, but there's nothing quiet about the way she wields a blade. She backs away, eyes the screens, and sees that Jazzy's on the verge of bleeding out. She's smart enough to retreat to a safe distance as the win becomes official.

The stage is set for Roathy and me. He grabs the same sword that Longwei did, but I take my time in choosing. The axes don't feel right, and the other swords look too heavy. I can't imagine fighting with a spear, and there are a few maces I'm not even sure how to work. My eyes settle on a pair of metal claws. I've never used brass knuckles, but my uncle definitely taught me how to box. I slide my hands into the metallic gloves and flex my fingers. The right hand has a moon-shaped shield. The left has dagger-sharp knuckles and a trio of silver claws extending out.

It was made for a southpaw, for me.

I take my place across from Roathy and wait. When Defoe gives the signal, Roathy does exactly what I thought he would. He comes flying forward, lashing the sword in wild, too-quick blows. I use my shield hand to ward off the first few, and then slash down under his third swing. I don't have to look up to know I just spilled his guts on the floor. Roathy reacts to his avatar's pain, pulling away from me and limping. He lunges one more time, and I bat the sword down with my right hand. His blade nicks my shoulder, but the forward step allows me to put all my weight behind the punch. The nyxia slides harmlessly through Roathy's neck, but my fist crushes his trachea.

The real Roathy and the avatar collapse together. I take a step back as the adrenaline pulses through me, the thrill of victory, the taste of pain, but it doesn't last long. Roathy's down. He's gasping for air, and the sound of his wheezing breaths are dying things. Defoe's there a second later with two medics at his side.

Isadora, Roathy's roommate, is shouting. Defoe has to grab her by the shoulders to stop her from following the medics out of the room. I should feel horrible, but I remember Roathy's face at the start of the fight. If he could have, he would have done the same to me. Destroy or be destroyed. I look up at the other challengers, and their faces are downcast. Some of them are looking at me like I'm different now, like there's a darker side to all of this that I've just unveiled. I slide the gloves off and climb out of the pit, trying not to think about black holes and broken things.

At lunch, the scoreboard shows my dominance. I should be thrilled, but Roathy's absence digs under my skin. I was just playing the game. I didn't want to hurt him. I pick at my plate and repeat the phrase in my head: *I didn't want to hurt him. I didn't want to hurt him. I didn't . . .*

1.	EMMETT	41,900	points
2.	LONGWEI	36,750	points
3.	AZIMA	32,900	points
4.	KAYA	31,450	points
5.	KATSU	30,400	points
6.	BILAL	29,300	points
7.	JAIME	26,200	points
8.	ISADORA	25,080	points
9.	JASMINE	22,050	points
10.	ROATHY	21,324	points

As we make our way to the Rabbit Room, Roathy's still not with us. I keep glancing back, hoping to see a medic escorting him down the hall. But the blast doors close once we're inside, and the competition is set to begin without him. Defoe signals from the front of the room.

"Longwei, your team is without a player. According to the rules, your treadmill will begin at a faster rate because of your loss. Good luck."

Their team shoots dark looks in my direction, like I knew the rule and purposefully put Roathy in the med unit to give our team an advantage. It's completely unfair, but I don't say anything because Defoe already taught us about Babel's concept of fairness. Kaya gathers our team around, but the bad vibes are on our side of the room too. Isadora keeps her distance from me, and Jaime keeps glancing over nervously. Kaya ignores all of it.

"Emmett, I want you to be our rabbit today."

I stare over at her. The idea of being ordered around right now annoys me.

"Why me?"

"You have the quickest reactions," she replies. "We'll run along the back. You stay up front. Call out every obstacle you see and give us time to react. Sound good?"

It takes a second to realize what Kaya's doing. She's putting her faith in me, showing the others she trusts me. She wants them to forget what I did to Roathy and remember what I've accomplished so far in the Rabbit Room. I nod my thanks to her as Defoe steps up onto his platform and the rubber floor starts to roll.

The other team is sticking with their bunched strategy, except that now Katsu is at the front of the line and Longwei already has one hand on his back for support. Kaya and the others fall back to one side, and I take my place at the front. Our path begins through the forest, and my eyes are darting around.

A tree falls onto the path in front of us and I call it out. Swinging to the right, I hurdle the only section without branches. Right after that, a pair of creeks, and then a series of low-whipping branches. I call every obstacle out, and I'm feeling good about our pace when I hear a shout. My head snaps back as my arms keep pumping.

The back walls have come to life. Another forest view trails us, with trees vanishing as we progress. A second glance reveals two wolves padding after us. Defoe promised the game would evolve, and it has. Obstacles ahead, dangers behind. Without warning, the speed of our treadmill picks up. We haven't lost anyone, but it's like our imaginary runner has spotted the wolves and is eager to get away. The pace winds us through more obstacles, and I hear Kaya command the group to move forward.

They join me as the pace picks up to a sprint. I look back as one of the wolves breaks free of the screen. It's massive, bigger than those from the days before, and unlike earlier versions, it doesn't look like it will vanish anytime soon. We duck a few series of branches and Isadora stumbles. I miss her outstretched hand and watch as the wolf pounces. It pins her to the ground and she screams. The two of them slide straight to the back of the room. Our side pulses and the speed increases. Sweat streaks down my face.

On the other side of the room, Katsu finally falls. I can hear him shouting as he zooms toward the back wall and his team is down to three. They don't have any wolves, I realize. Their forest screen is alive and vivid along the back wall, but there's nothing chasing them.

Our second one has materialized on the back of the treadmill. It sprints along our left flank, whipping under branches and over stone rises in pursuit. Kaya slides our team as far to the right as possible, but we're struggling to run and keep an eye on the wolf at the same time. Kaya wanted me to be the rabbit today, but I have a better idea.

Focusing, I transform my rubber band into the dagger I saw Defoe use the first day. It's heavy in my sweating hand. I tighten my grip and drift behind the others. Knowing it's suicide, I steady my strides and veer over to the wolf. Before it can leap at one of us, I'm leaping at it. My dagger lands above its shoulder, and the collision knocks the wind from my lungs. The wolf and I spin end over end, but I keep hold of the dagger and wrap my other arm around its neck. It snaps wicked-looking teeth at my face, but vanishes when we hit the back wall.

Our side lights up, but my sacrifice leaves the others free to sprint without distraction. Longwei's team has been running faster for longer, and pretty soon Bilal loses his footing and goes flying backward. Longwei can't quite make the leaps, and my team holds on long enough to eliminate Jazzy in the canyon section of the map. I lie back, staring at the ceiling, arms up in victory. These wins always feel the best. Kaya's the first to compliment my move with the wolf. Even Jaime admits it looked awesome.

Azima offers a hand to help me up, but Longwei shoulders past her and kicks me right in the face. My head snaps back and blood splatters the floor. My eyes tear up and I feel my face go from massive pain to completely numb in heartbeats. Before I can even think about getting up or fighting back, Jaime and Azima are there, pushing him away. Longwei holds his ground long enough to shout at me.

"You cheated. You only won because you cheated."

Jaime gives him another shove. "Back off, Longwei. Back the hell off."

Longwei turns and starts walking away. Every single bone in my body wants to rise. I want to stand up and end him. He might be smarter and faster, but I'm bigger and stronger. I've seen him fight and I know his style. But the group, and Babel for that matter, have already seen me do the hurting. I need them to see me this way, as the victim. I hold a sleeve up to my nose and let Kaya inspect it. Defoe's crossed the room already.

"Need a medic?" he asks.

I shrug my shoulders. "He just kicked me."

"I saw. I'll speak with him. That kind of violence isn't permitted. Do you need a medic?"

"No, I don't think so. It's not broken, is it?"

Defoe shakes his head. "Go get cleaned up."

Kaya helps me stand. She keeps her arm around me as we walk. Instead of the usual tired silence that comes at the end of each day, the others swarm around us, either worried about my nose or excited about having a little drama for once. Jazzy's the first one to take sides.

"No hard feelings from me," she says. "I didn't think you cheated at all, Emmett."

"Thanks, Jazzy."

Bilal nudges my shoulder. "Emmett, do you want me to make you some tea?"

"Tea?" I ask. "Will it help my nose?"

He shakes his head. "No, but it tastes *very* good."

I laugh. "Nah, I'm good, man. Thanks."

Azima leans into the conversation. "If he does not want the tea, I will drink it."

Bilal looks surprised. "You—you would like some of my tea?"

Katsu laughs. "As long as you're taking orders, Bilal, I'll have a mimosa. Just make sure you put one of those little umbrellas in the glass. I love those things."

Everyone laughs. We walk the long hallway together, and I realize I'm at the center of the group. Only Longwei walks ahead of us, apart. I should thank him for what he's done. Without him, I'd still look like the bad guy. In his frustration, he replaced me. Hitting someone when they're ready for a fight is one thing. Sucker punches, though, are the lowest of the low.

At the end of the hallway, he turns to look back at us. We're close enough to see the anger in his eyes. He sweeps his front tuft of hair to one side and disappears up the stairs.

I file the look under *E* for *Enemy*.

When Sabbath finally comes, I sleep like the dead.

Waking up is just a reminder that my muscles are sore and my brain is tired. The competition and the adrenaline push the pain out of sight, out of mind. My first deep sleep brings all the bumps and bruises back to the surface. When I limp into our shared living room, I find Kaya sitting cross-legged on the couch. She closes her book, picks up her nyxian mask from the table, and laughs her way into it.

She says, "You look like a grandpa."

"I feel like a grandpa." I take the seat next to her. "Big plans for your day off?"

She pats the book in her lap. "Alice and I are getting into trouble."

I raise an eyebrow. "Alice?"

She holds up the cover. A girl with blond hair and a blue dress looks like she's getting into all kinds of I'm-a-girl-with-blond-hair-in-a-blue-dress trouble. A handful of absurd characters are chasing her into it too.

"I'd read along with you, but it looks like it's in Japanese."
Kaya's eyes light up. "Do you really want to read it?"

I glance at the shelves. "Is there an English version?"

"Sure," Kaya says. "But who needs that when you have me? Get comfortable."

When I've got my feet kicked up, Kaya begins. She goes back to the beginning, even though I can see a dog-eared page marking her progress halfway through the book. As she reads, she pauses for suspense and changes her voice for different characters. Only person who ever read to me like this was Moms. Something about that thought makes all this feel like more than an alliance. It has the faintest taste of family to it.

And I was right about Alice. Girl's getting into all kinds of trouble.

"Wait," I say, interrupting. "She just started shrinking?"

"Yes," Kaya says, tracing the line with a finger. "Drinking from the bottle made her *really* small."

I frown. "Not very realistic."

"You didn't complain about the rabbit with the pocket watch."

"Because he sounds kind of cool."

Kaya glares at me. "Do you want me to keep reading or not?"

I laugh. "Yeah, yeah."

Before she can start again, our door hisses open. Defoe strides into the room, takes one look at us, and nods at me. "Come with me, Emmett."

He gives the command like a king would. I groan to my feet and wink back at Kaya.

"Thanks for reading. Promise you won't read on without me?"

Her whole face unlocks. "Yeah, I promise."

Defoe directs me out of the room. I'm guessing whichever rabbit hole he's leading me down won't come with magical elixirs. We walk through hallways and it's an effort to keep up with his long, purposeful strides. I find myself side-eyeing our mysterious director of operations. Nothing shakes the guy. He always seems in control and he always sounds confident. Only his hand stands out as a weakness. Up close, I can see just how shriveled it is. Since day one, he hasn't bothered to hide it. The bones look malformed and the skin looks permanently burned.

"What happened to your hand?" I ask. It's none of my business, but it's about time we tested him back. I want to know what kind of skeletons he has in his closet.

He holds the hand up, considering it.

"I sustained the injury in an encounter with an Adamite."

My eyes widen. "Really? You've seen them?"

"So have you, Emmett." He glances over. "On the videocast."

"But you've seen them in person. You actually fought one?"

"It wasn't meant to be a fight. It was supposed to be a peaceful discussion."

"And it did that to you?"

"Yes, but are you familiar with the phrase 'you should see the other guy'?"

I nod. "Of course."

"Well, you should see the other guy," Defoe says, throwing me that dangerous grin of his. I think back to the video of the Adamites. A squad of high-tech marines got destroyed by just a handful of them. Still, I find myself believing Defoe. He has an undefinable danger to him. Babel needs us because they can't overcome the Adamite forces and defenses to mine the nyxia they want, but for all we know, there are millions of Adamites on Eden. It's possible that an individual fight could favor a human, especially someone like him.

"You don't cover it up or anything," I point out.

"No," he says quietly. "It's a reminder."

"Of what?"

"I don't have to be perfect. I just have to be better than the other guy."

He leads us up a spiraling staircase. It's strange to walk and talk together like normal people would. I kind of admire the guy. He's a golden standard in a new age. But the deeper, instinctual feeling is fear. Underneath all his shine, I know Defoe is power and chaos.

"You don't wear a mask."

He glances over. "Not my style."

"But how does everyone understand you? Without the mask?"

He raises an eyebrow, like a magician weighing whether or not he wants to let me in on the trick. After a few more paces, he lifts his good hand and taps his cheek twice. "I have a permanent translation insert in this molar. Our most advanced tech. Perks of being the boss."

So there's even *more* to Babel than what we've seen so far. Makes me wonder what's still in store for us.

"Am I in trouble?" I ask. "Feels like I'm being taken to the principal's office."

"Not exactly. We just have to monitor the health of our contestants. With only ten of you on board *Genesis 11*, it's vital to keep you alive and well."

"My health? But I feel fine."

"How did you feel when you hurt Roathy?"

I take my time answering. "I didn't mean to hurt him, if that's what you're asking."

"You didn't?"

"Not for real. I just wanted to win."

"Winning is important," Defoe says. "I understand. This is just protocol, Emmett."

We continue in silence. The hallway narrows into an almost normal-sized door. It opens up into one of the ship's comfort pods. The room is filled with plush cushions and calming colors on the walls. Except now the view is of space. I walk over and squint out. It reminds me of black holes.

"Take a seat, Emmett. Dr. Vandemeer will be in shortly."

Defoe helps himself to an espresso. The machine coughs black liquid into a ceramic cup. He swirls sugar in and stirs. Even the coffee makes me think of black holes.

"My attendant's name is Vandemeer too," I say.

"Same person."

"But he's not a doctor."

"Of course he is," Defoe says, turning.

The door gasps open and Vandemeer enters. He offers a friendly smile but looks completely transformed. He's wearing glasses now and a little white coat over his uniform. Like Defoe, he's got a data pad in hand. "Hello, Mr. Atwater."

Defoe salutes us with his coffee and exits.

"So you're a doctor?"

"Of a sort," Vandemeer replies. He takes a seat opposite me. His face is full of odd angles, and he keeps his receding hair cut short. It's the first time I've seen him this way. Most days he's gliding alongside me, appearing one moment only to disappear the next. After a few clicks on his data pad, he looks up at me. "So, you were involved in an incident the other day."

I nod. "It was an accident."

"Certainly," Vandemeer agrees. "And how did it make you feel?"

Oh. He's one of *those* doctors. I let air out through my nostrils as I look away, out into space. It's so full of unknown that it looks empty. I don't want to hash out my feelings with a psychiatrist. He went from friendly insider to brain thief in about two minutes. When I don't respond, Vandemeer tries again.

"Emmett, every employee fulfills multiple roles on this ship. My roles both happen to deal with comfort. I act as your attendant during part of the day and a doctor during the rest of it. I'm assigned to you, but I can't help you if you're unwilling to speak to me."

"I don't need your help, all right?"

"All right. Certainly. Can I show you something?"

I glance back at him. With a sigh I say, "Sure."

He flips the data pad around. His finger taps the center of the screen, and I watch the footage from earlier in the week. I sidestep Roathy's blow and crush him with my left hook. He topples, and the camera watches as I back away. My face is completely, utterly, terrifyingly blank. "Did you notice what we noticed?" Vandemeer asks.

I nod once.

"So I'll ask you again. How did it make you feel?"

"Horrible," I say. "I didn't mean to hurt him. I felt bad about it."

"And yet it didn't show on your face. You masked that emotion."

"I didn't mean to. I was just . . . I don't know. Everything here is so simulated."

Vandemeer nods knowingly. "Exactly, Emmett. One of our biggest concerns with the training design is the simulated aspect of it. We were worried that it would form a distance between the participants and their actions."

"Okay," I say. Where's he taking me? I hate feeling like I'm being led somewhere, like I'm a dog with a pretty collar. "If you already knew it would happen, why's it a big deal?"

Vandemeer turns the data pad back around. He swipes the screen and continues looking at me. "Because we projected these symptoms for day one hundred and twelve."

I stare at him. "So, what, you're worried I'm some cold-blooded murderer or something?"

Vandemeer shakes his head lightly. "Of course not. Are you worried that you are?"

I roll my eyes. I hate the whole let's-turn-your-question-into-my-question thing. I glance back out to space and remember the recurring dreams. Destroy or be destroyed. I'm not a murderer, but I do want to win. More than I've ever wanted anything.

After ten days, Babel's already worried they brought damaged goods with them. I try to imagine how they think of me. A poor kid from Detroit. If they did their homework, they know I'm not in any real gangs. I hang out with the Most Excellent Brothers, but they're harmless by Detroit standards. Still, to the higher-ups and the Richie Riches I bet I look like your everyday street thug.

"Look," I say. "When I get pushed, I push back. That's how I was raised."

"And that explains your lack of reaction?" Vandemeer asks.

"I guess I didn't feel like I was wrong, because it was self-defense. You saw how he came at me."

"I did; you're right. So you felt that you were defending yourself?"

"Yes."

"And that completely removed your empathy for him?"

"Not completely. I felt bad on the inside. But it doesn't show on my face because my instinct is to push back, to protect myself. I guess I wasn't sure I was safe yet."

Vandemeer frowns. "But he was down on the ground at that point, Emmett."

I laugh, knowing I have him now. "You ever been in a fight?"

"No, have you?"

"A few times," I say. "Seen a bunch too."

Vandemeer spreads both hands. "And?"

"Well, the first guy on the ground isn't always the one who loses the fight, Doc."

"I see. So this was all . . . instinct?"

"Right. I was defending myself, and that doesn't stop when the guy hits the ground. You let up then and you deserve to get hurt. That's all it was. Case closed." He's not quite convinced, so I decide to throw in a little extra. "I keep having this dream." I try to look distant, like I don't want to share it. "I don't know what it means."

"Do you want to talk about it?" he asks.

I give him a weighty glance. "I don't know."

"Come on, Emmett. It might help make things easier."

I nod. Now sharing the dream was *his* idea. People love it when something's their idea.

"I kept getting sucked out into space," I say. "There were these black holes that looked like the other kids. I just kept getting pulled into them, like they were destroying me."

Vandemeer makes a note on his data pad. He's typing rapidly and nodding now, like it all makes sense. He keeps asking me questions; I keep feeding him answers. We dance our way to the conclusion that my life on the streets made me defensive, but that I shouldn't put a wall up between myself and my emotions. I leave out the part in my dreams where I'm the black hole, where I'm the destroyer. I am what Babel wants to believe I am. It's better that way.

DAY 10, 2:18 P.M.

Aboard *Genesis 11*

Vandemeer releases me, but the words dig under my skin until I find my feet moving in a different direction. Not back to my room, but down. Level after level until I see the signs for the med unit. The orientation labeled this wing as off-limits, but I need to see Roathy. He's been stuck in the med unit since I put him there on day seven. I tried not to feel too guilty, to convince myself that this was just another part of the game, but Babel arranged our second round in the pit as rematches. Everyone fought the same opponent they did in the first round. Roathy's avatar appeared next to mine just long enough to register a forfeit. Points trickled into my score and guilt tucked into a corner of my heart. I was telling Defoe the truth. I never wanted to hurt the kid.

The medical wing's a bright honeycomb of rooms. Six of the seven doors are swung wide open. The sheets on each bed are folded with perfect hospital corners. Light glances off polished medical instruments. My stomach turns a little. Hospitals always remind me of Moms.

I swallow the feeling and push past the empty rooms. The seventh door is a sliver of light. I pause by the opening to look inside. Isadora's sitting with her back to me. Her hair's pulled up in a topknot and I can see the crowned eight tattooed on her neck. My eyes trace the delicate lines before noticing the reach of her outstretched hand. She holds Roathy's limp hand in hers. His eyes are closed, and a monitor ticks off the beats. He's alive, but God he looks small.

I almost leave, but think better of it. Just because Babel wants a cutthroat competition doesn't mean I can be less than the person my parents raised me to be. I knock twice.

The door edges open as Isadora turns.

"Hey," I say. "How's he doing? I wanted to come down, talk to him."

She rises and all of her beauty sharpens into a weapon. She stares at me with all the fierceness I saw from her when she was driving a knife into Jazzy's stomach.

"Leave."

"I just came to say I'm—"

She turns her wrist casually. A nyxian bracelet slides off, smoking into her hand and reforming in the shape of a dagger. My heartbeat doubles as she grits her teeth in warning.

"You need to *leave*."

I'm a lot of things, but I'm not stupid. I raise both hands and back out of the room. I can feel her eyes trailing me until I reach the stairs. I take calm and steady breaths as I make my way back home. Kaya's words make more sense now: *If we team up, it'll feel like we're coming back every day to a safe place. I want to feel like I'm coming home.*

Back in Detroit, we all knew which places you could and couldn't go. There were invisible lines drawn around every block, and consequences for being in the wrong places at the wrong times. We learned the rules because learning the rules meant staying alive. Isadora's threat is a much-needed reminder. Some of the places on this ship aren't safe. Some corners are more dangerous than others. I make a mental note to learn the new rules, and soon.

Kaya's waiting for me when I get back to the room. Before I can share more than a few details about what happened, though, she cuts me off.

"You need to take a shower," she says. "Maybe two showers."

"For real?"

She leans over, sniffs twice, and pretends to faint back onto the couch.

"That's messed up, Kaya."

But she just lies there, pretending to be knocked out. I throw a pillow at her and she still doesn't move. "Fine. I'll shower, but you want to check out what Alice is doing after?"

She opens one eye. "That's a great idea. Hurry up!"

I laugh before heading into my room. Kaya's quickly becoming my favorite. Obviously, it's pretty easy to like Bilal. He's quick with a compliment, and always polite, but he acts that way with *everyone*. If it had been Longwei on the stairwell that first morning, I think Bilal would have joked and smiled with him too. Or he would have tried.

But with Kaya, it's like she *chose* me. First as her teammate, and now as her friend. There's something completely foreign about having someone just like me for no reason. Back home you had to earn your way into things. A sweet jump shot or a well-told joke. Get your reputation and you got your friends. Kaya's changed the rules, and I think that's a good thing.

After I towel off and dress in Babel's plush bathrobes, I find Kaya waiting in our shared living room. As I sit down across from her, though, I can tell she's a world away from the person she was just half an hour ago. A dark mood has pushed through her defenses. Her jet-black hair bunches against the arm of the sofa, and her little arms are wrapped tightly around a pillow.

"I can't stop thinking about what Roathy said at the beginning. About all of us being poor."

I take a seat at the end of the sofa. "He wasn't wrong."

"But he wasn't right either," she says. "That's not why Babel chose us."

Kaya glances at me. Her eyes are like two dark little pools. I try not to think about the fact that she's really pretty. All this time she's treated me like a brother; I want to treat her like a sister. Past all the beauty is a surprising sadness.

"Why'd they choose us?"

"We're all broken. They picked us because we're broken."

I don't like how close to the truth that sounds. The words have me shifting in my seat, feeling all kinds of uncomfortable. Not sure what else to say, I take a shot at cheering her up. I reach out and pat down my arms and legs before offering her a smile.

"You sure about that? No missing pieces far as I can see."

"You're broken," she answers quietly. "The same kind of broken as me. We're the same color, you know? It's not the worst color to be, but it still hurts."

I glance away. Vandemeer might have the degrees, but it feels like Kaya can see things he doesn't. She's right. I am broken. I should have been able to piece myself back together by now, but I spend all my time bracing for the next collision instead. I think about Moms going from warrior to wounded as the disease spread through her kidneys. I think about all the teachers who thought that because I was quiet I wasn't worth the effort. I think about PJ flirting with Shae Westwood even when he knew I was crushing. Life's thrown shots at me from every direction. Through all of it, I learned that distance is its own kind of armor.

Maybe that's the real reason I signed up with Babel. To put distance between myself and the next collision. A small part of me wants to leave now, put distance between myself and Kaya's knowing gaze. It's like she's seeing something in me that I've been trying to ignore my whole life.

"You can really see all that?" I ask.

"Like colors," she says with a nod. "It's been like that since I was . . . little. Different kinds of brokenness have different colors. All of the others have a color. Longwei, Jazzy, and Bilal are all red. That's burden. All three of them are carrying a lot of weight on their shoulders. Azima's white. She's searching for a peace that she's lost. And Roathy's black, because he's never known *any* peace. Katsu and Isadora were both betrayed. It's like gold, but the color's all faded. Then there's you, me, and Jaime. We're all blue."

It all sounds so strange, but I can't help asking, "What's blue?"

"Forgotten," she says. "We're the people the world wants to forget."

Her words hit so deep and hard that it's all I can do to release a breath. She reaches out and pats my leg, like she knows exactly how it feels to be *this* lost in yourself.

"So they chose us because we're broken, not because we're poor," she says.

"What's the difference?"

Kaya smiles now. "The pieces of broken people can be put back any which way. If we were just poor, they'd have to break us first, to make us into what they want."

I snort. "I had the distinct impression that they *were* trying to break us. Throw pennies to beggars and watch them fight. That kind of thing."

"That's the way it feels now, but it won't last. Babel want to make us *into* something. They want to carve us the right way." She sighs. "Besides, I don't care about the money."

That stops me cold. I care so much about the money that it's hard imagining someone who doesn't. I pegged Jaime as the one who didn't really care about the money, not Kaya.

"But I thought you said you were broken?"

Kaya's eyes drift back to the ceiling. "I am. Money won't fix that."

"Then why come?"

"Eden."

She makes the word sound like a promise, like a dream.

"I wanted to go to Eden. Can you even imagine it, Emmett? Another planet. With different species and people

and places. There's not much left for me on Earth. I wanted
to go as far away as possible. Where better than a new
planet?" Her eyes squeeze shut for a second. "But they don't
tell you the pain comes with you. They don't tell you that
hurt travels at light-speed too."

She slides from the couch, squeezes my shoulder, and
disappears into her room. I sit on the couch for a while
after that. I hate how right she is about all of it. When Babel
chose me, I let myself believe it was because I did something *special*. My whole life had been one bad break after
another and it finally felt like I was getting mine. Kaya's
words cast a shadow over that.

I'm about to call it a day when someone actually knocks
on the door. I stare for a few seconds, thinking I imagined
the noise, but another knock sounds. What now?

I cross the room and scan my suit, and the door gasps
open. Bilal frames the entry.

"Hello, Emmett."

"Hey, man. Everything all right?"

"Of course," he says. "I just came to formally invite you
to my room."

I raise an eyebrow. "Right now?"

He laughs nervously. "No, apologies, it is an open invitation. Come any time."

"To your room?"

He nods. "Exactly."

"Like . . . to play games or something? Help me out here,
man. I'm lost."

Bilal frowns now. "Games? I suppose we could, yes. It is
just an invitation."

I laugh now, completely confused. "An invitation for what?"

"My . . . it is . . ." He takes a deep breath. "Maybe I've been unclear. Where I am from, it is a custom to open your home to friends. I just want you to know my home is open to you and Kaya. I think highly of the two of you and would enjoy your company. That is all."

"Oh. Thanks, man. I appreciate that."

He nods, like the visit's been a success, but then he just stands there, waiting.

"Did you mean right now?"

"No, of course not." He blushes again, backpedaling. "Good night, Emmett."

I wish him good night and can't help laughing when the door shuts. He's awkward as hell, but I like the guy. I slip into my room and spend the next few hours working on manipulations. I try to imagine the others with their feet up while I have my head down and my nose to the grindstone. Eventually, though, the exhaustion has me tucked in hours before my normal bedtime. I lay there, trying to keep my mind focused on the highlights of the day.

I want to pass out to the image of Kaya reading me books, or Bilal extending awkward invitations. But I lose the fight. My mind clings to the image of Isadora. My dreams are filled with crowned eights. They multiply, circling me, and each one's holding a dark, dark dagger.

DAY 11, 9:45 A.M.

Aboard *Genesis 11*

As the new week begins, Longwei changes his method of attack.

Instead of physical violence, he demonstrates his hatred by destroying me in every single morning competition. He's first in all of our nyxia manipulations. He aces our quiz on the predominant mammals in Eden. He even surprises us in the water tank. Instead of manipulating his nyxian ring into goggles, he makes a special pair of shoes. We all crane our necks as he slips on the webbed padding and dives into the pool. I'm not sure what they are or how he made them, but he swims like he's an Olympian and crushes my times.

After each task, he looks over until I meet his eyes. It's like he's making sure I know that all of this, all his effort and all his skill, is now directed solely at me. Instead of being angry, though, I find myself smiling. I like this version of Longwei. At least this version feels human.

When lunch rolls around, I'm second on the scoreboard,

but the discussion revolves around the afternoon event. Running in the Rabbit Room will be replaced by another competition for the next nine days. Everyone's discussing the possibilities like it's going to be fun. But so far Babel's had us digitally murder each other, swim through storms, and run through exhausting obstacle courses. I doubt the next event will be midnight bowling or putt-putt.

"What if it's, like, flying little spaceships?" Jazzy suggests. "I'd love to fly something."

Katsu wags his fork. "No way they let us fly a spaceship."

"As long as it's not the Rabbit Room, I don't care what it is," says Bilal. He looks tired, like he hasn't been getting enough sleep. I guess we all look that way. "I hate the Rabbit Room."

I glance over, surprised Bilal's even familiar with the concept of hating something.

"Only because we always win," Azima teases him. "I *love* the Rabbit Room. I love to run. And I have never seen such lovely trees before."

Bilal frowns. "You ran into one of those lovely trees. Remember?"

"It was still lovely," Azima answers. "I wonder why they make us run so much. Will we run on Eden?"

Out of the corner of my eye, I catch Kaya looking deep in thought, like she's disappeared into a place where none of us can follow. Today her hair's in a thick braid that drapes over one shoulder like a sash. It takes her a minute to remember she's in a world with other people.

"Azima asks a good question."

Kaya's voice is so quiet that it silences every other conversation.

"I did?" Azima replies.

"What are they preparing us for?" Kaya's eyes are lost in calculation. "The nyxia tasks make sense. They're preparing us to use the substance we have to gather. I'd imagine it can be reduced into a certain form that's easier to transport into space. And swimming. That means there will be rivers or oceans. The Rabbit Room is either to keep us in shape or to prepare us for running from place to place. But why are they having us fight?"

"Didn't you see what happened to the marines in that video?" I ask.

Jazzy makes a face. "But we don't have to fight 'em. Mr. Defoe said the Adamites like us. We're their welcome guests."

"Maybe there are other species," Bilal suggests. "Maybe we have to fight those."

"Every action has a motive," Kaya says firmly. "I know the next task too. We haven't learned how to mine the substance. That's coming next."

Katsu shrugs his massive shoulders. "None of this matters if you're not in the top eight."

He's in the top four, feeling safe. Roathy and Isadora have the lowest scores. Every day Roathy doesn't return, his score drops and my guilt rises, but Isadora's the real surprise. Her scores weren't great to begin with, but now she's mentally checked out of the competition. She is Longwei's opposite. The only similarity between them is their isolation, their distance. But while Longwei listens to each conversation and files the information away to be used later, Isadora doesn't seem to hear a word.

She stares at the distant blast doors, waiting for Roathy to come back. Last week, I overheard Kaya trying to cheer her up. Isadora snapped for her to go away. She and Roathy didn't even know each other before boarding the ship, but his injury's made them thick as thieves. It's as if seeing him wounded drew Isadora to his side. It reminds me of the dudes who showed up to school with broken bones. Girls who didn't usually give them the time of day were lining up to sign casts or carry books.

All it means for Isadora is that her score is dropping almost point for point with his. A part of me feels bad for her, but a bigger part of me says that her loss is my gain. One less person to have to keep an eye out for. The thought leaves me feeling cold, guilty.

Defoe arrives a little later than normal. He's back in his smoke-threaded suit and looking like the whole world is bending backward to give him what he wants.

"New teams for the afternoon session," he announces.

Kaya nods like she expected it. A glance shows that Azima is distraught. I don't really know how to feel. It makes sense for Babel to mix us up, to not let us get too close with any one team or group. But I liked being on a team, and I liked winning as a team. Now the game changes.

"Emmett, Longwei, Roathy, Katsu, and Jazzy."

I can't help but glance over at Longwei. His eyes are locked on mine, and he's not happy. Finally, I think, an event he can't beat me in. The thought makes me smile. I just have to hope he doesn't stab me or something. We're short a teammate because of Roathy's absence, but even without him, we'll still have a good chance of winning. The only misfortune is being set against Kaya. My friend and ally, but also the group's best strategist.

"Kaya's team. Do you want to go first or second?"

I'm surprised to hear Defoe call them Kaya's, but her teammates don't question it. She's made a name for herself in the Rabbit Room. Longwei may have the highest score, but she's the one people rally around. She's smart and kind and quick on her feet. We watch the other team circle and listen as she whispers a plan. Jaime surfaces from their huddle.

"We'll go second," he announces.

Defoe turns and leads us straight down to the Rabbit Room. Bilal groans with disgust as the blast doors open. I'm wishing I hadn't eaten so much. How much more can they make us run? As we arrive, though, it's easy to see that the room's changed. The mesh net has been removed. Overhead, ceiling panels hang open to reveal wires and hardware. Spindly white cords dangle from the ceiling like spiderwebs. I count five thick cords. One for each member of the team.

"Initiate drill sequence," Defoe commands.

The lights in the room dim. Each thick cord branches off into five nerve endings. At the end of these smaller wires are dime-sized white circles. As we watch, the cords float upward and arrange themselves in a halo. No one moves, because it's like watching a science-fiction movie come to life. Most of Babel's technology has been an upgrade of what we have back home. This is the first time the tech makes Babel seem as alien to us as the Adamites are.

Who are these people? I glance over and catch Kaya's raised eyebrow. At least I'm not the only one thrown off by Babel's endless gadgets. I file it away under *L* for *Look Into It*.

"First team, you're up," Defoe says. "Complete the tutorial and begin your task. In order to win, you must accomplish the task faster than the other team. Good luck."

Longwei leads us out to the cords. Katsu makes a joke about mind control, but no one laughs because it feels too close to the truth. Up close, I hear electrodes firing and feel a strange warmth beneath the sentient cords. Taking a deep breath, I step beneath the nearest set and press up onto my tiptoes.

One by one, the little circles suction to my face. The first one lands and the temperature in the room goes up twenty degrees; a second later I'm sweating into my suit. The next circle attaches, and a whispering gasp of smoke sounds. The third one makes the room smell like sulfur. The fourth gives me cotton mouth, a taste like rotting cigars. And when the last one lands, my synapses all fire at once and I lurch into the unknown realities of elsewhere.

A sliver of my brain holds to the knowledge that what I'm seeing isn't real. On my left, Katsu, Longwei, and Jazzy look like wax sculptures. None of them move or talk or breathe. *This isn't real,* I think again. But then the rest of my brain attacks the sliver. It *feels* real. I put a hand up and part the rising smoke. My eyes drag across a landscape of barren hills and rock-strewn barrows. The sky isn't much of a sky. More of a misty overlord pressing down on any and every thing.

"Cool," someone says. I look over to find Katsu kneeling

on the ground. He's holding a shard of volcanic glass. He snaps it into two pieces and laughs. *"Really* cool."

Behind him, Longwei's moving now. Jazzy stands to one side, her eyes pinched shut.

"You all right, Jazzy?" I ask.

Her eyes open, and she smiles. "Yeah, sorry. The heat. It kind of feels like home."

I shoot her a smile as we start to explore the surroundings. There's something contagious about being thrust into the unknown that has us laughing and pointing like little kids. It's impossible to see much beyond two hundred meters, though. I can feel the ground pulsing like it's alive. It reminds me of the first day Defoe gave us our nyxian rings, like something waits in the stones. We're all exploring the foreign landscape when the biggest truck I've ever seen bulldozes through the misty nothing. Its wheels are twice my size. A white-railed staircase and matching ladder are built into the front of it.

As the driver pulls around, I see that the huge rig is broken up into three parts. The front end features a driver's hatch and an intricate nest of high-tech panels and switches. The middle section looks like a shadowy, robotic bird perched inside a cage of metal beams. Behind it is a loading bed that could easily fit two or three houses. A miniature rover roosts there, loaded down with its own mechanical goodies.

Smoke continues to dance around our ankles as the driver parks and descends the ladder. He's just like one of the marines from Babel's first video. Hair buzzed, utility belt brimming with gadgets, and a voice deeper than the idling truck engine.

"Welcome to the nyxian mining orientation video. Are all trainees accounted for?"

We all look around. For the first time, Roathy's absence stings in the other direction. I glance at the others guiltily before Longwei says, "Yes, sir."

The marine straightens. "I'm Lieutenant Light. Behind you is the finest piece of mining equipment you'll ever see. This machine is a hell of a lot smarter than you are, so most of the time you just let it do its thing. Whenever you arrive at a dig site, the first step is surveying the deposit. Everything starts with the command panel."

He walks us over to the truck and slides away the metal siding. The lights and clockwork underneath look as indecipherable as hieroglyphics. There's a mess of buttons and an empty black screen. He presses and holds a silver button for three seconds. "All functions require a three-second activation as a protection against accidents. This button initiates the surveying process."

Hatches between the wheel sets open, and a dark cloud of drones sweeps past us. We can hear a low buzz as they start laser-scanning the terrain. As they work, digital imaging maps itself onto the screen in front of us. Babel's bells and whistles keep getting more and more absurd.

The drones return to their hatches, and the marine brings our attention back to the screen.

"There are two readouts for every nyxia mine. The first one shows the depth and width of your deposit." A 3-D image displays a jagged underground hive of nyxia. The black spirals down some three hundred meters and stretches about half as wide. As we watch, a pink blip pings along the surface of the deposit. The marine stubs a finger at it. "That's your origin point. The very center of the deposit and, therefore, the best place to start mining. However, it's always best to consider the second screen before you begin the mining process."

He makes a show of pressing his finger to the screen and swiping left. The black hive is replaced with a diagram of crisscrossing red slashes. They're not nearly as numerous, and most of them are gathered in the deepest corners of the mine.

"As with most underground operations, there are firedamp pockets. The key thing to remember is that red is bad. Very bad. Your commander will have to keep an eye on where they are so that you don't drill right into one and get yourself blown to shit. Some of the smaller ones can be siphoned, but the computer indicates pockets that are too dangerous to get close to."

He swipes the screen a second time and the images merge. A black spiral of nyxia tainted by red gas pockets that, according to this dude, are waiting to blow me up. Great.

"The computer will make the safest decision. Keep that in mind. If your engineer sees a way around the gas pockets that will be more lucrative, that decision is up to him to make. As long as you don't endanger the lives of your team, you can deviate from the computer's decisions." The marine presses a pinkish button and counts off three seconds with his other hand. When his final finger ticks off, the truck lurches to life. We all stumble away as the engine revs and the wheels turn and the whole thing rumbles forward. Driverless. No one reacts, because self-driving cars are standard issue. It's the unloading of the drill that catches our attention.

The system controls lead the truck slightly to the left, and it heaves to a stop after about fifty meters. The marine holds out a hand to stop as a metallic screech sounds over everything. We watch the silver wings spread on their own. Huge, spiked talons extend and bury into the ground. The rest of the metal contraption slides out after them, unfolding like a massive claw.

Katsu says, "Are you guys even seeing this? This is amazing!"

Thirty seconds later, our drill hovers above the soil ominously. The thing is fifteen meters high. We shuffle to the side as the truck reverses to give the looming device a wide berth for digging.

"You'll want teams of five," he says. "Your commander monitors everything. He or she should give instructions and keep everyone working toward the goal. Second job goes to your jackjack. There's space in that drill for a driver. The jackjack has to be quick with his hands, strong, and responsive to even the slightest change beneath the surface. You need someone calm too. If shit hits the fan two hundred meters underground, they need to have ice in their veins. Two people are needed to set up your conveyor shaft, and the last person will transform nyxia into our ideal cargo dimensions. Any questions?"

Longwei raises his hand. "How do we communicate with each other?"

The marine nods stiffly. "Hold down the button on your shoulder."

We each reach for it. After three seconds, helmets spawn from the fabric at our necks. I feel mine stretch over my forehead, and then a clear visor encases me inside the suit. My breath fogs in front of me. As always, Jazzy speaks what's on everyone's mind.

"This is *amazing,* y'all."

"Totally," Katsu chirps back through the comm. We all look like *real* astronauts now.

The marine asks us if there are any questions, but I can't think of anything. We're all still in the middle of the shock-and-awe stage. Katsu was right and wrong earlier. They aren't letting us fly spaceships, but they are handing us the keys to million-dollar mining equipment. Babel's trusting, but I guess they have to be. We're their only shot at more nyxia.

After a short silence, the marine salutes us.

"Your first task is to excavate an operational tunnel. You will need to dig down to a depth of exactly one hundred and fifty meters. Good luck, soldiers."

He vanishes into the mist. We snap into motion, but it's a frantic and unsure kind of activity. We have no idea where to really begin, so we all huddle around the digital readouts and pretend we understand what they mean. The ground is vibrating in a steady rhythm with the truck's engine. Long-wei stands over the readout for a second and then pushes past us. He takes a handhold and begins climbing up the metal beams tented over the drill. When he reaches the top, he flips open a capsule and disappears inside.

"Why does he get to go in the drill?" I ask.

"I'm in the drill because I'm the best," Longwei replies.

My eyes widen. I forgot about the helmet comm. Katsu

laughs like an idiot at me. A few seconds later, the drill roars to life. We all watch the teeth spin with menace. It's impossible to hear anything but each other now. Longwei's voice pipes through again.

"Keep an eye on the readouts. If you see the gas pockets getting closer, say something."

Hydraulics hiss and the drill plunges down into the earth. Mud peels out in slick strips and we watch the silver drill bit vanish. We gather around the readout and spot the white of our drill appear on the diagram. The very tip slices into the black-labeled nyxia, and behind us the sound grows to painful decibels. The whole world shakes.

When the drill's halfway underground, I realize that this is very, very boring. There's nothing for us to do but watch the little blips on the screen.

So we watch. For almost an hour. Once, we have to warn Longwei of a red pocket that's growing five meters below and left of his current position. He presses a button that dispenses the gases and continues down. He's ten meters away when another sound cuts through the deafening rumbles. The three of us whip around as a pair of dark forms slouch through the fog.

"We have company," I say.

The screech of the drill lowers to a whine. Longwei asks, "What?"

"Monsters," Jazzy says. "On the surface."

The word *monsters* makes her sound like a little kid, but the things looming in our vision make me *feel* like a little kid. They are monsters. They move on all fours, their gait shuffling and drunken. The closer they get, the more muscle I can see in their chests and wide forearms. The closest thing I can think of in our world is a gorilla, but the word feels wrong. Instead of fur, they have diamond-shaped scales and daggered claws. Their shoulders come to jagged points, and their long tongues flicker from the deep pits of black mouths.

I'm the first to step away from the safety of our truck and toward the intruders. Focused on the image, I transform my nyxia into the shielded glove from the pit. A second manipulation forms in the shape of my jagged iron knuckles. I slide the weapons on as the animals lope toward our drill. A glance shows Jazzy walking in step with me. I'm not sure why I expected her to be afraid, but she's got her chin raised and a weapon ready. Katsu stands frozen by the truck.

"Wake up, Katsu. We need your help."

Heat's flooding up from the hole Longwei's cut into the ground. Smoke gathers and scatters as one of the beasts pauses by one of the supporting legs of our drill. It drives both clawed hands downward and the metal dents. The beast pounds again as the other stops, regarding us quietly. They're just twenty meters away now. My steps continue closing the gap.

"Hey!" I shout. I don't have a real plan, but if these things destroy one of our supports, I know the drill won't be able to keep cutting to the depth we need. "Hey, over here!"

The other lizard's attention swings, and it crosses the distance between us in a heartbeat. I slide right and let my jagged spikes rake across an exposed forearm. Most of the blow is turned away by the thick scales, but I catch skin at its elbow joint, and the beast roars with pain. Blood spits out, and I'm thrown to the side by a lowered shoulder. Jazzy screams and slashes her short sword down, severing the beast's outstretched hand.

The monster roars again and is backing away as the second one darts forward. I block two blows with my off hand and then it lands one on my hip. And *everything* shatters. I feel bones rattle and the air leaves my lungs and I feel like I'm falling through the world. The animal roars as it towers over me, but a massive sword plunges up through its exposed chest. Katsu thrusts it fully in, dodging the frantic claws until the thing gasps, coughs a death rattle, and dies. We're all panting, and I know I can't move, not even to stand. I lie back in the dirt.

"Everything all right up there?" Longwei asks.

"Just keep drilling," Katsu snaps.

The whirring of the drill picks up, and my pain doubles. I reach a hand down and groan at the slightest pressure. A strike from the creature dented metal. My bones don't dent. The hip is shattered, and shards of it feel like they've been shot like bullets into the rest of my side.

"What do we do?" Katsu asks in panic. "Jazzy, what do we do?"

Jazzy is far calmer under pressure. A glance shows her running back for one of the med kits. The edges of my vision are blurring as the edges of my pain sharpen. This is the worst thing I have ever felt. Worse than my concussion last year. Worse than the broken noses I got playing football. Worse than all the dislocated shoulders I got ballin' with PJ over the years. Jazzy yells something through the comm, but I can't make out the words.

I feel everything shrinking away. And then it stops.

We trade dirt for rubber, misty fog for dangling wires. The Rabbit Room comes back into view, and my pain vanishes. The others come snapping back to reality with me. Defoe's there with a pair of attendants. They disconnect the white cords and hand each of us a bucket.

"What's this for?" Katsu asks.

"The brain and the body don't always agree," Defoe explains.

On cue, Jazzy vomits. Katsu drops to his knees and does the same. Longwei and I are staring at each other, faces tight, like this too is a competition of wills. Something punches me in the stomach; I feel the taste of it rise, and I break first. Longwei wins again, but the spoils of victory leave him hurling into a bucket too. The attendants provide us with towels and water bottles as the other team steps in to replace us.

Bilal offers a hand to me. "And I was hoping *not* to throw up today. You all right?"

"Yeah." I'm still rubbing my hip bone. My brain can't accept that it's not shattered. I can feel the virtual reality dragging at my senses and stomach. I almost tell Bilal about the lizard-gorilla things, but catch myself. Why warn him? It's his team versus our team. He's watching me awkwardly, so I just say, "Good luck. It's a little weird in there."

He nods and joins the rest of his team. We're ushered out of the way but allowed to watch from the back of the room. The white cords attach to their hosts, and soon all five of them are floating in midair. Did we float like that? I'm not even sure how it's possible, but their hands are twitching and their legs walk them through that other world. They never move more than a few feet left or right, but it still looks a little frightening. Like watching human puppets on strings. Azima bends down and scoops a handful of invisible soil. Bilal points into the distance. It's not hard to imagine his eyes lighting up as he sees the truck for the first time.

I watch for a while before leaning back and closing my eyes. For some reason, I feel more tired than I ever did in the Rabbit Room. Like my brain and body worked harder entering another reality than they did running through a physical obstacle course.

Our group stays quiet, and I actually manage to fall asleep before Katsu wakes me up and the others start snapping out of the simulator. Just like us, they vomit into buckets and stagger around drunkenly. It's as miserable to watch as it was to feel.

Defoe announces, "Congratulations to team two. You reached the next stage five minutes faster than team one. The victory goes to you."

My shoulders slump. I wonder if Roathy's absence made the difference in round one. More likely Kaya was the deciding factor. We all expected Longwei to act like a leader, but he jumped in the drill and forgot about the rest of us. Usually, it's the kind of problem I'd take to Kaya for help, but this is the one time she won't be offering her advice, the one time our alliance is suspended. Azima starts to brag about their victory but ends up puking in the middle of her sentence. After that, both teams weave through the halls in silence.

The scoreboard looms on our left.

All eyes flicker over to it. Our daily reminder of success and failure:

1.	LONGWEI	50,750	points
2.	AZIMA	49,900	points
3.	EMMETT	48,900	points
4.	KAYA	41,450	points
5.	KATSU	41,400	points
6.	BILAL	40,300	points
7.	JAIME	37,200	points
8.	JASMINE	33,050	points
9.	ISADORA	29,080	points
10.	ROATHY	21,324	points

The damage of the day isn't awful. Third place and with a huge cushion over Isadora and Roathy. I remind myself that this is only the eleventh day of our voyage. The goal isn't to get comfortable. It's to work hard enough that if I'm the next one sick or hurt, I still won't have to worry about falling out of the top eight. Knowing that's the best advice I can give myself, I head back to the room after dinner and force myself to practice nyxia manipulations.

Faster, and faster, and faster. I push past my own limits so that when I do put my head down on my pillow, I fall instantly asleep.

DAY 12, 8:23 A.M.

Aboard *Genesis 11*

Roathy makes an appearance at breakfast. Everyone welcomes him back, wishes him well, but he ignores us. He still can't eat solid foods, so he blends a handful of fruits from the buffet bar into a smoothie and sits down with Isadora. She leans in and kisses his cheek. Kaya sees it and glances my way. Isadora's continued attachment to him is worrying. If Roathy's counting me as an enemy, then that means Isadora's counting me as one too. I glance their way a few more times and can't help feeling jealous. I want to be looked at like that. I want to be wanted.

Defoe arrives for morning exercises. As everyone's gathering to leave, I try to take the high road one more time. Isadora rejected my apology, but I still have hope for Roathy.

"No hard feelings," I tell him. "I was just playing the game."

A smile cuts across his face. Roathy looks at me the way he looks at everyone. Like he can see the strategy hidden beneath my apology. My whole body tightens as he leans in close and whispers in a voice only loud enough for my ears, "If you're going to hit someone like that, you better make sure they don't get back up."

He raises an eyebrow and walks away. Bilal sees it all and backtracks to me.

"Everything okay?" he asks.

"Yeah," I say. "Roathy's all talk."

Bilal looks even more worried. "I don't think he is, Emmett. You have to be careful."

"Nothing I can do about it now," I say. "Come on, we're falling behind."

Roathy's return isn't the only surprise. Our normal manipulations are replaced with a different kind of test. We've been pushed for focus and speed so far. Today Defoe wants to test our strength. A row of geometrical shapes runs along the back wall of the room. I spot cubes and spheres and pyramids and cylinders. They're all the black-hole color of nyxia, and as the row sweeps from left to right, they get bigger and bigger in size.

"Longwei," Defoe calls. "Step forward."

He does. His tuft of hair looks messy today and his eyes are red. As with all of us, the simulator drained him of energy. We watch him set his hand on a sphere the size of an apple.

"On my command, transform it into a 3-D shape of equal size. Ready?"

Longwei nods.

"Cube."

We watch the air ripple and a cube clatters to life. He moves on to the next one. Cylinder, cube, cube, sphere, pyramid, and so on. Longwei's about three-fourths of the way through the line when he stops in front of a sphere the size of a beach ball. There are only six objects left.

He reaches out, closes his eyes, and collapses. He twists onto his back and starts to writhe like someone has him hooked up to a transformer. I move forward to help, but Defoe holds out a hand. "He has to get out of it himself," he warns.

I curse under my breath. Even if I don't like Longwei, it's hard to watch his body get pulled around on marionette strings. It lasts for thirty seconds. When his eyes finally open, he gasps in thick lungfuls of air and lets out a terrified scream.

Longwei, the toughest and hardest one in the group, screams until a pair of attendants remove him from the room. Defoe calls Azima forward next.

She makes her cautious way through the objects. It's the first time I've ever seen her show any fear, any restraint. She looks like a child reaching into the unknown, a darkness where sharp-toothed danger waits. Her collapse comes halfway through the exercise. Invisible forces crush her, pin her, and wring the life from her. After about ten seconds, she comes gasping back to us. Azima doesn't scream, but she can't get back to her feet on her own. Bilal rushes forward and drapes her arm around his shoulder. Together they limp to the door.

What the hell is this? Kaya's name is called next.

"No," she says.

Defoe raises an eyebrow. "No?"

"No."

"Kaya, if you do not participate, you cannot earn points."

"That's fine. I'm not comfortable with this drill. I will forfeit it."

Dead silence shrouds the room. For the first time, Babel's methods are being questioned. They only have the authority we give them, and right now Kaya's putting her health over her points. I remember that the money we all so desperately need doesn't matter to her. I know she wants to go to Eden. She wants to see another place and escape a life of sorrow on Earth. So she wants to win. But right now she's saying no. Mad respect.

Defoe's expression tightens. "Five hundred points docked. That penalty will double every time we participate in this activity and you do not." His eyes dart to me. "Emmett."

Kaya glances over. Her eyes are dark pools, and I see the sadness there that I saw during our conversation on the couch. She's not trying to be rebellious; she's just terrified. Whatever the first two saw behind Babel's dark curtain, she doesn't want to see. I don't either, but competition is competition. Every point matters. I nod to her before stepping forward.

The longer I've had my ring, the less I've felt the nyxia's temptation. It still feels alive and vibrant, but I've ordered it around long enough to not be frightened of it. The first sphere of nyxia I set my hand on has a stronger lure by far. I can feel the vibrating pulse of something inside the substance. Then I hear Defoe say, "Cube."

Focused, I press the image forward and watch as the sphere sharpens into a cube. Each successive block has a

stronger influence over me. I'm only six objects down the
row when I start to feel the nyxia pressing back. Only
through intense focus can I push past its defenses and transform the object into a pyramid. My breathing slows and my
heart feels like it's barely beating. I move past the one that
Azima struggled with. Then the next one, and the next one,
until I've passed Longwei's mark.

I am stronger than you, Longwei.

Pride comes before the fall. The third to last object cuts
me away from the world.

I am drowning in the deepest waters. I am being pulled
too fast for my body. I feel my arms moving in and out of
their sockets. The drag slows, then stops, and now something outside me pushes its way in. Claws explore the deepest places, touch the parts of me I will never see. In that
impossible dark, I see a face . . . just before the lights return.

My lungs beg to be filled. I scream until they take me
away.

Vandemeer sits with me in a comfort pod. He's patient
and kind. I try not to look out into space because the black
nothing has a face now. Vandemeer notices and presses a
button, and an image of looming snow-capped mountains
replaces it. Everything with Babel is so damn point-and-
click. It's digging under my skin.

"Who are you people?"

"Just people," Vandemeer answers.

"Nah. My friends are *just* people. PJ and the Most Excellent Brothers, they're just people. Me? I'm just people. But
you guys? No way. What do you want?"

"Money," Vandemeer says. "It's always about money, Emmett. Babel wants to be the richest and most powerful corporation in the world. I joined them for the same reason. They paid the best and had the most resources. Everyone likes to be on the winning team."

And what about the losing team? I want to ask him. I want to know all the things they don't want me to know. The secrets that were digging under my skin that first day, the fears my pops had about them, they're all resurfacing. This flight must be costing them billions of dollars. So what do they want? The nyxia? Could it really be that simple? Spend a few billion to make a few hundred billion?

"What just happened to me?" I ask. "What was that?"

"Nyxia is an interactive element. You can manipulate it using your thoughts and intent. Every person is capable of manipulating the substance, but there are thresholds. We've discovered that if you try to manipulate too much, nyxia reverses the manipulation process. It's as if the substance is trying to take your skin and blood and bones and make . . . something else."

I stare at him, horrified. "So, what, we're just being used as experiments?"

"Of course not."

"Then what *was* that?"

"We've tested it extensively," Vandemeer says. He gives me a strange look, then reaches for his watch. With a few clicks, he turns it off. "Off the record, we discovered the limitations during the first mission. One of our men tried to manipulate an entire mine. He was devoured."

"Meaning what?"

"You felt it, inside of you?"

I shiver and nod. "Yeah."

"Imagine that it's not a safe, tested amount of nyxia. Imagine what you just went through multiplied by thousands."

"Sounds horrible."

"The video was difficult to watch. The victim did not die well," Vandemeer confirms. He turns his watch back on. "My suggestion would be to take it easy. You pushed yourself pretty far today. It might be wise to participate in the exercise and withdraw when you've reached a safer point. That way you can get points, but not . . ."

"Feel like I'm being killed from the inside out?"

"Yes," Vandemeer says. "That."

"Great advice, Doc."

Vandemeer frowns at that. It makes his face look even more slanted and sharp.

"Emmett, I really am here to care for you. Kaya's and your health are my primary concern on this ship. Do you understand that?"

"I appreciate it, Vandy. But at the end of the day, you're one of them. Aren't you?"

Vandemeer leans back in his chair, glances at his watch, and nods.

"Yes, Emmett. I am a Babel-employed doctor, first and foremost."

I stand up and brush by him as I pass. "Glad we cleared that up."

Old habits die hard. I didn't steal too much as a kid, but I was always looking. Always thinking about how a watch could slip from a wrist or how a pair of shoes might magically disappear from the school locker room. Spend enough time in the same old pair of jeans and everything seems worth the risk of getting caught.

But aboard *Genesis 11* there are some things that are a little more valuable than a fresh pair of kicks. Since day one, I've found myself eyeing Vandemeer's utility belt. He uses his data pad for access in the ship, but he also has a secondary identification card with an identical scanning pattern on it. He doesn't ever use it; I guess it's more of an emergency thing. Usually it's tucked safely into the back of his belt, but now it's in my pocket. A part of me just wanted to see if I had the chops to do it. But the real reason? I want to explore the rest of the ship. Babel clearly has secrets. Maybe even a handful that Vandemeer doesn't know.

I know I need to dig, to find out what Babel's got in their dark basement. Knowing what's coming might be the only thing that gives me an edge on the rest of the competition. It's my one way to pull back the veil on Babel. Answers are waiting. I just have to find them.

DAY 18, 11:23 A.M.

Aboard *Genesis 11*

Roathy's presence has haunted my week. He lurks and lingers, but every time I look over, he just walks away. Of all the competitors, we're probably the most alike. I see so much of myself in him, but one wrong turn's made him an enemy. I know he'll try to take revenge, but I have no idea what revenge means for a kid like him. If I were in his shoes, anyone who kept me from getting crucial points would have a target on their back. I get this gnawing feeling that when he does take revenge, nothing about it will be fair. The not knowing is the worst.

Babel's been running us through a series of mining tutorials. When we accidentally blew Longwei up in a simulation, the repetition started to make sense. We're not just learning how to use expensive equipment. We're learning how to stay alive as we do the job we've been hired to do.

Unfortunately, our team has gone through more growing pains than Kaya's. Girl's way smarter than the rest of us and we've been losing points each day. Longwei blames us, but he has no idea how to be a part of a team. I don't get too mad because I know we'll be racing through digital forests next week. In that competition, Kaya's strategies work for me. The hit-or-miss points make the individual competitions more important. Our continued battles in the pit are opportunities I have to cash out on.

As we enter the jungle gym of an arena, I glance over at the scoreboard:

1.	LONGWEI	62,750	points
2.	AZIMA	61,900	points
3.	EMMETT	58,900	points
4.	KAYA	53,450	points
5.	KATSU	51,400	points
6.	BILAL	50,300	points
7.	JAIME	47,200	points
8.	JASMINE	43,050	points
9.	ISADORA	39,080	points
10.	ROATHY	32,324	points

I've slid a little. Kaya's been making her way back up the scoreboard too. Really, if Isadora and Roathy weren't so low, I'd be feeling the pressure. But the scoreboard goes both ways. If I push myself, there's no reason it can't be my name in first place. The avatar screen loads, and I'm feeling juiced. Deep down, I've been looking for a fight.

Azima and Longwei go first. Azima plucks up her spear and Longwei sticks to his sword. He's improving, but that doesn't matter against Azima. She's a snake striking from high grass. For the first time, I notice how good her footwork is. She slides left and right, pushes off for her strikes, and shuffles away from each of his swings. And her shoulders too. She dips to change the angle of her attack or twists to bring the spear in from the opposite side. It's musical, almost. Longwei fights for all of twenty seconds before his avatar drops.

Next up are Roathy and Isadora. Defoe looks curious to see how the lovebirds will handle being pitted against each other. But when he gives the signal, Isadora drops both her daggers. Roathy steps forward and cuts off her imaginary head. They rejoin us on the sidelines and put their weapons away. So much for the dramatic lovers' duel.

A digital me flickers to life on the screen. Jaime fills up the other half. I can't help but smile. Jaime's not all bad, but our first standoff still looms between us. Deep down, I've been waiting for this fight as long as he has. He walks over and picks up the short swords Roathy used. I slip into my knuckled gloves and stand across from him.

He looks angry. Good. Anger burns both ways.

Defoe gives the signal and we circle.

Unlike Roathy, Jaime's not a lasher. I parry his first testing blow and jab at his rib cage. He swipes my strike away and we turn. My uncle taught me to fight patiently. Let people make mistakes and then press forward. Jaime's almost too cautious to make any. He tests me with another strike, I test him back, and then he finally overextends on a lunge.

I crunch down my off hand on his wrist, sidestep his riposte, and rake claws across his shoulder. He staggers back and I press now. Strike, circle, strike.

"You've never been in a fight," I grunt. "You've never had to fight."

And I know it's true. The way his body moves and the way his eyes stay wide instead of going tight. This guy's never fought anyone. He loses grip of one of his swords, and my killing blow is an uppercut on his chin. Babel's fixed my weapon so that my real hand can't hit his real face, but that doesn't stop Jaime from falling down onto the mat. He looks furious, but by the time he can stand back up, his avatar is dead and I'm the winner.

"You don't know anything," he says, pushing me hard in the back.

I go from dying embers to fireworks in two seconds. The speed of my turn shocks him. Nyxia snaps excitedly in my jacket pocket like it's feeding off my anger. I think about splitting open that bottom lip, but I smile instead. This is a long-term game I'm playing.

"I know I'm going to win again tomorrow. Every time we stand across from each other in here, I'm going to win again, and again, and again. Count on it."

Defoe arrives to break up a fight that isn't going to happen. I take note. He doesn't usually sweep in to break up competitive banter. He always arrives after the damage is done, like he enjoys seeing how the tasks test and stretch us. But with Jaime he comes in before I can do anything? I file it away under *S* for *Suspicious*.

I set my weapons down and watch the last two fights with the others. Kaya outfoxes Katsu, and Bilal lands a great killing blow on Jazzy. We leave the weapons behind and move on to lunch.

Eighteen days aboard *Genesis 11* and our imaginary deaths aren't bothering us anymore. In fact, we're all joking about it as we eat chicken sandwiches. Vandemeer was right. It feels unreal. The consequences don't compute because we know that tomorrow we'll fight again, that the sword wounds and the throwing stars aren't going to really hurt us. I wonder if we'll be able to flip the switch when it comes to real combat or real mining or real anything. Babel's plan is to make us numb. Execute the task without emotion. Complete the mission.

Babel's endgame is a mystery, but there are no secrets when it comes to the scoreboard. I'm in third place and I need to stay there. We finish up lunch and head down to the Rabbit Room. As expected, the lights are dimmed and the white wires are waiting to whisk us away to the virtual reality of virtual Eden. Before we can discuss strategies, Longwei crosses the room and plugs in. His body's floating before the rest of us can follow.

"Real nice," I mutter. "The captain who forgets his teammates."

"Dude's a little intense," Katsu says. "We should offer him a massage."

Jazzy joins us. "He doing it all by himself, then?"

"Maybe," I say, "but I'd at least like credit for whatever His Magnificence pulls off."

"Me too."

The voice is so close that my body goes rigid. Roathy lopes past like a jackal, his eyes never leaving mine, his laugh echoing in my ears. He knows, for just a second, that

I forgot he was there. And I know that he could have transformed his nyxia into a knife and tucked it neatly into my
back.

I ignore his crooked grin and take my place beneath
the wires. One by one, my senses leave here for there. Our
drill's in the ground and Longwei's the only one not standing with us. A massive hand slaps against my clear face-
plate, and I almost fall trying to scramble away from it.
Katsu laughs through the comm and holds up the severed
lizard hand from the first day.

"You should have seen your face," he says.

Scowling, I turn back to the drill. "Longwei, are you in
there?"

It's different today. For the last few simulations we've
been thrust right into tutorial sessions—all kinds of new
lessons and tools—but today looks like we're picking up
right after day one's progress. Inside the pit, we hear the
hydraulics of the drill. There's no answer from Longwei
and no sign of the monsters.

"Longwei," I say, louder, "unless you plan on coming in
second every time, we'd love to know what's going on so we
can actually help."

"I'm coming back up," he says. "The drill has to retract
to start the next step."

A glitch opens up to our right and Lieutenant Light
ghosts back onto the set. Then the hole in the world closes,
he smiles, and it's like nothing ever happened. He gestures
at the drill.

"Now that you have your drill in place, it's time for one

team to start shearing and for the other team to set up your secondary tunnel. Follow me."

We trail him back to the readouts on the side of the truck. He points at the results of Longwei's efforts. The drill is a white line diving down into a black sea of nyxia. It's a little crooked here and there, but it looks fine otherwise.

"Not bad, but your driver has to be stronger on the grips as he goes down. The straighter the tunnel, the easier your job is. That bottom area? That's where all the nyxia will collect now. Everything your jackjack shears off the vert-walls funnels down to the bottom. The secondary tunnel will allow you to extract the nyxia as the jackjack expands the initial dig site."

He holds and presses a blue button. I count off three seconds before there's movement on the display screen. A blue dot appears along the surface fifty meters away from our original entry point. As we watch, a matching line cuts diagonally into the ground until it connects at the lowest point of our tunnel. The marine steps away.

"Now all you have to do is press the blue button again. The minirover will initiate, and you'll have your second-ary tunnel under way. Your task today is to begin mining the main shaft, set up your conveyor belt, and extract one pound of nyxia. Oh, and one other thing." He sets a massive hand on the gun in his holster. "As you've noticed, some-times drilling attracts the tars. You may have also noticed they hit like hammers. Just make sure you activate the de-fense system on the console whenever you have approach-ing bogeys. Good luck, soldiers."

He walks off into the mists again. Before we can discuss anything, Roathy jabs the blue button. Three seconds later, metal grinds at the back of the truck. We round the corner and almost get decapitated by an extension ramp. It lowers onto the ground, and a seriously souped-up go-kart wheels off on its own. A swirl of dust follows it for fifty yards, and we watch as another miniature drill unloads itself from the vehicle's metallic back.

"Katsu," I say. "You and Jazzy take care of the secondary tunnel."

Katsu nods. The two of them jog off in that direction, and I realize I can actually order people to do things. Glancing over, I also realize I've left myself alone with Roathy. His expression is amused, like he's daring me to give him an order. He smirks before saying, "Don't worry. I'll go with them."

He takes off and I'm left alone. I return my attention to the digital layout. I can see everything. Swirling red pockets underneath the surface, the main drill fully retracted, and even the activated rover hovering over the blue dot on our map. I watch the little blips for as long as I can stand, then turn back toward the main drill site.

"How's it going, Longwei?" I ask.

"I don't know," he says. "It's stuck."

"What's stuck?"

"The drill. I'm pressing down like I did yesterday, but it won't move."

I start walking that way, when Katsu cuts through the head comm.

"Emmett!" he shouts. "Hey. Activate the defense thing. The lizard-gorilla things are back. The tars or whatever! A *lot* of them incoming."

I scramble back over to the control panel and find the switch labeled DEFENSES. I double-check that it's the right one and flip it. Metal screeches as two turrets unfold atop our truck. It happens as fast and unrealistically as it does in video games. In *KillCall,* you can set down a gun turret and it just pops to life and starts shooting. Apparently, that's what happens when Babel designs things. The two guns sweep for a target and start firing. The report is loud, but not so loud that I can't hear the distant cry of wounded tars. Katsu and Jazzy cheer into the comm.

I head back over to help with the drill. "Want me to take a look, Longwei?"

His answer is quiet. "Yes."

I start scaling one of the legs of our metallic drill stand. Careful to keep my balance, I tiptoe across webbed metal to the hatch. With a twist and a pull, I pop the top and glance inside. Longwei's face is streaked with sweat. His mask is completely fogged and his hands are wrapped tight around two black levers. He looks up and presses the levers forward to show me.

"It won't go down," he says.

"Have you tried the other levers?"

He shakes his head. "This is the lever to go down. The other levers are for the side drills. There's no point in using the side drills until I take it back underground."

"Just try them," I say. "Maybe it will reactivate the levers that aren't working."

"That doesn't make sense," he says.

I frown before glancing off toward the others. From this height, I can see the rover and their vague shapes in the fog. "Jazzy," I call. "How's the secondary tunnel coming?"

"About halfway down," she says, accent thicker than syrup. "We're doing good, but we might need help settin' up the conveyor. It's kind of weird."

I look back at Longwei. He's still stubbornly pushing at his black levers. I press the button on my shoulder, and the helmet retracts back into the padding. My comm vanishes with it and I'm breathing in fresh air. "Longwei!" I shout. The helmets were muffling everything. Even though the drill isn't digging, the engines hum and the pistons snap restlessly. I lean down and shout louder, "Longwei, let me try. It's okay. They need you for the conveyor belt."

I can see the war happen inside of him. He loves winning about as much as he hates me. Give up and he admits his defeat, but keep acting stubborn and we keep losing to Kaya. After a second, he nods to himself and unbuckles. I give him a helping hand out of the jackjack seat.

When he's up top, he presses his own helmet button. Wind tosses his front tuft of hair and he wipes away sweat with the back of his glove.

"I could have done it," he says. "I didn't need your help."

"I know. You would have figured it out." I look back at the truck and decide to tell the lie that Longwei needs to hear. He can't accept his own weakness, but he'll be more than happy to use mine as an excuse. "I can't understand the monitor. You can. We need you commanding us. Call everything out, all right?"

We both reactivate our helmets. The heat intensifies as I climb into the cockpit of the drill. The seat is hot and the air is hot and I'm sweating balls inside my suit. I take my seat and the world is one vibrating earthquake. I try to calm my breathing as my teeth start clattering together.

There's a ton of digital readouts in front of me. I don't know what they mean, but I know I've got to get this thing down and mining or we're toast. The black levers are useless, so I start pulling and pressing other things. The drill responds when I wrap a hand around the silver joystick on my right. Everything vibrates a little more. I press it forward and metal whirrs. On my display, the right drill spins. That's a start.

I take hold of the joystick on my left and turn both at the same time. Both the side drills spin, and Longwei's trusted black levers retreat into the dashboard. My chair leans back and the display adjusts so that I'm almost lying down to look up at it. Down by my feet, a silver panel lights up like a game of *ElectraDance*. I punch both feet down and the drill lurches to life. The bottom windows go dark. On my monitor, I can see the tip of the drill moving into the shaft and my side drills a few meters from first contact.

There's a brief hiss and then I'm rag-dolling as the drills corkscrew into the walls of nyxia on my left and right. My display shows it falling in thick strips. I'm just trying to keep hold of both joysticks when the left one starts to glow. The metal goes bright white for a second, then nothing. The right one repeats the process. I keep pressing deeper into the hole and my two side drills gobble up everything in reach. Even with the insane vibrations and the rawness of

my hands, I feel like I'm playing the coolest video game
ever.

I'm fifteen meters deep when the left side of my display is taken over by Lieutenant Light. He's twelve inches
tall, but his voice is just as deep. "Don't forget to use your
pulses when the side drills fully extend, soldier. And if you
push her too fast, you'll advance without shearing away the
maximum pull. Good luck."

My eyes dart around the rattling room for pulses. What
the hell are pulses? Both of my handles light up at the same
time. I realize they're signaling that the drills are, as the
marine just reminded me, fully extended. So where's the
pulse button? I probe upward with my index finger and find
a button. Laughing to myself, I say, "It *is* a video game!"

The next time my grips light up, I squeeze the trigger
and a thunderclap echoes out. Stone explodes on the displays, and even my glass windows are pounded by the falling debris. In spite of the heat, a chill goes down my spine.
That was a lot of power. A lot.

"Emmett." Longwei's voice. "You've got a gas pocket ten
meters down. It's on your left and it's only two or three meters into the rock. I'd immobilize that drill in five meters."

"Copy," I say, because that's what they're always saying
in video games like *KillCall* or *Gadget Swing.* I let the drill
ride out a few more shears and then pull my left joystick in
to my chest. The drill retracts, and I guide it steadily past
the gas pocket. Longwei clears me, and I go right back to
thunder and vibrations on both sides as the world gives way
all around me. It's been a long time since I felt this useful
doing anything.

We come vomiting out of the simulator about thirty minutes later. Jazzy had to climb halfway down the tunnel to get our conveyor unkinked, but everything else went flawlessly. Longwei led us and even Roathy helped. Our team set an amazing pace because he shifted into new roles wherever he was needed.

We wait restlessly for Kaya's team to finish their section and are rewarded by Defoe's smile. "Congratulations on your first victory, team one. You're all dismissed for dinner."

Kaya offers her compliments, and we're all walking back when I feel it. Coasting along my right shoulder, just out of view. Roathy's trying to deliver the message he's been sending me all week. *I'm here. I'm watching you. I will take my revenge.*

My patience is a thin, twisted little thing, though.

I whip around, grab two fistfuls of collar, and shove him up against the nearest wall.

Only it's not Roathy; it's Jaime. His pale green eyes go wide, and I can tell I banged his head hard against the wall. Kaya and Bilal are backtracking, eyes on me like I'm a bomb they have to defuse. I release Jaime's collar and mutter, "Just don't follow me like that."

"I was just walking," Jaime says. "It's a hallway. We were all just walking, lurch."

He gives me a look that could rival Longwei's and slides past. I watch him walk, watch the others turn to follow after him. When they're gone, I lean my head up against the cold metal walls and close my eyes. I think about space, about drowning in darkness, about being the threat that others fear. Am I their Roathy? Do I make *them* worried? It's been thirty seconds and I've already lost the thrill I felt inside the drill simulation. Now I'm just scared. Now I just feel lost.

The only good thing about being a black hole is that other black holes recognize you.

"Come on, Emmett," Kaya says. She came back for me. She takes my arm in hers, like I've just forgotten the way home. "Do you want to eat dinner?"

"No," I say. I'm not hungry. I'm not anything.

"Me neither," she says. "Come on."

Patiently, she guides me back to our rooms. She leads me over to my closet and looks the other way as I change into my pajamas. Then she actually tucks me into bed.

"Don't leave," I say. "I don't want to sleep. I always have these dreams."

She nods. "One second."

As she slips out of the room, I realize I'm crying. It's more than just the darkness I feel lurking inside. I miss Pops and Moms. I miss going to normal school with its normal expectations and normal people. I want the city smells and factory stacks on my way to school. I would even pay good money to babysit my cousins at this point. Anything to feel normal again.

Kaya returns with three books stacked in her arms. She climbs onto the empty half of my bed, sits on top of the covers, and leans against the wall. "I'll read to you."

I smile until she shows me the covers. They're all in Japanese. The pictures are startling. The first one has a skull in one corner and features a shirtless boy, face buried in his hands. On the cover of the middle book is a white guy with the transparent outline of a hatchet etched through his hair. They both look like the opposite of bedtime stories. Not nearly as playful as Alice.

"Why'd you pick such scary books?" I ask, half laughing.

She shrugs. "They had boys on the cover. I don't know!"

I smile again. The third option features a boy and a girl. The boy is leaning against a massive tree. The girl is seated on the roots, reading something. The whole scene is bathed in golden light, and they're looking off into the eager distance. "That one. Read that one."

Kaya tosses the other books onto the floor. She crosses her legs and begins.

Like the first time, she makes the story come to life. Her voice is so vibrant and full that I can feel myself being pulled away from Babel's dark world. I find myself racing through the woods with the characters, crossing a bridge into some imaginary land. I hear breathing and laughter, sounds softer than the falling leaves Kaya describes. She reads until I fall asleep, until I'm no longer afraid.

DAY 19, 7:58 A.M.

Aboard *Genesis 11*

1.	AZIMA	65,900	points
2.	LONGWEI	63,750	points
3.	EMMETT	61,900	points
4.	KAYA	60,450	points
5.	BILAL	57,300	points
6.	KATSU	54,400	points
7.	JAIME	49,200	points
8.	JASMINE	45,050	points
9.	ISADORA	42,080	points
10.	ROATHY	34,324	points

At breakfast, conversation revolves around Azima.

It's the first time that she's not wearing her traditional bracelet. The dark space of her wrist looks naked without it. Katsu makes a big deal out of it, pretending there's a new competitor on the ship. He introduces her by a Japanese phrase that simply translates as Lovely Flower. Azima laughs until Katsu claims that their ex-competitor Azima has agreed to donate all her points to him.

"I am the king again," he proclaims. "And you are my loyal subjects."

Azima threatens him with a fork. "Those are my points. You cannot have them."

"What was it?" I gesture to my own wrist. "The bracelet you wore."

"A reminder. My people were the last nomadic group in Africa. We stopped our wandering, but I wear the beads as a reminder that we are a people born for *motion*. The beads tell my story. A girl also wears them to attract a worthy man."

Jazzy scrunches her nose. "So you were trying to attract a worthy man?"

"I was," Azima says between bites. "In the beginning."

"What does that even mean?" I ask.

Azima considers me. "I made a deal with Mr. Defoe."

"We all did," Katsu replies. "It involved a lot of money, as I recall."

"No," Azima continues. "I added something. I wanted to be allowed to pursue a husband if I found one of you to be worthy of me."

Three of us choke on our food. Awkward silence dominates the table. Pursue a husband? Azima's eyes are narrowed with a wide smile that her nyxian mask hides. I find myself avoiding eye contact, just in case that's the deciding factor in who she chooses.

"Don't worry. It is our way. A woman must be strong. A woman must learn to defend herself. She must rise into womanhood with purpose. If she does this, only a worthy man can approach her father for marriage." We all stare again. Azima is serious. She wants to get married. Possibly to one of us. "I have worked hard to make sure my husband is held to a high standard. Being invited on this mission raised that standard even higher. If I were still living in my village, my parents would search for a young man of equal ability, someone who could keep up with me. It's only natural that I consider those who were honored with invitations to this mission. You have achieved what I have achieved."

"Well, which one of us is it?" Katsu asks, puffing his chest out. "You've seen my work with the ax. I don't want to say I'm the obvious choice, but . . ."

"No. None of you, because I'm the strongest warrior." She points her fork at the scoreboard. Her name glows at the top. "You can't protect me. In fact, I will have to protect you. The only realistic option is to marry myself."

We all laugh when Katsu offers to officiate the ceremony. Defoe arrives, though, to break up the fun. We're escorted to the wall of nyxian objects again. One by one, we're punished in a nyxian prison. The only two who don't come out screaming are Jazzy and Roathy. After getting rag-dolled for ten seconds, Jazzy straightens, takes a deep breath, and returns to the line without saying a word. I guess it isn't a huge surprise. She's always the calmest under pressure.

Roathy's resistance to the nyxia feels different. The darkness takes him, but he shrugs it off, like he's been through way worse than a mysterious force grinding through his insides.

When it's finally my turn, I take Vandemeer's advice because I don't want what happened last time to ever happen again. So I convert the objects until I start to feel the nyxia pushing back, too big to control. I step away from the objects and nod over at Defoe. "I'm done."

His face tightens. "Your loss."

Points trickle into my score, and Defoe calls Kaya. She refuses again, and we wait for Azima and Longwei to finish the challenge. Both of them are too competitive to stop early. After Azima gets her dose of torture, Longwei pushes as far as I did before hitting the floor, harder and longer than last time. We watch his body flail. He gasps back to us, but doesn't scream this time. Instead, he stands up and points at the blocks angrily. For once his anger isn't directed toward any of us. It's aimed at Defoe. "You shouldn't ask us to do the impossible."

"Impossible?" Defoe replies. His questions are always poison-tipped and red-clawed.

"The objects are too big," Longwei says. "It's designed to make us fail."

"It's designed to push you beyond your current limitations."

Defoe stands beside the very last object. It's a cube that comes up nearly to his hip. He sets his hand on the dark surface and closes his eyes. The substance shivers into another shape.

"Impossible?" he asks again.

He sets his hand back down on the top of a nyxian pyramid and transforms it into a sphere, a cube, another pyramid, and finally back into a cube. Each time, the transformations get faster and faster. I see sweat trickle down his forehead, but otherwise the performance is effortless.

"That is amazing," Azima whispers.

"But not impossible," Defoe says in reply. "Unlearn your idea of impossible."

Hell of a show-and-tell, I think. Hell of a mistake too. Before, we didn't know what he or any of the Babel employees were capable of. Now we do. We know he's strong. Stronger than us. Fighting him with nyxia would be impossible. I file it away under *D* for *Danger.*

We cross over to the pit. My eyes flick to the scoreboard, and I'm thankful for Vandemeer's advice. I didn't get tortured by the nyxia, *and* it didn't cost me much in the standings either. As we funnel inside, I find myself looking forward to another fight with Jaime. I made a promise yesterday to our finely groomed friend, and I intend on keeping it.

The other fights just quicken my pulse. All the results are repeats, except this time Roathy drops his swords and sacrifices himself to Isadora. By the time Jaime and I take our place in the center of the arena, I'm a dangerous, dangerous man. He stands across from me, with his perfectly combed hair and pale green eyes. He looks pissed off. He's gritting his teeth and white-knuckling the grips of his swords. Trying to pump himself up for a fight.

People think that works. I used to do it whenever I played PJ one-on-one in basketball. And he'd crush me like a grape. Most of the time, the only thing that matters is skill.

Defoe gives the signal. Jaime doesn't dance this time.

He lashes out with his right sword and follows immediately with his left. He keeps up the rapid blows and pushes blindly forward, trying to rock me back on my heels. It's a desperate tactic. I ward off the first four blows, set my feet, and use his imbalance against him. A quick duck sets me up to rip a good shot across his rib cage. His avatar bleeds. I could just step away and let the wound leech away his health bar. But I don't do that. I want to punish, to finish, to destroy.

Jaime crowds me again, swinging an off-handed lash. I block, put two jabs into his stomach, and slide. My footwork is perfect as I step into a final, punishing hook. He doesn't flinch, though. He's supposed to flinch. Instead, he moves into my swing and brings up one of his swords.

If this was real life, Jaime wouldn't have a jaw.

If this was real life, I'd be short an organ.

The pain rips through my stomach and our legs buckle. Simulated pain feels a lot like real pain. Jaime and I are a sweating tangle of limbs. Pain sears through me again, and Jaime's eyes go wide in terror. I panic, thinking I've hurt him the way I hurt Roathy. I trace his stare back to my own stomach, though. The pain triples. A bright, scarlet circle is spreading there. His blade's plunged through my suit and into my stomach. This isn't a simulation. This isn't fake. This isn't happening to my avatar, then translating into my brain. A real sword is in my real stomach.

I fall backward. When I try to speak, it comes out as a bloody cough. A crowd of masked faces, the slap of foreign tongues, and then a quiet, nyxialess darkness.

DAY 21, 1:37 A.M.

Aboard *Genesis 11*

Vandemeer is lounging in a space chair in the corner. The Dutchman never *really* lounges. He's always sitting with a leg crossed or with his arms folded or with a pen twirling between his fingers. I pretend to read a book as he monitors my numbers on his data pad. He's been sitting there for the last twenty-four hours. I almost took it for genuine concern. But then I remembered he's with Babel. This is his job. I'm his meal ticket. Nothing more.

"When can I leave?" I ask again.

"Mr. Atwater, you had internal surgery. A blood trans-fusion. Your injuries are serious."

"When?" I repeat.

He sighs, swipes his data pad, and shrugs his square shoulders. "Another week."

"I can do some of the tasks. The nyxia manipulations, at least."

"No," he says. "You can't."

"Yes, I can."

He sighs again. Standing, he fetches an orange from the food bin in the corner. He crosses the room and hands it to me. "Peel this," he commands.

He sets the orange in my open palm. I frown in concentration and begin working the peel away. I can feel sweat trickling down my forehead after I've pulled off just a few thick sections. Halfway through, my hands are shaking. Vandemeer snatches it from me and peels the rest.

"Tired?" he asks. "Hurting?"

"I'm fine." I lean back in bed and breathe unsteadily. I feel empty. "I can do this."

"Maybe if you were willing to take the appropriate painkillers," Vandemeer tries again.

"No," I reply. "No drugs."

"At least tell me why you don't want them."

"Doesn't matter. It's not an option."

Vandemeer sighs. He's been digging at the corners of the truth all day, but my past is my own. Babel has their hands on a lot of me right now, and I don't have to give them anything else. They don't need to know that I've brushed shoulders with drug addicts at school and in my neighborhood. I've seen good dudes go down dark roads, and a while back I promised myself I'd never follow in their footsteps. Painkillers seem harmless enough, but I still see it as the beginning of something I'm not looking to get started. I file it away under *N* for *No Thanks*.

Vandemeer glances back down at my medical charts.

"Have it your way. You'll just have to let your body heal. You can't compete like this."

"I could handle it."

"No, you couldn't."

"Try me."

Vandemeer's patient veneer cracks ever so slightly. His eyes show a flash of annoyance.

"Lift your arms."

Gritting my teeth, I hold both hands out.

"All the way up," he challenges.

I get them up to my shoulders before I feel it. A slashing pain that runs its way to something worse, something with real fire. I hold my hands up defiantly until Vandemeer forces them back down to my side.

"It would be far more impressive if your heart rate weren't through the roof." He takes a towel and gently wipes the sweat from my forehead.

"I can do it," I repeat. "Just let me try."

"If anyone could, it would be you," Vandemeer says. "But you're not going anywhere. Not until I clear you. Rest. Heal. We'll begin therapy in a few days and you'll be allowed to rejoin the others." When I start to complain, he sets a hand on my shoulder. "Emmett, you're not going to lose. I've watched you. You're too tough. You want this too much to lose."

My eyes meet his. "It doesn't matter."

"Of course it matters," he says softly. "I know how much it matters to you."

"If you did, you'd let me back in the game."

He shakes his head. "You'd earn a handful of points. You'd overextend yourself and your body wouldn't heal. An injury would just land you right back in the med unit."

"Whatever," I say. "Just let me sleep, then."

Frustrated, Vandemeer deliberately reaches down and turns off his watch.

"You're going to have to *trust* me," he whispers. "Have you ever considered that I might benefit from your success, Emmett?"

I throw him a dark look. "Like, you want my money?"

Vandemeer laughs. "No, not like that. You might have noticed that Babel believes in healthy competition."

"Healthy? I'm in a hospital bed."

"You know what I mean," he replies. "You aren't the only ones competing."

He can't be serious. "What? Best doctor gets a bonus? How does that even work?"

"We were allowed to choose," he says. His cheeks color in embarrassment.

"Choose?"

"I chose you and Kaya. We receive a large bonus if we are the primary caretaker of the top performers. The better our patients do, the more money we get."

I nod. Of course. Babel's fundamental belief is competition. Give a person an incentive and then remind him that someone else is working toward the same reward. They'll both work twice as hard, and Babel only has to give out one prize at the end. It's smart, but it means that the higher-ups don't just see *us* as chess pieces. They see *everyone* as chess pieces. Vandemeer's an actual flesh-and-blood doctor. He gave up other pursuits to have his strings pulled by Defoe on *Genesis 11*. All for a fat bonus. Deep down, he's no different from me.

Vandemeer nods once and heads for the door. I call out just before he leaves.

"Do you know what happened? With the sword?"

Vandemeer's features darken. He really doesn't like that I got hurt. I know now that it's more than just false concern. His success depends partly on mine. Maybe he really cares.

"Someone used a piece of nyxia to recreate the sword," he answers. "It was swapped with the blunted version we keep in the armory. The copy wasn't great, but it didn't get noticed."

"It was Jaime," I say.

Vandemeer's face betrays nothing. "They're still investigating."

Back to diplomacy and the careful, calculated responses of a Babel employee. He might want me to trust him, but he's a little too much of a chameleon for that. I file away our conversation under *W* for *Wishful Thinking.* The door hisses open and shut as he leaves.

I close my eyes. In my mind, I can still see Jaime. The step forward into my punch, the forward thrust of his sword. I can also see the surprised look on his face. A stubborn part of me calls it acting. The realistic part of me thinks he didn't have a clue. It's not hard to trace the sword back to Roathy. He used it in the fight before. He could have manipulated it at any point, knowing he wasn't actually going to fight Isadora. All he had to do was switch the blades and hand them to Jaime. I hate having so much anger and no direction for it.

Either way, I'm stuck in here. And they're out there.

There's no scoreboard in the med unit. I can only imagine
the truckloads of points they're all snagging in my absence.
I have no idea how long I'll be in here, how far behind I'll
be. I press a button that dims the harsh fluorescence overhead. In the softer glow, I open the English version of the
book Kaya read to me. Apparently I asked Vandemeer for
it when I was first brought down to get stitched up. I've
never really read on my own. Too many cousins to babysit.
Too many nights watching Moms sleep on the couch. Sitting there and listening for her next breath. And the next.
And the next.

I never thought of escaping into a book.

So as I read, I'm surprised how quickly the words take
me from the hospital bed and into the woods. I'm the one
swinging into imaginary lands on hanging ropes. I like it
there. But I don't like it when I'm the one facing the bully
in the school hallways. I don't like it when my friends leave
me and I'm all alone. The words of the book echo.

Words about being tricked, about being invited into a
new world, only to be abandoned. The character in the
book feels stranded, like an astronaut left alone. I wonder
why Kaya hasn't visited. Or Bilal? Setting the book aside, I
flip the lights. I don't like the words in the book or the way
they make me feel. I close my eyes against the pain in my
side and the ache in my heart.

Sleep comes eventually, mercifully.

The slightest twist sends fire up my side.

"Careful," preaches Vandemeer.

He has me move patiently through yoga exercises. Lunges and squats and deep breaths. Without painkillers, it's a slow process. Far slower than I want it to be. Already six days have passed. Vandemeer refuses to tell me the scores, and the others don't visit. Not even Kaya. I'm the lonely astronaut from the book.

"Why didn't you just use nyxia to heal me?" I grunt. Vandemeer has me flat on my back, lifting my legs six inches off the floor. It's second-level hell.

"Doesn't work," he says. "If nyxia causes a wound, we can't use nyxia to heal it."

"Seems limited."

I sit up. He motions for me to spread my hands slowly while dipping my chin.

"It's the way the substance works," he says. "Nyxia was purposed to cut through you. If we try to use nyxia to heal the wound, the substance refuses. It's smart enough to recognize its own work and it won't undo that work. Make sense?"

"That's creepy. You understand how creepy that is, don't you?"

Vandemeer coaches me through a deep breath and a neck roll. "It's an interactive substance. The matter is far more clever than Babel likes to admit. We don't quite know how it all works, but we're learning every day."

"So the nyxia is all connected?" I ask.

"How do you mean?"

"You said it knows that nyxia was used to cut me open. So doesn't that mean it *knows* what the other nyxia did? Like they're connected somehow?"

"Or the new nyxia recognizes a change in your cells. We don't really know."

I shrug my shoulders back.

"Seems stupid to put that much faith in something you don't understand."

"Electricity, gasoline, vaccinations. You can't make progress without taking risks."

"I guess," I say. "But are you sure we aren't all going to get cancer or something?"

"Everything causes cancer," Vandemeer deadpans. "Except for nyxia. We've tested it."

"On what?"

He steeples his fingers. "Classified."

I laugh. Then my ribs feel like they're being kicked by a pair of giants. I collapse to the floor in pain and Vandemeer tosses a towel at me. "Great job today. You're close."

"I'm ready."

He ignores me. "Let's run a few more diagnostics tomorrow. Your range might still be limited. Fighting in the pit won't be easy, but most of the other tasks should be fine. Sound good?"

"Yeah, yeah. Sounds good."

"In the meantime," Vandemeer says, tapping his data pad, "I have a surprise for you."

A screen unfolds from a compartment in the wall. It looms over my hospital bed. I give Vandemeer a confused look. "You missed your first scheduled call home. I took the liberty of setting you up for one while you're down here. The call will patch through in two minutes."

"Are you serious?"

He smiles. "I'm serious."

With that, he backs out of the room. I forgot that I'd get to see them. I hadn't realized how much I missed them. I miss Moms handing me my book bag every morning and pulling me in by the neck to give me a kiss. I miss Pops reclined in his favorite chair, reading out box scores from yesterday's games. We may have been poor, but at least I knew what I was waking up to every day. The next three years will be an experiment in the unexpected and unpredictable. I stare at myself in the reflection of the black screen. I'm not ready for this, for any of it.

Two minutes of waiting feels more like thirty.

Then light flickers to a steady glow. I didn't realize I was holding my breath. I try to settle against the too-soft pillows as pixels resolve and my pops fills the screen. I can't help searching for Moms in the background, but she isn't there.

A smile splits his face. "There he is. My boy."

"Hey, Pops," I say. "I miss you. You and Moms both."

My face hurts from smiling, from trying not to cry. He apologizes for Moms. He doesn't have to say why she's not there, because I understand. It hasn't been easy for her to travel, and I'd guess Babel's communication center is a road trip for them. He's quick to remind me that she loves me, to say the words she'd say if she weren't so sick and tired and beat down. It guts me to know that just three weeks has put me a few million kilometers away from them. I hate that I can't smell the factories or his thick-scented soap. Smiling, he rubs a finger and thumb over the edges of his mustache.

"What's this?" he asks. "You working a little facial hair?"

I run a finger above my own identical lip. The stubble there is thicker now.

"You think I should shave it?" I ask.

"Up to you," he says. "Just make sure you use shaving cream. Take a close look at which direction the hair is going and shave with the grain. Not against it. Got it?"

I nod. "Thanks, Pops."

He's all smiles. "So tell me about everything. How is it?"

"It's fine," I say. "It's hard, but we all started out not knowing anything."

"So you're doing well?"

"I was," I say. "A few bumps since then, but I'm getting into my zone."

He nods encouragingly. I don't have the stomach to tell him that I almost died. All it would do is make him lose even more sleep.

"Well, it's just the first few weeks. A season isn't won

or lost in the first couple games. Remember the Lions' last run?"

"They started out 0–4," I answer.

"People overreact. Thought the world was ending in Detroit. They made their run, stuck to their plan, and won it all."

I'm nodding. He's right. Even if I'm down a few thousand points, I still have a long way to go. The others are going to get sick, injured. All I have to do is keep steady. Be better than two other people. Do that, and I return to Detroit as a king. Thinking about Detroit just has me thinking about PJ, and my boys, and before long my heart's hurting even more.

"Who'd they pick up in the draft?"

"This back out of Wisconsin," he answers. "Great motor on him."

"How we lookin'?"

He grins. "I think it's either us or London this year. Should be a hell of a season."

Hearing about Detroit fills my heart up. I ask for more.

"PJ keeps coming by," he says. "Asking about you. He's a good kid when he's not trying to prove he's unbreakable. I always think of him as the kid who jumped through our window."

I grin. Like most of our childhood stories, the window thing was my fault. I pointed out that superheroes are born through trial. How could we know whether or not PJ was superhuman without a few experiments first? I had him run timed sprints, lift my dad's weights, and jump through a window at full sprint. His parents kept him away as long as they could after that. Which was about a week. We were too close to separate. The memory feels like it happened to somebody else in some other life.

"I miss him." I think about the fact that none of the other competitors have visited me. I thought of Kaya, Bilal, and Katsu as friends. But they haven't visited, not once. "I miss all of you."

"We miss you too. But right now, you have a mission," he reminds me. "You work hard and keep your head up and we'll be right here when you get back. All right?"

I nod, but can't quite meet his eyes. He believes in me more than I could ever believe in myself. "Pops," I say. "Can I ask you a question?"

"Anything."

I ask what's been gnawing away at me. "Am I a bad person?"

The playfulness vanishes from his face. He looks at me like he's checking for scars.

"Did someone tell you that? These Babel people?"

I shake my head. "No, I just feel it. I get so angry. At the other kids, at myself."

"Emmett." He says the name like a reminder of something forgotten. "You're the best of me and you're the best of her. Ever since you were little, that's the way it's been."

"I don't feel that way," I say.

"You're off in space fighting a war against nine other people. You can't expect to always feel like yourself. Just don't lose who you are. Are you a bad person? Of course not. Does that mean you'll always do the right thing? Of course not. No one's perfect."

"I just want to win. More than anything."

"Win or lose"—he shrugs, like they're the same—"I'm proud of you. We all are."

Would he be proud of me if he knew what I did to Roathy? Or how I provoked Jaime because he was different? I feel the shame bottlenecking in the narrow alleys of my heart.

"Hey, that reminds me," he says. "Your moms started treatment. These doctors that Babel suggested are amazing. She—"

But the feed gutters out before he can give me a taste of more hope. I stare at my reflection in the blank screen. A lonely astronaut in the pitch. I lie back and snag my player from the bedside table. I scroll through songs for a while.

The one I choose has thick beats that blend at the beginning before smashing against each other in the chorus like titans. All my chaos runs into the music. I play the song three times, louder and louder, until all I can hear is music, the pulse and the beat.

DAY 28, 5:30 A.M.

On the morning I'm scheduled to return to action, I wake up to a shadow in the doorway. Smooth as silk, Marcus Defoe glides into the room. I haven't seen Defoe during my recovery. I look around for Vandemeer, but he's gone. Defoe pauses at the foot of the bed.

"Back to full health?" he asks.

His tone makes it sound like we're at a bus stop and he's asking about the weather.

I nod. "I'm ready."

"Good. You're falling behind."

Everything in me wants to ask how far. Or to tell him it isn't fair, that I've been cheated. But he doesn't care about that. It's all a part of the game to him. I stay silent. I try to look unconcerned. I want him to believe I can make up every point. Secretly, I want his approval.

"I'm here on personal business," Defoe says. He swipes his data pad and a door hisses open on my right. I've spent a full week in this room and I've never even noticed it.

A Babel guard shoves a bound and hooded figure into the room. My heart thunders inside my rib cage. What is this?

The man's legs buckle, and he falls to his knees on the floor of the med unit. Defoe unmasks him. Gray hair slicked with sweat. Pudgy, unshaved cheeks. I watch the blood trickle from his nose, dripping down to stain a white collar. He's one of the attendants. I've never bothered to look at their faces. Except for Vandemeer, they've all been the same.

"Emmett," Defoe says. "This is Dr. Karpinski. He attempted to have you killed."

Everything inside me goes cold. I'm a moonless night, the darkest cave.

Karpinski whimpers. The sound stirs something darker and colder inside me. He's stocky and well into his forties. Why would he want to kill me? Everything about this is wrong. He looks like a tortured soul, but I don't care. I want him to be punished for what he did.

Defoe's watching me.

"He tweaked the footage afterward, but the trail inevitably led back to him. He's Roathy and Isadora's caretaker. He hoped to help them by fixing the competition."

My hand instinctively settles on the spot where the sword plunged past my ribs. Karpinski doesn't ask for mercy or forgiveness. He just breathes thick breaths and stares at me with blank raven eyes. Defoe tosses something. It slides to a rattling stop at the foot of my bed. A sword. Karpinski's dead eyes flicker down to it.

"This is how things will work, Emmett," Defoe explains. "In China, Dr. Karpinski would be tried and executed. In most of the United States, he'd be given a life sentence without parole. Were he an Adamite, he'd be Gripped to the Eternal Tasks of the Maker."

My mind won't stop spinning. What does Defoe want? I try not to look at the sword at my feet. I try not to think about how it might feel in my empty hands.

"And while there are several international treaties regarding the fair use of space, we're a little outside of everyone else's jurisdiction. This is our territory, and our laws are different."

"How?" I ask coldly.

"We've activated Primal Law in this case. Do you know what that means?"

"First. It means first."

"Precisely. In this case, the first affected. The chief offended. Dr. Karpinski planned and executed an attempt on your life. You are the first. Thus, the judgment lies with you."

"I don't understand."

Defoe nods at the sword. "Do you think that Dr. Karpinski deserves to die?"

My fists tighten. "Yes."

"Then swing the sword."

I bend down to pick it up. The handle is nyxia, but the blade isn't. Light shivers down its silver length as I hold it out. Karpinski deserves to die, but I don't know if I deserve to kill. The blade weighs so little; it would be easy. I fix my eyes on him.

"Why did you do it?" I ask.

He looks at the ground. "They made me do it. They threatened me. I didn't know."

"Dr. Karpinski forgets he's an adult," Defoe says. "Even if his recruits asked him to do this, he made his own choices. He's the responsible party."

I look back at Defoe. "What happens if I don't do it? Will he go to trial?"

Defoe shakes his head. "Primal law. If the most offended can forgive, so can we."

"So, what? He just gets locked away?"

"Of course not," Defoe replies, like it's obvious. "He returns to duties."

My grip on the sword tightens. "That's not fair."

"Then make it fair," he replies. "You can't complain of fairness when you're the judge."

"So either I kill him or he just walks free? That's stupid."

"If you want to give the sentence, you should swing the sword."

My shoulders feel the weight of Defoe's challenge. He's asking too much of me. Dr. Karpinski stares out, already half a ghost. This is another test. Babel wants to know what kind of judge I am. Karpinski's crime is a dark thing that will bleed me for as long as he's alive. A potential murderer will roam the same halls I do. He could strike again. Next time, he might succeed.

"This is the only way?" I set the blade against his neck. Karpinski doesn't even react to the cold touch of it. A part of him is already dead. Defoe nods an answer.

"The only way," he echoes.

I nod back to him. The decision is easy. *You're the best of me and you're the best of her.* It's only true because Pops said it's true. I let the sword drop to the floor. It clatters at Karpinski's side like a broken promise. I feel like I'm handing the weapon back to Karpinski, turning my back and showing him where to plunge it. Destroy or be destroyed.

But I won't kill for them. Babel wants a willing executioner. They want me to be the hand that plucks the rotting grape from their pristine vines. They can go to hell. My pops would want more than this for me. I have a feeling he'd tell me to be the bigger man, no matter what.

Defoe strides forward. "This is your decision?"

"Yes."

Karpinski avoids my eyes. His shoulders slump and his whole body collapses down on itself. Defoe snatches up the sword, admiring the sharp edge of the blade.

"Dr. Karpinski, you've been shown mercy." Defoe brings the sword down in a casual arc. At first I think the swing misses, but then Karpinski cries out and blood fountains down his shoulder, onto the tiled floor. He doesn't have free hands to stop the flow. His ear is gone, just like that. "You will not die today, but you are marked. Tamper with this process again and I will float you into space with the waste containers. Do you understand me?"

Through his whimpering, there's a quiet agreement. Defoe cleans the blade and his eyes flicker back to me. "You've been cleared, Emmett. You may return to competition today. If you'll excuse us, I'd like a few more words with Dr. Karpinski."

His words open the door at the end of the room. I make my way to the exit and Dr. Karpinski cries out. I'm almost out the door when I realize that he's begging for me not to go. I leave him and that horrible place behind.

When I get back to my room, it takes everything I have to steady my breathing. I hate Karpinski for trying to kill me. I hate Defoe for trying to force me to be less than I am. This is an injustice, a darkness, that I can't just file away. The endless cabinets of my mind don't feel big enough now. It's never failed, not since Grammy taught me how to do it.

I was nine. We played together like boys do. Six of us running through dirt, pretending it was grass. Throwing a football, pretending it had air. I was fast then, a little taller and a little stronger than everyone else. You don't get tired when you're young. You just run and run and laugh and shout until your head hits the pillow. And so I ran. Go routes and slants and posts, always jumping a little higher, always slipping free of awkward-armed tackles. One too many touchdowns later, they got mad. It started small. *It's not fair,* one said. *You're too fast,* added a second. My two teammates abandoned me. One against five. These weren't the Most Excellent Brothers either; these were friends of proximity. Before you even really know yourself, the friends formed by the shortest walks.

I forget who pushed me first. I forget the names they called me.

But I'll never forget that first punch. It came from the right. One second nothing, the next second a two-ton train. I spun. They came. I fell. They kicked. It went on until I looked broken enough to stop. They let me up. God, what a mistake. Nine is too young to know the rules. Later I'd know. You *never* let them back up.

I don't even know if I got my hands on the right one. I just know that when I had him, I wouldn't let go. I didn't stop swinging until it was just us, and the dirt, and sirens. It was a mess. Charges and accusations and fingerprints. I was too young for juvenile court, but not too young to be looked at sideways, to hear the way they whispered. It all fueled my anger.

It wasn't until later that Grammy took me by the hand. She led me out to her garden, just a corner plot under a rusted fence, and had me sit down in the grass. I sat and so did she.

"Oh now, Emmett," she whispered. "You're hot with it, aren't you?"

I cried and she let me. There was never shame in crying, not in front of her.

"Your grandfather didn't live long enough to teach you, but I will," she said. "He had reasons to be angry too. Every day gave him new ones. But you can't always beat the stuffing out of your reasons. Most times, his reasons didn't even have a name. You understand me."

I didn't, but I wanted to understand her so badly that I nodded.

"Good, because I won't say twice. So what your grandfather did, every time it came up, was file it away. I used to hear him sometimes. *'I* for *Injustice,'* he'd mumble. Thought he was crazy, but he wasn't. He'd store it up. File it away. Then use it on something else so he didn't lose himself to it." She set her hand heavy over mine. "Remember that. You lose yourself to anger and that's it. It's a lonely road, and a long one. But if you find a way to control your feelings, if you can take that anger and make sure you're the boss of it, then you won't be so bad off. So file it away. This one? Let's call it *C* for *Cowards*. How you like that?"

I liked it a lot. After, my uncle started giving me boxing lessons. If someone called me a name at school or shoved a shoulder into me on the street or ignored my texts, I filed it away. I would look forward to Sundays. I would dip and jab, opening up my files and punishing the bag with what the week had given me. It was a way out. For years, PJ would call me the coolest of cats. He always wondered why things didn't bother me more. *You should see your face,* he would say. *It's carved out of stone, man.* And it was.

I remember that as I consider Karpinski and Defoe. I can't control what happens, but I'm more than what Defoe wants to make of me. Babel might have all the keys, but they don't know what they're keeping in the cage. Not yet, but I'll teach them soon enough.

DAY 28, 8:31 A.M.

Aboard *Genesis 11*

Vandemeer escorts me down to breakfast. He looks excited about my return. It's not hard to figure out that he knows nothing about Karpinski. The attempt on my life is a lesson I won't forget. Karpinski claimed he was forced to do this by Isadora and Roathy. The other contestants want to win as badly as I do. But they went for the wrong guy. I don't forget and I won't forgive.

As we walk, it still feels like my insides are wound too tight, but I'm eager to be back, eager to make up lost time. We take the stairs that lead into the massive multipurpose cafeteria. I want to see the others, but I find myself more eager to see the scoreboard.

My eyes flicker there first:

1.	LONGWEI	97,750	points
2.	BILAL	91,300	points
3.	AZIMA	90,900	points
4.	KAYA	87,450	points

5.	KATSU	84,400	points
6.	JAIME	80,200	points
7.	JASMINE	75,050	points
8.	ROATHY	74,324	points
9.	ISADORA	74,080	points
10.	EMMETT	64,900	points

I'm stunned. The math makes sense, but I'm completely stunned. My heart races as I realize how far behind I am. It's all relative. Others will get injured, I remember. Others will be sick. But that doesn't take away the feeling that I'm in a bottomless pit without much of a rope.

I'm ten meters from the table when they finally notice me. All of them look like they're seeing a ghost. I trace faces for signs of guilt, for avoidance or embarrassment. All are too shocked that I've returned to give anything away. Only Kaya shows emotion. She looks furious.

Katsu's the first to speak. "We thought you were dead."

"Takes more than that to kill me," I reply.

That brings out a few smiles. Roathy and Isadora exchange a glance. Seen and noted.

"Seriously," Katsu says. "They wouldn't tell us anything. You didn't look good when they took you away, man. I can't believe they let us think you were dead."

Kaya rises to give me a hug. As she does, she whispers into my ear. "Vandemeer told me I couldn't visit. They didn't tell us anything. I'm so sorry. I didn't want you to be alone. I tried to visit almost every day, Emmett, I really did."

I nod and pretend it's not a big deal. But I can feel it burning in just about every direction. The idea that Vandemeer, after all the trust we built in the med unit, would purposefully keep Kaya from visiting is messed up. And if Vandemeer was just following protocol, what's Babel get out of keeping me isolated? As I pull away from Kaya's hug, I'm not even sure who to blame or who to be pissed off at. I start in on breakfast instead and half listen as Katsu makes me promise to show him the scars.

Defoe doesn't note my presence as he arrives to escort us to morning activities. We're back to speed drills with nyxia manipulation. I finish in the bottom three for every single one. I'm rusty and slow; the others have had nine more days of practice. I keep pace in the classroom session but lose ground again in the swim tank. My lungs aren't used to the exercise. My score stays as far back from the others as it was at the start of the day.

In the pit, I'm matched up with Azima. A nice welcome back to the competition.

I was wrong about her. She's not a snake striking from the grass. She's three snakes. Her lashes come too fast for me to block. I'd love to blame my injury, but as I backpedal and miss parries, I know she's just that good. And only getting better. On the fifth strike my avatar drops, and Azima raises her arms in triumph.

The morning has me sweating and tired. I don't lose the same amount of ground I lost while in the med unit, but Vandemeer was right. I'm not ready. Not well and not whole. My struggles continue in the afternoon. We're back at the simulated mining site. The others move at a rapid-fire pace. They have plans now, strategies for maximizing their efficiency. Longwei's in the drill, and eventually they relegate me to nyxia manipulations.

We lose easily. Katsu mutters something about weak links. His words shouldn't hurt my feelings, but they do. That night I dream-walk through empty rooms that get smaller and smaller. As the rooms shrink, I shrink with them. I wake up right before I'm reduced to nothing.

The next day is even harder. I have to give up halfway through my swim when the left side of my stomach feels like it's been set on fire. Vandemeer suggests a forfeit, but I refuse. Instead, he applies a balm to my wound as we cross over to the pit. The pain subsides just in time for Azima to make me look like a weak and wounded thing. I try to use the trampolines to draw out the fight. Play a little hide-and-seek. Azima's better at seeking than I am at hiding, though. I catch a spear with my neck and head to lunch.

As I gnaw on a piece of chicken, it's hard not to stare at my score. I'm not catching up. I'm getting farther and farther away. Is it even possible that once I was in first? The thought almost makes me laugh. Longwei doesn't look at me anymore. To him, I'm not a threat. To the others, I'm only worthy of pity. They've given up on me too. I want to give up on myself, but I remember Pops working night shifts and Moms getting side-eyed by doctors who didn't think we could afford their treatments. I remember that if I don't do something soon, I'll go home with pocket change instead of treasure chests.

Wanting something and actually making it happen are two different things. Focused, I still screw up a piece of our machinery at the drill site and don't manipulate our nyxia deposits fast enough. The other team destroys our time. My teammates don't hide their glares. Defoe gathers us around, and I'm the ghost in the back of the room.

"Another Sabbath arrives," Defoe says at the end of the exercise. "A well-earned break. We'll open the recreation room like last time. Sleep in and treat yourselves to rest."

I drift to the back of the group as we walk through the sleek hallways. My image reflects back to me along the walls and I wonder who I'm looking at, where the real me has gone. Of course, Kaya drifts back to me. She lets her shoulder bump into mine.

"I missed you," she says.

"Yeah? Funny way of showing it."

Kaya's eyes go dark. "Vandemeer wouldn't let me visit. That's protocol on board the ship, Emmett. Babel's call, not mine. Anytime someone gets injured by nyxia, they have to be quarantined. Only their chief medic can see them. What? Think I'm making all of this up?"

Her explanation makes sense, but it's been a long day, and I feel like I deserve to be angry at someone, at something. I shrug my shoulders and start walking. "Whatever."

She grabs hold of my arm with more strength than I thought she had. I stop short and she waits until I look her in the eye. "You don't have to act tough around me."

I shake out of her grip. "Why do you even care? Answer that."

"Because we're teammates, Emmett. Because we're friends. Because we're the same color. You think I forgot any of that?"

"Kaya, I don't even know what that means."

"You're blue, Emmett, the same broken as me. Remember? We're both forgotten. People look past us or through us or around us. I'm blue too. I know what it feels like."

I shake my head, and I can tell that frustrates her.

"For me, it was both of my parents," Kaya says, voice quiet as dying. "We were very poor. We had to move to a new apartment. They took me there, unloaded all of our things, and put me to sleep. When I woke up, they were gone. They left my things. And a note."

Her words break me. I can see how hard it is for her to talk about, how hard it is for her to admit that someone left her behind. But instead of crying, she tightens her jaw and lifts her chin. She stares me dead in the eye and waits stubbornly for me to say something. I don't want to be liked, not by her and not by anyone on this ship. I just want to go home and fix the world I left behind. I want to save Moms and Pops and myself. Making friends complicates that.

Kaya doesn't back down, though.

"I know something happened to you too," she says. "You don't have to tell me what it was or why it happened. But you want to know why I care about you? Why I like you? Because I made a promise to myself when I was little. If I ever saw someone who was blue, like me, I'd never leave them. So I'm not going to leave you just because you had a bad day. I'm not going to leave you just because you're mad at everything. We're not just roommates anymore, Emmett; we're family. I'm right here, and I'm not going anywhere."

She stares at me, and all I can do is look away. I can feel my carefully gathered armor falling to the ground. I don't want anyone to know my secrets, to see through me like this.

"You really came every day?"

"As often as I could."

I nod at her. "I'm sorry. Today was hard."

"I know, but you're not that far behind. I've done the math, Emmett. This isn't a game of thousands. We're still a long way away from the final scores."

"But every point matters."

"You're right. So let's keep earning them. I'll practice with you tomorrow for our Sabbath. You've gotten enough rest in the med unit. Let's sharpen you back up."

I glance sideways at her. "You'd really do that?"

She laughs. "Have you even heard a *word* that I've said? You're so stubborn."

"I just don't get it."

She hooks her arm into mine. "I like you—what's there to get?"

For the first time, I don't challenge her words. I need something good right now, and it feels like her words are all I have. We wind our way back to the room and set a time for training tomorrow. Before we part ways for showers, she shows me something she's been working on. It's a bulky camera, more vintage than vintage. It shines nyxian black.

"My grandmother had one," she says. "Come here."

She flips her grip on the camera and slips an arm around my waist. I put mine around her shoulder and we both smile into the flash. The camera spits out a little square picture. Kaya snatches it, waves it in the air, and hands it to me.

"I don't need to see it to know it's a good one. You keep it."

I set it on the dresser and watch as the picture comes to life. We look worlds away from this competition. We look like real friends. If only a shower could wash away reality. I stand naked before a mirror afterward. My stab wound is a scrape of lighter skin just below dark ribs. A readout of vital signs dances to life. It claims I've lost twelve pounds. I can see it in my ribs and my cheeks. The mirror screen scans the interior of my stomach. Everything flashes green.

But there's a broken that the mirror can't see. I feel it now more than ever.

Distracted, I snag my player and open up the back. Vandemeer's access card gleams with possibility. Knowing Kaya, she'll want to stay up late and read together. Tomorrow is Sabbath, so we don't have to worry about bedtimes or getting rest for the next day. But I think I can make our evening way more fun. I throw on street clothes and slide back into the living room. Kaya's waiting there with a book, but she sets it aside when I wave the access card in her face.

"You stole it?" she asks, eyes wide.

"A while ago," I reply, tucking it into a zip pocket. "It's his backup card."

Kaya drums her fingers nervously. "Have you used it before?"

"Not yet. Want to do a little exploring?"

She grins beneath her mask. "Let's see how far the rabbit hole goes."

Together we check the hallways. No signs of Vandemeer. No Babel techies roaming the night. Most of our fellow competitors are safely tucked away in their rooms. I lead Kaya down the nearest passage. I haven't gotten to use the card yet, but that doesn't mean I haven't done my homework. Ever since I first snagged it, I've kept my eyes open for corridors and tunnels and stairwells.

We go down a few flights of back stairs, and I stop in front of my first discovery.

"I present to you a normal wall," I say dramatically. "Except when used by a magician."

I punch the side of a random panel and it opens. Kaya gasps as a hidden hallway is revealed. "Cool," she whispers beside me. "But how'd you know it was there?"

"A magician never reveals his secrets."

She frowns at me and stamps a heel down on my big toe.

"Ah! All right, all right!" I point down at the floor. "Scuffs on the tiles. Why else would there be scuffs on the tiles in this random spot? Easy find."

She makes an appreciative noise as the dim lights ahead of us brighten. It reminds me of the energy-saving overheads they installed at the Food First near my house in Detroit. They'd dim whenever someone hadn't walked down an aisle in a while. Took about three months for them to break. The yogurt section was all blacked out and the store was slow to get things fixed. I always pretended I was on secret missions to locate snacks. The only goal for *this* mission is to have fun, but the same feeling steals through me. I feel invincible.

"What do you think they use them for?" Kaya asks.

"Shortcuts, I guess. I'm sure there are a bunch of them around the ship."

Our path dead-ends and I pop another panel. We slide out into a wide hallway that leads to a massive black-bolted door. I unzip my suit pocket, pull Vandemeer's card, and thrust it at the sensor. The light goes green, the door slides, and we're through. Kaya looks a little wide-eyed.

"You're good at this," she says.

I wink at her. "Babel's not the only one with secrets."

She laughs at that, but as we keep moving, she notices things I don't. Like how big the ship must be and how Babel has woven nyxia into the walls and wiring of every hallway. She's always got her mind on the bigger picture. I've never been good at zooming out that far. It's no surprise she's always got a strategy for everything. Ahead, the passage forks.

"Your choice, Alice," I say.

She doesn't even answer, just starts skipping happily down the left passageway. Laughing, I jog-step to catch up with her.

"This is seriously so cool, Emmett."

"I owed you one. For not giving up on me. I kind of hoped this would make us even."

I can tell she's smiling. "I wouldn't have ever done this on my own."

"What are best friends for, if not to make you do stupid things?"

She blushes at the words. I mean them. This place is dark enough without friends. I need her. I didn't realize it before, but I probably don't stand much of a chance of surviving this competition without her. We walk quietly, lost in the moment, and I almost forget my own rules.

"Whoa," I say, yanking her back by the collar. "Back to the wall."

I show her. With my back pressed flat, I ease around a corner. Above us, a black-orbed camera hovers. Even as we pass beneath it, we can see the blinking robot-red eye. I motion for Kaya to cross to the opposite wall, and we repeat the process, pressing ourselves tight and slipping beneath another camera. At the end of the hall, another black door looms.

"How'd you learn to do that?" she asks.

"Midnight raids on the snack closet."

I swipe the card again and there's a gushing suction of wind. We both step into an antechamber. Above us, air hisses through metal vents. We wait a few seconds as the room's sensors adjust to our presence. I just hope Babel isn't eyeing the readouts too closely. I won't be surprised if they come sweeping in to end the fun. It's worth it, though, to have a little freedom before they do.

The second door groans open and I step up to the edge. The room looks like a mechanical center. A bunch of pipes and empty air and wiring. It's all lit up, with about a thirty-meter drop.

"Dead end?" Kaya asks.

"I don't think so," I say, holding a hand out into the room.

Inside the air lock, I can still feel gravity's pull, but as soon as my hand crosses the threshold it goes weightless. Kaya watches it float upward and raises an eyebrow.

I laugh, let out a whoop, and leap into no-grav air. It's breathtaking. The lightness, the freedom, the fear. I glance up as I float across. The whole room is a vertical shaft. Only

fifteen meters across, but about one hundred meters from
top to bottom. The first leap lands me on the far wall. I
reach out and grab one of the metal supports, pinning myself there. Kaya comes soaring gracefully out, her angle
higher than mine, her face priceless. She adjusts her body
and grabs a handhold about five meters above me.

"Where do you think it leads?" she asks.

"Let's find out."

I shove off the wall and go flying past her. She laughs
and follows. We zigzag our way up the shaft, swimming
through the air, dancing absurdly, and acting like kids for
the first time on *Genesis 11.* Above me, Kaya gets a grip on a
second black air lock. I angle my body and push off toward
her. My aim's too high, but she snags my leg and pulls me
back down.

"There's no place to scan," I say. Kaya carefully slips her
feet beneath the exposed edge of the frame and bends at the
waist. There's a fist-sized circle punched into the center of
the door. I watch her stuff a hand inside and feel around.
And then she freaks. Her hand is stuck and her face twists
with terror. I panic-reach for her shoulder and try to pull
her away when she breaks into laughter.

"Got you," she says, winking.

"You're the worst."

I push off the wall and let myself float away. We spend
an hour exploring the place. There are only two air locks
in the room. The one we came through and the one we
can't get through. Kaya spends most of the time looking at
it, wondering why there are no scans on this one like there
are on the other one. Eventually I lure her away with jelly

beans I saved from the cafeteria's snack bar. We tell stories and throw different flavors at each other, laughing until we feel sick.

I keep waiting for Defoe and Babel guards to show up and spoil the fun, but they never come. Even as we head back to our room, nothing. Kaya laughs excitedly when we're safely back on the couch, and we both dig into the thrill of having gotten away with something. We listen to songs on my player and shuffle cards until we're too tired to think of anything but falling asleep. Until all the pain and anger and frustration feel a few million kilometers away.

DAY 50, 11:47 P.M.

Aboard *Genesis 11*

They say pain is weakness leaving the body. If that's true, each of us is becoming strong enough to carry worlds on our shoulders. The days of competition start merging together. We win and lose in the Rabbit Room, but each race feels like a continuation of the last, like we'll always be chasing each other through simulated forests.

Virtual mining explosions and pain sensors remind us that one day the consequences of our mistakes will be more than broken pixels. Babel demands perfection because perfection will keep us alive on Eden. There's such a predictable rhythm to the schedule that I only notice when the lyrics change. The day that I start learning more about my competitors.

On the fifth Sabbath, Bilal invites me to his room to play cards. My first instinct is to turn him down, thank him, then retreat to the safety of my own room. But I realize it'd be nice to kick my feet up and do something mindless. It's not like Bilal's an enemy. From day one he's been open and kind to me. I accept the invitation and follow him upstairs.

"Longwei lives in the other room," he explains. "But he doesn't enjoy company."

Their living space is identical to ours. The only difference is that Bilal's door stands wide open. A glance inside shows his clothes neatly folded and his possessions organized on the bedside table. I nod in that direction. "Your door broken?"

He shakes his head. "I asked them to rig it that way. I want everyone to feel invited."

I can't help smiling at that. He's such a weird kid. We both take seats at the table and Bilal starts shaking a deck of cards out of one pack. I watch him separate out the jokers and shuffle twice for good measure. He sets the cards neatly aside and looks up at me.

"Now we just have to wait for the others."

I stare at him. "What's that?"

"I invited everyone. It will be wonderful to play a *big* game."

I bite back my frustration. I should have known. Bilal doesn't leave people out. He doesn't spend time counting his enemies like I do. I glance back at the door and feel the awkwardness creeping up my spine. The first knock sounds and Bilal stands. Jazzy waves her way into the room and takes the seat closest to me.

"I've been *dying* to play some cards," she says.

Kaya's next, and Katsu arrives shortly after. It starts out like any shared meal or competition. We laugh at a few jokes, but before long the humor fades. Jaime arrives, followed by Isadora and Roathy. The sight of them in a place I wanted to call safe has my stomach knotted. Everyone pulls up chairs or sits on cushions. Azima is the last one to join us, and just like that everyone's gathered, sitting around the same table, except for Longwei.

And something magical happens.

Bilal explains his favorite game, deals the cards, and performs a spell on us. All the tension eases out of our tight shoulders and nervous hands. We flash full houses and struggle to make our flushes and laugh when Katsu sneaks a queen out of one sleeve. For a time, we aren't competitors vaulting through the endless dark. We're kids sitting in the back of a classroom. The teacher has given us free time, and something about it tastes eternal.

We play for hours. Long enough for the lighter conversations to take on weight. Jazzy is the first one in the group brave enough to talk about home, about the world she left behind. I listen and everything in my gut says it's a mistake—she's giving us her secrets, making herself vulnerable—but at the same time I find myself spellbound by her honesty.

"My parents always had me competing in 'beauty and brain' pageants, but I kept finishing third or fourth. After a while, my family went broke from the travel expenses." Bilal deals another hand. Everyone glances at their cards, but we're all waiting to hear the rest of Jazzy's story. "All that wasted money. We didn't really miss it until we found out about Mama's breast cancer." We watch as she lifts the familiar strand of fading pink-tipped hair. "Is it bad luck if the pink washes completely away?"

No one answers. We all look down at our cards. A minute

passes before Katsu lets out a massive belly laugh. Azima tries to quiet him with a stern look, but he ignores her. We all watch as he stumbles toward the door. "Just wait," Katsu says. "I'll be right back. No one move!"

Azima scowls before reaching out and squeezing Jazzy's hand. I'm still dissecting the gravity of the moment. Kaya's shared her backstory with me, but only because we're a team. That makes it feel different somehow. We have learned bits and pieces about the other competitors, but I can't imagine opening up my weaknesses for the others to exploit. We sit in silence until the door opens and Katsu bursts back into the room. He's holding a delicate box. I can tell he's almost out of breath. We all watch as he opens the box and slides it to the center of the table. Everyone leans in to get a look.

"Higashi," Katsu announces. "My last piece. It's made with real wasanbon."

I hear Kaya make an appreciative noise. The cookie's small and delicate. At least, I think it's a cookie. It's carved in the shape of a boat and colored mint green. Jazzy raises an eyebrow.

"I'm confused," she says. "What's this have to do with me?"

Katsu closes the lid to the box. "Roathy said we're all poor, didn't he?"

Eyes swing in that direction. Roathy offers a single shrug in answer.

"He's right," Katsu says. "I mean, come on, Babel clearly picked the most ragged bunch of kids they could find. So just consider this another leg of their competition. The saddest story gets my last higashi. Right now, Jazzy's the leader in the clubhouse."

He slides the box slightly in her direction before taking a step back. I'm expecting everyone to reject the idea, but Azima leans over the table excitedly.

"I would do anything for sweets."

She explains she's part of the first generation of the Rendille people to settle fully in Kenyan cities. Once, she says, there was no greater sin to her people than stillness. They slept under the stars, raced the sun to the horizon, and went wherever the water waited for them. She tells us that even her name, Azima, means "magically charmed into motion." A name usually reserved for boys, it was given to her because she never stopped moving as a child.

Movement is in her blood, in her bones, but the elders decided that their people's survival depended on being still, on becoming modern. So she watched as uncles and aunts moved to cities and lost their minds sitting at desks and staring at screens. Her family was reduced to a life of boxes, and eventually to caskets. Each relative buried in cities as foreign to them as any star.

"I'm afraid," she says. "I know this mission brings me great honor, but what will happen when I go home? What man would dare to ask for my hand now that I have roamed through the stars? My life will never be the same."

She laughs nervously at the silence that follows her confession. We deal another hand of cards and pretend her fears don't sound a lot like ours. Instead of sliding the higashi in Azima's direction, Katsu launches into his own story.

"Dad left when I was three. He lives in America. Mom

was never the same after that. I have this permanent image of her just staring out the front windows of our apartment. I lived with my grandmother for a while. I don't know. Doesn't feel like there's much to go back to."

Jaime nods his understanding. The movement catches the table's attention. He glances awkwardly from us to the higashi before clearing his throat and starting in.

"My family had a farm," he says. "Life was good. Living in a mountain town. It was simple, but we had a bad year, and the neighbors hated us. We went bankrupt. Lost everything."

I fold a hand of low cards and side-eye Jaime. I want to call him out on it, accuse him of lying, but he pulls out a faded photograph. "This is the last picture we took on the farm."

He passes it around. The edges are so worn that the picture's shapeless now. His mother's a beautiful woman. Jaime clearly got his pale eyes and sharp chin from his father. All three of them stand on a farm with cows roaming in the background. I stare at the picture long enough to miss my turn to bet. When I finally look up, Jaime's watching me. He offers a polite smile, and I realize I've been an asshole this whole time. His parents really *were* farmers. He told the truth. Bilal deals another hand as the shame of it buries me, but I'm too much of a coward to say I'm sorry.

Katsu saves me from embarrassment. He laughs loudly and snatches the photo.

"Major points for using a prop, Jaime," he says. "But I still give Jazzy the edge. There's just nothing quite as sad as toddlers in tiaras parading around a stage."

Jazzy and Jaime share a smile at that. Katsu shoves the box farther in Jazzy's direction before eyeing the rest of the table. "Who's next? Who will claim the final higashi? Keep in mind that's a gift from my grandmother, you clowns. So you better take this seriously. How about you, Bilal? Why'd you invite us all here in the first place?"

I'm not sure Bilal likes the new game we're playing, but he's too polite to turn Katsu's invitation down. He smiles before saying, "Hospitality isn't optional. It's the expectation of every honorable man. This is what my parents taught me. It is who my father raised me to be."

He goes on to describe the hilltop village he's from in Palestine. Two of his best friends were a pair of sheep. The longer I listen, the more I can feel the distance between us. I don't understand people like him. His home was burned down twice. His family lived through actual famines. It's impossible that someone with his story could have ever learned to smile. But that's all he ever does. There's a heaven in him no darkness can take.

When Bilal finishes, Jazzy slides the box his way. "I know when I'm beaten."

My friend traces the lid of the box with idle fingers before looking directly at me.

"What about you, Emmett?" he asks. "Can you take the box from me?"

I shake my head. "Doubt it, man."

He smiles. "Let us decide."

I can feel the weight of their gazes. I've made a living out of back corners and side streets. There's never been a stage I felt like I belonged on, but Bilal's quiet attention convinces me that everything will be all right. The words come trickling off the tongue.

"Moms got sick a few years ago," I say. "Kidney failure. She's moving up the list because of Babel, but it's been a bumpy ride. Pops does his best, you know, but it's like his bosses are happy to watch him kill himself for each dime. I don't know, man. I got good people in my corner, but it's like I'm living in a world where most people would prefer if I sat down in the back row, took what the world gave me, and kept my mouth shut. But that's just the way life is, right?"

I shrug my shoulders to say that it's over, that's it. Bilal nods like he knows exactly how I feel. He starts to pass the higashi my way, but pauses when Roathy rises to his feet. I'm half-expecting him to leave and call all of this a waste of time. Instead, he starts to speak.

He was born in the Triarch Empire. The massive conglomerate of countries bordering China has proven itself an economic power in the past decade, but Roathy tells us he's one of thousands of kids who've grown up homeless on the streets, fighting each other for scraps in trash dumps and alleyways. "The worst fights," he says, "were always against the dogs."

As he continues talking, I realize I understand him a lot better than I understand Bilal. Roathy's not the type to smile at a world that's forgetting him. I get that, and I get him. The truth makes him dangerous. He left a life that he can't go back to. When he's done, Bilal looks between the two of us, unsure of the polite thing to do. I nod in Roathy's direction.

"I think he wins."

"Not so fast," Katsu says. "Kaya and Isadora still have to go."

There's a little noise of protest from my left. Kaya's eyes are dark and forbidding above her mask. I know what she'll say even as she opens her mouth to answer.

"There are some competitions I don't want to win."

Katsu looks annoyed by that but says nothing. The attention of the room shifts Isadora's way. She stands and crosses the room, accepting the box from Bilal's gentle hands. A little gasp sounds as she flips the lid, snatches the candy, and plops it in her mouth.

We hear the crunch. Dust powders the air around her lips.

She says, "I don't have to tell my story to know I would be the winner."

With that, she leaves. Her departure tolls through our group like midnight in a fairy tale. The magic Bilal created for us starts to slip through every finger. Roathy follows Isadora out. The rest of us stay and play cards, but we're no longer laughing. Hushed conversation revolves around Isadora. She's always been the quietest in the group, but that doesn't mean she hasn't left clues here and there. She apparently told Jazzy once that there's nothing more important to her than being a mother. And occasionally she and Katsu mourn the fact that they're missing the approaching World Cup.

It's only after these facts are fully examined that we turn the conversation to the *real* mystery about Isadora: her tattoo. Everyone's seen the crowned eight etched on her neck by now, but it's clear we've each heard very different explanations.

"It's the number of her favorite soccer player," Bilal explains.

Azima shakes her head. "She told me it's the day her mother died."

"I thought it symbolizes making it into the top eight," Jazzy offers. "Isn't that why there's a crown?"

Katsu laughs at that. "How would she have known about being in the top eight? You think she got the tattoo after boarding the ship?"

"She's the youngest in a family of eight," Kaya says firmly. "That's why she originally got the tattoo. She always felt like she was in last place. That's what she said."

When we question Isadora the next day, her eyes narrow playfully. "I would have thought it was obvious. Eight. The number of fools it takes to figure out the meaning of a tattoo."

One night of playing cards has drawn the colors out of the dark world Babel's trying to build. We still dig and fight and scrape for each point, but there's something human beneath every mask now. I know some of their secrets, some of their stories. I know now that I'm not the only one who comes from a broken world and I'm not the only one who's desperate to fix it.

Only Longwei continues to hold himself apart. As the weeks pass, he never sits down to talk with anyone. He doesn't play cards on Sabbaths. He doesn't tell stories about his childhood. His actions still speak volumes. He enters every event like a man possessed. Failure is not an option.

Second place is a mark of shame. Even in silence, Longwei is proving Kaya's theory right. We all are. She said each one of us was broken. She claimed she could see it in us, bright as paint on a canvas. Hearing the truth of that in each of our stories has me wondering how Babel chose us.

I remember getting called out of algebra. The principal took me to a conference room. There were three of them. All in suits. It scared the hell out of me.

When I sat down, they slid the first contract across the table and said I'd been chosen. Wasn't I lucky? I'd been drawn from a lottery out of thousands of applicants.

Funny thing is, I know I never applied.

DAY 99, 4:35 P.M.
Aboard *Genesis 11*

As we get closer and closer to the Tower Space Station, we learn that this is a competition of highs and lows. Bones break, ankles twist, muscles pull.

Babel pushes us over cliffs and expects us to fly. Sometimes we do.

I stand in front of the mirror. There is no longer a gut for my suit to tighten. The ribbed leather six-pack actually represents the muscles underneath now. Babel and Karpinski took my soul's softness in weeks. It's taken a little longer to remove the physical softness, to carve me into something hard and powerful.

Vandemeer waits in the living room with Kaya. Every morning we train. Every night we study Eden and the Adamites. Every day the two of them help me claw my way back up the scoreboard. Our alliance is earning its weight in gold. After crunches and push-ups, Vandemeer quizzes me on the climates of Eden. The more I learn, the more of a mystery their world seems. Eden isn't Earth. The Adamites aren't humans. The similarities are there, but underestimating the differences might get us killed. It helps knowing that almost the entire Adamite population lives in one massive city. It helps knowing their average age of mortality is more than double ours. Even little things, like the fact that they never communicate through head nods or hand motions, could matter when we're on the surface and face to face with another species.

We walk down to breakfast together. The others have changed too. Katsu's still massive, but muscle has formed in his arms and chest. Kaya was right about him. There are days where he can't hide his sadness behind clever jokes. On those days, he's darker and more bitter than any of us.

Bilal has actually grown a few inches. He's tall and goofy-looking now, but still always smiling. Jaime's face has thinned. The change emphasizes his cheekbones, makes him look even more like a medieval prince. I've been slowly setting aside my natural distrust of him. He's been slowly forgiving me for all the early accusations. Only Azima looks the same. She claims this kind of chaos is in her blood. She says she was born to survive far crueler conditions.

I used to think that was true of me.

Vandemeer's training isn't only physical. It's mental too. One lesson that won't stick is his request that I don't obsess over the scoreboard. In spite of his reminders about psychology and positive thinking, I glance at it after every activity, every meal, every anything:

1.	LONGWEI	370,900	points
2.	BILAL	363,300	points
3.	AZIMA	362,750	points
4.	KATSU	361,450	points
5.	KAYA	348,050	points
6.	JAIME	325,200	points
7.	EMMETT	295,350	points
8.	ISADORA	288,080	points
9.	JASMINE	280,050	points
10.	ROATHY	274,324	points

It took weeks to catch up and solidify my position. But getting here won't be enough. A twisted ankle or a punctured lung or a broken bone can stop my point flow at any time. Now the focus is on building a lead and keeping my distance from the bottom two. If there's one thing I've learned, it's that no one's safe. Not until they tally up the totals and we unload for Eden.

Another thing I've learned is that none of my competitors are the lazy rabbit from Aesop's fables. They all keep running. They all wake up in the morning with purpose.

Everyone has a specialty that keeps netting them points. Azima never loses in the pit. Bilal and Jazzy have set themselves apart in the classroom. Katsu is one of the most clever nyxia manipulators, and Kaya's always one step ahead in strategy. Jaime's a little good at everything and Longwei's a lot good at everything. I know I can compete with any of them, but I'm forced to take it all one step at a time. It's a game of small victories, little milestones.

This morning, Defoe has us gripping. Of all Babel's exercises, it's my favorite. A flat-topped podium stands between two competitors. Defoe manipulates nyxia and hides it beneath a tablecloth. When he pulls back the curtain, we fight for control of the nyxian item.

I take my place across from Bilal. A deep breath lets me push away every thought. I go to a place of cold stones and still waters before Defoe makes the pull.

A smoked-wood clock. Bilal and I both reach for the nyxia at the same time, but I'm faster than him. I can feel him in my mind, shouldering and reaching for a handle on what I already have in my mental hands. I let my eyes close and hold tighter to the image of the clock, with its black numbers and gold ticking hands. When I have it there firmly, I shove back against Bilal and manipulate the substance into a leather-bound book.

"Time," Defoe calls.

We both open our eyes and my creation sits on the podium, title and all.

Bilal shakes his head in disbelief but says, "Nice pull."

Points trickle into my score. Small victories, I remind myself. I got the points and Bilal didn't. I just need it to happen a few hundred more times. Most days I can beat everyone except Longwei. His strength in this exercise feels like stepping in front of a two-ton truck. Dude still doesn't smile when he wins. I'm not sure he'll smile until a spaceship sets him down on Eden's foggy shores. Maybe not even then.

Bilal and I walk to the end of the line and watch as Longwei lines up across from Katsu. He closes his eyes, keeping his whole body completely still. We watch Defoe pull the covering and barely catch a glimpse of shape and size before Longwei grips it. Katsu groans as Longwei's trademark gold medallion clatters onto the podium. He doesn't even smile as Defoe dismisses us for the day.

"How do you do that?" Bilal asks. "You always leave me stranded out of the gate."

"I don't know. It's all about focus. You can't be thinking about anything else."

This is the line I toe every day with him. Bilal, who comes up to my room on Sabbaths and tells me stories. Bilal, who reads Kaya and me lines from his favorite poems, who never stops smiling at everyone. But he's already in second place. So do I help him? Do I answer his questions if I'm the one playing catch-up?

"I don't know about you, but I'm exhausted," Bilal says. "If tomorrow wasn't Sabbath, I'd probably have taken the day off to get my knee looked at."

His knee's been bugging him for a week. His medic thinks it might be a torn meniscus. An injury like that could keep him out at least a week if it needs surgery. After my time in the med unit, I don't wish poor health on anyone. But we all get injured. Jazzy was out for a week with a high ankle sprain. Isadora was sidelined with some kind of space vertigo. Babel's well-oiled engines push on with or without us. Only Longwei hasn't needed a day off.

Which makes sense: he's more machine than man.

"You're sitting in second," I tell Bilal. "I'd be happy to trade places. Those first few weeks cost me an arm and a leg. I'm barely keeping my head above water."

"I've just been lucky. Keep going, fathom?"

I nod. "Trust me, I fathom."

Fathom and *lurch* and *seat-talk*. The slang's developed in the past few months. A hybrid of Earth lingo and something we're creating ourselves. Everyone's added phrases to the mix from their corner of the world. Jaime was the first, calling me a *lurch* the day I flipped on him. That and *lurk* alternate as the best way to remind someone they're acting like an idiot. I threw *fathom* into the bunch. Azima gave us *seat-talk*. Jazzy started the popular *go suck on an egg*. I speak the same language as her and I wasn't even sure what that meant. The new slang gives our group the feel of a family. Like most families, we have rivalries and fights and skeletons piling up in the closet. Like most families, we fall apart more often than we come together.

"Hey, get that knee looked at tomorrow," I tell Bilal. "I'm going to be catching up on sleep, so I'm not sure I'll have time to hang out unless it's at breakfast."

Bilal nods and we bump knuckles. He splits his way and I split mine. Kaya's waiting in our room for me.

"So why'd I just lie to Bilal? I always feel guilty doing that. It's like lying to an angel."

"He is an angel," Kaya replies. "Which is why he's a bad fit for tomorrow's activities."

I roll my eyes. "Let me guess . . . more exploring?"

The competition's not the only thing that's changed. Kaya's interest in Babel has grown into an obsession. I almost blame myself for it. Discovering the no-grav room only made her more curious. I dream about moving up the scoreboard. Kaya dreams about what's behind Babel's locked door.

It doesn't help that Vandemeer started printing journals for us to read. He calls it positive-reinforcement research.

He thinks giving us more information on Babel and the Adamites will have us believing we're going down to Eden. The dense reads that were supposed to set Kaya's eyes on Eden have done the opposite. She keeps finding new things that feed new suspicions. She's convinced Babel has something hidden, and she thinks we're the detectives who are supposed to solve the riddle. It's not hard to understand her obsession. She thrives in finding solutions to problems. The door's the one mystery she hasn't solved.

She forces me to take her down to the no-grav room even though we've never made it past the second air lock. Judging from the look on her face, tomorrow will involve more exploration. Really, every time we come back without a Babel marine escort I'm surprised. Vandemeer doesn't miss much. Maybe he noticed the missing card and hasn't said anything because he knows Babel's consequences for errors have a cost. An image of Karpinski bound and on his knees rises in my mind. If that's how Babel handles their own stepping out of line, it'd be wise of Vandemeer to keep his mouth shut about losing it.

"More exploring," Kaya confirms. "But this time I've got a surprise for you."

I laugh. "Whatever you say. I've got an appointment to call home and an afternoon in the steamer. Want to meet up at the usual time?"

She nods. "Sleep well, Emmett."

DAY 100, 10:33 A.M.

Aboard *Genesis 11*

Meals are unpredictable on Sabbaths. Everyone's schedule changes so drastically. People eat late or early or not at all. Once, Katsu slept through the entire day. He woke up just in time to start another week of Babel's endless grind.

So it's only by dumb luck that I bump into Bilal on the way to breakfast. We exchange good mornings and stumble downstairs together. Naturally, Longwei's the only other person awake this early. Our annoying leader doesn't even look up as Bilal and I walk the length of the buffet. It feels so normal to joke with Bilal and sit down for a meal that I almost don't notice how weird he's acting. He's always been a little awkward, but today he's straight jumpy. His normally tidy hair looks chaotic. As I chew on a piece of bacon, I realize he's blushing. Sweating too.

I point at him with my fork. "Hey, the hell's wrong with you today?"

His eyes flick over to the other end of the table, in Longwei's direction. He's standing at the buffet, back to us, picking through the deviled eggs. Bilal turns back, content knowing that whatever he wants to share won't be overheard.

"Last night, Azima kissed me."

I stare at him. "Sorry, I think your mask's broken, Bilal. It sounded like you said that Azima *kissed* you last night."

His face goes a deeper shade of red. "I did."

"Azima? Kissed you?"

He nods. "On the lips."

The widest smile splits my face. No wonder he looks like the world's ending. Bilal's probably the nicest kid in the world, but it's not hard to imagine this was his first kiss. Laughing, I reach out for dap. Bilal pounds my fist, half laughing himself, but then he shakes his head.

"I should not laugh. It is not honorable."

"Kissing?" I ask. "Dude, nothing wrong with a little kissing."

Bilal shakes his head again. "But I must ask her parents for their approval."

"Good luck." I thumb back. "He's a few million kilometers that way."

"Exactly," Bilal replies, face lined with concern. "It's not right to—"

The sound of a crashing plate cuts him off. We both look up like startled birds. Longwei's standing by the edge of the table, his deviled eggs a smash of white and yellow on the floor. But he's not looking at the fallen plate or the mess. His eyes are locked on Bilal. It takes a second to realize that he's blushing too.

"Can we help you, Longwei?" I ask.

His fists are clenching and unclenching.

"But *I* kissed Azima."

All the color drains from Bilal's face. The two of them stare daggers at each other as I burst into laughter. It's too funny not to laugh. All this time Longwei's built himself up as the untouchable competitor. He works harder and smarter and faster than any of us, but with just four words he's shattered all my illusions. It's hard to even imagine him kissing someone. He doesn't usually do anything that won't earn points on the scoreboard.

But a glance at Bilal cuts my laughter off. The stare he's leveling Longwei with is a furious one. It's not even the presence of anger, really. It's the absence of his normal smile.

"Look, guys," I say, trying to play peacemaker. "I'm sure it's an honest mistake."

Longwei ignores me. "I kissed her first."

Before Bilal can answer, Longwei storms out of the room. I have to fight back the laughter because, seriously? He kissed Azima first? That's his argument? Bilal's taking deep breaths as I scramble for the right words. Thankfully, he finds them first.

"How could she?" he asks.

I shrug. "It's not 2020 anymore, man. Girl's got the right to kiss who she wants."

"No, not that," Bilal replies. "I agree that it is her right. But Longwei? How could she ever kiss Longwei? I have to take a shower. I do not feel clean."

He starts walking off in the wrong direction.

"Bilal." My voice pulls his attention. "That way. You have to go that way."

He nods once and changes direction. "Longwei, of all people . . ."

I wait until he rounds a corner before dying from laughter. I'll have to thank Azima later. This might have been my favorite moment aboard *Genesis 11*. I still remember her giving a speech about finding a man worthy of her, but I didn't realize she'd been conducting interviews. Neither of her choices surprises me. Longwei's name has been first or second on the scoreboard since the beginning, and Bilal's the nicest person I've ever met. It doesn't hurt that he's competed well too. Both of them are worthy, in their own ways, but I have a hard time imagining Azima settling for either one.

Sighing, I make a mental note to talk to Bilal later. Knowing him, he'd never actually take revenge on Longwei, but I'm sure he'll run circles in his own head about all of it. I start in on a second helping of breakfast when Vandemeer tracks me down.

"Ready to go down to the Contact Room?"

We walk the halls together. Vandemeer gets Sabbaths off too, but sometimes he spends them working with us anyway. I couldn't have asked for a more determined medic. He's always preaching to me about not checking scoreboards, but as we walk down to the Contact Room, he's eyeing every single one.

"It's a Sabbath, Vandemeer. The scores aren't changing anytime soon."

"I know," he says, smiling. "Just proud of your progress."

"Yeah, well, let's not freak just yet. There's a long way to go."

"How positive."

Vandemeer swipes us into the Contact Room. A handful of techies sit in front of glowing screens. I catch glimpses of lunar alignments, solar charts, the works. I've been escorted through a couple of times now to make calls home and I still can't make heads or tails of any of it.

Vandemeer nods me toward the feed room and strikes up a conversation with one of the techies. But as I open the door, I realize there's already a call in progress. Jazzy sits in the reception seat. A woman fills the screen in front of her. She's strikingly thin, and her entire head's been clean-shaved. Cancer couldn't take the bright blue from her eyes, though. Both of them look my way, and it's not hard to see where Jazzy gets her looks.

"My fault, Jazzy. Didn't realize I was early."

I start to leave, but Jazzy waves me in. "Emmett! Come meet Mama!"

Something about her excited smile pulls me forward. She's only got one minute left on her call home, and she's inviting me into it? Jazzy slides over to make room and throws an arm around me as I sit. "Mama, this is my friend Emmett!" she says.

The woman flashes a pageant smile. "You takin' care of my girl up there?"

I can't help smiling at the familiar southern drawl. "Yes, ma'am."

"He's one of the good ones, Mama," Jazzy says, surprising me.

Before Jazzy's mother can ask another question, I quietly excuse myself to let them say goodbye. Heat's crawling up my neck and down my back as I hover by the doorway and wait for their call to finish. I've never thought of Jazzy as a friend, but I guess she's not like Roathy or Longwei. She's always been kind to me. The only thing I have to hold against her is that she might be the one who takes what's mine. I've never thought of her as a friend because I've kept both hands gripped on the idea that she's competition, nothing more.

Her call cuts off and she stands. I watch her take a quiet moment to collect herself. That's something I've always noticed about Jazzy. She knows how to take her deep breaths offstage. It's the reason she can always be so composed and ready for whatever's next. As she leaves the room, she gives my arm a passing squeeze. "Glad you got to meet her," she whispers.

Her departure leaves me feeling guilty. I hate that she's just a name on a scoreboard.

Vandemeer appears at my side. "One minute until they feed through."

I nod and take a seat as he closes the door. We've had five or six calls now. Sometimes the signals are too weak to establish a connection. Moms hasn't shown up for one of them, because she's started treatment. Babel's kept their word, they've fast-tracked everything, but that means she's fighting hard now to get better. It means she's too sick and exhausted to make the long-distance trips to Babel's comm center. That doesn't make her absence any easier. Every time the screen turns on, I hope she'll be sitting there next to Pops. Hope's a funny thing that way. No matter how many times she's not there, I always have more for the next time.

When the screen loads, though, it's just Pops.

"My boy," he says. "You look great, Emmett."

It must be summer in Detroit. He's wearing a classic black tank and has his hair cut short. I can picture him in the barbershop chair, telling Terry summer's coming and he's got to look good if his wife's about to be back in dresses.

"Last time you said you were in grind mode," he says. "Work paying off?"

I forget the details I've given to him and the details I've kept hidden. He knows someone got stabbed by accident. He doesn't know it was me. He knows Babel's offering us lottery tickets. He doesn't know how much fine print there is. I'm not sure if it's childish or grown-up, this fear of mine. A fear of telling him the full, unfiltered truth. I just think it's time I shouldered my own burdens instead of letting him do the heavy lifting.

"Yeah," I say, smiling. "I've been climbing back up the scoreboard. Doing well."

He nods, tells me to keep going, always pushing me to be better. Sometimes I get so caught up in what's going on aboard *Genesis 11* that I forget there's someone Earthside, praying and hoping and dreaming of what might happen if I pull this off. He told me to do it for me, to fight for *my* future, but he has no clue how badly I want it for him, for Moms.

"So everything's okay?" he asks.

"Still have work ahead of me, but I'm healthy and I like my chances."

Pops smiles at me like we're not a billion kilometers away. He looks ready to ask more, about the ship or about me or about space. But I'm tired of this place. Far too tired to waste our precious minutes on any of it. "How's Moms?" I ask. "I miss her. I miss you both."

"Good. Real good, son. The treatments seem like they're working."

We never say the words. *Chronic, failure, death.* We talk about her sickness without talking about it. I was still little when Moms first found out about her kidney disease, when she first started spiraling down. Pops shouldered the load after she lost her job, after the insurance money ran dry. It was all so hard for me to understand. I'd get mad that she was so tired. I thought it meant she didn't care about me. The older I got, the more I understood, but sometimes you hold those strikes against people in the darkest corners of your heart.

I nod. "She's not working, is she?"

"Not yet, but she misses that desk job she had in Moore Square. She's trying to get back to it, you know? It made her feel normal. For a while there, she'd come back home and talk about it. You know how she usually is about work."

"Work ain't for home," I say, smiling.

He laughs. "Exactly. So she's better, but still no traveling. That's why she's not here. Babel's station is about a six-hour drive. I don't think she can handle that kind of distance, you know? But the other day she asked if I'd take her to the store, Emmett. That's when I knew she was turning a corner on all of this."

"The store?"

"She wanted to buy work clothes. Man, she looks some kind of fine in business casual."

I cock an eyebrow at that. He's right. That is a good sign. At some of the lowest points, she'd talk about giving clothes away. Acted like she didn't have much use for them, not the direction she was heading. The idea of her buying clothes is a great sign.

"There's this one dress," Pops is saying. "Whoo . . . It takes me back. . . ."

I groan. "Pops. Really?"

"Hey, it's the reason you're here in the first place."

"Five minutes," I remind him. "We get five minutes, and this is what you talk about? There's something wrong with you—you know that, right?"

He laughs again. "You'll see what it's like one day, trust me. Anyway, she's getting better every day. I'm doing fine. She couldn't come today, but I do have a surprise for you."

I watch him lean over and rap his knuckles on a side door. A few seconds later it gasps open and PJ McQueen steps into the room, his grin wider than the screen, his eyes darting and excited.

"My *due*! Look at this guy!" PJ sits down next to Pops, still grinning. "Hey, Emmett. I know that you were getting tired of me domming you in pickup games, but you didn't have to leave the solar system out of shame, man."

Laughter shakes my whole body. "Please, PJ. You're good, but you're not that good."

"Right, right. Guy goes to space, gets a big head, acts like I don't rain j's for days."

I laugh again and glance over at Pops. "What were you thinking, bringing this clown in? He's supposed to be on a strict training program, Pops. Scholarships start next year. Have you taken your two thousand free throws today, PJ?"

PJ makes a face. "Come on, I could take off one day to talk to the celebrity."

"Celebrity? I don't know what Pops has been telling you, but I'm not a celebrity."

"Course you are," PJ says. "Whole world's going nuts. Babel went viral last week."

I frown. "Viral? What?"

"The Babel Files," he says. "Everyone at school's talking about it, man. All these girls started claiming they had things with you too. Don't worry—I shut down the rumor mill and set you up nice for when you come back."

I shake my head in confusion. "What are you talking about?"

PJ grins, giving his shoulder a dust-off. "Well, I told most of the girls to get lost. But I think Shae Westwood's down to date. Just call me your intergalactic wingman."

"Not that, PJ," I say. "The other thing. What are the Babel Files?"

"An article," Pops answers. "Haven't they shown you the article?"

"No." I shrug. "We're in space."

"Oh man," he says, clapping his hands together excitedly. "It's pretty cool. There's a whole page about you. They snagged your last yearbook photo and interviewed some teachers."

My mind's spinning. "There's an article about me?"

"Yeah, you and all the other recruits. It was kind of cool. You always talk about these kids, and now I know what they look like, you know? Gave me a face to go with the stories you always tell. I see what you mean about that Longwei kid."

"But," PJ interrupts, "not one mention of the Most Excellent Brothers? For shame, man. That was our time to shine. I expect name drops in future interviews."

I laugh again. "But who published it?"

Pops opens his mouth to respond, but as his lips move, the sound cuts. I hear a bass vibration and then a little high-pitched whine. His voice patches back, scrambles, and mutes a second time. After thirty seconds of interference, I jump up and open the door.

"Hey," I call to the nearest techie. "Sound isn't working."

The woman frowns at her glowing screen before detaching from her station. With another frown, she crosses over to the doorway. As she reaches the entrance, the screen flickers twice, and when the image returns, the sound does too.

". . . morning or something like that. But like I said, they're going nuts over it." There's a pause. "Emmett? You there, Emmett?"

"Seems to be working now," the techie says.

I scramble back into my seat. "Yeah. Sorry. You were cutting out some."

"Oh, okay. Well, like I was saying, Vegas is taking bets

on you guys. They have no idea what they're betting on, but it's kind of cool. And you won't believe—"

The screen vanishes. In the corner, I see that the five minutes has elapsed. In the mirrored dark of the screen, I look exhausted. Sighing, I push myself up and move back through the Contact Room. Vandemeer's waiting outside. I almost share my suspicions, but I remember that even trustworthy Vandemeer is being watched. He still wears Babel's watch and needs Babel's paychecks. He's at their mercy as much as I am. So I tell him that Moms is getting better and list off a few of PJ's stat lines from playing varsity as a freshman last year, but I don't mention the glitch or my suspicions.

I don't tell him that I noticed how the sound cut when Pops went into details about the Babel Files article. I don't tell him that I think the glitch happened on purpose, because nothing on this ship ever breaks or malfunctions. If Babel wants something to work, it works. So what was he saying that they don't want me to know? Whatever it is, I brace myself. Just one more thing to keep an eye out for, one more change waiting on the horizon.

DAY 100, 2:45 P.M.
Aboard *Genesis 11*

The best thing about having Sabbath off is the steamer.
I hunker down inside, naked and sweating and relaxed.
Detroit could get so cold. My guilty pleasure was simple:
hot showers. Sometimes I would walk straight home from
school and strip down. Didn't bother with soap or sham-
poo, just wanted to disappear into warmth. Hot water only
lasted for a few minutes back home, but it was still my favorite part of the day.

Babel's devices never fail. If I go to take a steam bath,
there's steam. If I want to disappear into the simulator and
pretend I'm in the Alps, I can. They're not a company with
faltering technologies or half measures. Knowing this is
comforting and disturbing. Comforting, because I know
we'll get to Eden. After seeing all their bells and whistles,
I have no fears of dying in a freak explosion or a botched
landing. Disturbing, because Babel isn't a company with a
plan B. They're more likely to have plans A through Z, and

I'm not even sure we know all of plan A yet. It's like looking at a puzzle that's missing twenty or thirty pieces.

When I feel my fingers start to wrinkle, I press and hold the release button. Hatches glide outward and fog gasps ahead of me like moon mist. I take a quick shower and towel off before doubling back to the cafeteria.

I was hoping to find Bilal again, and I do, but he's far from alone this time. I'm not even all the way down the stairs before I catch the first snatch of excited conversation.

"This means we're famous," Katsu is saying. "If the whole world's reading about it."

Jazzy says, "I always wondered what it'd be like to be a celebrity. I started hating pageants after a while, but there is something fun about being onstage."

I round the corner and everyone looks up. Katsu jumps to his feet, raising both arms like he just finished a marathon. "Emmett! We're famous, man! You can call me Hollywood!"

"Hollywood," I repeat, eyeing him. "This about the Babel Files?"

Katsu smacks my arm excitedly and looks back at the others.

"He heard about it too. This is amazing."

I slide past him and take the empty seat across from Azima. She's braiding Isadora's hair, and Isadora is braiding Jazzy's hair, and Jazzy is drawing a tattoo on Jaime's arm. It's the kind of thing that only happens on Sabbaths. They're the deep breaths we all take between endless sprints. The only time we can kick our feet up and act like normal people.

Bilal waves at me from the far end of the table. He looks showered and normal again, but I can still see a little red in his cheeks. He's halfway through a slice of pie. I make an effort not to look at Azima after looking at him. Naturally, Longwei's not here for the festivities. He tends to vanish whenever there's a crowd. I notice that Kaya and Roathy are absent too.

"How many of you heard about it?" I ask.

"All of us," Azima answers. "One way or another."

I nod. "I wonder why they published it."

"Who cares why they published it?" Katsu replies. "I'm famous. When I go back to Japan, I'm dating supermodels. Racing sports cars. I'll be that guy they show at sporting events, you know? The one the announcers talk about for a few minutes. With the big sunglasses."

Isadora laughs. "I don't think we're that kind of famous, Katsu."

"Why not?" he asks. "We're like . . . sexy astronauts!"

Jazzy makes a face. "Do you always have to make it weird?"

"Yes," Katsu replies proudly. "I'm here to make it weird. Everyone knows that."

"He has a point," I say. "About us being celebrities. We're the youngest people to ever go into space. Pretty sure that's a big deal."

"You really think so?" Bilal asks through a mouthful of pie. "We'll all be famous?"

Jazzy shoots another look his way. "You're the nicest kid in the world, Bilal, but you have the worst table manners I've ever seen."

He finishes chewing and smiles. "My family didn't have a table."

Before Jazzy can get too embarrassed, Azima says, "I don't want to be famous."

"Really?" Isadora sounds shocked. "If you're famous, you can do whatever you want. You can go to all the parties. Get the best seats at restaurants. I want to be famous."

"Famous people are corrupt," Azima says. "They are unhappy. Everyone knows this."

"I don't want to be famous either," Bilal chimes in quickly. "Too much attention."

I notice him looking hopefully in Azima's direction and have to hide a laugh. Katsu looks around the rest of the table in shock. "Then the two of you can live your quiet lives while Isadora and I go to parties. Emmett? Jaime? You two coming dancing with us or not?"

Jaime shrugs. "I don't really dance."

Katsu groans before turning to me. "Emmett. Please. Please say you'll party with me."

"In Japan or Detroit?"

He laughs. "Let's meet in the middle."

"So . . . the ocean?"

He laughs louder now. "You're all officially invited to my middle-of-the-ocean party. We'll eat all the best food and dance on yachts and whatever else famous people do. And just to make sure Jazzy comes, we're making it a sexy astronaut theme."

Everyone laughs at that. For a while, they talk about their favorite celebrities. Bilal's obsessed with some philosopher in Palestine. Isadora confesses that she wants to date the entire Brazilian soccer team. I get caught up listening for a while and almost forget I've got somewhere to be. I excuse myself and head back to our room, hoping I haven't kept Kaya waiting too long.

As I come back in, I hear her shower running, so I sit down at our table and pull one of the reports on the Adamites. This one's a random scientist's theory on Adamite mythology. Once I would have fallen asleep after the first paragraph, but Babel's tests have made my mind sharper. Things that were once hard are becoming easy. I wonder if this is the student I could have been without all the distractions. If I could have come home and spent hours doing homework instead of babysitting cousins. I file it under *N* for *Never Know.*

When Kaya's ready, we take our normal route. Same checkpoints and cameras and secret panels. I'm pretty sure at this point either of us could do it blindfolded. If Babel's watching, they haven't said anything about our nighttime fun. Maybe they don't care if we do a little exploring, so long as we don't get into any real trouble. Or they know what Kaya can't accept: we've reached the limits of our exploration.

As we walk, I catch her up on the day's news. She hasn't heard about the Babel Files yet, and she's apparently known about Azima's interest in Bilal for a while. I'm always surprised to find out that she spends time with the other competitors, but I guess it makes sense. When I run out of news, she shares a new strategy she's developed for the Rabbit Room. I laugh because it's the kind of brilliant plan only Kaya could devise.

We wait in the antechamber and then enter the no-grav zone. Kaya doesn't play around on the walls anymore or throw jelly beans. The fun version of Kaya has slowly been replaced by the obsessed version. Her fascination with Babel has made her all business. I keep catching myself hoping we'll get through the door and have an answer and finally be able to move on. Kaya pretends it's this great adventure, but secretly I think she just wants an answer to the riddle of the door. She pushes herself directly up to the second air lock and latches her feet on the exposed frame. All I can do at this point is follow.

"Notice anything about my necklace?" she asks.

Throughout the competition, Babel's given us more and more nyxia to use. I keep three bands on one wrist and a ring on the opposite hand. Kaya's the only one who keeps hers in the form of a necklace. Little nyxian charms dangle beneath her collarbone, shaped like stars and hearts and wings. I glance at it and give a nod. "Your sunflower's missing."

"Well done," she says. "I needed it to manipulate this." Reaching into a pocket, she removes a perfect black cylinder. "Took me a few weeks to get it right. Give it a try."

I take the cylinder from her and line it up with the door slot. It's a perfect fit. Kaya gestures for me to press it fully forward, and I push in until it draws flush with the rest of the door. We both hear a little *click*. Clockwork mechanisms grind to life. My eyes go wide as the door slides open.

"You're a genius," I say, stunned. "A genius, Kaya."

We float into an antechamber, and the gravity falls thick

over our shoulders. We each drop to a knee, and it takes us
a few seconds to stand. The next door has a handle.

"Should we keep going?" I ask.

"Of *course* we keep going. I've been imagining what's
back here for *months*."

Together, we cross the threshold into a new, brightly lit
corridor. It looks like every other one, but our careful progress reveals no cameras. The hallway runs twenty meters,
then hairpins. A slow descent. We walk twenty more meters, then hairpin again. There are no stairwells, no scuffed
floors, nothing.

"They didn't use nyxia in these hallways," Kaya remarks.

I nod, though I hadn't noticed. The walls are some kind
of nanoplastic lined with the occasional metal support.
Something about the layout puts me on edge. I'm about to
tell Kaya we should go back when a door appears around
the next turn. Like the walls, it has no nyxia woven into its
frame. There is a scanner, though. We come to a stop before
it. I don't swipe it open.

"Finally," Kaya whispers excitedly. "We finally get to see
what's back here."

I try to look excited, but something's off. This door is
different from the others.

We stand there awkwardly until Kaya glances over.
"Well, go ahead."

"I don't know if we should," I say. "I don't have a good
feeling about it."

Kaya looks at me like I'm crazy. "Emmett, we've spent
weeks—no, *months*—trying to get in here. If we stopped

now, it'd be like reading to the end of the book and not finishing."

"Doesn't feel right."

"But we're literally *right* here. We can't stop now."

I swallow and nod. "Your call."

The card scans and the door releases.

The brightness inside forces us to squint. I blink twice before picking out shapes, vague and ethereal. My eyes adjust slowly. Jointed mechanical arms extend from the high ceilings. Five, ten, twenty at least. They hang ominously throughout the room, ending in sharp drills and glinting saw blades. Staggered along the walls are plasma screens. I can't decipher the diagrams or numbers flashing green across their surfaces. Blue light pumps through everything like blood. It borders the white floor panels and circles the joints of mechanical tools.

Kaya takes the first step inside. On cue, the tiled floor snaps from white to black. It looks like a shadow has fallen, like some towering monster looms above us now. The lights lose their reflection, and in the fading glow we see what the room is for.

A man. Three straps run crosswise, suspending him tightly to the far wall. His face is half hooded, down to the upward curve of his lips. A pair of snaking white cords feed into the corners of his mouth. Matching white cables disappear into his bare chest, his arms, his abdomen. Just below his throat is an open wound. The edges of it are smoking and rotten. It almost looks like *something* was lodged there and *someone* ripped it out.

Kaya and I are drawn into the room the same way neigh-

bors are drawn to a burning house. Babel forgot to put up
police tape; we can go as close to the fire as we want to.
There is no noise except for the slow, steady pulse of a monitor. The beats are so spaced out that I find myself waiting
and waiting for the next one to sound.

"He's alive," I whisper. But who is he? And why does
Babel have him here, like a captive?

"Look at the scars," Kaya says, soft and sad.

His skin looks like faded clay. It must have once been a
rich and beautiful color. Along his arms, I notice the burns.
Skin has bubbled up in some places and been stripped
away in others. His entire left shoulder is colored with faint
bruises. It doesn't need to be said, but Kaya says it anyway.

"They've been torturing him."

We come to a stop. Not quite close enough to reach out
and touch him. My eyes trace downward. They left under-
garments, and a strange, stony armor over his kneecaps. I
point to them.

"What are those?" I ask.

Kaya kneels, making a thoughtful noise. "I've seen
crosses like that."

"Crosses?"

She holds out both arms. "Crosses."

And she's right. A central stone has been molded to each
kneecap. From it, jagged arms reach up and out and down.
I squint to get a closer look. The metal looks grafted into the
skin, almost like scales. I circle around to the side and hear
Kaya suck in a breath.

"Be careful," she whispers.

"I am."

At an angle, I get my first impression of how big the man is. Not tall, but compact and muscular. He's thicker from front to back than most tree trunks. I doubt I could get my arms fully around him. His shoulders are unnaturally broad too. On his elbows I spot stones that match the ones on his knees. They mesh perfectly with his skin. For the first time, I realize he's not human at all. This is an Adamite. Here, on the ship.

"Kaya, it's one of them."

"An Adamite," she confirms. "How could they do this to him?"

The monitor beeps, startling us both. We each catch the other's look of panic. There's a moment of embarrassed smiles. But a movement wipes them from our faces.

Though a strap stretches below his chest and across his biceps, the captive's hand begins to rise. The monitor ticks into the silence. The hand climbs like a ghostly drawbridge. I'm close enough to notice everything: how the veins thicken, how the frail hand tightens into a powerful fist, how the man's lips part ever so slightly. I stand in horror before him, unable to move, unable to speak.

The charms along Kaya's neck tremble with movement. They rise impossibly into the air, turning on their clasps like little planets. Kaya's staring down and my jaw drops. We watch the invisible hands slide the nyxia up, millimeter by millimeter. We're both terrified, but Kaya's instincts finally kick in. She slaps a hand over the charms and pulls the necklace back to her chest.

A thunderclap breaks the silence.

Kaya drops with it and lets out a strangled, high-pitched

cry. I feel a presence snake into the air, and I'm forced back as something big and powerful tears across the distance separating us. It is wind and rain and chaos. I fight forward as Kaya starts to scream.

Voices sound in a distant world. The man strapped to the wall tightens his fist, and Kaya's eyes go wide. The necklace tightens, digging into flesh. I'm there, scrambling to help, but my hands can't get between the nyxia and her neck. There's a click as one of the charms snaps off. It claws into the air, and the captive manipulates it into smoke, gathering the substance around a fist. I'm shouting now: for help, for anyone. Kaya's eyes are bloodshot, her face terrified. Her hands fight and claw, but neither of us can pull the necklace free as it tightens, tightens, tightens.

I'm already crying, but I scream when the nyxia's drawn upward. Kaya's body is pulled into the air until her toes are barely touching the floor. I try to pull her body back down, but I'm not strong enough. The force is too powerful. Kaya's stopped clawing at her neck. One hand falls limp to her side. Then the other. I hear a rattling noise, and I shout at the top of my lungs as the lights of the room flash twice. The man on the wall spits a curse through gritted teeth.

Then Defoe is between us.

His charcoal suit ripples. One second it's fabric, the next black plate mail. He clamps both hands over the man's fist. Shadows slash out in every direction. Defoe grunts, then rams his nyxia-enforced shoulder into the captive's stomach. Pinned and blind, the man can't brace for the blow. Defoe rams the shoulder again, and air gushes out through the man's thick lips. With a jerk, Defoe rips the nyxia away from the captive. Another quick manipulation melds it into his armor. He sets his feet and delivers three more blows: gut, gut, and groin.

Kaya collapses to the floor. I get my fingers between her and the necklace and rip it away. Dark red lines are dug there like trenches. Defoe wheels around, nyxia shivering back into his suit as he ducks and lifts Kaya by an arm. I put my weight on her other side and we drag her out of the room. Darkness fills the edges of my vision.

This isn't real; this can't be happening.

"She's not breathing!" I shout. "She's not breathing."

She's not moving either.

"God, she's not breathing."

Defoe gets the door closed and he lays her down. Footsteps sound overhead. Kaya stares, eyes red, at the ceiling. Vandemeer and the other attendants turn the corner. Hope tears through me. They can save her. They have to save her. I stumble back as they slide in around her body. Vandemeer starts CPR. Someone preps a crash cart. They let electricity course through her. Vandemeer breathes into her lips. His hands pump over her chest. I wait for the movie ending. The gasping breath. The eyes snapping open and blinking. A promise that it's not over.

It doesn't come. Vandemeer backs away. His face looks shattered.

"Time of death, 9:02."

As they escort me away, I get one final look at Kaya. She looks like a fallen petal, snapped too soon. No one closes her eyes, so she keeps staring out at the world she's left behind. I remember the second book we read together. A bridge to imaginary lands. I remember new worlds meant to be explored together, but I also remember the lonely astronaut and his dead friend. His empty heart and her haunting absence. I don't need to pretend I understand the boy in the book. Not anymore.

DAY 100, 10:15 P.M.

Aboard *Genesis 11*

"You're certain?" Vandemeer asks me again.

I nod. "It was an Adamite."

"Aboard the damn ship," he says softly. His eyes flicker down to his watch. He's always weighing his words carefully, because Babel is *always* listening. For the first time, I realize they're watching him as much as they're watching me. "This is the first I've heard about it."

"They had him tied up. They were torturing him. That's why the Adamite killed her. He thought she was one of them. So he killed her, trying to escape."

Vandemeer looks uncomfortable. "Why were you down there, Emmett?"

I have no answer. To say it was Kaya's fault feels like a betrayal. She's the one who kept digging. She wanted to keep going. But if I had never stolen the card, she'd still be alive.

Is that what he wants to hear? Guilt buries me deeper and deeper with each passing second. Not knowing how to speak any comfort, Vandemeer busies himself with my hand wraps for the thousandth time. I have hundreds of tiny cuts from trying to rip the nyxia necklace off. The real injuries are beneath the surface, though. I will never forget the red circle dug across her thin neck. I will never forget those dark, playful eyes shot with red. I will never forgive myself.

Sleep's impossible. Vandemeer hooks me up to machines, forcing my hand. I wake screaming from nightmares every hour. Drugged and ragged, I'm not ready for Defoe's visit when it comes. I have no idea what day it is, how much of the competition I've missed. I can barely tell if I'm really still alive. He appears at the foot of my hospital bed, and light shivers across his suit.

"Emmett," he begins. "I've come to discuss your punishment."

The thought almost makes me laugh. There's nothing he can do to punish me. Whatever he takes won't be enough. Does he even know who Kaya was to me? Does he understand the kind of person we lost? He can't punish me and he can't forgive me. No one can.

"Rod and reproof," Defoe continues. "Erone has delivered the rod of discipline. The rod answers for past mistakes; the reproof instructs future action. Together they bring wisdom. I hope Kaya's death has taught you the meaning of our rules, the purpose behind our boundaries."

Anger burns through me. I'm to blame, but Babel's hands aren't clean on this one.

"You were torturing him," I say. "That's why he attacked us."

"We were performing tests," Defoe says. "As the Adamites have done on our people."

"He killed Kaya because he thought she was one of *you.*"

Defoe stares at me. His face gives away nothing.

"So it's our fault that you ignored the rules? Is that really what you think?"

Tears streak hot down my face. No, it's not what I think. I know the part I played in all of this. Defoe spins his data pad and shows me the boldly lit scoreboard. My score's taken a massive hit.

"We've subtracted thirty thousand points. Ten for stealing from your medical attendant. Ten for disobeying space protocols. Ten for endangering the lives of *everyone* on this ship."

"You think I care about my score? You really think I care about that?"

Defoe straightens his already straight tie. "So this is how you'll respond? Kaya died and now you'll quit? I would have thought her life was worth more to you than that. For the record, the Adamite has been removed from the ship. You will not mention his presence to anyone else. You will not break our rules again. And if I know you at all, you will not insult Kaya's memory by quitting. She would have expected more."

He sweeps from the room. I lean back in my bed, hyperventilating. For the thousandth time, the image of Kaya breaks me in two. I hate that Defoe's right. I hate that he's the one who had to remind me of who she was and what she'd want. I know I'll fight for her. I know I'll keep going, even if I don't deserve to be here when she's not.

Defoe thinks he knows me. He knows I won't forgive myself for this, but he doesn't realize that I won't forgive Babel either. Beneath their song and dance, Babel's just as dark and dangerous as we always imagined they were. Their treatment of Kaya's death. The tortured Adamite. All of it.

They're willing to do whatever it takes to get what they want. My heart rate soars just thinking about it. I thought we might have control. That if we played hardball, we could dictate terms to Babel because we're their meal ticket on Eden. But that's not true. Without them, we're stuck off-planet. Billions of kilometers away from home and without a single speck of control over what happens to us.

The truth is stunningly simple. We're slaves. Babel has the food, the money, the spaceship. Babel will dictate which of us travel down to Eden. If we're good little boys and girls, maybe we'll get to go home. Kaya's death has made the truth clear. I know there's only one thing I can do, for her and for myself and for my family.

If Babel's going to keep us in chains, I'll go where they can't follow.

I'll go to Eden.

DAY 101, 8:01 A.M.
Aboard *Genesis 11*

Babel's efficiency knows no bounds. The next morning, Kaya's name has been struck out on every scoreboard. The others discuss it as I sit down for breakfast. They think she quit. I can't make myself say it. They deserve to hear it from someone other than Babel, but I'm too ashamed to even look them in the eye. I fill up a plate of food to kill time, but I don't eat a thing.

Defoe arrives. His black suit could be an attempt at mourning, but his eyes and his voice aren't sad as they deliver the news. To him, Kaya was just a potential employee. I hate him for it.

"Last night, Kaya was killed in an accident."

The truth strikes like lightning. The others stare. My mouth begs to explain, to say that this was Babel's fault, but Defoe silences me with a look. He allows time for the others to react. This will be a lesson. No one is safe. Anyone can fall, even the smartest one in the group. I hear the others whisper, and I hate myself for saying nothing. This isn't right.

"Only nine remain."

He allows this to sink in as well. I want to hate him for it, but I thought the same thing when I woke up this morning. One less person to take my spot. I couldn't shower away the guilt of thinking something like that, not with all the hot water on *Genesis 11*.

"This does change our outlook. We didn't plan on losing any of you before arriving at Eden. Without Kaya, we have only three female competitors remaining. Our on-planet projections show that at least three are necessary for optimal team function. We believe this would happen organically in the competition, but Kaya's death has forced our hand."

I'm too tired, too lost to understand. Roathy slams a fist into the table. The others look on edge, so Defoe goes on.

"Jazzy, Isadora, Azima—you will move on to Eden."

The three of them look shocked. Azima wasn't likely to lose, but Jazzy and Isadora were in the bottom four. It was going to be hard enough for me to catch one of them after my punishment. Now I can't even do that. I glance up at the scoreboard:

1.	LONGWEI	373,900	points
2.	BILAL	365,300	points
3.	AZIMA	364,750	points
4.	KATSU	363,450	points
~~5.~~	~~KAYA~~	~~351,050~~	~~points~~
6.	JAIME	328,200	points
7.	ISADORA	292,080	points
8.	JASMINE	283,050	points

9.	ROATHY	277,324	points
10.	EMMETT	268,350	points

My points have been subtracted. Babel's penalty for my guilt is such a small thing. I'm just nine thousand points behind Roathy, but it feels more like ninety thousand. If Kaya's not here, how can I possibly go on?

For a second, I'm worried about winning, about money, about home. The second burns by quickly, though, as I remember Kaya's crossed-out name on the scoreboard. I hate Defoe for turning our eyes to the competition instead of to her. I hate that we're thinking about beating each other instead of honoring the person we've lost. The person I killed. It's the kind of hate and anger that can't be turned into anything else, that can't be converted into fuel.

As the week goes by, I lose everything. The swimming tank makes me feel like I'm drowning. The classroom lectures are a distant voice. In the pit, I can't force myself to throw a punch. Bilal sits beside me at every meal.

"If you want to talk about it," he says, "I'm here."

He doesn't dig deeper when I shake my head. He doesn't ask about the points I lost or what happened. He just stays by my side and honors Kaya's absence with his silent presence. I can barely find the words to thank him.

Defoe is the only one who knows what happened, and he's the only one who carries on like nothing has changed. I realize that, for him, nothing *has* changed. I file it away under *A* for *Asshole.* He escorts us down to the Rabbit Room on yet another endless day in what feels like an endless week. I stand there like the dead until Jaime says something about needing a new strategy. I burst out laughing. It's abrupt and frightening. I can't help but belly laugh, though, as I remember one of the last things Kaya told me before she died. Her new strategy for the Rabbit Room.

"All right," I say. "This is what we're going to do. For Kaya."

Azima, Isadora, Jaime, and I line up near the center of the room. Defoe swipes his data pad and the room churns to life. The digital forest flickers on the wall screen and the race begins. Isadora swings over to the far left as we planned. She sets a steady pace as Jaime, Azima, and I transform our nyxian rings into thick handheld shields. As the pace picks up, we drift toward the center of the room, where the mesh tennis net divides us from the other team. On my signal, we all leap over it and into enemy territory.

"For Kaya!" I shout.

My battle cry is echoed, and the other team looks terrified as we come crashing into their formation. It's chaos. I ram Longwei and kick my legs out to trip Bilal. Jazzy almost ducks away, but Azima snags her by the arm, and the whole group falls in a tangle. Someone's foot hooks around my neck, but all I can do is laugh as we slide helplessly to the back wall. The room lights up like fireworks.

Isadora's still running for our team, though, and a few seconds later the tread floor stops.

Defoe looks radiant, clapping as he walks over to us.

"Finally, someone is thinking outside the box."

He's looking at me, like it was my plan.

"It was Kaya," I say firmly. "She came up with it."

"For Kaya," Azima repeats.

She slings an arm around me and the others crowd close. They speak the phrase as we all leave the Rabbit Room together. That evening, I linger in the multipurpose room. I'm afraid to go back to our room without Kaya. I'm afraid to wake up to my first Sabbath without her as my teammate, as my friend. The others eventually retreat, though, and I'm forced back to where I first met her.

My suit glows and the door slides open. I go to my own room and start undressing. The mirror doesn't indicate that my heart's been broken. It doesn't have a measure for my hopelessness either. It just ticks off the beats and counts the calories, like those are any way to measure life. I sit on the edge of the bed until I hear knocks. The sound echoes through the walls. I drag my suit across the room and scan it, and the door whisks open.

My friends come storming inside.

Katsu holds an open carton of ice cream. "Sleepover!" he shouts.

Bilal is carrying pillows and blankets. He tosses them down and gives me a hug. Jazzy, Azima, and Jaime file into the room behind him. "Thanks," I whisper. "Thank you so much."

Bilal nods over to Jaime. "It was his idea."

Jaime looks over and nods once. "We didn't want you to be alone."

His kindness levels me. I reach out a hand and he shakes it.

"I'm sorry about everything," I tell him. "All that stuff at the beginning."

He shakes his head. "It's nothing. It's in the past."

After Jaime explained his idea to the others, Katsu went

down to the kitchens and stole the ice cream. Bilal found movies to watch and Jazzy gathered the extra pillows.

The night blurs. We eat out of a massive carton of ice cream and watch old Disney cartoons that are in all the wrong languages. Everyone honors Kaya, saying something nice about her. I'm surprised how often she offered her kindness to the others. I selfishly believed she only spoke to me that way, but in just a few months she helped each of them when they needed it.

I fall asleep on the floor next to Bilal. Katsu sleeps beside him, snoring like a plane engine. Jazzy and Azima sleep on my bed, while Jaime retreats to the couch. Kaya's absence brings the broken boys and girls together, even if it's just for a night.

INTERLUDE

THE BABEL FILES
MARCUS DEFOE

"This isn't some punk reporter digging for cash," Roman explains. "They published it in *Time*. Some of our objectives are already toast, on principle."

Our coordinator of Earthside operations runs a hand through already disheveled hair. Roman Beckett is all hot air and urgency. He made partner because some of his initial operations decisions thrust Babel Communications into its current ascent. Bright fires can still burn out, though, and this mistake might be unforgivable.

I have the article pulled up on my data pad. Twenty-three sprawling pages that document the lives and background of every single competitor we recruited. The information is almost as good as the information we had. All in all, the intelligence is stunning. The fact that they tracked us on every single house visit reeks of betrayal. Roman's job is to flush out defectors and keep the company's secrets in the pockets and vaults where they belong. He didn't do that, not this time.

In the digital square above him, Katherine Ford sweeps a sandy lock behind her right ear. She's our technology queen and development specialist. Roman has spent the last twenty minutes trying to ease some of his burden onto her shoulders, and she doesn't looked pleased.

"Our cryptography programs were running," Katherine explains. "This happened on your side of things, Roman. Don't try to implicate any of my departments in this."

"I know that, Katherine," Roman snaps back. "They did it old-school to avoid detection. Actual film. Typewriters too. A nanosecond upload and straight to digital press."

"Bunch of quacks," David Requin croaks. "Nothing better to do."

Requin. He's a cold man, as cold as they come. I resist rubbing my eyes. Too much time staring at screens. This meeting shouldn't even be happening. We were still a few months away from our next call, but the emergency demanded our attention. Now the whole world knows we've taken recruits into space. Every major news network is running special segments with their own angles on what we're doing and what devious webs connect the children we've recruited.

"Quacks?" I ask quietly. "Just because someone spied on *us* for once, that makes them quacks? You're being narrow-minded again, Requin."

Requin just shrugs. "You know what I mean. All it does is feed the junkies who get off on this kind of thing. They want to pull back the curtain and see the wizard. Good for them. They don't know that we have twenty curtains and twenty wizards. We've got so many trapdoors, sometimes even I forget where they are. So I say go ahead. Let them think they know the half of it. It doesn't change any of our plans. Don't forget, we're all alone out here."

Roman nods along, but Katherine's eyes are sharper. She sees what I see. This article isn't a bruise that will fade; it's a sore that will fester.

"You understand what this means, don't you?" I ask. "They knew enough about us to know what we would know and how we would know it and how they could avoid us. Quacks? They sound more like prospective employees to me."

Roman snorts. "You've got to be kidding."

"Of course I'm kidding. Not every problem can be paid to go away. This article puts a microscope on us, Roman. It's an open door to other companies too. If two paycheck journalists can put a bag on our head and take a few swings, what do you think someone with an actual bankroll will try to pull?"

Roman doesn't snort this time. He huffs an "I'll handle it."

"No, you won't." I tap my data pad. A blue circle appears in the corner of their screens. "I've attached the public explanation, answers to expected questions, and an objective board for our broadcasting team over the next few weeks. First step, we start fast-tracking the financial benefits to the families. Let's get some press on our generosity. The implementation can start tomorrow."

Roman looks furious, but all three of them tap their screens to download. Green arrows race around blue circles, and the documents duplicate onto hard drives. They scroll through the abstract summaries. Requin's the first to finish. "Excellent. Well, that settles that."

Katherine nods. "Next time, I'd prefer Roman solve his own problems."

"Agreed. I have my own circus to run," I say.

Roman's neck is bright red, but he keeps his mouth shut for once. His first smart move today. He's not dead in the water, not yet. But he should have seen the journalists and he should have sniffed out what was going on. When you get lazy, mistakes happen. We've all made mistakes in the past, but these days they seem to be happening only to Roman. Babel doesn't shelter the weak. We amputate, rebuild, and conquer. Roman knows that, and he knows how close he is to being cut away.

"Speaking of circuses," Requin says, dropping the subject with a grin. "We're ready for you, Marcus. The Waterway is fully operable now. Hell of a fun ride, even for an old man."

I can't help but smile. "You better not be cheating."

Requin snorts a laugh. "Don't need to cheat, old friend. Not this time."

"Care to make a wager on that?" I ask dangerously.

The question wipes the grin off his face. Our bets are planet-sized. Just two years ago Roman lost a stable of Picassos to Katherine at the Kentucky Derby. I've never lost a bet, because I make a habit of knowing the outcomes before I set my money on the table.

Requin pushes back. "How about a specific bet?"

"How specific?" I ask.

"Picking the commander."

Katherine smiles. "Can I get in on this action?"

"No, not fair," I answer. "This is a bet for half-blind mice."

"Fine," Katherine replies. "I'll leave you two to your gambling. I've a company to run."

Her screen blinks black. Roman follows suit, thankful for the excuse to leave, and it's Requin and me, alone on the call. Every minute is costing millions, so I cut to the chase.

"Erone nearly broke free of his bonds. A couple of the recruits swiped an access card. He got his hands on some nyxia, but I was there in time to stop it. We lost Kaya."

"Maybe you should be more careful," Requin suggests unhelpfully. "If he'd managed to overcome you, he would have torn the ship to pieces."

"Doubtful," I say. "Knowing Erone, he would have followed the flight pattern back so that he could tear your ship to pieces. He's fond of me. He hates you."

"Well, I did abduct him," Requin laughs.

"Anything else?"

Requin frowns. "Wait, what about our bet?"

"No, thanks," I say. "I don't make bets I know I'm going to lose."

"And how could you know that?"

"I'm up early every *morning*." I let the word hang in the air. Requin chuckles like a child caught stealing snacks. "You know how the saying goes, early birds and all that."

"So you admit defeat?"

"Yes. At least until I can find the aces I normally keep up my sleeves."

"Until then." Requin nods, and the connection goes black.

PART II

BLACK HOLES

DAY 188, 7:48 A.M.

Aboard *Genesis 11*

1.	LONGWEI	686,900	points
2.	KATSU	633,450	points
3.	BILAL	529,300	points
4.	AZIMA	528,750	points
5.	JAIME	519,200	points
6.	JASMINE	474,050	points
7.	ROATHY	470,324	points
8.	EMMETT	468,350	points
9.	ISADORA	413,080	points
~~10.~~	~~KAYA~~	~~351,050~~	~~points~~

Vandemeer waits in the living room. For a few weeks after Kaya's death, he and I were lost to each other. He neglected his duties and I neglected mine. We seemed to snap out of it together. His allegiance to Babel became secondary to me. For Kaya, we fight together.

I'm pretty sure that Vandemeer thinks if he can get me to Eden, he'll be able to forgive his failure in protecting her.

I don't want to tell him it won't work. It never works that way. Guilt like this doesn't leave. You can set it aside, but it's always there, waiting.

After warm-ups, I walk over to Kaya's door and bow my head. I don't know Jesus or God all that well, but I imagine we're closer to them up here in space. Maybe they can hear me, even if we're not on speaking terms. I say the same words every day.

Vandemeer eyes me afterward. "What do you pray for?"

"Rest."

"Who do you pray to?"

"I don't know."

Breakfast comes and goes. We all treat each other like friends until we're forced to be enemies. Going back and forth is more tiring than just hating each other. Sometimes I think Longwei has it right. He doesn't waste time on friendships. Maybe that's why he's so good. All his energy goes into treating us like enemies. Maybe it's easier that way.

But Kaya's death changed me, changed everything. I can't go back to cold competition and ruthless winning. I don't want to go back to that. Kaya made us laugh and smile. She offered help to anyone who asked for it, even those who were afraid to ask. For her, I try to be better. Bilal keeps offering to talk about it, but I can't share my shame with him.

The grueling months have transformed every competition. New strategies, new trends, new ways to get hurt. Most of the rooms carry Kaya's legacy with them. She had a brain that broke each challenge down into compartments and solved them like simple puzzles. Watching the others copy her tactics after all this time makes the hole in my heart a little bigger, a little deeper.

Following routine, we make our way down to the pit. At this point, everyone's deadly. Practice makes perfect, and Babel has made us all effective killers. The only question is why.

Babel's other edict has changed things too. The girls are immune now, guaranteed spots. Vandemeer has been hung up on it for months. He doesn't think the new ruling's ethical. He spent weeks combing through my contracts to try to get the ruling overturned. But there are so many hidden twists gridlocked in Babel's clauses that he eventually gave up. I don't bother worrying about why Babel pushed the girls through, or whether or not it was fair.

None of that matters. Babel spoke. And when Babel speaks, the rules are set in stone. All I can do is try to win in spite of them. It's not easy. Isadora no longer has to fight for herself. Instead, she fights for Roathy. Against the other girls she slacks off. But against us she fights tooth and nail for each point. The two of them keep to themselves most days now.

Overhead, Kaya's avatar flickers briefly onto the screen. It takes eight seconds for the forfeit to register and the points to add into Azima's score. Eight seconds is long enough to take me back to that bright room full of dark things. I shake the vision out of my head as Kaya's avatar is replaced. I hate that my image of her has slowly shifted to this digital, Babel-made projection. She was more than that, more than they could ever capture with pixels and lights.

Next up, Longwei and Bilal.

For a few weeks, Longwei tried to carve a new rival out of Bilal. He wanted to go to war with my friend over Azima's affections. But there's only so much hate you can build up against someone who won't hate you back. Any chance of solidifying a rivalry was ended by Azima's new belief that the Adamites could be the most eligible bachelors down on Eden. It took a few days to help Bilal get over his heartbreak at hearing that pronouncement.

Our first- and third-place contestants salute at center. Defoe gives the signal and Bilal presses, only to have Longwei melt into the backdrop. Our eyes follow the action as Longwei trampolines up to the second level and darts out of sight. From our vantage point, we can still see the top of his head bobbing along the outer rim. Then Longwei trampolines up to the third level. Ducking low, he circles back along the square, padded ridge. Bilal's making his cautious way along the second tier, checking all the nooks and crannies that people normally hide in. He's taller than Longwei, more visible. We all watch as their paths near a point of intersection.

And then Longwei leaps.

His front tuft of hair flops up, and his eyes look wild as he takes flight. Bilal's hatchets go up, but not quickly enough. The impact jars both weapons from his hands, and he goes stumbling toward the edge of the second tier. Before he can recover, Longwei plants a kick into his lower back and Bilal flies. We all gasp as he goes over the edge. The angle's all wrong as he juts out a leg just before impact. My stomach pinwheels when the bone snaps clean in two. Bilal collapses in a blooming red puddle. We all stare at the very,

very white bone that's slit upward through his black suit.
The sight is enough to turn us all inside out.

I run forward. The pain registers on Bilal's face, and
high-pitched shrieks tear from his lungs. I can hear the attendants just behind me. Before I can get to him, Longwei
hops down. Instead of helping, though, he brings the nyxia-
blunted sword down on Bilal's neck. Overhead, Bilal's avatar loses its head. The real Bilal is screaming with pain,
and Longwei begins to walk away. Rage turns everything
red. I veer away from Bilal, knowing the attendants are
there, knowing they can do more for him than I can. Longwei doesn't realize I'm coming. A second later, I lower both
shoulders and blindside him. The collision shakes me from
jaw to hip. We go rolling and I end up on top of him.

"You bastard."

He tries to squirm, but I'm bigger than he is. I pin his
arms back with my knees and rip the nyxian mask from his
face. It clatters away and I land a downward jab. His head
snaps against the floor. He's spouting Mandarin as his nose
bloodies. I ignore him, sweeping his hand aside and punching down again. Twice more and his eyes daze.

I'm shouting at him still, screaming every curse I know,
when Vandemeer pulls me off. I manage to land a kick
against Longwei's ribs before Vandemeer can push me away
and walk me out of the pit. I don't look at the others, but I
can feel their stares as I'm escorted out of the room.

DAY 188, 1:13 P.M.
Aboard *Genesis 11*

Vandemeer doesn't come down too hard on me. Instead, he makes me do yoga. I inhale, exhale, stretch, roll shoulders, and find the anger fading to the distant corners of my brain.

"I have to go see him," I say when we're finished.

"Bilal?" Vandemeer asks.

"When I was down there, I thought everyone abandoned me. I won't let him feel that way."

"Your wound was directly caused by nyxia. It's standard protocol to not allow visitors in those situations. Bilal's injury happened naturally. You'll be allowed to visit him, all right? I'll take you down after the Rabbit Room," Vandemeer offers. "How does that sound?"

"Sounds like shit." Points before people, that's what Babel's teaching us. That's what I used to think before Kaya. "Sounds like I care more about my score than I do about my friend."

"Think about it, Emmett," Vandemeer replies impatiently. "He's going into surgery right now. He won't be able to see you and you won't be able to see him. Not until to-night. No sense in you wasting an opportunity to keep fighting. You've worked too hard."

I grind my teeth together. He's right. Still makes me feel like a lurch, though.

"Are they still at lunch?"

"They're due in the Rabbit Room," he says. "I'll take you down."

All I can see in my head is Bilal's bone jutting into the open air. As we walk, Vandemeer tries to remind me of the climates we studied earlier. I'm too distracted for that, though.

I ask about Bilal instead. "How long will it take him to recover?"

Vandemeer grimaces. "Earthside it'd take him a year."

"But here?" I ask. "It wasn't a nyxian injury like mine."

"No, it wasn't. Here it will be much faster. Nyxian pins and plates. Advanced blood treatment and muscle rebuilding. He'll be back in a month."

"That's an eternity."

Vandemeer stops me in front of the Rabbit Room. "I know you like him. He's a good kid with a good heart. But there's only so many more spots left for the trip to Eden. We've been working hard to make sure one of those spots goes to you. No letting up, all right?"

I give him a guilty nod and join my team. With Bilal in the med unit, the teams are even for once. Not that it matters. The past few months, our team has ruled the Rabbit Room like tyrants. Another way to honor Kaya's memory. We use her strategies and we never lose.

Breaking the illusion that we were in separate rooms running separate races changed everything. Now the tennis net has to be guarded. Now the groups have to figure out who to send over to the other side. Defoe's stopped having digital wolves chase us. We're the wolves now.

A glance shows Longwei's still feeling dizzy. I'm surprised he's here at all. I volunteer to cross over to their side. It's always better to be aggressive with a wounded creature. Jaime and Isadora will guard the front end of our border and Azima is chosen to run on our safe wing. Defoe stands on his platform like an overlord. With a flick, the room kicks to life.

One of the keys now is deception. If the other team sees a shield, they assume you're on border patrol. If they see long poles, they'll know you're trying to cross over into their territory. I manipulate my nyxian rings into a shield and fall in line with Jaime and Isadora. Three shields makes us look like we're turtling. All defense with hopes of having Azima outrun their runners.

Our eyes have to flicker from the screen to the other team, to the screen and back again. It sharpens the senses when you have to fear everything around you. We watch Katsu and Roathy drift over to the border. They run in stride with us, just a few feet away, with only the mesh net separating us from them. Both have their nyxia formed into standard padded shields.

Katsu shouts, "Look at these lurches! They don't stand a chance."

"We'd be more scared," I shout back, "if you could actually jump over the net, Katsu."

He laughs loudly. Our attention is forced forward, though, by low-hanging branches that materialize from the front screens. We dip and duck. I use the distraction to transform my shield into a staff. I plant a knee until the treadmill's whisked me to the very back of the room. In a smooth sideways motion I leap into enemy territory.

It takes Roathy a few precious seconds to notice. He calls out the breach, but I'm already across and dangerous and hungry. Playing the wolf is my favorite game. Move too early and the whole team converges to eliminate the threat. Move too late and you put your team in impossible situations. Fifteen meters ahead and ten meters to the right, Longwei's running guard with Jazzy. Katsu and Roathy are dead ahead. If either drops back, Jaime and Isadora will double up on the straggler.

Our positioning is perfect. My adrenaline spikes just thinking about Longwei. I want another shot at him. My staff isn't nyxia-blunted. Swung hard, it could break a bone or two. Up ahead, the trail descends toward the ravines.

My eyes flick back to Jaime for our signal. He starts to raise a fist when Isadora takes her padded shield and slams it down into the back of his legs. He lets out a cry of pain and whips past her. He hits the back wall before he even knows what happened. Isadora transforms her shield back into a ring and stops running.

With a quiet nod at Roathy, she lets the treadmill carry her out of the race. I mutter a curse as Roathy and Katsu climb the barrier. They stumble onto our side and Azima sees them. She's helpless, though. Isadora's betrayal is blinding. Blinding because she's adding an element to the game that shouldn't exist. Our team is our team. We leave rivalries at the door and always compete.

But her spot's guaranteed for Eden. We should have known she'd take advantage of that for Roathy's sake eventually. I take a glance around and know the numbers will only get worse. It forces me to pick up my pace. Jazzy and Longwei run down a narrow center shelf. Both wield nyxian balancing poles like me. Jazzy's the one who invented them, said her middle school track team used something similar. The flexible shafts help us vault impossible distances. Or swat at a competitor's legs. The addition has made Babel's course far more navigable.

Out of the corner of one eye, I see that Roathy and Katsu have Azima cornered. I focus on my footing and drive my pole down into the rubber. It jerks, tightens, and springs me two meters into the air. On my right, a cry sounds. Azima has her arms wrapped around Katsu. The two of them roll into the nearest canyon, and only Roathy's left on that half.

When the lights flash, I know I'm alone. Three against one.

My feet land with a shocking thud. Then I'm sprinting. Three bounding strides draw me nearly even with Longwei and Jazzy. Before Roathy can cross back to our side, I edge my way toward the center and plant the pole again. My forearms absorb the shock and I'm airborne. Time stands utterly still. I lose my grip on the nyxia, but instead of falling, it transforms. I'm too lost in the adrenaline of my leap to give any direction. Darkness blooms like a gasp of smoke from a grenade. A war cry tears from my lungs and my body goes parallel with the floor.

Longwei's twisting his shield around, but the blackness descends on him before I do. My nyxia drapes over his shoulders and cinches like a net. He crumples as I land. My shoulder collides with Jazzy, but somehow we both keep our feet. She shoots me a terrified glance and then drives her pole into the ground. I know if she leaps away, I'll never catch her. Desperately, I lash out and give her lower half a hard shove. She screams as the angle of her flight lands her in the nearest ravine.

I leap left, quick-step through a patchwork of crevices, and straighten. Adrenaline turns into laughter. The lights flash as Jazzy and Longwei are eliminated. I am a titan falling from the sky. Roathy's pulling himself over the mesh barrier. I laugh again and launch myself. He rolls to the side, but it costs him his footing. He flatfoots his next jump. I keep running and pump both fists when he shorts it.

The treadmill flashes to a stop. I go down on both knees and raise my arms in victory. Jaime and Azima come flying from the back of the room to dogpile on top of me. Isadora scowls at me from the back, but I don't care. I feel like I've conquered galaxies; I feel like I'm supposed to be going to Eden. It's the first time since Kaya died that I feel like I deserve to win.

DAY 189, 2:13 A.M.

Aboard *Genesis 11*

My ascension is short-lived. Bilal's pale form lays me low. His X-rays show more hardware than bone. Babel's surgeons have left him with finger-thin scars in five different places. His right leg's been shaved clean of hair. I never noticed how much of it he had. Like me, he's becoming a man in the deep black of space. Like me, he's stuck in a med unit millions of kilometers from home, from the people he needs at a time like this.

He wakes up once, eyes wide and dazed. But his words are clear enough.

"Emmett," he rasps. "Hey, do me a favor."

I take his hand and give it a light squeeze. "Anything. What you need?"

"Longwei. Tell him he is an asshole."

Laughter rips from my throat. Bilal manages half a smile before shaking his head.

"Just kidding. Tell him I know it was an accident. I forgive him."

I swallow as Bilal squeezes my hand and leans back, eyes closing.

"I don't want him to feel guilty," he adds, drifting off.

I can only smile. If I were in his shoes, I'd be pissed, but Bilal is Bilal. I sit with him, stealing little slivers of sleep, until morning comes. I know I need to leave or forfeit breakfast.

"I'll come back. Every day. Like Kaya did for me. I promise, I'll be back."

As I pass scoreboards, I try not to look at how tight everything is. I'm just barely above Roathy now. If the competition ended today, I'd be going to Eden. But there's still time, and I have work to do. Even with the penalties Babel gave me for Kaya's death, I'm so close I can taste it. It's like Kaya's hand is on my back, giving me a shove, telling me to do the impossible.

And after my performance in the Rabbit Room, I know I'm meant to go to Eden. I can rise above this. I eye the scores again and know that a month out will have Bilal dropping like a stone. His score will plummet, and even if I do beat out Roathy, he might beat out Bilal. A part of me wonders how I would even survive Eden without my two favorite people.

Longwei hawks a glance at me. I don't look away. Instead, I survey the damage. He has a black eye and a few other prominent bruises. As far as I'm concerned, it's not punishment enough. He breaks eye contact and I turn my attention to breakfast. The table's mostly quiet. Quiet is always a sign of Katsu's sour mood. If he's not joking, we usually don't even talk at breakfast.

"Bilal?" Azima asks. "Is he okay?"

"He slept all night," I say. "Recovering from surgery."

"A choice time to get injured," Katsu says bitterly. "Good for us, I guess."

"Don't be a lurch," I throw back. "He's really hurt. It could happen to any of us."

Katsu wags his fork at me. "It won't happen to me. I have a secret strategy."

Jazzy leans over. "You do? What is it?"

Katsu pats his gut. He's slimmed down some, but he's still got all of us by forty or fifty pounds. "Keep on as much padding as possible. Less likely to break the bones underneath."

We laugh into our cups. The sound dies quickly, though. That happens a lot now. Jokes aren't as funny as they should be. Joy slips through our fingers because we're grasping and reaching for everything else. We're past being broken. Now we're at the stage where Babel is gathering the shattered pieces and making us into something. I catch glimpses of it in myself, in the others. Defoe plans for us to be more. I think about my friends sitting in algebra or running laps in gym class. How could they ever be as fast, as hard, or as smart as we will be? They don't want like we want. They won't die for what we would die for. They haven't seen what we will see.

But then I remember Bilal. He's not a product of Babel. He has a joy they can't touch.

"Longwei," I say, remembering my friend's request. "Bilal said he forgives you."

Everyone stares. Longwei turns slowly. "For what?"

"He knows it was an accident," I say, trying to keep the hatred out of my voice. "He didn't want you to feel guilty for hurting him. Just a message he wanted me to pass along."

For just a second, Longwei's determined front breaks. I see some deeper and darker pain in his eyes, but he looks away, focuses on his breakfast. The others are quiet.

"It's unfair they pushed some people through." Her eyes flick briefly to Isadora. "Bilal is a good person. If someone deserves a free pass to Eden, it's him."

Before I can agree, medics spill into the room. Vandemeer looks like someone hosed him awake with cold water. I panic, scanning the table. Only Roathy and Bilal are absent. The other medics gather their contestants, and I fear the worst has happened. Another death, another Kaya.

"What is it?" I ask.

Vandemeer nods toward the exit. "The Tower Space Station. We've arrived."

DAY 189, 8:28 P.M.
Aboard *Genesis 11*

We gather before a sheer black wall near the back of the ship. It has the characteristic shine of nyxia. For the first time, we see the entirety of our crew. *Genesis 11* is a small village of astronauts and medics, techies and marines. They watch as Defoe marches us into the room.

We're lined up in order, first to last, between the nyxian wall and the crew. My stomach tightens with anticipation. Word works through the ranks that there will be thirty more days before the contest is over and we're ready to leave the ship. A new challenge awaits. Whatever the design, I know it will be harder. Babel always demands more, never less.

My eyes slip over to the scoreboard on our right:

1.	LONGWEI	689,900	points
2.	KATSU	640,450	points
3.	AZIMA	532,750	points
4.	BILAL	532,300	points

5.	JAIME	520,200	points
6.	JASMINE	478,050	points
7.	EMMETT	473,350	points
8.	ROATHY	471,324	points
9.	ISADORA	415,080	points
~~10.~~	~~KAYA~~	~~351,050~~	~~points~~

Eight out of ten will go. I'm already ahead of Roathy, but it's not the kind of lead that lets you sleep comfortably at night. My eyes drift up to Bilal's score. He's performed so well, but this final injury might keep him out for a few weeks. I know I can beat Roathy, but what if we *both* catch Bilal in the process? I've made promises to myself, to Moms and Pops, to Kaya's memory. I'm going to Eden. But if I can, I'm taking Bilal with me too.

Outside, metal kisses metal. The ship shudders, and I can feel the vibration in both legs. Defoe is delivering us with surprisingly little pageantry. Even though our most important accomplishments are written in bold on the scoreboard, there are other successes that have been set aside and forgotten. We are space travelers. Astronauts. When I'm older, I'll tell my kids about this voyage. No one else, not PJ or any of the Most Excellent Brothers, can say what I will say. They cannot tell the stories I will tell.

But Eden's still out of reach. Thirty more days, I think, just thirty more days.

I glance over at Bilal. His attendant's wheeled him into the room, and a hard, nyxian cast covers his leg. Even injured, he's still smiling beneath his mask. Always smiling. The sound of grinding metal ceases. We all stand a little taller, straightening our shoulders. Defoe separates from the crowd to stand before us. His nyxian suit shimmers like the fine edge of a knife.

"Thank you," he says with a wide, sweeping gesture. "To the crew for their precision, to the medics for their care, to the competitors for their fortitude. We've just completed a voyage that marks a new era in man's ventures into space. It is an honor to be at the helm of a mission such as this with people such as you. Today, the days that precede it, and the days to follow, will be recorded in history alongside the other markers of human progress. You will be remembered."

Our medics step forward to stand behind their pairings. There is an empty space on my right where Kaya should be standing. Vandemeer pats my shoulder kindly as Defoe dismisses the astronauts and techies. They drift back into the underbelly of the ship, and when the last footsteps fade, Defoe continues.

"We are now entering the next phase of the competition. You will have thirty more days and no more Sabbaths. In that time, you will be able to add to your overall scores through a competition called the Waterway. There you will learn to navigate similar conditions to what you will see on Eden. The only major difference is that you will do this as a team."

We all stiffen. A few sideways glances. We are not a team. We have our friends and enemies here, but in no way are we a team. And if we have to work together, how do we gain ground? How do we get points or keep others from getting points? I glance back at the scoreboard and smile. Is it possible I just beat Roathy on a technicality? If he can't gain ground, then being a thousand points ahead of him is a great place to be.

Roathy and Isadora look like they're thinking the opposite. His face is tight and furious. Hers is a softer, prettier kind of rage. Good. I want them angry and unfocused and trapped. I want them separated and broken. I want them to pay for what they tried to do to me.

"Shall we begin?" Defoe asks.

The question takes us back to the beginning. We've come a long way, but we still know nothing. Nothing of what waits behind this wall, nothing of what Eden is really like. The walls grind to life. Our collective breath catches as one turns to two. The slightest sliver of light separates the seamless edges of the retracting walls. It sounds like a massive engine throwing out revolutions. We watch and wait as the gap grows.

The room opposite ours is high-ceilinged and brightly lit. A man walks forward as soon as the gap is wide enough. He's old, with something familiar in his face. His hair is fine silver, but disorganized by a hand constantly running through it. Downcast eyes, crooked nose, stress lines. He wears a nyxian suit that matches Defoe's. As the walls continue to part, and as he and Defoe shake hands, we see them for the first time.

The sight is heartbreaking. It's like looking at ourselves in a fun-house mirror. The base image is reflected back, but all the details are distorted. They are ten to our nine. They wear nyxian masks too, but the faces and eyes above them are painted with different colors and different expressions. We stare at each other, speechless.

Ten of them. There are ten of them. There were ten of us. Anger burns up my throat in the place of oxygen. I do not want these ten people to exist, because their presence can only mean one thing. We aren't the only ones vying for a chance to travel to Eden. We aren't the only *Genesis*. Each new face is a new threat. One more person in my way.

Babel's changed the game again.

DAY 0, 8:42 P.M.

Aboard the Tower Space Station

I want them to be an illusion. They're not.

One girl stands in front of the others. Dark hair rests over one shoulder in a thick braid. The months in space haven't faded her deeply tan skin. Both eyes narrow and I can tell she's taking our measure, drinking in the details of our team. I wait for surprise or fear or concern, but it's like we're a new challenge, a new Rabbit Room. It's like she's already figuring out how she's going to beat us.

Behind her stands a redheaded girl who's tall and gangly. Two other girls have dark skin and dark hair; one looks like she's from India and the other from the Middle East. They have two boys bigger than Katsu. One's a good five inches taller than me, and all muscle. His shoulders are broad beneath a face that any sculptor would find worthy of stone. The other boy's big and meaty, his face a mess of freckles.

Like us, they also appear to have a pair of lovers. Two blondes, both stunning. The girl's got the brightest blue eyes

I've ever seen outside a magazine. The boy styles his hair up like a famous soccer player. The last two boys stand shoulder to shoulder, though they look nothing alike. One's short and cruel-looking, a thick brute of a boy. The other's got golden curls above a tan face. His eyes are so startling that they look like a new color, a green swallowed by blue. The two of them are picturesque opposites, Jekyll and Hyde.

On the wall to our right, something clicks and rattles. We take our eyes off each other long enough to watch the scoreboard change. Ten more spots are added. The names shuffle and the points organize. We all watch as our standing in the competition changes:

1.	*MORNING*	1,070,200	points
2.	*LONGWEI*	689,900	points
3.	*KATSU*	640,450	points
4.	*PARVIN*	570,200	points
5.	*HOLLY*	542,700	points
6.	**OMAR**	540,000	points
7.	*AZIMA*	532,750	points
8.	**BILAL**	532,300	points
9.	**JAIME**	520,200	points
10.	*NOOR*	515,050	points
11.	*JASMINE*	478,050	points
12.	**ANTON**	502,290	points
13.	**EMMETT**	473,350	points
14.	**ALEX**	472,200	points
15.	**ROATHY**	471,324	points
16.	*ISADORA*	415,080	points

17.	*IDA*	390,400	points
18.	**LOCHE**	357,500	points
19.	**BRETT**	327,000	points

My heart stops beating. I can't take all the information in at once, so I break it down, forcing everything into more manageable pieces. First, I'm in thirteenth. Not exactly a lucky number, but it seems like a solid place to be.

Second, bold names. They've italicized the leaders and the rest of the girls. After Kaya's death, Defoe guaranteed their passage. But my passage? Far from a guarantee. My name is bold on the scoreboard, and that's what really matters. Mine and eight others. We're the last ones fighting for spots. I realize that if my name is bold, that means I can lose my spot. At least three will be eliminated. I'm closer to the bottom three than I want to be. I am in danger.

The last piece of information comes as a guilty afterthought: Babel removed Kaya's name from the scoreboard. Her absence there almost levels the walls I've been rebuilding with Vandemeer. I squeeze both eyes shut, whisper a prayer, and promise I won't forget her, even if Babel does. The rest of the room is silent. No one speaks for a long minute. We knew Babel would change the game, but this kind of change was unimaginable.

Longwei finds his voice first. "That is total bullshit."

I can't help but laugh. His score, so insurmountable in our eyes, has almost been doubled by Morning. I find the name on the suit of the girl with the dark braid, the one standing apart from the others. As we watch, she turns and walks the lines of her team, whispering to them, either informing or rallying. It's obvious that we don't have anyone like her.

We have Longwei, who is talented and hateful. Jaime, who performs each task competently but never demonstrates an excellence worth following. Azima, who hasn't once volunteered to lead in our group competitions. Katsu, who can't take anything seriously. The rest, myself included, have not scored well enough to demand respect. If Bilal wasn't hurt, I'd peg him as the most likely person to rise into a leadership position.

"Genesis 11, meet Genesis 12," Defoe announces. It takes a moment to realize that *we're* Genesis 11. We never identified that way because the challenge has always been an individual struggle. Defoe goes on: "They are your competition. Genesis 12, I am Marcus Defoe, one of the Babel Communications CEOs. Please know that both teams have been through the exact same training. The same courses in the Rabbit Room, the same battles in the pit, the same explorations of simulated Eden. The scores you see are a reflection of what you did with that same opportunity. That being said, our numbers for the descent to Eden have changed."

Fear thunders back through me. The game is changing. Air leaks from Babel's promises.

"One of the contestants aboard *Genesis 11* died during our flight. It was agreed then that we would appoint three captains for three different mining units. We are likely to take the top three for those positions. So even if you have already qualified for Eden, you still need to fight. Our three captains will have their salaries doubled, in perpetuity.

That's your incentive. The rest of you are fighting to go to
Eden. Each unit will be made up of five members in order
to maximize nyxia extraction and mobility on Eden. That
means fifteen out of twenty will go."

One more person eliminated. I glance back at the scoreboard. I'm clear of the bottom four by just a thousand
points. Everything is crumbling. Defoe retreats, and the
silver-haired man takes his cue. His voice is deeper than
a well.

"My name is David Requin. We've done our best to sim-
plify things on the scoreboard. Those of you in italics are
safe. Your flight to Eden is virtually secured. Congratulations." He pauses and begins listing those who aren't safe.
"Jaime, Anton, Emmett, Bilal, Alex, Roathy, Loche, Omar,
and Brett. Step forward."

Feet shuffle as we obey. Five on their side. Four on ours.
Bilal looks like an easy target in his wheelchair. If he misses
a few weeks, he's seriously in trouble now. I glance at the
scoreboard again. Loche and Brett are in the deepest hole.
I scan the fronts of their suits. Loche, the lover with pretty,
spiked hair. Brett, the lumbering boy with the freckled face.
I dismiss Omar. He's way too far ahead. But the other two?
They might be my biggest threats.

The two opposites. Alex, athletic and curly-headed, is
just a thousand points back. Anton, short and wicked, is
well ahead. I have new enemies to add to the old ones.

Requin and Defoe let the uncomfortable moment stretch
its legs. As the seconds pass, my nyxian rings dance with
nervous energy. They want to transform, into sharp blades
or steady shields. I am back to the thin line between black

holes. Am I the danger? Or are they? Anton smiles wickedly at us and I decide it's them. They're the dangerous ones.

Requin explains. "You're all fighting for spots. Bold names are still on the fence. As long as your name is bold, you have a mathematical chance to join the italicized names and secure a spot on Eden. But bold also works in the other direction. If your name is bold, it's still mathematically possible that you can lose your spot. All of you have thirty days to decide your fate. We reserve the right to remove *anyone* who cannot meet our standards in the Waterway. If you can't operate there, we don't want you on-planet. Is that understood?"

Everyone nods. It feels like the beginning did. Everyone's a threat.

"Medics," Defoe calls. "Escort your participants to their new quarters. The first round will begin in the morning. Contestants, get your rest. You'll need it."

We're led through the Tower Space Station. Morning walks at the front of their group. The rest march behind her like eager soldiers. They don't look defeated or tired. A few of them, maybe, the stragglers, but the rest of the group looks excited about what's ahead. I hear them laughing together. Our group walks in silence. Even Katsu doesn't make any jokes.

Our new rooms are smaller, ten separate compartments honeycombed around the same living space. Genesis 12 files into identical rooms on the floor below us. I have hundreds of questions about the station, but I don't ask them because I know Vandemeer doesn't know either. Genesis 12 was a surprise to him. I can still see the gears turning in his head.

First the enslaved Adamite. Now a secret group of contestants. What else have they hidden from him? From us?

We split from the others. Vandemeer scans us into the room. He pulls out his data pad and punches a few buttons. One of the walls starts to retract like a window curtain.

"Thirty days," Vandemeer reminds me. "Just in case you need an incentive. This is what you're fighting for. This is where you're going."

The edges of the window are dark. The frightening black of space. But at center, Eden. It's breathtaking. A darker blue than what I remember of Earth's portraits. A sea that hides its dangers in darkness. The green and brown of its continents are more broken up, dashed in twos and fours and twenties by fat-tongued rivers. Swirling white storms cover up mountains and plains, islands and jungles. It is familiar and foreign all at once.

Vandemeer nods at the new world. "There is no one on this ship who can take that away from you. No one but yourself. Remember that. Fight for it. For yourself and for Kaya. You *will* go down to Eden, Emmett."

DAY 1, 9:45 A.M.

Aboard the Tower Space Station

We form single-file lines and follow Defoe and Requin down to the Waterway. A natural hype snakes its way through both groups. Their crew definitely looks more organized, but that might just be the effect of Morning marching fearlessly through the corridors. I try to mimic her calm and focus, but Katsu starts in with the smack talk. The back-and-forth feels so much like home that I start grinning. It reminds me of PJ walking out to half-court before rec-league games, finding the best player on the other team and calling their number.

"Look how cute they are," Katsu says. "Marching in step like little ducklings."

"At least we know which group is the good-looking one," Anton jabs back.

"Good-looking?" Katsu laughs obnoxiously and points a finger at Anton. "I've found things in gutters that looked prettier than you, little man."

Anton's cheeks burn red. "If we were in Russia, I'd slip

you into a river, nice and quiet. It'd be easy. You don't look like the kind that floats. Straight down to the mud, big boy."

Katsu laughs even louder. "You're just adorable. Like an action figure."

Anton's cheeks grow brighter, but Morning shoots him a look from the front of the group. It cracks like a whip. Anton bites his tongue and keeps walking.

Defoe and Requin lead us through a network of tunneled hallways. The path ends in a massive hatch that opens with a scan from both their access cards. Lights drone above, reflected in the dashing rapids below.

A river. Babel has a damn river on their space station. We stand on an observation deck above the foaming trenches. The Waterway is about one hundred meters wide. It winds through artificial rocks and twisting plant life. Dark blue, it rolls out some two hundred meters before coiling around a corner. Below, two boats bob at anchor.

I look over and I'm surprised to see Bilal being wheeled into the room by his caretaker. He looks like he's been through seven hells down in the med unit. His eyes are sunken and withdrawn, his frame stick thin. I'm amazed he's even here.

"Welcome to the Waterway," Requin says, sweeping us down a narrow ramp.

Babel's made makeshift docks and gangplanks. Defoe leads Genesis 11 to the left; Requin leads Genesis 12 to the right. "Later, gargoyle." Katsu blows a kiss at the little Russian.

Before Anton can call back, Morning pushes him across the gangplank. She's a head taller than him and stronger than she looks. Katsu can laugh all he wants, but their team seems more focused than ours, and it's not hard to see that it's because of her. I watch her stand at the top of the gangplank as the others file past. They nod their respect to her. She's what Kaya would have been for us if she were still alive.

As we cross our own gangplank, my stomach knots. We're in more trouble than I thought. *I'm* in more trouble than I thought. Genesis 12 is what Defoe could have made us, but we weren't fitted together like a puzzle. We were pitted against each other like gladiators. There's too much bad blood between us now to change that.

The boat is yet another marvel of Babel's endless innovation. Every railing is sleek, every floorboard flawless. Though the wooden planks smell freshly lacquered, they still groan beneath our weight like good planks should groan. Standing at center is a nyxian throne. A captain's chair, more likely, but it looks regal as all get-out. Webs of nyxia weave from the chair's base and along the wooden planks, lashing the throne to eight nyxian consoles that are built into the ship railings. I find myself searching for oars or sails or ropes, but there's nothing. Just the captain's chair and the consoles.

"Welcome to your tutorial session," Defoe says, pulling all eyes back to him. "The ship is a replica of a watercraft the Adamites use on Eden. These next thirty days will require you to navigate the Waterway, ward off predators, and participate in ship raids. We want you prepped for everything that could happen on Eden. Water travel is a necessity on the planet to be held. You will be tested three times a day. All competitions are on the Waterway."

"How much are they worth?" Isadora asks. Roathy stands behind her like a gaunt shadow. They're worried, and they should be. "How many points?"

"There are two team matches a day, worth three thousand points each. That's a total of one hundred eighty thousand points. Every member of the winning team will receive the bonus. The losing team gets nothing. The third event every day will be individual nyxia battles. That is where you can climb or fall within your own ranks. Fathom?"

Defoe makes our slang sound like it's his. We all nod because we all fathom. The bulk of the points will be through teamwork, but there are still opportunities to draw blood from our own. I glance over at the other ship. Requin is standing to one side as Genesis 12 explores their vessel. Morning's pointing out things and directing her team to certain stations. We need to get moving. Defoe's noticed it too. He claps his hands together with finality.

"You have thirty minutes to familiarize yourself with the ship, establish a captain, and determine which nyxian stations each of you will man during the coming weeks. Genesis 12 has one more participant than you do, so they will be sitting out one person each day in a rotating order." He glances over at Requin and lowers his voice. "Choose your captain first. The back station should be manned by the strongest nyxia manipulator in the group. Pure strength and stamina. Front station needs to be able to scout. Drivers are right and left. The rest you'll need to figure out yourselves." He glances at his watch. "Make that twenty-nine minutes. Get to work."

Defoe exits and the arguments begin.

"I should be captain," Katsu says.

Longwei rounds on him. "I'm in first."

"You're in second," Katsu snaps, thumbing at the score-board. "And points don't matter."

"Points are the only thing that matter," Longwei replies.

"You're not a leader." Katsu looks around and shrugs. "You don't even talk to us. How are you supposed to lead us? No one will follow you."

Longwei sweeps his front tuft to one side and goes quiet. His eyes stay sharp and angry. Before Katsu can claim the captain's seat, Jaime steps forward.

"I should be the captain," he says. "I can multitask better than anyone. And I'll actually take the command of the ship seriously. All you do is tell jokes, Katsu."

"Raise your hand if you remember *anything* Jaime's done better than anyone else," Katsu says. When the others hesitate, he smiles over at the Swiss. "That settles that."

"What about me?" Azima suggests quietly. "I can lead."

A new round of arguments follows. Frustrated, I look back to the other ship. A few steps takes me to our right railing, close enough to hear Genesis 12. They're not at stations yet, but they aren't arguing over who should be captain either, because their captain is already seated in her chair.

"Omar, you're at the back station," Morning instructs. "I'll add my strength to yours as often as I can. Anton and Alex, wings, please. You work together better than anyone."

Her commands aren't challenged, just obeyed. They've

already chosen who will sit out for the day. Ida, one part of the runway-good-looks couple, stands on the dock. The rest move silently to their stations. Morning's about to give another command when she notices me watching. She raises an eyebrow, shoots me an unexpected wink, and waves goodbye.

I'm still staring when she twists one of her wrists. The nyxian bracelet slides off. Darkness floods out like smoke, spreading and forming a wall between our two ships. It doesn't swarm over us or anything, but the sound cuts completely off. Aside from Defoe's tricks, it's the most impressive thing I've seen anyone do with nyxia, and she made it look easy.

I turn back; our team is still arguing. "I'll be the captain."

It's now or never. With a flick, I let my nyxian rings transform. They gather around my knuckles dangerously and settle into fists, sharp with iron and padded black.

"Anyone want to fight me for it?" The ship goes quiet. "Katsu? Longwei? Jaime?"

I've crushed them in the pit. It's the one place where our scores don't matter. They know the damage I can do. When no one says anything, I point to the front of the ship.

"Defoe said we need eyes. Jazzy's had the best vision in the Rabbit Room all year, she's always calm, and she's aced all the pattern tests. Any objections?" None. Jazzy nods at me but doesn't move. "Go ahead, Jazzy. Take a look at the front console and try to figure out what it can do."

With a nervous glance at the others, Jazzy slips to the prow. Good. Next I point at Katsu and Longwei. "You're the two strongest manipulators. We need one of you powering the ship and the other as one of our drivers. Which one do you want?"

"Power," they both say.

I try not to sigh or roll my eyes. "Longwei, you were always the strongest on the grips and got the furthest on the 3-D shapes exercise. Head back to the power console. Katsu, you're the quickest with technical stuff. There's no one I trust more to drive us than you, but you need a partner. Who do you want?"

He eyes the rest of them. His anger vanishes as he considers my question. Giving him a choice has made him forget that I just stole the captain's chair. It's a tactic I think Kaya would have used. One wrong word or objection could take us back to the beginning and remove me from leadership. I wait patiently as he thinks about each person. Eventually he shrugs.

"I'll take Jaime."

Jaime smirks. "Thought I hadn't done anything to impress you."

"Exactly why I want you on my team. So I get all the glory when we dominate the Waterway."

"Yeah, yeah. Go to your stations," I command.

They do. Only Roathy, Isadora, Azima, and Bilal remain.

"Roathy and Isadora, you want to work together?"

"We don't answer to you," Roathy replies.

"No? Then we'll start each day off by throwing you overboard. You'll get no points."

The two lovers exchange a look. I'm not sure I could actually order the crew to do it, but I know they're in a tight spot. Isadora's already guaranteed passage to Eden. Roathy isn't. If this part of the competition depends on teamwork, he'll need us to move up the scoreboard. They're both going to have to play by the rules for now, even if they don't want to.

Isadora nods. "Keep us together. We'll work better that way."

"Head to the back right and left stations. You'll have to figure out what they do." My eyes return to Bilal and Azima. "Bilal, can you man a station?"

He nods. "I can't move, but I'll strap my chair to the console for now."

"All right, you and Azima on the front stations flanking Jazzy. Let's get moving. We're already five minutes behind Genesis 12."

I stride over to the middle of the ship, amazed that this worked. They actually let me be their captain. I take my seat, and at first it's just any other cold-backed chair. Chills crawl up my back, goose bumps down my legs and arms. Then the nyxia clicks to life. I'm *aware*. Of the water beneath the boat, of the metallic machinery and cogs, of each of my crew members. I can feel them through the nyxian links, like we're all part of the same body.

"Hello?" I ask.

"A little louder, Captain," Bilal says.

I clear my throat. "Better?"

Affirmatives all around. My words aren't loud enough to be heard naturally over the river, but they crackle through the nyxian links like a wireless headset. Before I can give the first command, Morning's sound barrier dissolves. We all look up as their boat roars into the water, engines humming like a freight train. Babel has set up ropes for our tutorial area, but they're using what little room they have to move and turn and test. Black smoke trails their ship. The competition doesn't start for another twenty minutes, but I already feel a few laps behind. Time to get moving.

"Let's get a report from each station. Clockwise, all right?" Everyone agrees. "Jazzy, what's going on up front?"

Her hands are tight on the grips of her console. Each station has a sort of foxhole carved out in front of it. The depression has her standing tall enough to see over the ship's railing, but short enough that my view isn't blocked.

"I've got pulse scans," she replies. "Watch."

She punches the button. The others lean over the railing to get a look. A smoky substance crawls from the prow of the boat and spreads over the water like fog. It runs one hundred meters ahead before fading to nothing. Jazzy shifts her shoulders and we all see a digital readout on the mirror-black surface of her console.

"Can you tell what the markings mean?" I ask.

She nods. "Just have to tap the screen and it explains. River depth, currents, all that."

"Perfect—all right, moving clockwise. Azima, what's your station do?"

She's posted on one of the diagonal stations that Defoe didn't explain. We all watch the nyxia connected to the railing in front of her extend up and out. Her manipulation takes the shape of a harpoon gun. "Looks like I'm playing defense," she says. "Should I fire at Genesis 12?"

She grins back at us and we all laugh. I shoot her a smile and say, "Soon enough. How about you, Jaime?"

"It's a little confusing because we're not moving yet. The first option is for rudders and steering, I'm pretty sure. The second one, though, says something about suction."

We watch him tap the screen. A second later the ship gives a sharp tug. The ropes anchoring us to the makeshift dock start to uncoil. We all hold tight as the ship drifts to the right, veering against the current as it crawls toward the massive metal supports of the observation deck. Jaime's eyes go wide as it lurches again and the whole boat tilts. There's a loud suction sound and our ship crawls up the wall. We're turned terrifyingly on our side, but no one goes flying overboard. The bottom of our ship has a full grip now. We're hanging in defiance of gravity.

"You're fired!" Katsu booms from the other side of the ship. We all laugh again.

"Can you get us back down, Jaime?" I ask.

Jaime manipulates his station again and the boat slides smoothly down the wall. With a splash and a toss, we're back in the water. I cock my head back to the right.

"What about you, Roathy?"

"Same as Azima," he reports. "A defensive station. She used one of the presets, though. It looks like these four stations can manipulate into anything. Watch."

His console stretches past the railing, forming up and out like Azima's did. Instead of a harpoon, though, his nyxia turns into a giant hand. It's almost as big as we are, and mimics Roathy's movements. He waves and it waves. A second later, the massive middle finger extends to flick us off.

"Useful, right?" Roathy asks innocently.

I can't help but laugh. "Definitely useful. Great. Longwei?"

"Do the others first," he replies. "My station will make things loud, I think."

"All right," I say. "Isadora?"

"Defense station," she says crisply. She doesn't play our game, though. We wait for her to give us a demonstration and she just stares back defiantly. I could call her out for it, but it doesn't matter. Pops taught me to pick my battles. She wants to win for Roathy's sake. She doesn't have to laugh and tell jokes so long as she fights and works when the races start.

"Fair enough," I mutter. "Katsu?"

"Station is a go, Captain. I'm starting to get a feel for Jaime across the link. We'll figure it out before the end of the day."

"Check," I say. "And Bilal?"

"Defensive station," he says with excitement. His nyxia transforms into a metallic cannon. He taps his fingers twice and a double shot of laser particles launches into the wall like fireballs. The substance dissolves when it hits, but not before leaving smoke rings on the thick ramparts of the Waterway. Katsu lets out an appreciative whoop. "I don't need both legs to fire a cannon. Station is ready, Captain."

"All right, Longwei, let's start moving."

A second later, the engines roar to life. On our right, Genesis 12 wheels in a circle, kicking waves out in every direction. Above them, a digital clock ticks the seconds down toward our start time. Just seven minutes. The practice area is small, but right now small is good.

"Katsu and Jaime, take us toward the rope and then turn us to the right."

For the first time, I get a feel for them working across the nyxian link. Their communication is running along another current. I have access to all of it as the captain. I'd only need to reach out to tap into their link. The engine gives another roar, and we ease our way forward. Jaime and Katsu are tight-gripped on their consoles. We all wait, a little breathless, as the ship approaches the rope barrier. Our front starts to turn, but a little too late. The ropes stretch a good three meters before we wheel back toward the practice square. Not perfect, but it's a start.

"Good," I say through the link. "Pulse scan, Jazzy."

She punches it again. A second later, her screen lights up with information.

"Ship forty meters away, docks one hundred meters away," she reports.

"Longwei, power us across this diagonally," I say. The other ship is moving in a similar direction, but we can get there first. "Bilal and Isadora, transform your stations into big hands. If the other ship crosses our path, give them a nice push in the opposite direction."

Jaime and Katsu hold the rudders steady as Longwei puts more power into the ship engines. I reach through the link and find him, straining to fuel us. I'm not sure what to do exactly, but I set my mind behind his and give a push. The boat leaps forward. We cut across the square three times as fast as we did before. Genesis 12 changes its course as we come flying through, missing us by a good ten meters. Bilal waves at them as we pass; Isadora shows them an angry fist.

"Another turn," I announce. "Let's make it sharper this time."

I pull off the throttle, leaving Longwei on his own. The boat slows down as Katsu and Jaime whip us back hard to the left. A few of the crew stumble to a knee, but it's a perfect turn, and we're facing the Waterway again.

"Perfect," I say through the link. Looking up, I see our time has nearly slipped down to zero. The other crew is still wheeling in circles in one corner of the practice area. "Let's set up by the entrance to the Waterway. Ease off our use of nyxia, save our energy."

Longwei rolls us slowly that way. It takes half a minute, but our nose eases up against the ropes and we're in a starting position. I stand and walk the ship. It feels like a captain thing to do. I tell Jazzy she's got free rein to tell me anything at any time. I tell her to be louder and more vocal than she thinks she needs to be. I remind our defensive stations that Babel doesn't believe in easy competitions. They're going to send something at us and they need to be ready. Jaime and Katsu are having a little argument about the rudders. I don't interrupt; they can figure it out on their own. Last, I talk to Longwei.

"How is it?" I ask.

"It's like riding a bike. Easy, but I can tell I'll get tired eventually."

I nod. "Did you feel it when I added my strength?"

"Our speed almost doubled. How often do you think you can do that?"

"As often as I can," I promise him. "When we start—"

There's a thump and our ship rocks from side to side. We all look up. Genesis 12 is anchored right next to us. Alex, with his golden curls and otherworldly eyes, gives our crew a playful wave. Morning stands at the back of the boat with her power choice, the big statue of a kid named Omar. They're in discussion too. There are only forty seconds left until we start, but Anton can't resist crossing over from his station.

"Same boat," the little Russian calls. "Same course. Same training. What will your excuse be when we smoke you today, and the next day, and the day after that?"

My eyes drift to Morning. A flat smile rests on her face. She knows Anton well enough to know when his anger is working against him and when it works against the opposition. Right now, she'd like him to get under our skin, to rattle us into mistakes. What would Kaya do in a situation like this? I want to be a leader, but I know I'm not her.

"Aren't you supposed to be on the front of the boat?" Katsu asks.

Anton stares back at him. "What?"

"They typically carve grotesques onto the prow. How'd you break free?"

Anton's cheeks burn fire-red. "You're pushing the wrong person."

Katsu laughs. "Have you ever read about Napoleon? Cute little guy, always angry?"

It happens fast. Anton flings out a backhand. A slash of

black crosses the distance between our ships and Katsu's face whips back like he's been slapped. Before any of us can react, Anton thrusts out both hands, and darkness forms around Katsu like a prison. Inside the black, Katsu screams. Anton's face is bright with anger and joy. Azima rushes forward, trying to pull Katsu out, but she can't get past Anton's creation. We hear the screams again.

Morning starts forward, but I move faster. I plant a foot on our railing and leap across. Anton's face twists to fear as he sees my flight over the gap and above him. He tries to redirect his nyxia but isn't quick enough. The collision rocks my jaw, but I wrap both arms around him as we go rolling across their deck. Anton lets out a strangled cry as the other crew members lurch forward. I transform my rings into a single claw and hold the blade at his neck. He stops squirming and I tighten the grip of my legs around his.

"Let him go," I grunt.

"No," Anton spits. "He deserves—"

I press the point of a knuckle to his neck and slide it an inch. Blood spurts. A gargling rasp escapes Anton's lips. "All right, all right! Just stop!" I lighten my grip enough for him to recall his creation. The nyxia retreats in the air above us, reforming in rings on his fingers. We're both breathing heavily and sweating. I don't let him go, though, not while I'm still aboard their ship and surrounded by their crew. We take our feet awkwardly, my bladed knuckle still sharp at his neck. The others are staring at us, but I look past them and at Morning.

"If he does that again to someone on my crew, he's dead."

Her head tilts slightly to the left as she considers me.

"You wouldn't hurt him."

I smile like a madman. "Just try me."

There's respect in her eyes. I can tell I surprised her. After a second, she nods.

Back at the railing, I shove Anton away. Curly-headed Alex catches him, and Genesis 12 watches helplessly as I plant a foot on the railing and leap back to my ship. I stumble on the landing, but Isadora and Azima keep me from falling. As one, we look back across the gap. If there wasn't hatred before, there is now. Eyes locked on Morning's, I sound the command.

"Return to stations. We have a race to win, everyone fathom?"

My team answers with a war cry. I am the captain. Not as smart as Kaya, not as talented as Longwei, but willing to leap overboard for any of them. Maybe that's all it takes.

Azima dusts off Katsu and I make sure he's okay as Defoe and Requin arrive. A railed walkway runs along one side of the Waterway about thirty meters above us. They look down from it, fully aware of what just happened and obviously unconcerned. They want a fight; they want us to compete. They like the early blood. Defoe addresses us.

"One lap," he calls down. "We'll start with a single lap. The first team back to the tutorial bay wins. This is not a boarding exercise, just a race. Please remain in your boats for today."

Requin punches a button and the ropes release.

"Hit it, Longwei!" I shout.

Engines roar and both boats kick ahead.

"Pulse scans, Jazzy." It takes me a second to mentally

trace my way back to Longwei's console. When I've got the trail, I add my strength to his and we go flying forward. The link is a small drain on my energy, but we nose ahead of Genesis 12 as the rapids grow choppier. "How we looking, Jazzy?"

"Shallow rocks directly ahead," she reports. "We need to sweep right, to the far wall."

"Do it," I command.

Katsu and Jaime link together and start us in that direction. I spare Genesis 12 a glance. Their route doesn't take them quite as wide. They'll be ahead by a bit. The river dips the nose of our ship, and we get our first solid toss from the currents. "Keep scanning, Jazzy."

"Emmett!"

The call comes from Bilal. He's pointing ahead. A hatch in the distant ceiling has fallen open. It's right before the turn in the river, still a ways off, but Babel's up to something. We all wait and watch as Longwei and I push the ship past jutting rocks and into a narrower portion of the river. Something dark falls from the opening, flutters, and takes flight.

"Incoming!" I shout. "Convert to long-range weapons."

The dark mass splits. Two of the birds head toward Genesis 12 and the other two are making a line for us. Jazzy gives another report of shallow water as Bilal converts his console into a cannon. Our ship splashes back toward the center of the Waterway. Overhead, the birds are getting closer and flying lower.

"Orders?" Bilal asks.

"Take aim when you're ready. Roathy? Isadora?"

"Cannons are ready," Isadora answers.

"Fire!"

Our ship rocks with the concussion. Laser particles whip into the air, crackle with heat, and break apart the incoming birds. One sweeps lower to avoid the shots, but the other dodges right into a second blast. We see the wide wings tangle, and it splashes into the river. Bilal gets a second shot off, but the remaining bird slashes away and past us.

"Keep an eye on it," I call. "Keep firing if you have it in sight."

"The next stretch is pretty straight," Jazzy pipes back. "Can't see around the bend yet."

"Longwei, how you doing?"

"Let's increase the speed," he answers. "Add to it and we can hit this straightaway hard."

I glance over at Genesis 12; we're a few lengths behind them, but nothing we can't change. I reach through the link and find Longwei. Together we pump the engines and our speed jumps. Defoe and Requin are moving overhead, watching our progress from a distant checkpoint. They look pleased, but it's hard to tell as we pick up speed and the rapids splash brightly against the sides of the ship. Within seconds we're passing Genesis 12.

Behind, a pair of laser cannons fire. "Bird's back," Roathy grunts. Another round of shots pulse into the air. "It's coming around your way, Bilal."

"Can you make a net?" I ask, struggling to concentrate. Even forming words causes my focus on the nyxian links to slip. "Wait for it to get close?"

Bilal replies with an affirmative. I watch him reshape

the nyxia as we approach the first turn in the river. "Can you scan around the corner, Jazzy?" Katsu asks.

He and Jaime are focused. Not a word the whole time, except through the sensitive nyxian link they're sharing. Jazzy tries to direct her pulse scan that way, but it dissipates before it can reach that far. "We're going in blind," she says. "Forty more meters."

We're all bracing tight when the bird comes diving out of the sky. It's right on top of Bilal as he pulls the trigger and a nyxian net springs out beautifully. The metallic-looking bird croaks in surprise as the sprung rope collapses and tightens. A second later it plunges into the river. There's a whoop from the crew.

"Nice shot, Bilal," I say. "Longwei, do you want me to pull back a bit?"

"No," he grunts. "Look how far ahead we are."

I glance back. He's right. We're about thirty meters in the lead and distancing ourselves every second. Genesis 12 is still battling their birds. We can actually win this, I think. But the thought vanishes as we round the corner. Jazzy calls out the danger, and every crew member turns to look. A wall of rocks stretches across the entire Waterway. On the other side of it the river continues its winding course, but I see no way through.

"Kill the engines, Longwei!" He does it, but we've still got too much speed. "Katsu and Jaime, can you skid us to a stop?"

"We can try. Everyone hold on," Katsu says. "Jaime, cut right on three."

Everyone gets a good grip on their console. I realize I've been gripping the arms of my chair tightly the whole time. I hear a dull scraping sound as our engines cut. Both Katsu and Jaime yank on their consoles at the same time. The ship wheels too fast, though, leaning over to Katsu's side like it's going to flip us.

"Jaime, hit your suction!"

The turn has us slowing down, but I can feel the ship lurching in its progress, wanting to capsize. Jaime taps his console just in time. There's a whooshing suction and the boat evens out as his side tries to pull us to the closest metal ramparts.

When we rock back to a normal position, I say, "All right, release it." He does. The rest of the crew is breathing heavily, panic in their eyes. "Jazzy, what are you seeing?"

She leans to one side and shows us. "It's straight across, no openings. Maybe we can climb over it with the suctions?"

Standing, I take a look at the stretch of rocks, thinking it might just work. Azima squashes the idea, though. "It's too uneven. We'll tear the ship apart."

Jaime nods in agreement. "I don't think it can be crossed that way."

"Then what?" I ask.

We're all looking helpless when Genesis 12 comes pumping around the corner. They've dealt with their birds. I wait for them to see the rock wall, to cut their engines, and stop like us. Instead, they hold their steady pace and head straight for it. We all watch and listen as Morning commands them.

"Hold! Not yet!" They're twenty meters from the rock face when she shouts, "Now!"

Genesis 12 nose-dives. We watch nyxia spread up from every console like armor. The eight stations form a sleek black dome that seals the entire ship. At the same time, the boat submarines down beneath the water's surface, beneath the rocks, and out of sight.

Just like that, they're gone.

"Holy . . . ," Katsu whispers through the comm. "How do we do that?"

Jazzy scrambles through her console, but before she can find the button, the scraping noise sounds again. "What is that?" I ask. "Are we beached?"

The answer comes splashing over the side of the ship. Jazzy screams as the first bird lands on the floorboard with a *thunk*. Its eyes are boiled red and its body looks half metal, half nightmare. It snaps at Azima with a sword-sharp beak. She ducks a shoulder but can't dodge the sweep of the bird's outstretched wing. The blow knocks her hard against the railing. She slumps down, but before it can snap her in two, the light of a pulse cannon colors it white. The cannon shot nails the bird in the chest, taking it writhing overboard.

Roathy nods at us. "I think I got it that time."

We're all breathing heavily as we return our attention to the course. Jazzy finds a screen she didn't see before, and the nyxia submarines over us. Carefully, Jaime and Katsu navigate through the underwater cave and pop us out the other side. We're too far behind, though. Genesis 12 is a distant speck rounding a distant corner. We should be proud, but when we cross the finish line it's as the second-place team.

There's no pride without points. The scores have changed even before we arrive. I want to say something positive, to act like a captain, but as we dock, nothing heroic comes to mind. Anton doesn't even need to taunt us. Their celebrations are mocking enough. We head back to our rooms, trying to ignore their victory and our failure.

DAY 2, 8:15 A.M.

Aboard the Tower Space Station

The next morning I'm the first one out in the common area. It feels like the captain thing to do. Wake up first. Think about how to change the game and beat the odds. I know I have just twenty-nine days to prove I'm worthy of going to Eden. Even the air I'm breathing has a taste of finality to it. This is the end of all my hard work. If I win, it's the beginning of something more.

I take a seat in front of the window that faces Eden. It hangs in the dark of space like a quiet promise. The sight of the foreign planet makes me think of an old song by the Alabama Shakes. I scroll through my player until I find it. It starts with light echoes of sound before the instruments raise up and Brittany Howard's voice blasts every note with color.

I remember the music video for it too. A black astronaut wakes up in space and realizes he's slept his way through the universe and deep into the empty nothing. He sits in the command chair trying to contact home, but there's only his voice, only the realization that everyone else is gone. Until some foreign sun strokes the horizon. You don't find out what happens to him, but there's a strange hope in that golden light.

Someone taps my shoulder just as I throw the song back to the beginning.

It's a surprise to see Morning. She's fully suited up, minus the nyxian language converter. Without her mask she looks like a completely different person. The intensity of her eyes is thrown off by the soft shape of her chin, the casual smile on her lips. She points to the empty seat next to me and I nod her into it. A quick glance shows that the room's full of empty chairs she could have chosen. The idea that she wants to sit with me has me curious. I tug out an earbud as she folds her legs up beside me, her eyes taking in distant Eden.

"I can't believe we're this close," she says.

"Some of us are closer than others."

She nods at that. Her place on Eden is guaranteed. Her captainship too. It should have her relaxed and coasting through the last thirty days, but I get the sense she's got other goals in mind. There's something larger riding her shoulders, some burden I can't quite grasp. My goals are far simpler: make the final cut and get the hell home.

"You American?" she asks.

My mask sits on the nearest table. I realize this is the first time in a while I've had a conversation without it. "I'm from Detroit. You?"

"San Jose," she replies. "We moved all over, though."

I nod before giving her name tag a side-eye.

"Morning. Never heard that name before."

She glances back at Eden. "Mi abuelita chose it. She said I was like a brand-new day."

It's such a pretty line that I don't know what to say back. Quiet carries the next thirty seconds. The Shakes are still trembling through my earbuds, loud enough for Morning to notice. She nods over. "Can I listen?"

She leans a little closer as I hand her the stray earbud and spin the song back to the beginning. Thirty seconds ago the track was about space and loneliness and other worlds. But as we work our way through the smashing lyrics, each new line sounds like it's describing the distance between the two of us. On the scoreboard we're a few galaxies apart. But here and now our shoulders are pressed together and our heads are nodding in rhythm. It's the kind of moment you share at a high school lunch table, not looking down at a foreign planet.

I'm glad she doesn't tell me how perfect a song it is. She doesn't ask who sings it either. She does the opposite of what most people do: she just listens. I can feel my heart slamming around my chest as the song finishes. I fumble for something to say, but she gets there first.

"That's an old song. I didn't hear morphing in any of the lyrics."

"Nah," I say. "I don't have any of that new-age stuff."

"In love with the classics?"

I smile over at her. "I'm actually a fifty-three-year-old man. I just look young."

For the first time, she grins. It's not the smile she's been wearing since she walked in the room. Seeing the new look

is like finding a secret bonus level. I can't help grinning
back.

"Fifty-three?" she asks. "What's your secret?"

"Lemon juice." About five years ago, I remember Moms
actually trying to use lemon juice on some age spots. Pops
dogged her about it for weeks. "That's all I packed, actually.
No clothes, no books, nothing. Just a bunch of lemons. Trying to stay young, you know?"

She laughs at that. "So you're good-looking *and* funny?
Let me guess: they handed out senior superlatives on the
ship and you were voted Mr. Congeniality of *Genesis 11*?"

I hitch on the idea that I'm good-looking. She speaks the
words like they're simple, straightforward facts. Like it's
something I'm well aware of. My brain scrambles for an
answer, but I get caught up on thoughts of Kaya. In two
minutes Morning's assumed the same comfort with me that
Kaya did in the beginning. The only difference is that Kaya
made me feel calm and Morning makes me feel chaos. My
right hand's shaking so much that I have to keep it pinned
out of sight.

"No chance of winning Mr. Congeniality," I finally say.
"Bilal swept that award, I think. Kid's so nice he snagged
all our votes. Honestly, it's the only thing our crew can ever
agree on. How about you? Most Likely to Be a Future Presi-
dent?"

She blushes and shakes her head. "They follow me because they trust me. From what I saw yesterday, I'm pretty
sure that's true of you too. That's why I wanted to talk. I
just—I don't know—you impressed me yesterday. Protecting
your crew like that. You care about them a lot."

"Not really," I say, which makes her laugh. "But Kaya cared about them. She always cared about everyone. After she died, I couldn't just treat them like enemies. It felt wrong to act like who she was didn't change me, you know?"

She looks at me like she doesn't know. I remember that Genesis 12 has no idea what happened to Kaya. In their minds, Kaya's death is nothing more than a mysterious asterisk. Morning's smile fades as she considers the expression on my face.

"What happened to her?"

"It was an accident. A bad one."

She's quiet for a while before saying, "The two of you were close."

"Might as well have been my sister."

Morning reaches over and sets her hand on mine. I let my eyes fall to the floor. She gives a little squeeze, and for a second I imagine a world where we're not about to spend twenty-nine days fighting each other tooth and nail for every point.

A little smile parts my lips. "Damn. Why's your hand so cold?"

She shoots me the most scandalized look ever and tries to pull away, but I'm quick enough to snatch her hand back out of the air. It's thin and callused and dark-knuckled. I take it between both my hands and rub warmth back through each joint. There's a long moment where we both just watch the way my hands move over hers. Our eyes meet and . . .

. . . the door opens, and we about hit the roof.

My other bud rips from her ear and we both retreat a few steps, like we're putting distance between ourselves and a crime scene. Defoe's gliding through the doorway, fingers whipping across the surface of a data pad. He takes in our awkward postures and smiles.

"Making friends?" Our silence has him laughing. "Pardon my intrusion."

He taps a sequence and wake-up alarms thunder out. Assistants follow him through the entry as the other contestants rise. Morning puts a little more distance between us before standing there with her arms crossed defiantly. I try to think of something to say, but her Genesis 12 crewmates come pouring out of the lower rooms, and it's like I've vanished. I move to the opposite end of the room and wait for my own teammates to come. The moment's gone, slipped through my fingers. I stand there for a while, trying to catch Morning's eye, but her nyxian mask is back on and she's wearing that hard, stony demeanor with it now too.

She's doing what I should be doing. She's putting on the necessary armor and preparing for war. But as Genesis 11 files down to join us, and even as we head to the Waterway, I can't shake the thought of her hand in mine.

DAY 4, 11:57 A.M.

Aboard the Tower Space Station

For more than forty-eight hours now, my world has been reduced to two things: Morning and losing. We haven't shared any private moments. No listening to songs together. But we've made a sport out of locking eyes, out of looking away. It's all made me feel guilty, because my team keeps losing to hers.

Genesis 12 stays one or two steps ahead of us in every competition. The gap doesn't feel that big. We perform well, but we are always a mistake away from winning every challenge. We fight off birds and shock-eels. We navigate tricky currents and submerge into pitch-black caves. Always, though, Morning is mastering some new aspect of the game. Like Kaya she figures it out and then teaches it to us through defeat. I have never missed my friend more, never needed her at my side as much as I do now.

We don't make a habit of socializing with the enemy, but the handful of conversations that do happen are very educational. Their crew has one clear similarity to ours: Babel plucked all of them out of poverty. It's obvious that each contestant has their own desperate reasons for wanting to make it to Eden. It doesn't matter if they're from Colombia or India. The story reads the same. Winning will change *everything* for them back home.

And even though they always win, Genesis 12 keeps working hard. They take meals together, discuss strategies, and train during free hours. When I suggest the same for us, the practice sessions go miserably. Roathy and Isadora are a plague. Katsu and Jaime aren't taking any of it seriously. We lost these fights months ago, I realize, in the dark rivalries that Defoe forged between us.

But not all is lost.

As we watch the members of Genesis 12 climb the scoreboard, Babel gives us a chance to stand on our own. An event that depends on no one but ourselves. The day begins and ends with the Waterway challenges, but in between we fight. All the toys from the pit are set out on the docks. Megascreens descend from the Waterway's walls, and we watch one another die as pixelated giants. The water challenges are a distant glimpse of Genesis 12. In the duels, we get to know them in an up-close-and-personal kind of way.

Holly, the redheaded girl from Ireland, has a nightmare of a right hook. Her footwork's even a little better than mine. Their Egyptian giant, Omar, crushes Katsu on the first day using a mace I'm not even sure I could lift. Then there's Anton. He fights with knives, dirty and quick, and he's as dangerous with his right as he is with his left. He loses to Azima the first day, but dices Jaime up like a stuffed pig the next.

Luckily, not all of them can fight. Parvin and Noor were clearly relying on the same kind of strategy Kaya used in the pit. They're accustomed to bleeding someone, avoiding them, and hiding out. But our fights take place on the rocking docks of the nyxian ships. There's nowhere to run unless you want to fight underwater.

Alex, the tall, curly-headed Colombian, isn't bad. Like Bilal, his reach and length help, but he's not disciplined enough to beat the better duelers. On the first day, I stood across from their other big boy, Brett. I was worried until I saw him move. Lumbering and sloppy. I slid past a half-assed lunge and hit him with a deadly shot across the chin.

My other pursuer, Loche, loses both of his first matches. He curses every time he loses, and even Babel's translators have trouble forcing some of the Australian phrases into something I can fully understand. I wouldn't have to worry about either Loche or Brett, but Morning's stubborn streak of victories might not stop. Already Alex has pulled ahead of me. Which is why the duels are even more important. I have to stay ahead of Roathy if I want a chance of going to Eden.

The worst part is Bilal. It's not hard to do the math. Each fight he misses is costing him. Slowly I'm moving up the scoreboard as he goes through physical therapy and gets fitted for a walking boot that will help him return to action. At this rate, one of us isn't going to make it to Eden.

Today I fight Morning. Her first two fights took a combined ten seconds. I pluck up my boxing gloves and cross the gangplank. She's already waiting there, dueling hatchets in hand. When she sees I'm her opponent, she reaches up

and clicks her nyxian mask off. She sets it aside and gestures for me to do the same.

Since that one early morning, we haven't talked. Morning's been too busy training her team toward perfection.
But the second her mask comes off, there's a smile on her
face. It's the kind of smile you get when you're picking up a
date, not when you're about to get surgical treatment from
a pair of hatchets.

"I like you," she says quietly. "I like your music. I like
your jokes. None of this is personal, but as long as you're
standing there and I'm standing here, you're not gonna win."

"And I was hoping you'd cut me some slack."

"Never," she says. "Honestly, I wouldn't mind walking
around Eden with someone like you, but you're gonna have
to earn your own way. Fathom?"

I raise an eyebrow. "That's my word."

"Take it back," she replies, giving me that secret-level
grin. "If you can."

We both put our masks back on. I watch her, arms up in
a defensive stance. I trace the movements of her muscles,
the shuffle of her feet. I know she will strike, and that when
she strikes, it will come faster than I imagine, in a place I
could not have guessed. Her eyes give nothing away because she doesn't glance where she wants to attack, a mistake too many of the others make. Her eyes are locked on
mine.

She feints wide, switches her stance, feints inside, and
then ducks forward. The twist her body gives to avoid
my swing would be poetry if the final couplet weren't her
hatchet in my neck. She spins before my second swing can

come across and plants the second one in my stomach. Above, my avatar collapses. Damn, she's fast.

"Four seconds," she whispers.

As she slides past, she bumps my shoulder playfully. I trudge across the gangplank to join the others and try to keep my cool. I watch the next few matches without much interest. Isadora bests Brett, Jazzy loses a lopsided duel against Omar, and Bilal's avatar forfeits to Anton. It's not until the final match that I feel my attention drawn back to the boats. Loche, the Australian boy with the pretty hair, stands across from Longwei. Before they can fight, Morning runs down and crosses the gangplank. She whispers something into Loche's ear and runs back across. The Aussie gives a tight smile and advances.

All of us lean over the railing to watch, like a whisper from Morning will result in some kind of miracle. But Loche looks more uncoordinated than ever. He dodges a sweeping stroke from Longwei's sword, barely parries another, then ducks close. He doesn't swing, just wraps his arms around Longwei's chest and gives himself a shove over the railing. We watch them plunge into the dark blue, out of sight. Their splash settles, and there's nothing but dark rapids.

Our eyes flicker to the avatar screen. Loche's figure looks calm, heartbeat a bit quick, but still alive. Longwei's is thrashing wildly on the screen. His heartbeat is flying and his oxygen levels are plummeting. Loche is going to drown him.

I shove past the others and stand next to Defoe. "You can't let him drown."

"He won't drown. We have a system in place."

Longwei's avatar is starting to turn blue. We watch as his struggling arms get weaker and weaker. I glance back at Morning. Above her mask, the look she returns is hard and unyielding.

"Is that what you told him to do? That's cheap."

Morning doesn't flinch. "You'd do it, if it was the only way you could win."

I shake my head and look back at the screen. Longwei's avatar doesn't have a pulse. Below, Loche's golden hair bobs up out of the water. Under one arm, he's holding an unconscious Longwei. Divers appear from nowhere, fit an oxygen mask over his head, and pull him out of the Waterway. I rush down the stairs.

I might not like Longwei, but he let me be his captain, and being captain means being there for moments like this. I stand by until they revive him. His eyes are bloodshot and his throat is bruised. He stares at the lights overhead like he's not sure what happened. I sink to his side and put a hand on his shoulder.

"You're all right, Longwei," I say. "You're going to be okay."

His whole body shudders. The medics start asking him questions, working on his breathing, but as they do, Longwei's hand falls atop mine and squeezes. He doesn't say thank you, but he doesn't have to say it. When they clear him, we walk back up to our rooms together.

"Did I lose?" he finally asks.

I laugh. "Barely, Longwei. Just barely."

After his attendant promises me for the third time that he's going to be fine, I storm out of the room in search of

Morning. I don't know why I'm so mad, but I can feel the rage like it's bone-deep. I know she wants to win and lead her team to Eden, but Longwei could have died.

I knock on her door for a few minutes, but there's no answer. When I backtrack to the lobby, I find curly-haired Alex shuffling a deck of cards. His eyes are tracing Eden's oceans.

"Where is she?"

Alex glances over. "Who?"

"Morning. I need to talk to her."

He nods now. "She said you would. She's down in the Tower's Rabbit Room. Working out or something. She said to tell you to come find her if you asked."

I thank him and move toward the stairs. I've used the Rabbit Room here once or twice too. Either loosening up muscles before the day starts or getting in some extra training. The lower down in the station I go, the less I see of Babel's techies and marines. Vandemeer explained that these are their long-term employees. Some of them have been stationed out here for close to a decade. I end up walking a lengthy hallway that branches out into a handful of odd corridors.

In the distance I spy Morning leaned up against the door to the Rabbit Room like she's been waiting for me all this time. Her arms are crossed and she barely looks like she's broken a sweat. Her mask hangs from the utility belt at the hip of her suit.

"Hey, I need to talk to you," I say.

She pushes off the wall and meets me halfway. "Same."

"Look, that stuff that Loche pulled—"

Morning cuts me off with a hand gesture and a look. I'm about to say something else when she crosses the distance between us, comes close enough that we're breathing the same air, and drops her voice to a whisper. "Let's do our talking where there aren't cameras."

There's something intoxicating about how she slides away and gestures for me to follow. She moves down one of the side corridors, gives me a lingering over-the-shoulder look, and ducks into one of the mechanical rooms. The invitation might as well be blasting through speakers, but I stand there staring at the empty doorway because I have no idea what's going on.

Does Morning want to talk, or does she want to *talk*? I may have bragged otherwise to the Most Excellent Brothers, but I've never really done that kind of talking with a girl like Morning. It's one thing to flirt with Shae Westwood or Samantha Givens at a basement party. That kind of talk with those girls was a second language. It never had any weight because we were just kids. It was never about anything more than the moment. Morning's different somehow. I realize my preparation for situations like this is a stash of song lyrics and movie scenes. I wipe the sweat from my palms and follow after her.

Two steps inside and everything's clear: she has something else in mind.

Morning waits at the back of the room, her hands on her hips and her mask on. She's not alone. Anton glides out of the shadows with one of his knives leveled at me. He gestures for me to keep walking as Omar blocks the exit. The Egyptian manipulates his nyxia until it stretches across the entrance with a static snap. The room's sounds echo louder now, like we're cut off in our own world. My eyes flicker between them before settling on Morning.

"Why all the James Bond spy stuff?"

As I ask the question, I realize I'm mad. Mad that she led me on and embarrassed I let my imagination color so far outside the lines. Morning doesn't flinch away from my stare.

"We need to talk to you," Morning says. "Without Babel listening."

"So that's why there are three of you and just one of me?"

"Omar insisted on coming. We're just being careful."

"Right. So if I don't want to talk, you just let me go?"

Anton spins his knife. "There are other ways to get the information from you."

"Shut it, Anton," Morning says, stepping forward. "If you want to leave, then leave. I brought you here because I know I can trust you. I know we can ask you questions and you won't go running off to inform Babel."

I glare at her. "You sure about that?"

"Of course I'm sure," she says. "I've seen how you look at them, Emmett."

"Whatever." She's right, but I don't like how this is going. "What do you want?"

"The girl," Morning says. "How did she die?"

"Kaya. Her name was Kaya."

"Kaya," Morning corrects herself. "How did Kaya die?"

"I told you it was an accident."

"Right, but there are accidents and there are *accidents*. Whose fault was it?"

The words catch in my throat. For a second I think about lying, but Kaya's memory has made me better than that. "It was our fault. We were exploring an off-limits part of the ship."

"And what?" Anton asks. "She got sucked out of an air lock?"

I hesitate again. This was Defoe's one command: don't tell the others about the Adamite. It's possible they'll use whatever I say against me. It's possible they want one more person disqualified. But I know Morning well enough now to know that's not the way she'd want to win. She thinks she can earn her crew's way down to Eden. Nothing she's done has been backhanded, because she can win the right way. I realize that other than Vandemeer, no one else knows how Kaya died. It's been a burden I've carried on my own shoulders. But here and now? We can talk off Babel's radar.

"An Adamite killed her."

Air hisses through Anton's teeth. The Russian circles nervously, knife tossing from one hand to the other. Morning's considering my words and what they mean.

"Why would an Adamite kill her?" she asks. "Babel told us they love children."

"He was blindfolded. He had no idea who he was attacking. Babel had him strapped to a wall. In a torture room. He lashed out at Kaya because he thought she was one of them."

Anton curses. From the back of the room, Omar says, "You were right, Morning."

Morning nods. "So there's more to the story than Babel's telling us."

"There always was," Anton says, seething. "Their whole show is wizards behind curtains and trapdoors. Just give the order, Morning, and I'll get the information."

She frowns, but eventually nods. "Do it. Just be careful."

A wicked smile splits his face. "You really mean it?"

She nods again. "Go."

He pockets the knife and heads for the barrier Omar has thrown over the door. The Egyptian steps aside, and the sound of Anton's echoing footsteps cuts off once he's through. I turn back to Morning. "Want to tell me what the hell's going on?"

"Did you hear anything about the Babel Files on *Genesis 11*?"

"Yeah, all of us did. It's an article, right? Someone back home wrote it about us?"

"Exactly. Did you ever read the article?" she asks.

I shake my head. "How could we read the article? We're out in space."

"Anton," she replies. "He got me the file. We read it together. The person who wrote it had a lot of theories. About us. About Babel. Everything. Did you ever get the sense that maybe there's something bigger happening here?"

I think about that. There's been an army of red flags raised along the way, but nothing that indicates a specific direction. "Babel's corrupt and powerful. What else is there to know?"

"We're not sure," Morning says. "But we want to find out."

"Look, I'm glad someone's got time to play detective, but I don't. You might be sitting pretty on the scoreboard, but

I still have to earn my way down to Eden. I'd love to help you. I'd love to get justice for Kaya. But right now I have to focus on making the cut. So unless there's anything else you want to ask me, I'm going to head back upstairs and prep for the next challenge."

Morning eyes me for a second, then nods to Omar. He pulls the nyxian barrier back into a ring and slides it over his finger. He considers the two of us for a second, then slips out of the room. I listen until the sound of his footsteps fades. Morning looks at me, and all the hardness in her expression is gone.

"Those are my brothers. They're just being overprotective."

"No kidding."

She reaches out and sets a hand on my arm.

"You're right. It's not fair for me to drag you into this while you still have other things to worry about. But I meant what I said, Emmett. You're the one I trust from *Genesis 11*. I can tell you're an honest person. I like that about you."

No one ever taught me how to take compliments. All I can do is nod. "Thanks."

"I wish you'd been with me on *Genesis 12*."

After four days of painful losses, I've been wishing the same thing. I can't help thinking now about what that might have been like. What that could have meant for me, for us. But if I had been on *Genesis 12*, I would have never met Kaya, or Bilal, or Vandemeer. I wouldn't be the person I am now without each of them. And I don't want to wish that away.

"Can't change things now."

Morning gives my arm a squeeze before letting go.

"I want you with me on Eden," she says. "I really do, but I made promises. When we found out about your crew, I promised my team that I'd fight every second of every day to get them to Eden if they just trusted me to lead them. I don't break my promises, Emmett. Not even for you."

DAY 9, 6:20 P.M.

Aboard the Tower Space Station

We float down the black river in silence. We've been roaming through the unlit rapids for thirty minutes now. Too long for my comfort. Babel has every light in the Waterway clicked off. Defoe claims it will simulate one of Eden's moonless nights. The only light comes from Jazzy's sonar system. Little green blips in a dark, inky sea. The only sound is the river. When we talk it is in whispers so quiet they sound more like thoughts. "We're twenty meters from a rock. Need to drift left ten meters to hit the next strait."

We feel the subtle change in direction. There's a flash of light in the distance, then nothing. "Was that them?" Azima whispers.

No one answers. We started in one direction along the Waterway and Genesis 12 was sent the opposite direction. We caught a glimpse of them on the radar about five minutes ago and have been stalking them ever since. But somewhere in a rocky switchback, we lost them. I've got Jazzy throwing out fake radar signatures every ten seconds.

Bilal's sitting by her console, helping read the terrain. We drift for another five minutes before Jazzy whispers excitedly, "I've got them." On her screen, I can see a little red dot burning through the black. "Fifty meters ahead, tucked against that big rock."

The rock looms like a deeper, darker shadow. Ahead, the river divides into smaller sections. I take a look over Jazzy's shoulder and notice they're waiting at the tightest squeeze in the river. The rock they hang from has them poised above the choke point, a perfect ambush.

"Let's anchor here," I command. "No noise. Jazzy, ten-second scans."

The work is done in silence. When we're nestled against the nearest rocks, I gather the crew at the center of the ship. Their faces aren't recognizable in the black.

"How do we know they aren't throwing a false signal?" Jaime's voice asks.

"We don't," I answer.

"It's a solid choke point," Katsu's voice says. "I bet they're just waiting for us."

"So why don't we bait them?" Longwei asks. "Go through the strait, make just a tiny bit of noise, and surprise them."

"What's the point?" I ask. "Sure, we know they're coming, but they've got the upper ground. We'd be sitting ducks."

"Then we split up," Longwei says. "Look at the scans— these rocks connect to the big rock. Half of us climb up that way. Someone grabs the flag and drops down to ours. We win."

"For once," Katsu mutters darkly.

"It sounds great and all," I say. "But I can't even see your faces right now. How are we supposed to climb up there?"

There's a pause. Then Longwei says, "Skillfully."

Little breaths of laughter.

"All right," I say. "Let's do it."

It's agreed that Katsu, Longwei, Bilal, and Jazzy should stay on board. The rest of us prepare for what will be a treacherous, slippery climb. Jazzy runs the scan and freezes the screen. We memorize the rock formations and pinpoint distances together. Azima suggests using nyxia for a little extra grip. It takes a few minutes, but we each manipulate the best pair of grip gloves we can in the darkness.

"Everyone ready?" I ask.

The affirmatives are quieter than river splashes. We grope for solid rock and lower onto our stomachs as quietly as possible. The path isn't straight or even. My stomach and knees are rubbing raw as we make our way forward. Even when the path widens, I stay low and keep crawling. I can feel the slickness left and right of me. The slightest slip would ruin our surprise and send us into the river. I'm sure Babel has their divers on hand, but I don't want to risk it if they don't.

In spite of the pitch black, we find the first mound of the big rock their boat is gripping. Azima runs into the back of my legs as I trace the lightless scene for anything odd, but it's useless. Too dark. We keep crawling. I hear fabric snag on a rock behind me and freeze. We all wait like statues, but nothing happens. Three more meters and we're at the edge of the rock. A glance over reveals the deep shadow of their boat. I reach out and touch it just to be sure. Holding my breath, I crawl back in the opposite direction. Roathy and the others are flat on their stomachs. I make sure the angles are right and set my flashlight on the back of Azima's boot heel. I flash a handheld light twice and flatten again.

We hear the faintest sound of our ship's engine. Jazzy guessed one minute to get around the lip and into the strait at their slowest speed. I count the seconds as shadows shift.

"All right, Azima. We'll all climb up the side," I whisper. "But you're making the grab."

"On the back of the captain's chair, yes?" she asks.

"Yes." There's a soft engine thrum on our left. "Thirty seconds."

Green dots blossom above us. I blink a few times.

"What are those?" Azima whispers.

We watch them swirl in the air like fireflies.

"They look like eyes," Isadora says.

Genesis 12 descends. Something heavy crushes me against stone. My arms get pulled back and someone ties off my hands. The others struggle, but not for long. We're all pinned to the rock face and gagged before we can cry a warning. Their headgear glows with enough light to see the features beneath. Anton stands above us, his hair slicked back with wet.

"We have the ducklings," he whispers. "Now we get the goose."

The green glow of their gear fades as they slip back to their boat. We watch the shadows vanish over the lip. A second later, they release their suction and splash down into the water. The boarding party takes our crew easily.

Our flag is claimed. The lights click back on and we wait as Anton and Omar take their time removing our bindings. Morning orders her crew to undo their nyxian transformations before we can get a look at the night goggles they used.

Longwei and the others look up at us, confused about what happened. All we can do is shrug back as Defoe and Requin appear on the platforms above. They lead everyone through a side hatch. We walk by one too many scoreboards on the way back, one too many reminders of how we've failed.

1.	MORNING	1,151,200	points
2.	LONGWEI	701,900	points
3.	KATSU	658,450	points
4.	PARVIN	624,200	points
5.	HOLLY	614,700	points
6.	**OMAR**	612,000	points
7.	NOOR	572,050	points
8.	**ANTON**	568,290	points
9.	AZIMA	553,750	points
10.	**BILAL**	532,300	points
11.	**ALEX**	532,200	points
12.	**JAIME**	529,200	points
13.	**EMMETT**	494,350	points
14.	**ROATHY**	489,325	points
15.	JASMINE	484,050	points
16.	IDA	447,400	points
17.	ISADORA	427,960	points
18.	**LOCHE**	420,500	points
19.	**BRETT**	387,000	points

"This isn't working," Katsu says heatedly. "I mean, no offense, Emmett, but we haven't won once with you as the captain. Tonight was awful. Just awful. They always have a plan."

"If you had such a great plan, why didn't you share it?" I fire back.

"Because I'm the *driver,* not the captain. You're supposed to come up with the ideas."

The other members of our crew have stopped walking. Genesis 12 passes by, and Anton claps for us. "Another valiant effort! Keep at it, you guys!"

Katsu starts after him, but Longwei and Jaime grab him. When Genesis 12 is out of sight, he rounds on me instead. "This isn't working," he repeats.

"We've been close," I say hotly. "Every time. If you just give me a few more days—"

"Close isn't winning," Katsu says. "Look, it doesn't even matter that much to me. I'm going to Eden. But the rest of you need to figure it out. They've won eighteen straight. That's fifty-four thousand points. If we keep losing, you're gone. End of story."

He storms off. I look at the others. Jaime gives me an apologetic look but says nothing to defend me. Even Bilal is avoiding eye contact. I decide to wash my hands of it.

"If that's what you want, vote in someone else," I say. "I don't care."

I stand there, heated, as the others walk away. I feel left behind, pissed off by their rejection, and halfway buried by the scoreboard. Loche's gaining on me with my every failure. I take a few minutes to cool off before following after the others. I just need to sleep it off. We all do. Maybe they'll realize in the morning how close we've been to winning.

Raised voices catch my attention. I thought the others were long gone, but an argument crashes its way from one of the side corridors and echoes through the main hallway. I follow the voices until the words, and the two people fighting, are clear as day.

"You act like I'm not trying," Roathy accuses.

Isadora's voice is quieter, but far fiercer too.

"Are you trying? I don't know. It's like you quit on me. There's two weeks left, Roathy, and you're not making *any* progress. If you don't want to be with me, just say it."

His voice is annoyed. "Of course I want to be with you."

"Then act like it," she snaps. "I can't do this alone. That's what will happen. I'll have to go down without you and I'll be alone for *all* of it."

"Isa, I'm trying."

"Try *harder*," she snaps. "That's what I need. I need you to try harder."

There's silence, and footsteps, and I barely manage to slide into an adjacent room. From the shadows, I watch Isadora storm out. I wait for Roathy to follow, but he doesn't. After a few minutes, I ease out of my hiding place and glance around the corner.

They were in one of the comfort pods. Roathy stands quietly by one of the porthole windows, looking out at the endless black. I wait by the entrance. There's a second where I think about doing what Kaya would have done. Talking to him, encouraging him, and making sure everything's all right.

But then he unleashes a frustrated scream and flings the contents of the nearest table away. Ceramic mugs shatter against the wall, gasping white clouds of dust into the air. He doesn't stop there. He keeps wrecking everything, and I force my feet to move, away from him and down the hall. Even when I reach the safety of my room, Roathy's outburst stays with me.

Babel's game is coming to a close. Roathy's screams might as well be prophecies. When the game ends, there will be winners and losers. I always thought things would get clearer as we arrived at the finish line, but I was wrong. We're all reaching for the same prizes. The finish line will be chaos. It will be the final and dying efforts of the desperate.

And I'll be in the middle of all of it.

DAY 10, 8:03 A.M.

Aboard the Tower Space Station

The next morning they vote someone else as captain, and I do care. I know I led them well, and I know in the end it wouldn't have mattered. I'm not Kaya. I don't have her clever tactics or strategies. It isn't enough to care about my team and sacrifice myself for them. I failed.

It makes me resent Morning and Genesis 12 even more. In the three days that follow Katsu's promotion as captain, we manage a single victory. The taste of it is enough to have the rest of the crew believing he's the magical difference that will start netting us points.

I know the truth. Genesis 12 has to sit one competitor out each day on a rotating basis. We won on the day Morning sat out. When she's in the equation, she tips the scales. It's that simple. We needed to win the afternoon session too, but Katsu got us beached and slaughtered. Still, one victory has the crew asking Katsu about strategies and believing we're about to turn it all around. One look at the scoreboard on day fourteen shows that Katsu's leadership is more false hope:

1.	*MORNING*	1,184,200	points
2.	*LONGWEI*	710,900	points
3.	*KATSU*	667,450	points
4.	*HOLLY*	644,700	points
5.	*OMAR*	642,000	points
6.	*PARVIN*	645,200	points
7.	*ANTON*	595,290	points
8.	*NOOR*	593,050	points
9.	*AZIMA*	565,750	points
10.	**ALEX**	556,200	points
11.	**BILAL**	535,300	points
12.	**JAIME**	535,200	points
13.	**EMMETT**	506,350	points
14.	**ROATHY**	498,325	points
15.	*JASMINE*	490,050	points
16.	*IDA*	468,400	points
17.	**LOCHE**	441,500	points
18.	*ISADORA*	439,960	points
19.	**BRETT**	411,000	points

Yesterday, Omar's and Anton's names italicized. They're officially safe, out of reach. Seven of us remain; four of us will not make it. Vandemeer agreed to sit down with me and crunch numbers. It didn't take us long to figure out that Alex is pretty much out of reach too. Neither Vandemeer nor I have any false hopes about our ability to beat Genesis 12 on any kind of regular basis. They'll win the majority, if not all, of the remaining games.

We also figured out that I'm unlikely to catch Jaime. I'm a far better dueler than he is, but there's too much ground to cover in too little time. I'm far more likely to catch the one person I don't want to catch: Bilal. He had a little setback with his leg and he's forfeited every duel so far. Even if he does make a miraculous recovery, how many fights could he actually win?

The only other threats come from below now: Roathy, Loche, and Brett.

Roathy's actually keeping pace in the dueling. He fights each duel like it's the end of the world. My own victories are the only thing keeping him at bay. And Brett's too far back. The biggest threat looks like Loche. He continues to climb each day. The Aussie isn't even performing that well in the duels, but at this rate it might not matter. The math doesn't lie.

We have seventeen more days. Two competitions each day. That's 102,000 points. Morning will be gone for two of those days, or four of those competitions. If we can win those, we'll grab twelve thousand points. If the past thirteen days are any indication, Genesis 12 might actually take the remaining ninety thousand that are up for grabs. I have a 65,000-point lead over Loche. Normally, I'd call that insurmountable, a done deal, but because of Morning, it isn't. The duels will fluctuate our scores some, but in Vandemeer's best projections, I beat Loche by a few thousand points. In the worst-case scenarios, I lose by the same amount. That's too tight for comfort.

So I'm focused as we climb aboard today, knowing we're almost halfway through the last leg of the competition. Katsu's renamed our stations. He calls Jazzy our eyes. He calls Jaime and me the hips, always pairing it with a grin.

He calls Longwei the backbone and our four defensive stations fists. I don't really care what he calls them; I just want
to scrape together one or two unexpected victories. Longwei fires up the engine, and we drift out to the starting
point. Genesis 12 is already there. Anton and Alex stand
together by the nearest railing. Both look confused as they
point at the scoreboard.

"Alex, have you noticed anything . . . unusual?" Anton
asks with playacted curiosity.

"The scoreboard," Alex says. "It appears to be broken."

Anton grins. "How do you mean?"

"It seems only the Genesis 12 members are allowed to
gain points. Very unfair!"

Our crew doesn't respond. Even Katsu's done with talking trash. There's only so much you can say when your
record is as stunningly bad as ours is. As we wait, I get a
feel for Jaime across the nyxian link. My console reads like
a high-tech computer screen. I organize all my controls into
a single row of icons, ready to suction or push or dip at a
moment's notice. The driving's strange. The grips are super
sensitive. On the first day I had us sliding all over the place.
But Jaime and I have found our rhythm now. It helps that
all of our early hatred has completely faded.

Today, Requin comes alone. His silver hair is a mess, but
he's smiling. He offers his hollow smile a lot these days.
He's proud of his crew. "Today's race will be three laps."

Without another word, he activates the Waterway. The
ropes vanish and we get a good kick off the start. Jazzy
pulse scans, and we wait for her to call out the course. Genesis 12 hums alongside us, nosed just a bit ahead. Omar and

Longwei can get about the same out of their engines. The difference is always what Morning can do with the power she's given.

"Nothing on the scans," Jazzy says.

"Be prepared for anything, defensive stations," Katsu commands.

We maintain the course and Jazzy reports ten seconds later. We're humming along, setting a solid rhythm with the current. "Still nothing," she says.

I glance around and realize we're all strung tight. We've learned how Babel works by now. The less of an obstacle there seems to be, the bigger the monster lurking around the corner. But as we continue picking up speed and round the first bend, Jazzy reports no obstacles again. I glance up and realize we're moving too fast for Requin to follow. Another glance shows him two hundred meters back, waiting by the observation deck. Usually they fast-track to the closest choke point and watch how we handle it. Not today, though. Which means . . .

"Speed!" I shout. "We need as much speed as we can get."

Twenty meters to our right, Genesis 12's already adjusting. Omar and Morning double their engines, and they've nosed ahead by half their ship's length. Katsu's looking out over the water warily. "I don't want to get us in trouble around the next bend," he says. "If we go too fast, we can't stop ourselves from whatever's waiting."

I glance over. "There's nothing waiting. No choke points or obstacles. It's a speed race."

Katsu looks unconvinced. "Jazzy?"

"Still nothing."

Frustrated, I leave my console. Genesis 12 is pulling away as Katsu makes up his mind. There's still time, though. I pull Bilal from his station. Katsu shouts something, but I ignore him. My hands are barely on the grips before the nyxia transforms into my vision. A grappling gun. I take aim, adjust for speed, and fire. We all watch the black hook arc over the river, land on their deck, and snap tight. There's a distant click as the hook claws into the wooden railing.

"They're going to notice that soon enough," I say through Bilal's comm. "We have to divert everything to speed by that time. That's what they're doing."

A quick glance shows I'm right. All four of their fist stations are turned inward. They're pushing energy to Morning and letting her feed Omar. It's genius. And probably the reason Ida hasn't noticed the hook wedged two meters from her station. Genesis 12 is moving three times as fast, but the hook tugs us through the water with them. There's a groan from our ship as Katsu considers me with narrowed eyes.

"Fine," he relents. "All fists convert your energy toward me. I'll push it to Longwei."

The crew gives their assent, and before long our engines are pumping too. Morning keeps glancing back, wondering how we're staying with them, when Ida finally notices the grappling hook. Morning furiously orders Ida to get rid of it.

"Bilal, come here." He limps over. Our increased speed has forced the grappling cord to go slack. I coil it back overboard until it's a little tighter. Smiling, I offer Bilal a place to grip and take hold of it myself. "Did you ever play tug-of-war?"

It takes Ida a few seconds to dig the hook out of the

side of their ship. We wait and watch as she gets it free. She's got a good one-handed grip on it and is about to throw the metal overboard when we tug. The effect isn't as dramatic as I expected, but it hooks her arm and shoulder into a stumble. She loses balance and goes flailing overboard.

There's a loud cheer from Genesis 11. Without Ida, the numbers are in our favor. Soon we're flying down the obstacle-free Waterway. The speed feels dangerous, but Katsu and the rest of the crew can see that we made the right call. We finish the first lap with a solid lead.

"How are you doing, Longwei?" Katsu asks.

"Feeling fresh," he replies quietly. "And powerful. With all of you feeding me, it's very, very powerful."

We whip around another corner. Genesis 12 is floundering behind us. Isadora calls out their distance as one hundred meters back. They can't keep up without Ida. Everyone's honed in as we pass the starting point again.

"Should we slow down some?" I ask.

"No point," Katsu says. "We're winning. Let's not give them a window."

We're whipping around the second corner again when we see her. Morning stands along the metal ramparts to our left. Her suit and hair are soaking wet, her hands outstretched. Along the water's surface, she has shaped a staggering wall of massive nyxia black rocks. They stretch across nearly the full, seventy-meter length, leaving only a tiny gap at the far end of the Waterway. I have never seen someone manipulate so much nyxia. It's impossible.

Katsu's the first to panic. "Swing right! Swing right! We have to hit that gap!"

The engines cut and I feel Katsu join his power to Jaime and me. His mental hand is heavy as he redirects the rudders and yanks the nose of the ship toward the only opening. Morning watches as our boat turns too fast, heaves dangerously, and starts to tilt.

Jaime activates his suction, but it's not enough to stop our momentum. We all scream as the boat tips. Black water fills my lungs, I'm turned end over end, my ears scream, my eyes pinch closed, and something sucks at my body. I can feel someone slapping at my neck. Something crushes my legs. I am dying until an arm slips across my chest and pulls. I break the surface, gasping.

The scene is chaos. Divers are appearing through the hatched entrances and leaping into the water. All of us survive, but it takes two long minutes to pull everyone out. I look up as Genesis 12 comes flying around the corner. Morning rises out of a crouch. We all watch as she walks down the ramparts and sets a hand against the nearest rock. My eyes go wide as the whole thing topples with a shove. There were no rocks. The whole creation falls back into the water, and we can see that it's flat, two-dimensional. It looks just like the backdrops they use in theater productions. There's a smack and a splash as her team skids over it and onto victory.

Morning grins at our crew. Until she sees me. I watch the pleasure she takes in winning vanish. It's a simple equation. When she wins, I lose. There's a flash of guilt, and then the divers block my view of her. I don't wait for the chaos to clear, because I don't want to see her right now. We were beating them. We should have won and collected

crucial points, but as always, Morning's the only obstacle
that matters. Cursing, I leave the room.

After lunch, I punish Loche. We get matched up for a
duel and he tries to pull what he did against Longwei. He
wants to get close, wrap his arms around me, and take me
overboard. But if you get close to me, you get punished. Two
jabs have him staggering. Another brings him to a knee. I'm
eager for more, for blood. But as I move in for the kill, I see
Loche's face.

He's looking at me like I'm a monster, a black hole.

Something whispers in my ear to stop. Instead of finishing him off, I let my hands drop and I walk away. I'm not
a monster. I won't become what Babel's trying to make me.

We lose another capture-the-flag game in the afternoon,
and I find myself where I was when I started the day. Losing ground to Genesis 12. The rest of the crew is dejected.
Longwei punches a glass partition on our way back to the
rooms. He's in danger of losing his captainship on Eden
now. I'd feel bad for him, but at least he's going.

Bilal and I sit together in his room afterward.

We've spent the past few days ignoring the fact that
we're fighting each other for the last spot. It's always been
easier to pretend it's us against the rest of them. A few days
after his surgery, his doctor showed him the vid of me attacking Longwei. Something unspeakable formed then. He
looks and talks to me like a brother. I didn't want that.
There's too much pain and guilt when true bonds turn rotten. A branch can be cut away, but roots run deep and dark.
What I wanted didn't matter. When someone treats you like
a friend, that's what you become. His words have made

a brother out of me. My words have carved him into the same.

Which is why every conversation with him breaks my heart now.

"I will have to start fighting soon," Bilal says quietly. "But my doctor has advised against it. The leg can't take combat. Most days, I will lose. Everyone else is catching up to me."

I can only nod. "Maybe you can fight the weaker opponents."

He's quiet for a while. "You are going to pass me."

I shake my head. "You don't know that."

"What will happen will happen."

"Bilal, there's still time. Maybe our team will turn it around against Genesis 12."

"Do you think so?" he asks.

No. Of course not. "Maybe."

Bilal nods, like he believes it. "We must hope."

"And someone could get hurt. Alex, maybe."

Bilal looks shocked. "We must hope, but never for that."

I hope for it every day, pray for it every night.

"Bilal, it's either you or them. You know that, right?"

"I cannot wish harm on anyone," he says. "They have worked hard too."

I shake my head. "They don't deserve it like you. You're *good*. Better than me and better than them. That's why you deserve to go, no matter what the scores say."

He blushes. "Before I came, I slept outside. I had a rug for a bed, a shirt for a pillow. My best friends were sheep and my family was poor. The loser gets money too. Remember?"

I remember a promise on a piece of paper. I remember

Babel giving us their word about how life on *Genesis 11* would work. Those promises have been broken before, but I don't have the heart to remind Bilal of that. Instead, I say, "I remember."

"It is more money than my father has made his entire life," Bilal says dreamily.

My heart breaks just watching him. I make a promise to myself to find him if I *do* get to Eden. When I get back, I will take my paychecks to Palestine and split them with him.

"What will you do with the money?" I ask.

His marbled eyes are distant, lost. "I will buy my father livestock. I will go to school. Even a small part of that money will get us a house three times as big. Life will be better."

"I'll come visit you," I say, but it tastes like a lie. There are no guarantees in life, especially not out in space with Babel calling all the shots. "You'll have to teach me Arabic."

Bilal is teary-eyed. "I hope for these things. Not all is lost, yes?"

"No," I say quietly. "Not all is lost."

DAY 20, 5:23 P.M.

Aboard the Tower Space Station

I dream of Bilal. He stands in a desert and I am the wind, coming to devour him.

As Defoe promised, Babel isn't allowing any more Sabbaths. This part of the competition isn't about rest. It's about seeing who can survive the grind and come out the other side as champions. But today's the last day when we can call home, before the winners leave for Eden, so Babel schedules both our Waterway competitions in the morning and sets aside ten minutes in the afternoon for everyone.

Morning guides Genesis 12 to victory twice in the span of a single hour. After collecting our losses and eating lunch, Vandemeer sends me down to the Tower's version of the Contact Room. I don't know how to tell my parents that I'm still in the bottom four. I'm gaining on Bilal, but he won his first duel yesterday, against Parvin. He could still beat me. And Loche or Roathy might catch me. How can I possibly go home to them empty-handed?

The scheduled appointments are tight, so it's no surprise

to see Morning exiting the Contact Room just as I arrive. It is a surprise, though, to see her crying. When she sees it's me framing the entryway, she doesn't look embarrassed or apologize; she just comes forward and buries herself in my chest.

It happens so fast that I barely get my arms out and around her. She cries, louder and harder, and I stand there with a million pointless phrases running through my head. But I don't know why she's crying or what I'm supposed to say. So I just stand there and hold her, the way Pops always held Moms, the way both of them always held me.

When she finally has the strength to pull away, she keeps one hand on my chest and uses the other to wipe away tears. She sniffs twice, takes a deep breath, and looks up.

"I need you to tell me that everything's gonna be all right."

"What?"

"Just say it. Say everything will be all right."

I stare at her, then speak the words quietly. "Everything will be all right."

She swallows once, gives me a firm nod, and slips out of the room. I'm left with my head spinning. I can feel myself falling for her, but at the same time, I know she's the most likely one to send me home. One of us has to fail, and I'm hoping her dreams of bringing all of Genesis 12 to Eden don't come true. If I'm going to have any prayer of going, she has to fail.

I head into the Contact Room and prepare for my own goodbye. When the screen flickers to life, my heart almost breaks. For the first time, Moms is sitting next to Pops.

Tears rush down my cheeks, but I don't wipe them away. Her smile is every sunset and sunrise I've missed out here in the lonely black of space. She's wearing a summer dress, sky-blue and bright against her dark skin. Her hair's pulled up into a pretty bun. Her eyes shine with pride.

"My boy," she says, and her voice is sweeter than any song. "My brave, brave boy."

"Moms, I missed you so much."

Pops has his arm around her bird-thin shoulders. She leans into him and smiles wider.

"Your father's told me everything. We couldn't be more proud."

I nod. I want to tell her so much. It comes out all at once.

"We still have some time left, but I think I can do it, Moms. I think I'm going to make it. When I come back, we're going to be rich and I'm going to take y'all out for a nice dinner and buy you pretty dresses. Pops, I'll get you a car. Not a Ford. Forget Ford. I'll get you a Ferrari or something. When I get back, it's going to be different."

Moms nods. "We got the first few checks already. Everything's changing. And my treatments have been going well. These Babel doctors are so good, Emmett. I wanted you to know I'm at the top of the list. I get the next kidney transplant. It's such a difference, sweetie. All because of you. When you get back, win or lose, life's changing. It won't be the way it was. You just make sure you be smart and you be good, hear me?"

"You're already smart *and* good," Pops adds. "So be smarter and better."

"I've still got the key," I say through tears. "What do you want me to do with it?"

My father's face tightens. He's fighting off tears too. "Bury it. If you go down there, we're free. You're free. You'll be the first one to hand down something new. Bury the key on Eden as a sign, okay? A sign that all that's over and that we're starting new lives. Bury it for your sons and your daughters."

He's crying now and I'm crying more. Eyes swimming, I try to change the subject.

"Anything you want me to tell the aliens?"

Pops smiles. "Teach them football for me."

"Sing them love songs," Moms says. "Sing like we used to sing."

"I will," I say. "I promise, I will."

"Never forget where you came from," Pops reminds me.

"Or how much we love you," Moms adds.

"Never," I say.

On the corner of the screen, it ticks the final seconds we have.

"I love you."

"To the moon and back," they both say.

The feed cuts and I'm left alone, crying. A techie peeks in but thinks better of telling me to leave. I cry good tears and bad tears, missing tears and hopeful tears. When I finally pull myself together, each footstep sounds like a promise.

For Kaya, for them, for myself, for every Atwater there ever was: I'm going to Eden.

Determination pours into every bone and muscle. I can't

just sit still. Knowing we won't be back in the Waterway until tomorrow, I head down to log some time on the tread floor. Working out has become a release ever since Kaya died. Disappearing into the tanks for an hour of swimming keeps me from going insane. Running dulls the mental strain of fighting for every damn point. The crazy thing is that my father's been this tired for twenty years. I was born to grind. If I can just keep fighting, maybe it will be me who breaks those chains.

The altered Rabbit Room is empty. I slide off my nyxian rings and bands, thankful for a workout that won't involve someone swinging a weapon at me. A few taps on the corner of the big screen has the tread floor grinding to life. I input distances, elevations, and speeds. I hate running in silence, so I plug in my player and run to the rhythm of old beats. Which is why I almost don't hear them.

In the seconds between songs I catch the faintest breath of the blast door. My eyes flicker to the corner of the screen. I'm almost at the end of my ninth kilometer. Each breath comes unevenly. My calves are burning and the front of my shirt is soaked with sweat. I want to collapse. Instead, I straighten my shoulders and punch the power button. The tread floor carries me halfway to the intruders before stopping. I should have known they would come after everything I overheard.

Roathy and Isadora flank the entryway. The intent of their visit is clear: Isadora's shaped her nyxia into a fine-tipped spear. Roathy waves at me with one of his short swords. Neither weapon looks blunted. I glance to the corners and find the cameras there. Red dots in black bulbs.

It's tempting to signal for help, but I stand there and wait instead.

"'Lo, Emmett."

"Finishing Karpinski's work?" I ask.

The two lovers exchange wicked smiles. I expect Roathy to speak, but it's quiet Isadora who answers the question. The girl who saves most of her words for Roathy, and almost always in whispers. Since his injury they've been together, but I never pegged her as the leader.

"Karpinski? He's nothing." Her voice is cold and casual. "We tell him to go and he goes. Stay and he stays. He's a dog. A good dog sometimes, a bad dog sometimes. But only a dog."

Her words tie knots in my stomach. She doesn't sound like a kid. I've seen myself transform under Babel's bright lights. Eyes turned in, I must have missed how the others have changed. Where have calluses formed? What has Babel killed in them? What's grown up in those dead spaces? Isadora twists her spear casually, eyes dark and unblinking above her mask.

"You told him to kill me?" I ask quietly.

My hands are trembling. They notice, and they mistake it for fear. This isn't fear; it is anger. Something dark stirs in the empty air. I am a waiting pit, the beginnings of blackest night.

Isadora flashes a look of mocking sympathy. "You were in our way. That's really what it comes down to now. We can't risk you taking Roathy's spot. Not when we're so close."

Roathy holds up my gym bag. With a smile, he tosses it into the hallway and seals the door. All my nyxian rings and bands, gone just like that. They both tighten their grips on their weapons, and I know it will happen soon. He'll come first; she will follow. He'll swing low and she'll dart high. I know enough of their fighting styles to see the first few moves play out in my head. But my mind fails to form a counterattack. Without nyxia, I'm dead where I stand. Neither Isadora nor Roathy is a great fighter, but this isn't a fight. It's a slaughter.

"You can't beat us without nyxia," Roathy says.

Isadora nods encouragingly. "We know how this ends."

Before they attack, I grab the towel hanging over the mesh barrier. Slowly, I wipe the sweat from my forehead. They don't move. They just stand sentry over the door scans, waiting. Calmly, I drape the towel back over the net and lean down to tie my shoe. A flash of quick fingers pulls the little black coin from beneath my heel. I hid it there for a moment like this. I hid it there because I learned a long time ago that I couldn't trust *anyone*.

Today is not the day that I die. The thought beats like an anthem in my chest. *Not today.*

"They'll know you killed me," I say, standing. "There are cameras down here."

Isadora smiles. "We're not here to kill you."

"Just to hurt you," Roathy adds. "What do you think, Isadora? The leg?"

"A leg sounds perfect," she says. "We can give him and Bilal matching scars."

They're playing with their prey. As they speak, they begin to move. Slow, mirrored steps that bring them onto the tread floor with me. I palm the nyxian coin, waiting.

"You're making a mistake."

The power in my palm pulses, dances, hungers. It feeds on my rage and anger.

"Mistake?" Isadora laughs. "Roathy, where'd I promise I would take you?"

"To Eden."

"And what will we do there?" she asks.

"Start a new life."

"I always keep my promises, don't I?"

"Always."

Their circle tightens like a noose. Knowing I'm caught, Isadora lunges. The point of her spear darts at my neck. I roll that shoulder away, but the blow never reaches me. Half a meter from my face, it catches. I watch the metal point wedge into thin air. The shaft reverberates and flexes from the blow. Isadora's eyes widen just before a pulse of black air engulfs me. It is the darkest night. It hovers blackly and asks a question of me.

My body answers yes. The empty air snaps, and the lights blink back into my vision. Isadora and Roathy are still there, but now they exchange a nervous glance. My feet retreat on their own. I look down at the coin in my hand, but it's not there.

And that's when I feel it. In the air that I'm breathing and the thoughts that I'm thinking and the movement of every muscle, all charged with dark energy. I am in some distant corner, an observer. From that distance, I watch Roathy slash at me. His blows are turned aside. They panic. He and Isadora strike together; I do not flinch. I do not do anything at all.

Until my hand moves. Black flickers from the shield and completely surrounds Roathy. His screams are muted, but Isadora's cut through the silence of the room like a siren. When my hand falls, the nyxia reforms around me. Roathy looks like a broken doll at my feet. His nyxia is gone, consumed by my own. I am turned by an ungentle hand. Isadora's smart enough to transform her spear into a shield. Before I strike again, she stumbles to her right, one hand pressed to a cramp in her stomach, the other held out protectively over Roathy.

An angry part of me wants to end this here and now. With this power, I could break both her shield and her bones. The nyxia ignores this. It notices an open path to the door and pulls me toward it like I'm a marionette. Isadora weeps as the door scans open. I do not look back.

DAY 20, 7:21 P.M.

Aboard the Tower Space Station

Vandemeer finds me. The door to my room scans open. He glances in cautiously. His eyes note the nyxian rings I've removed from my gym bag and placed safely on the dresser. After what happened, I'm afraid to touch them. As he enters the room, Defoe fills the entryway like a shadow.

"Emmett," Vandemeer says quietly. "Are you all right?"

"Bad question."

He nods. "You're right. Bad question. We saw the vids."

"They came for me," I say. "They wanted to hurt me."

Vandemeer sits at the edge of the bed. "We know. We saw."

"Roathy?"

"He's alive. Recovering."

Relief floods through me. Two fears took over as I waited. First: I am at the mercy of a dark power I don't understand. Second: I am leaving a trail of destruction behind as I make my way to Eden. First Kaya and now Roathy. Vandemeer's words remove one of those fears. I point to the six nyxian rings on my dresser.

"It manipulated *me.*" I throw a dark glare at Defoe. "You have no idea what this stuff is, do you? You're treating it like a Lego set, but you don't have a clue."

When I got back to my room, it wasn't hard to figure out what had happened. The nyxia saved me. It wasn't just an extension of my desires. It took control. It acted like a living, breathing being. The most frightening part is that this living, breathing being felt a lot bigger than I am.

I've felt helpless before. In school and at home, I've felt what it's like to be powerless, and I can tell the difference between that and this. With this, the nyxia took what little I call my own and did what it wanted. I know it saved my life, but that doesn't mean I'm stupid enough to think it's a good thing. You should never give something that much control over you.

"It can be conquered," Defoe says with confidence. "We've had episodes such as yours. People have found themselves in the grip of the substance. We know the risks and have tested it extensively. It was my understanding that you cared about honoring Kaya's memory and being one of the competitors chosen to go to Eden. Above all else. Is that no longer the case?"

"Stop using her like that," I snap. "She's more than that."

Defoe shrugs. "Should I fetch the paperwork for your dismissal, then?"

"No," I say quickly. I hate how quickly. "No. I don't want to go home."

"Are you certain?"

"Yes." He turns to leave, but I'm not finished. "What's their punishment?"

Defoe turns slowly, a sleek eyebrow raised. "Punishment?"

"I had points docked after what happened. I got Kaya killed. Aren't there punishments for attempted murder? You saw what they wanted to do."

His lips curve into a feral smile. "I'll fetch the sword for you. The same one I gave you for Dr. Karpinski's sentence. We'll make a grand ceremony of the trial, but only if you're willing to swing the sword."

I don't know if he's serious, but I shake my head. It's only when Vandemeer heaves a relieved sigh that I realize how long it took me to answer the question. My hesitation pleases Defoe. Whatever he wants to carve me into, I'm closer than ever.

"Rest assured, they won't try anything like this again. The situation has been explained to each of them. Neither of them will risk the consequences again. You have my word."

Defoe shades out of the room and Vandemeer and I are left alone. He deliberately switches his watch off. "You know, I almost resigned."

I glance over. "What?"

"After Kaya died. After I found out about the Adamite. I was going to quit."

"Why didn't you?"

His eyes soften. "You. I don't trust Babel anymore, but I couldn't leave you, Emmett. It will be safer if we can get you away from them. If we can get you to Eden."

For a while, we don't say anything. I lean back and close

my eyes, but Vandemeer doesn't leave the room. He sits and reads beside my bed, like he knows I don't want to be alone.

He eventually says, "I'm glad you said no."

"I'm not."

"One day, you will be." Vandemeer's voice is as quiet as a bedtime story. "You will be glad that you are not like them. You'll be glad that you showed mercy to those who did not deserve it. Watching you gives me hope. If we are to send representatives down to a new world, they should not be people without mercy. Babel chose you because you're poor. They thought you would be easy to manipulate. Twice you've proven them wrong. Twice you've set the sword aside when they've asked you to swing it. When you look back, it won't be mercy that you regret."

He leaves the room, but my body's not ready for sleep. There's too much momentum in my thoughts to slow anything else down. I'm thinking about my call home. I'm thinking about how close my brush with danger really was. I'm thinking about Babel and all their secrets. My thoughts eventually drift back to the scoreboard. The numbers get clearer and clearer every day. Unless I change something, I'll be on Babel's first ship back home. A failed castaway with pockets just big enough for the consolation prize.

It has me realizing these could be my last nights with Azima, or Bilal, or Katsu. If I don't make the final cut, when will I ever see them again? Maybe back on Earth? For some reason, it's hard to imagine our crew getting together for a ten-year reunion. If I do fail, this week will be the final pages of an unforgettable chapter of my life. But I know I'm not ready for it to end.

My feet carry me out of the room. It's night, so the lights are dim and the stars are bright and the halls are empty. I move through the quiet until I'm standing in front of her door. I knock twice and wait there awkwardly. I'm not even sure how late it is or if she's awake or . . .

The door opens.

Morning's in a black tank top and sweats. Her dark hair hangs down past her shoulders. She looks up at me like she's trying to figure out why it took me so long.

"This is a bad idea."

She nods. "The worst."

Before all the reasons not to can bully their way between us, I cross the distance and pull her into a kiss. Her arms snake around my neck and I have her off her feet. I almost miss the bed as I set her down, as gravity presses my lips against hers, as she fumbles my shirt up over my back. Our kiss breaks for the second it takes my shirt to hit the floor. There's an understanding as we crash back into each other. This might be our only time together. This might be as much of an end as it is a beginning. The weight of that truth makes every touch and every kiss more than collisions. We steal eternities from each passing second. Our hands and our lips craft memories big enough for both worlds. Eden or Earth, I know I'll carry all of this with me wherever I go.

For the first time, it doesn't matter that we don't know what happens next.

It's enough to crash into something new, something beautiful.

DAY 27, 7:33 A.M.

Aboard the Tower Space Station

Sometimes mistakes should be made. Sometimes they should be made two or three or five times. The only catch is that Morning has promises to keep, and none of them are to me.

Fifty-two competitions in the Waterway and we've won six. One victory against Morning in all that time, and it was a fluke more than anything. During Morning's three absences, we managed a 5–1 record. If only there were more of those ahead. With just four days remaining, she will captain Genesis 12 for each of their remaining Waterway competitions. Vandemeer and I take a final look at the scoreboards, running scenarios. Today is the final dueling day. Other than that, there are eight more Waterway battles or races. Just nine events. Twenty-seven thousand points up for grabs.

1.	MORNING	1,286,200	points
2.	LONGWEI	755,900	points
3.	HOLLY	737,700	points
4.	OMAR	735,000	points

5.	*PARVIN*	711,200	points
6.	*KATSU*	703,450	points
7.	*ANTON*	681,290	points
8.	*NOOR*	662,050	points
9.	*ALEX*	634,200	points
10.	*AZIMA*	610,750	points
11.	*JAIME*	571,200	points
12.	**BILAL**	553,300	points
13.	**EMMETT**	551,350	points
14.	**ROATHY**	543,325	points
15.	*IDA*	540,400	points
16.	**LOCHE**	533,500	points
17.	*JASMINE*	511,050	points
18.	**BRETT**	495,000	points
19.	*ISADORA*	472,960	points

Five bold names and only one spot remains. Vandemeer looks over the numbers again. For the first time since I've known him, he is unshaved. He looks rail thin too.

"Four things need to happen."

"That's four things too many," I reply. He doesn't laugh. His face is hooded and pale. Neither of us sleeps well these days. "All right, what are they?"

"First, you have to beat Anton today."

"Done," I say. Twice I've beaten him, though he's nearly nicked an artery both times.

"Second, Longwei has to beat Loche."

I take a deep breath and nod. "He will. He won't lose three times. Not to Loche."

I wish I believed that. Vandemeer says nothing because

he's thinking the same thing as me. Longwei's fights have
been awful. He's been outmatched time and time again.
He's barely hanging on to his captaincy at this point. A lot
of our crew is heading the same direction.

Desperate and lost and helpless.

"What's the third thing?" I ask.

Vandemeer's eyes are tight. "You have to win in the
Waterway. Just once."

We both stare out the porthole window. Eden stands
bright against the dark of space. We know the odds of winning. We know it isn't likely, because we know Morning
doesn't lose.

"What am I supposed to do?"

Vandemeer tries to look confident. "Something amazing."

"Just one time," I say. "All right. And the fourth thing?"

"It's not something you can do."

I glance over. "What is it?"

"Bilal."

He doesn't need to say any more. Bilal's final match will
be against Holly. My friend's only won one duel so far, and
trying to compete hasn't allowed his leg to heal properly.
Holly's good. It's not likely that he'll win, but he's as desperate as anyone else. If he wins, I won't go to Eden. It's the
position I always hoped to avoid. Make friends in a place
like this, and eventually you have to root against them. But
Kaya taught me better. I'll be happy for Bilal if he wins. A
part of me believes that.

Vandemeer stands. "We should head down."

After Roathy and Isadora's attempt, they've been quiet.
I have no idea how Defoe threatened them, but it doesn't

matter. The numbers just don't work for Roathy to make it to Eden. He can't catch me, and he's going to get passed by Loche.

The morning challenge has us loading cargo. Nyxian blocks transported to a location at the other end of the Waterway. We start off faster than Genesis 12, but we burn out along the rapids. They pull a few clever submersions and are fully unloaded by the time we dock. Watching them win is like watching my future slip quietly through my fingers. Seven more chances.

I can't stomach a lunch, so I walk the Tower Space Station. I know what's at stake. I know what I have to do. The rest of it is out of my hands. I make a few circles around the station before heading back to the Waterway. The observation deck is empty except for Defoe. His eyes are distant, like he's looking past the course, through the station, and down to Eden. My arrival catches his attention.

"You're early," he says.

"Nowhere else to go."

His eyes flicker over to me. "We are nearing the end."

"Yeah, we are. Will you go down to Eden?"

He laughs. "I can't. As much as I'd love to, the Adamites will not allow it."

The river fills our awkward pause with quiet.

I say, "I'm not sure I'll get to go either."

"You need a win in the Waterway."

I shouldn't be surprised he knows that, but I am. "It's unlikely."

"Change the dynamic, then," he says. Footsteps echo behind us. The others are coming. "Change the dynamic.

Think like Kaya used to think. Remember her strategy in the Rabbit Room? You have to change how the game works. Morning keeps winning because she changes the dynamic first. Change it before she can and maybe you'll get your win."

I nod. "I still have to win my duel."

"Against Anton?" He flashes teeth. "Just get him riled up and let him overextend."

"Why are you telling me all of this?" I ask quietly. Shadows stretch in the hall behind us.

Defoe's lips purse. "You remind me of myself, Emmett. I came from nothing to where I am now. I worked hard for everything I have. It's also my belief that your presence on Eden will benefit our company. I've watched the other students. Morning? She's brilliant, of course. But Loche? He'll go down to Eden and treat it like a vacation. I can tell you'll work hard, Emmett. More than that, you're a loyal person. I'm not going to manipulate the results of the contest, but I can still hope to see someone like you on the surface for Babel."

He straightens as the others funnel into the room. Let the games begin.

Babel's scheduled it well. The early fights are of little consequence. Morning crushes Isadora like she's crushed everyone. She glances over my way after her fight and she's wearing the same look she's had for days. There's passion, and fear, and dark dread. There's a war happening inside her. One part wants me on Eden. The other part has promises to keep.

Ida falls to Azima's spear and Omar makes Katsu look

small again. Parvin and Jaime go tumbling into the water during their duel. In the chaotic splashing, Jaime catches her on the shoulder with his short sword. Then the first fight of consequence: Holly and Bilal.

My friend's still walking with a limp. He wears an air cast inside his boot, and he noticeably favors the leg. I can't fight the secret fear that edges into my heart as I watch them take their positions across from each other. What if he wins? What if Bilal's the one who knocks me out of the competition once and for all?

The two of them circle. Bilal knows he won't last long, so he fights aggressively, darting forward and hoping to score a lucky shot. But Holly's a great boxer. She wards off the rushes, dances around jabs, and punishes every mistake. My heart rejoices and breaks as her finishing haymaker ends him. I watch Bilal's avatar fall, and a horrible box is checked in my heart.

One out of four.

The next fight arrives, and I'm not sure either participant has calculated its significance. I consider pulling Longwei aside to make sure he knows the consequences, but he shoulders his way downstairs before I can. Not that he would have cared about my fate anyway.

Loche looks determined. His bright-blond lover, Ida, stands by the bottom docks calling for him to be brave, to win. Longwei shoots her an annoyed look. Even that amount of emotion gives me hope. The fight begins quietly. The two circle, and Loche looks for a way inside the reach of Longwei's sword. They exchange blows and circle twice more. Loche lunges under a sweeping strike, but before he can slip his arms forward, Longwei head-butts him in the face. The crack echoes over the water, and Loche stumbles, nose gushing blood and legs unsteady. Longwei takes his time after that, slashing at ribs, disarming Loche, and then putting silver right through the Aussie's heart. Loche's avatar drops and my heart soars.

Two out of four.

As Anton and I cross the bridge, I consider Defoe's advice.

Get him riled up, he said. *Let him overextend.*

The Russian is twirling his knives and humming some military marching song. I walk past him and turn so that I'm facing the observation deck. I fake a confused look.

"Wait, who am I fighting?" I ask, letting my eyes drift up to Defoe.

Defoe raises an eyebrow in return. "Anton."

"Oh," I say, looking right at Anton. "Where is he?"

Defoe doesn't answer this time. I can hear Katsu laughing as a flush creeps up Anton's neck. I crane my neck forward and squint.

"Oh, there you are! Sorry, didn't see you for a second."

My smile clinches it. I make it a dirty, I'm-better-than-you kind of smile. It doesn't make me feel good, but it has Anton pacing like someone just insulted his mother and his grandmother. Maybe his dog too.

When Defoe gives the signal, he flashes forward. And God, is he quick. I fend off the first two strikes, but he spins and leaves a gash on my upper arm. I can hear him cursing under his breath as he stabs, ducks, slices. He catches me four times in the first minute. There's not even a second to glance up at the avatars, but I know I'm losing, bleeding out.

In the end, though, Defoe is right.

Anton ducks to put his left blade between my ribs, and I absolutely crush him with a hook. Even with the protective nyxian padding, he whips with the blow. I plant a massive boot in his chest, and the gargoyle goes flying over the railing. His avatar's brain hemorrhages, and I win. He comes gargling and cursing to the surface, but his words can't touch me.

Three out of four, I think.

Just one more thing to do and I'm on Eden.

Vandemeer waits in the hallway and actually picks me up when I tell him. We walk excitedly back to our rooms, but the hardest part is still to come. That afternoon, we lose a round of capture the flag. The next morning, we lose a race that's completely underwater. My chances vanish like words on the wind. Vandemeer follows me everywhere. His encouragements sound small. Another afternoon comes, and this time Babel simulates storm currents. We get trapped by metallic tentacles so large that I don't want to see whatever creature they're supposed to prepare us for. Genesis 12 notches another victory, and Loche's score inches up to mine.

The idea that we could win a group event seems laughable.

Four, I think. Only four events remain.

One victory, I think. An impossible number.

DAY 29, 8:44 A.M.

Aboard the Tower Space Station

EMMETT	554,350	points
~~BILAL~~	~~553,300~~	~~points~~
LOCHE	545,500	points
~~ROATHY~~	~~543,325~~	~~points~~

I know what has to be done.

Morning didn't mean to help me, but her words are my answer: *As long as you're standing there and I'm standing here, you're not gonna win.* So far that's been proven right. She changes the equation; she tips the scales. It doesn't help that our team isn't a team. We are a group of going and not going, of winners and losers. As I stare down at Eden, I realize I'm the only gray in our group of black and white. Everyone else has had their fate determined. Unless Babel has some final twist, they all know where they're going.

I grab the brass key my father gave me and stuff it in a zip pocket. I skip breakfast and make my way down to the

Waterway. After boarding the ship, I do a few nyxia tests. When I'm satisfied with the distances and heights and manipulations, I sit down and wait. The others are slow to arrive, but my heart sings when I see Azima and Katsu arrive first. I wave them down.

"'Lo, Emmett," Katsu says.

"We don't have long, so I can't explain it fully, but I have a plan for today. Bilal's going to take my spot on the hip, all right?"

Katsu shrugs. "Whatever."

"Not whatever," I snap back at him. "Look, I know you've already got your spot, but I don't. I need one more win. If we lose the last four, I'm gone. No Eden."

Azima frowns, but Katsu only shrugs. He's feeling as defeated as the rest of us.

"That's how the game works," he says. "I want you to make it, but what can I do? Morning doesn't lose. They're good as gold for the last four games, Emmett. Sorry, man."

"Just promise me you'll do everything you can after it happens."

"After what happens?"

"Just promise."

"Sure, I promise."

I glance over at Azima. She leans in and kisses my cheek. "I will fight for you."

One burden off my shoulders. I heave a sigh and reach into my pocket, fish for the brass key. "If I don't get to go, will you bury this on Eden?"

Azima plucks the key out of my hands. "What is it?"

"It belongs to my family. If I don't get to go, I need someone else to take it. I'm the closest we've ever been . . ."
Azima and Katsu look at me in confusion. "Just take it."

Azima puts it in a zip pocket as the others arrive. There's
not much more I could have asked of them. Still, there's one
more person to talk to before we start. I spot Bilal at the
back of the procession. When he crosses the gangplank, I
pull him to one side.

"I need you."

His eyes are soft and sad. "I lost, Emmett. It's over."

"Friend," I plead. "My friend. I need you today. Will you
help me?"

He stares at me. For a heartbeat, I'm afraid he'll say no
and my only plan will be lost.

"One more time," he says. "And the next time you ask?
I'll say one more time again. And the next. And the next.
Forever."

I wrap my arms around him like the brother he is. I put
aside the thought that our forever might end in just a few
days. Katsu gets us started up. Genesis 12 looks relaxed
and ready as Defoe and Requin make their appearance on
the ramparts. Not even Morning glances over to note my
changed position on the ship. Fear thunders in my chest.
I'm afraid it won't work and I'll blow my one chance. But
I'm also afraid of what might happen if it does work. I'm
afraid of breaking something I don't know how to fix.

"One lap today," Defoe announces. "This is a bit of a
slower course."

Before they swipe the river to life and release us, I transform my station into the nyxian wall I saw Morning use on

the first day. It spreads like smoke between our ships and blocks us from view. With another twist, the nyxian rings melt from my fingertips and transform into one of the poles Jazzy had us using in the Rabbit Room.

I line up with the captain's chair and aim myself to the right. As Defoe gives the signal for us to begin, I get a running start. The pole wedges, then flexes, and I launch through the smoke wall. Even as Genesis 12 lurches into the river, my flight angle propels me right over Alex's head. Omar cries out a warning, but not before I've stumbled smack into Morning's captain chair. She's fast, already ducking a shoulder, but I knew she would and my arms are vise tight as I spin her into my grip, lock my arms, and shove off the chair. We stumble into Anton, bounce left, and we're airborne.

Morning screams as I tighten my grip, and we both plunge into the river. My ears flood and my neck burns with the slap of the water, but I don't let go. She wedges her elbows, claws at my suit, everything. I don't let go. After half a minute has passed, I start to laugh. Bubbles flood upward as I release her and fight for the surface. The divers are there, ready to drag us off to one side. Over the shoulder of my rescuer, I see Genesis 11 rounding the corner well ahead of Genesis 12. I've done my part. I can only hope my friends will do theirs.

When we're safely up on the ramparts, Morning shoves past me, her eyes dark and angry. She's been right this whole time. As long as she's in the equation, her team will win. All I had to do was take her out of it and roll the dice on my team pulling off the upset. I follow her back to the starting point. The ramparts give us a good angle on the final half kilometer of the river. The boats haven't appeared yet and won't for a while. I stare at the empty blue as Morning paces anxiously. Her eyes keep darting from the scoreboard to the river and back.

"You act like this isn't a good thing," I say. "Like you don't want me on Eden."

Her eyes flick over to me. "I made promises. You know that."

"You can't take all of them."

She just shakes her head and stares out over the water. She keeps pacing, and I know my fears were legitimate ones. She hates losing. She hates promising something she can't deliver. Since the start, I knew my success would mean her failure. It shouldn't, but she's given herself such a high bar that anything other than perfection feels like a disaster.

If I'd pulled off my victory in the duels or on one of the days she had to sit out, losing wouldn't be a big deal. But jumping across the ship and tackling her made everything personal. Now I'm the one who's brought failure to her door.

"They're going to win," she says. "I've trained them. They'll still win. I know they will. Loche . . . he needs to win. . . ."

It hurts seeing how aware she is of the math. It means she knows how close I am. It means that she chose them over me. It shouldn't hurt, but her words gut me.

"If they lose, then I get to go to Eden."

When she turns back, her face looks torn. This was always the choice: me or them. Promises of the past or dreams of the future. I want to tell her it's going to be all right, but now I'm not sure. I have no idea what will come around that corner. I have no idea what it will mean for me or for her or for us. Already I can see the broken pieces of what could have been.

"I didn't promise you anything," she says. "I promised *them*."

She points. Her crew is the first around the corner. My heart stops beating. Genesis 11 comes around too, but they're behind. With just five hundred meters left, they're behind. I stumble toward the railing to get a better view. The ships are getting closer, bigger. Genesis 12 veers to the right. We can't see from here, but the riverbed must be littered with shallow rocks. Their speed cuts, and Genesis 11 comes flying up on their right.

We watch the ships prepare for a collision. At the last second, Katsu jerks our ship to the left. The nose of Genesis 11 nails the back of Genesis 12. Even from two hundred meters, we hear the snap of wooden planks and the scrape of metal underbellies. Genesis 12 fishtails as Genesis 11 comes shouldering past. My crew swings left to miss a jutting rock and comes gliding free. I pump both fists into the air.

"Go!" I shout. "Come on! You've got this!"

Before Genesis 12 can right their ship, my crew comes rolling across the finish line. I slide down the nearest rampart and splash into the water. I'm half shouting and half gurgling as I swim to the docks. They come down the gangplank as I pull myself up, soaking wet and screaming like a madman. Katsu pulls me into a bone-crushing hug.

"How you like that driving?" he shouts. "Captain Katsu, at your service!"

Bilal wraps his arm around us. "That jump was amazing, Emmett. Amazing."

"You can bury this yourself," Azima says, shoving the key back into my hands.

We're laughing together when Defoe and Requin descend the staircase. Genesis 12 anchors behind us. I turn just in time to see Morning's fury. She won't meet my eye as she walks through the lines of her team, as she whispers the quiet words I've just made reality. Loche knows what this means too. Ida is crying as she shouts that she won't go anywhere without him. A look from Requin silences her. I want to feel bad for them, but I'm *going* to Eden. A thousand burdens have slipped off my shoulders. My journey goes on. I'll have another chance to honor Kaya, to pay my respects, and to help my family.

A scoreboard looms behind the two Babel leaders. On it, the scores have gone official. My heart beats so fast that it can't be the same one. Maybe I have an Earth heart and an Eden heart now. Two hearts, one for each world. They both skip a beat, though, when the eliminated participants are cleared off the board. All the work they've put in, gone just like that.

1.	*MORNING*	1,301,200	points
2.	*LONGWEI*	761,900	points
3.	*HOLLY*	752,700	points
4.	*OMAR*	750,000	points
5.	*PARVIN*	723,200	points
6.	*KATSU*	709,450	points
7.	*ANTON*	693,290	points

8.	*NOOR*	674,050	points
9.	*ALEX*	649,200	points
10.	*AZIMA*	616,750	points
11.	*JAIME*	577,200	points
12.	*EMMETT*	560,350	points
13.	*IDA*	543,400	points
14.	*JASMINE*	514,050	points
15.	*ISADORA*	475,960	points

Defoe steeples his fingers. "Thus concludes our competition. There are two more scheduled days, but all possible outcomes have been decided. Loche, Roathy, Bilal, and Brett. Please head upstairs. You'll have a final goodbye, but we need a moment to speak with those that will go to Eden. Please follow your attendants out."

A hatch opens at the far end of the dock. The medics are waiting in their pristine white dress suits. I catch a glimpse of Karpinski before spotting Vandemeer. He stands off to the side, beaming a smile at me. He's gracious enough not to shout or wave while the others are escorted out, but I know he knows, and I know he's proud of me.

Bilal stops at the end of the hallway. His dark eyes are wide as he waves back, smiling. Both my hearts break as he turns the corner and vanishes. Even losing, he's better than me. If I'd been in his shoes, I would have stormed down the hall and never looked back. The hatch closes. We straighten our shoulders, and Requin smiles down at us.

"Congratulations. We know what we put you through. We know the difficulties. But now comes the hard part. Taking all of this practice and putting it to the test. Reading about the Adamites is different than standing face to face with them. Where you're going, the wolves are real, the dangers are plenty, and the task is demanding." His smile widens. "But you're as ready as we can make you, and you just became *bloody* millionaires. So celebrate tonight. Eat good food and sleep soundly in your beds. You're going to Eden."

There are cheers and shouts. Hugs of delight and relief. But pain too. Morning's trying to look excited for the rest of the crew, but I can see guilt riding her shoulders. Isadora and Ida are lost; both are crying. It's not hard to see the difference between them, though. Ida huffs her tears like the world has ended and there's nothing she can do. Isadora's tears run down her face to splash onto clenched fists. She looks ready to destroy worlds.

Morning's the first to ask, "When do we leave?"

Defoe looks up from his data pad. "Tomorrow night. Pods will release at nine p.m. It's the best atmospheric window for your descent. Requin and I will use the time between now and then to form the teams of five we intend for you to work in while you're on Eden. You'll be equipped for the descent, supplied from our cargo satellites, and in constant communication with the Tower Space Station."

"But business tomorrow," Requin chides. "Tonight, enjoy yourselves."

DAY 30, 12:37 P.M.

Aboard the Tower Space Station

It's odd to pass through hallways without scoreboards. Strange not to be focusing on the next test. There's a freedom in it that feels like summer come at last. After dinner, I went hunting for Bilal. He wasn't in his room, though, and he wasn't anywhere else I had access to on the Tower Space Station. I crawled into bed knowing I'd have only tomorrow to say goodbye to him. Eden looked majestic out the porthole, but in the dark moments before sleep, it was a poor trade for my friend.

Vandemeer doesn't wake me up. No alarms go off. No lights click on reminding me it's morning. I sleep two hundred days, two hundred nights. I sleep to take back all that I lost aboard *Genesis 11,* and all I still have to lose. I sleep, and dream of victory, of falling like iron rain to a planet of fog-thick valleys. In each dream I'm given gifts no one can take from me.

When I wake up, it's to Vandemeer rummaging in a

corner. Seeing me, he apologizes, but when he tells me it's almost an hour past noon, I flip the apology right back.

"It's all right, Emmett. You slept about as long as I expected you to sleep. It happens in situations like this. There was a part of your mind that never slept on *Genesis 11*. An instinct that couldn't stop thinking and planning. That's gone now, so you slept fully. Don't apologize for that."

"I have to say goodbye to Bilal."

Vandemeer nods. "Of course. He's not in his room, but he has to be somewhere on the station. We'll find him after you eat breakfast. Or brunch . . . lunch? I don't know."

He's got something behind his back. I nod at it. "What's that?"

Vandemeer grins. "I was going to save it for later, but since you've spotted it . . ."

He holds it out. A present. Wrapped in old star charts, and he even managed to find a bow somewhere. I shoot Vandemeer a smile. "You didn't have to get me anything."

"No, but I wanted to."

"What is it? Money?"

He laughs. "I hoped to give you something a bit more valuable. Go ahead, open it."

The newspaper tears and the bow falls to the floor. I pop the tabs of a cardboard box. Inside is a black cord connected to thin, sticky padding. One end looks identical to the charger I use for my player. I look up at Vandemeer for an explanation.

"You might figure it out eventually, but okay, I'll save you the trouble."

"What's it do?"

"A nyxian charger. They don't exactly have electrical sockets down on Eden." He taps the sticky end. "Attach that to any nyxian source and plug the other end into your player. I've tested it a few times to make sure, but it'll charge."

I coil the cords up and set it on the bed beside me. "It's perfect, Vandemeer. I mean it. Perfect. Now I can share my tunes with the Adamites. They'll be forever in your debt. I just wish you'd given me a warning so I could have made you something."

"That's not necessary, Emmett."

I hold up a curious finger. "Yeah, if only there was something I could give you. . . ."

I duck a hand under my pillow and fish out the picture. It took some doctoring, and Vandemeer nearly caught me working on it a few times, but I finally finished it. I couldn't part with the original that Kaya gave me, so I made him a copy. It's the selfie she took with me all those months ago. My arm is wrapped around Kaya's shoulder. Her smile is all the flowers in all the fields. The version I copied looks like an old-school holographic card. The shifting colors and space suits make us look like superheroes.

"It's not wrapped or anything," I say, offering it to him. "But it took me some time to get the colors right. I hope you like it."

His hands tremble. "Yet again, you are full of surprises."

"This way we can both take her with us. Wherever we go. This way, we'll never forget."

Vandemeer nods. He sets the picture gently aside and gives me a hug. I file it away under *T* for *Temporary*. I'll see him again. I have to believe I'll see him again. Already there have been hard goodbyes. Moms and Pops won't hear from me for a year. Vandemeer can't follow where I'm going. Neither can Bilal. It doesn't bring me to tears, but it does feel like an amputation. Babel is taking parts of me that I never knew I needed. The person who lands on Eden will be less without them.

Gifts exchanged, we head to lunch. Vandemeer carefully fills my plate up with foods that are less likely to be thrown up during the descent. The decision makes me curious.

"We've been moving just as fast through space all this time, though, right?"

He nods. "Yes, and Babel's used nyxia to seal their launch pods too. If you throw up, it won't be caused by the force of the descent. It will be caused by the emotional shock. You'll be alone and on a foreign planet. That's enough to make anyone a wreck. Trust me."

After all this time, I do trust him. We sit in easy silence together. I catch glimpses of the other victors every now and again—Jaime even comes up to congratulate me—but the rest of the afternoon is a long and stretching quiet. We all know this is a solemn day.

For the first time, I let myself imagine Eden. It's full of uncharted wild. Populated by a species about which we know next to nothing. We will be the first in years to roam its plains and valleys, to navigate its rivers and cities. And when I come home, everything will be different.

It's late afternoon and my search for Bilal is just as fruitless as the night before. He either can't be found or doesn't want to be. Vandemeer shadows me as we search. The only people we run into are techies and marines making final

preparations for the launches. Frustrated, I return to my
room. There, we find a letter from Bilal.

*Babel says I will be given another chance. I'm not
sure what it will be, but perhaps I'll see you on Eden
after all. If I do not, then I will wait for you back
home. I am thankful to have such a friend. My home
is open to you.*

Bilal

"I don't think you'll see him before launching," Vandemeer says after reading it.

"Do you have any extra paper?" I ask.

Vandemeer fetches some, and I do my best to write
something back. When I'm done, Vandemeer takes the letter and promises me it will reach Bilal no matter what. I
want to search the ship again, but Defoe arrives. He sets
a knapsack next to the door and hands me a glowing blue
key. It dangles from a necklace like a dog tag.

"Your activation key," he explains. "The pods are indi-
vidualized. You'll need the key to enter the pod. Once it's
closed and prepped, you'll use the key to launch. Understood?"

I nod. "Got it."

"The pods won't launch without the key. They won't
launch with multiple people inside of them. They won't
launch until the door's properly closed. Remember that."
Defoe gestures to the bedside table. "Go ahead and remove
all of your nyxia."

It takes a second to slide off all the rings. He sweeps

them into a zip bag, only to replace them with a pair of boxing claws. The nyxian knuckles look sharp and shiny, brand-new. I can't help but pull them over my hands and flex my fingers inside the fine leather.

"Newly made," Defoe says. "Unlike the pair you've used, these are not blunted. They're sharp enough to slice through stone. Our gift to you."

He fishes through the knapsack. "And one other gift."

My name is patched onto the front of a fighter jacket. It looks like the kind of thing pilots wore way back when. On one arm, the Tower of Babel is patched above an American flag. Vandemeer helps me slide into it. A perfect fit. Defoe nods his approval.

He takes two steps forward and extends a hand. It takes me a long second, but I reach out and shake it. His grip is iron. "Congratulations, Emmett. Your contract has been fulfilled, and Babel Communications will begin providing your family with the money you've earned. Should you continue to fulfill that contract through your work on Eden, you will gain even more benefits based upon the agreement you signed with us. Your team will have quotas that can earn you these extra benefits. Continue to work as you have, and you will live out the rest of your life as a very, very rich man.

"You are departing from Station Twelve. Please arrive at your pod fifteen minutes before departure. You may bring the knapsack, the jacket, and any approved personal items you have. Consider this your official welcome into the ranks of Babel Communications." He steps back and nods to Vandemeer. "Doctor, I entrust him into your care. Good luck, gentlemen."

The minutes tick away like time bombs after that. Vandemeer doesn't say much and neither do I. When it's time, I sling the knapsack over one shoulder and walk down with him. The station looks alien somehow, like a stranger. Blue lights shine here and there, casting their glow over dark panels and sleek interfaces.

We're permitted into a section of the station I haven't seen before. An elevator takes us down four flights, dropping us off in a white-lit hall. The number twelve glows blue against a distant door. One of the Babel techies gives me a good prep about breathing and buttons, but the launch is mostly automatic. My only role, he laughs, is to not die from a heart attack on the way down. I don't laugh at the joke because I'm barely breathing as it is.

We're in a long, circular hallway. At one end, I spot Jazzy. She's outfitted like me, but alone. She waves and I wave back. On the other side, Morning waits. She paces back and forth. Every now and again she looks over at me. I'm expecting her to still be pissed off about what I pulled on the bridge, so it's a surprise when she waves me over. I glance back at Vandemeer for approval. He smiles and gives me the kind of wingman shove that would make PJ proud.

I stumble over and Morning watches, eyes dark above her nyxian mask. She glances over my shoulder at Vandemeer, then locks back onto me. I watch as she snaps the mask off.

"I've got two things to say to you." She leans so close that

it's just the two of us, in whatever world we've been making the past thirty days. She sets her hand against my chest
like she's trying to keep the walls from collapsing. "I *wanted*
you to win. After that second day, when you held my hand.
I *wanted* you down on Eden with me. You—I'm just glad it's
you, okay?"

She plays with the collar of my suit before shoving me
back a step. Her wildest grin flashes before she can slide
the mask on over it. I know there's still pain there. I know
she thinks she failed Loche and the rest of her team. I know
she'll treat that broken promise like a burden, but for now
it's enough that we're going to the same place together.

"Wait," I say. "What's the second thing?"

"I'm still mad as hell." She nods me back toward Vandemeer. "Race you to the surface?"

I nod once. Her smile's gone, but it feels like a new beginning. I take my place at Vandemeer's side and feel the
pride straightening my shoulders.

Not everything is lost or broken. There's still hope.

The techie announces that the door will open in five minutes and retreats down the hall. I unravel my headphones
and flip through songs until I find the one I listened to on
the first day. The one that annoyed Longwei to death. I'll
have to make him listen to it when we land on Eden.

I offer Vandemeer the other earbud and he takes it. He's
a little taller than me, but we stand quietly and listen to the
cuts and drops and bright voices. My stomach is rolling,
but it helps to know that when the song finishes, the door
will open. When the door opens, I go to Eden. The facts are
straightforward now.

A commotion sounds behind us. I don't look at first, but Vandemeer turns and the bud falls out of his ear. Voices are raised. Vandemeer says something I don't catch. When I turn, Karpinski is shouldering past one of the techies and down the hallway. My stomach clenches. So do my fists. His face is as hollow as ever. Why is he here? For me? Vandemeer has something pointed at him that I can't see. Karpinski holds out his hands pleadingly.

"I'm not here to hurt him," Karpinski begs. "I'm not."

Vandemeer's face darkens. "You need to leave, Karpinski."

"No," he says. "No. Emmett has to know. The others don't know."

The song reaches the bridge. One minute.

"I'm warning you," Vandemeer says angrily. "Don't come any closer."

Karpinski takes a few steps back. "Fine, but Emmett has to know. He's waiting for you. I don't know why, but he's waiting for you."

In my ear, the final chorus is playing. Trumpets boom. Thirty seconds.

"I mean it, Karpinski. You need to leave."

Karpinski goes on stubbornly. "It isn't over. There's one more chance. In the room."

He thrusts a fat finger at the glowing twelve. Behind us, the door hisses open. An identical door with an identical number waits. An antechamber. Vandemeer signals and the two techies grab Karpinski. They force him back down the hallway. My heart's beating fast as I put my player back in the knapsack.

"Be careful," Vandemeer whispers.

"I won. I get to go to Eden. No one's in there."

Vandemeer's face is veiled. "Just be careful."

A robotic voice echoes from the antechamber.

"Door closes in ten seconds."

I step inside. Behind me, there's another hiss. I dig through my knapsack as the door closes and start pulling on my nyxian knuckles. With my ungloved hand, I tuck the glowing blue key under my shirt. The nyxian jacket feels like it's waking up. Cleansing air gusts through the overhead vents. As the noise dies, the doors slide apart. Light pours into the antechamber. My body coils in expectation, but no attack comes.

My enemy waits in the dimly lit distance. Roathy looks every bit a demon. Dark is his suit; dark are his blades. He's framed by a view of space, by the promise that was taken from him. As I step forward and the second door hisses shut, he starts to laugh. With one curved blade, he points.

"I knew it'd be you," he says. "Twenty-five percent chance, but I knew it'd be you. They like to play their games with us. That's all this is. One more game to play."

"I won the game."

He grins beneath his mask. "Oh. They must have put me in here by accident, then."

They put him in here? This can't be right. Beyond Roathy looms the launch pod. It's carved into the bottom of the wall like a lodged bullet. I want to ask why they brought him here, but that's a dumb question. He knows why and I know why. He's here to finish Babel's game. One more test to pass. One last fight to win. If he's telling the truth.

I am the darkest starless corner of space.

"I know you've got the key," he says with a nod back at the pod. "They told me. Get it and we'll forget you were in the bottom four. Get it and you can go to Eden instead."

"Roathy," I warn, "we've fought more times than I can count. You never beat me. Just let me go and I won't hurt you. Isadora will be back in a year. You'll see her again."

His face pinches in disgust. "You're a lurch if you think that's how this works."

"I mean it, Roathy. It doesn't have to end this way."

"It's the only way," he spits back. "The only way, fathom? They saw to that."

I stop just five meters from him. "Who? Babel?"

"Fight or die, they said. If I let you go, the pod launches and the room vacuums. If I let you go, I get sucked out to space. This was always the plan. Always. We aren't going back."

My heart's thundering in my chest. It doesn't make any sense. The words from Bilal's letter echo. *Babel says I will be given another chance.* But why force us to kill? Why like this? I imagine Bilal in an identical room, facing Anton or Jaime or Alex. I know he'd never fight. He'd step to the side and tell the other person to go to Eden.

But what if Roathy's telling the truth? What if this was Babel's final plan?

One final fight to the death. Kill or be killed. Black hole or black hole.

"You said one out of four. The others . . ."

"Same thing. Bilal, Brett, Loche. Same thing. They might already be fighting."

"It doesn't have to end like this," I repeat. "They wouldn't vacuum the room, Roathy. That doesn't make any sense. Trust me. It's smarter to just let me go."

"You think there's anything Babel wouldn't do?" Roathy sets his feet and lifts both short swords. "I'm going to Eden. Isadora and I promised each other. You won't stop me."

I settle into my stance. My mind is reeling from the possibilities of Babel's final lie, but the rest of me moves by instinct. I know how the fight will go. I know his first swing, my first block. I know how he moves his feet and how I'll slide in response. We've danced this way too many times to forget the music. The only difference will be the blood, the dying.

I start forward, eyes fixed on his. I'm a sword slash away when I notice his eyes flicker up. There's a pulse of bright light behind us, and fire lances me from shoulder blade to hip. I drop to a knee as another pulses overhead. Roathy's blade comes slashing down, and it is a miracle that I get my off hand up in time.

His swing glances past and slits a bright red line along my right shoulder. I shove back and up and almost get my guts spilled by one of his lunges. He catches me under the armpit instead, and I nearly slip on the blood puddling at my feet. He sees it, my death, and I see it reflected in his eyes. I block, block, and slip. Before he can bring his short sword raking across my face, the nyxian jacket thrashes to life.

It is not by my command, but it saves me all the same. His blade is turned back by the forming shadow. On my knees, bleeding and coughing, I watch the substance seal me safely away from Roathy and his cannon. He shouts and swings helplessly. Every time he does, white sparks fly. The pulse cannon he created keeps firing, but my shield turns away each shot. Eventually I stagger to my feet, and the shield stretches with me.

"You coward!" Roathy shouts. "Come out and fight me."

Knowing the nyxia will hold, I slide off my gloves and calmly treat my wounds. The burn on my back is already numb. I'll need to have it cleaned or it'll fester. Neither of the cuts is deep, but that doesn't make them hurt any less. Carefully, I draw two strips from the nyxian shield. A quick manipulation makes them adhesive and I dress them over the wounds. I twist back into my gloves and crack my neck. Roathy waits.

I have to kill him.

But I can't kill him. If I kill him, Kaya's taught me nothing.

The thought has me breathing hard. If I can't kill him, then what? Do I hope that Babel was lying to him? That they wouldn't vacuum the room and waste their precious resources? My eyes flicker from Roathy to his pulse cannon. I assess the situation, take another deep breath, and set my feet. With a thought, the nyxian shield dissolves.

Before Roathy can start forward, it coils into a giant black bird. It looks like the one Katsu conjured in those first days, but bigger and darker. It flaps up in a chaos of wings, and Roathy's forced back a few steps. I use the distraction to slide left, angling my back to the pod. The cannon charges, but it doesn't fire as I put Roathy between me and it. Roathy slides forward, but this time I meet each of his swings. He's getting angrier and sloppier. I jab twice and he pulls back, changing his angle of attack. Behind him, the pulse cannon's gone silent. It's a clever manipulation. Roathy has it set to my body signature, but it can't track me with him in the way.

I keep up the jabs so that he doesn't notice my nyxian bird landing on it. The metal claws dig deep, and it strips pieces away. A metal screech pulls Roathy's attention, and I almost plant a claw right in his heart. He spins and back-pedals. I pursue. His face is transformed. The thirst for blood has vanished, replaced by desperation. He lashes out, and I crush his wrist with my right. One sword clatters to the floor. I press him before he can pick it up. Jab, jab, hook. The third shot brings blood gushing from his ribs. Behind him, my bird has the cannon crashing to the floor. Roathy presses a hand to his wound. Blood slips between each finger.

I lower my hands and he takes the bait. His sword stabs high, and I sweep it higher with my claw. A helpless noise escapes his lips as I steal in for an uppercut with my off hand. The little shield shatters his nose and sends him sprawling. Blood splashes out as he lands on his back and slides toward the entrance. The second sword clatters to the ground, and this is the moment.

Blood pulses in my neck as I stand over him. I could end it here. Be done with it forever. The nyxia aches for blood and justice and reckoning. It seems to know who Roathy is and what he's done. It wants to answer like for like. But Kaya gave me something Babel can't touch. Pops and Moms raised me to be the better man. Vandemeer praised me for showing mercy.

I will not be the executioner Babel wants me to be.

Roathy's still down and dazed. I cross the room and collect my things. Before he can crawl back to his feet, I manipulate my bird out of the air. A black square forms in its place. I pinch the corners before throwing them up and out. A thin smoke screen divides the room in two. Roathy and the entrance on one side, me and the pod on the other.

He's back on his feet now. He holds one hand over the mess of his nose and pounds the other fist against the wall I've created. Desperate, he reaches out and tries to take hold of the nyxia from me. But I've always been stronger than him in that. My manipulation holds as I concentrate on putting the final touches to it.

When I'm sure it's ready, I seal it off and stand in front of him, eye to eye.

Anger twists his features. He picks up a sword and slashes at the wall. He swings again and again, until his arms are ready to give out. There are flickers and sparks, but this is one of my best manipulations ever. Eventually Roathy sags to his knees and shouts, "Fight me! You're a coward! Fight me!"

"Coward?" I ask quietly. "I could have killed you, Roathy. You know that, don't you?"

"You're going to kill me!" he shouts. "When you leave, the room will vacuum!"

When I don't say anything, he takes his sword up again and stabs it forward. The point catches in the wall, but he keeps driving it forward with everything he has left. The wall shakes nervously, but I know it will hold. I made it strong for a reason.

"I wouldn't do that if I were you."

His arms are trembling with the effort now.

"Roathy, it's an air lock." I tap my side of the wall. "In ten seconds, I'm getting into that pod and launching down to Eden. Destroy this, and you have no protection against whatever Babel planned for you. If they were telling the truth, then this saves you. Goodbye, Roathy."

He lets the sword sag and his eyes meet mine.

"I will come for you. I will find you. I will *never* forget."

I look down at the broken boy and nod. "Don't forget any of it. Don't forget who put you in this room and why they put you here. Don't forget that I'm the one who had a chance to kill you and didn't take it. Don't forget that I let you live, when they would have let you die."

"Launch pod will release in one minute."

The robotic voice echoes. I leave Roathy screaming behind the black. He deserves better than this, but I doubt he'll be given it when Babel finds him. I cross over to the pod and dig under my shirt for the key. The blue light glows bright as I shove it inside. It clicks open and I give the handle a tug. I leave bloody streaks everywhere.

Inside is clockwork and lights. I stuff my knapsack below my seat and the hatch closes. Launch platforms line the inner rim of the ship. I can see the black of space above and below. Gunmetal gray loops in a thin circle. I lean forward against my straps and see that the other pods have deployed. Empty craters are all that is left. My breath catches.

Maybe Roathy was right. Maybe Babel really did intend to kill one of us. No matter what.

I search for Bilal in every single window. I pray and plead to whoever's listening for him to be alive. But there's only one other pod that hasn't launched. It's three over on the right, and a ghost waits inside it.

Isadora's face is a ruin. Not from one final fight, but because my pod is the only one left. She must have watched the others launch into space, one by one. This pod was her final hope that Roathy would be coming with her, and I've ruined that hope once and for all. I glance back into the room and see Roathy there, a mirror of her pain and loss and sorrow. But at least he's alive. At least my nyxian wall will save him.

"Launch sequence activated."

I thrust the key in before looking back at Isadora. The entire pod starts to shake as we lock eyes. She doesn't know what happened, but there's an accusation, a promise in her stare.

And then I'm falling. Black spins in the windows and claws at the glass. Flame lashes out, and I'm pulled chest forward through space. I say one more prayer for Bilal, and then the metal screams. I get a glimpse of Eden's dark-wine oceans before everything blurs to nothing.

ACKNOWLEDGMENTS

I still remember holding my first published book. I was in fourth grade and I had written *The Chronicles of Rascal*. Our elementary school class had the projects printed and bound. I turned the pages of a story I had imagined and made a promise to myself to never stop writing.

I'd like to thank the team at Crown Books for Young Readers for taking my childhood dream and surpassing all expectations. To Emily Easton, for having an even higher vision for this book than I did. Settling for anything less than my best writing wasn't an option for you, and I'm so thankful for that. I'm also indebted to Alison Impey and Regina Flath for the jacket design, Stephanie Moss for the interior design, and Alison Kolani for the copyediting. Phoebe Yeh, Samantha Gentry, and everyone at Crown Books for Young Readers, and Barbara Marcus, Judith Haut, John Adamo, Kim Lauber, Hannah Black and the rest of the marketing team, and Dominique Cimina and her publicity team at Random House Children's Books.

I'm really thankful for my wife, Katie. She's far kinder than I could ever be, and I'm always trying to learn from her example. Her hard work gave me the opportunity to write full-time while we were abroad. I owe that period of creativity and growth to her. More important, I get to laugh with her every night before I go to bed. What would this life be without those brief, eternal joys?

I owe a great deal to my family. Momma, thanks for reading my stories long before they made any sense. You always believed I had something worth saying. Daddio, thanks for diving into new worlds with me and asking the right questions. I owe my love of science fiction and fantasy to my brothers, Matt and Pat. Endless hours playing video games and slaying dragons finally paid off for us! So if you two are up for another run through Molten Core, I'm game. The Zaccardos deserve a hat tip here as well. Thank you for making me feel so welcome and always encouraging my dreams.

A great big thank-you to the teachers who inspired me throughout the years. I'm especially indebted to Susan Letts and Anne Dailey. Your mutual conspiring to land me in a creative writing class was such a demonstration of faith for a young writer. I've never forgotten it.

And the relationship between teachers and students works in both directions. I'm indebted to a number of *brilliant* students for reading my book in its earliest stages. The same teens who inspired me to write a character like Emmett eagerly dove into beta-reading on my behalf. Over fifteen students offered their sage advice and life experiences to help me form Emmett into a more fully realized character. If you ever need a reminder that you're capable of moving mountains, all you need to do is look at my first and final drafts. Thank you so much. I hope all of you keep writing, and reading, and thinking deeply: the world needs your brilliant stories.

To the members of the Cramp, thank you. Life is unpredictable, but on Thursdays, you're all there, waiting to talk shop about whatever project is on the table. The leaps and bounds in my writing career might look impressive to the casual observer, but it was really all of you lifting me on your shoulders and throwing me off a cliff, confident that I had learned to fly.

To Daniel, Wes, and Scott. You're a bunch of clowns, but you're my clowns. Half of what I know and who I am has shades of each of you in it. Thanks for always being there for me.

To my agent, Kristin Nelson, thanks for being such a warrior. From our very first conversation, there was no other option in your mind for this book than to be a smashing success. Such was your confidence and faith in me, and never once did that falter. Thanks for always taking up my fight.

That same gratitude should be extended to the rest of the amazing team at Nelson Literary Agency and their affiliates: Angie Hodapp, Jamie Perischetti, Kassie Evashevski, and Jenny Meyer.

Last, people always ask what I do for a living. In an effort to sound remotely normal, I tell them I'm an author, but in reality I'm a sub-creator. As such, my biggest thanks will always be to God. I look around at our world, which Gerard Manley Hopkins described as *charged* by His grandeur, and I'm stunned by the endless creativity. It's a pleasure to take all that He invented and try to make my own characters, stories, and worlds from it. There's joy in sub-creation, but always with a nod to the God who was clever enough to envision baboons:

"And you? You shall have a bubblegum butt. . . ."

GETTING TO EDEN was the first
step to the promised FORTUNE.

But SURVIVING EDEN may be
the biggest REWARD of all.

NYXIA
UNLEASHED

RISE TOGETHER
OR FALL APART.

SCOTT REINTGEN

TURN THE PAGE TO START READING!

CHAPTER 1

THE FALLEN

Emmett Atwater

Fallen angels were cast down to Earth and became demons. When Babel casts us out, it's in fire and blood and steel. As the descent begins, I hold on to one truth: I am more than what they would make of me.

It takes thirty seconds for the silence of space to give way as I break through Eden's atmosphere. It sounds like giant fists hammering the sides of the pod. Metal screams, and I start shouting every cuss word I know. The porthole windows dazzle: bright purple slashes and golden hooks against black backdrops. The patterns start to turn my stomach, so I close my eyes.

A snarl and a snap, then I get a nice gut shot as the drags deploy. Flame-resistant chutes explode overhead. My velocity cuts to nothing, but my heart rate's still spiking when the entire console flashes red. I lean forward and catch a glimpse of dark nothing before the pod drives, hammer-struck, into Eden's surface.

"Landing sequence complete."

I groan at the android voice. Grid lights flash from the console. They trace the contours of my body before winking out. My holographic avatar appears in the air. Burns on my lower back. The cut on my shoulder from Roathy's blade is a thin red slash. There are a few speckled internal stresses, but nothing with exclamation points.

"You require medical attention."

"You think? Let me out of the pod."

"Exodus Sequence confirmed."

The porthole windows are covered in mud, but that doesn't stop the walls from peeling back like the wings of a great metallic insect. Sweat-soaked, I stagger out beneath the hatches and take my first steps on a foreign planet. Turn and search, turn and search. I'm alone.

My launch pod flashes red beacon lights, but I see no answer on the dark horizon. Behind me are vague, mountain-like rises. Ahead, a strangled valley thick with trees and creeks.

I look up, blink, and look again. Two moons loom in the starless night. Their combined light creates the illusion of a bright, snowy evening. Every branch is pale-painted, every creek a whitewashed echo. I look back up. One moon is bigger and brighter, its surface marred by a series of bloody scars. The other moon is dime-to-quarter of the first. Hanging in the sky, they look like a pair of mismatched eyes set in a dark, endless face.

The moons watch me stumble to the nearest creek and plunge my hands in elbow-deep. A rippling shiver runs up my spine and sharpens the senses. My hands shake as I wash Roathy's blood from my hands. I scrub dark streaks from my suit, rinse my face, and try to forget the broken boys Babel wanted to bury in the stars.

I left Roathy alive, but what about Bilal? The others?

Shivering, I stumble back to the pod and hoist my knapsack over a shoulder. There's nothing else to do but walk, find the others. Did something go wrong with my landing? Or did Babel lie about this, too? The need to see another human face dominates every thought. I can't fathom the idea of sleeping alone on an alien planet. So I climb the nearest hill. And after that, another. My strides are light and long in Eden's lower gravity.

At the top of the next hill, I look back. My pod's beacon glows red, but there's still no sign of the others. I stare down at the strangled valley, brightened by both moons, and realize it's empty. The creek shuffles through the hills. A breeze clacks branches together like spears, but I don't see any animals. No birds fluttering between branches or fish leaping out of creeks.

Anxious, I press on to the next hill, and the next, and the next.

Finally I reach an overlook that connects to the other valleys. They honeycomb darkly out, each of them beaconless. I have no idea where the rest of the crew might have landed, or if they landed at all.

In the gloom, I look for a sign. A hole dug into a hillside or a tree snapped by a falling spacecraft. Anything. The landscape stares back, and a fear takes shape, nestling in the darkest corner of my mind: I'm alone.

Then a flicker. Bright orange against the pale moonlight. Not a pod beacon, but a fire. It's no more than a speck, but

I strain my eyes, scared to lose the sight. It flickers again, a bright flash, and then someone brandishes the torch like a flag. The movement's so human, so hopeful, that a ragged breath escapes my lungs.

I'm not alone. The others are here.

The way isn't easy, but I cut across the face of the valley, trying not to lose sight of the fire. I'm forced down a pair of steep hills and into the forest. I splash my way through ankle-deep creeks and finally plunge through the low branches.

They're waiting. Four faces washed in flame.

Morning stands apart. She's holding a crude and crooked branch tipped with fire. I don't know who she expected, but the sight of me dismisses some dark fear. There's something fierce about the way she tosses the branch back onto the pile and crosses the distance. I can barely get my hands out as she wraps me in a hug, head pressed to my chest like it belongs there.

Over her shoulder, though, I get my first good look at the others.

They look like the survivors of an apocalypse, not explorers knocking on the door of a new world. Azima's eyes are dark. She's wearing her ceremonial bracelet for the first time in months, and I understand why. Out here, anything that feels like home is a good thing. Jaime rests his head in her lap. I almost confuse it for something romantic until I see the wound. An angry red marks him from rib to gut. It's already stitched up, but that doesn't make it look any less nightmarish. His pale knuckles are painted with dried blood.

My heart breaks. For him, for whoever they made him

fight. The sight puts an end to my theory that Jaime was ever special or different. Babel's broken him just like the rest of us. My mind jumps to Bilal. Is my friend alive or dead? Was he put in Jaime's launch room? Anton sits nearby too. The little Russian's eyes look completely lost. What did Babel do to us?

Morning slides out of my grasp. She takes a deep and steadying breath, like for one second she was breathing me instead of air, before turning back to the others.

"We should get moving," she announces. "Our supply location is nearby."

"Moving?" Azima asks quietly. "Look at our boys. We need rest. We need sleep."

Morning considers that. "Does anyone feel like sleeping?"

Anton looks up. "I can't sleep. Not now."

Morning's eyes flick to me. "Can you sleep? After what happened?"

I realize she knows. She knows what Babel did, what they wanted us to do. If I close my eyes, I can still see Roathy on the other side of my barrier, begging to go down to Eden. It takes about two seconds to figure out *how* she might know.

"You?" I ask, stunned. "They made you fight?"

Her expression hardens. My question just confirms her guess. Now she knows what Babel tried to do to me, to them. "No," she says. "I didn't have to fight. It was in the captain's instructions. The computer told me to *monitor my team*. It said that some of you 'experienced additional testing.' After Anton landed . . . he told me what happened."

My laugh is harsh and short. " 'Additional testing.' That's what they called it?"

Morning nods. "I'm sorry. None of you should've ever had to go through that."

There's silence, a crackle of flame, deeper silence.

I ask, "So we just keep moving?"

Morning nods again. "The walk will tire us out. No point sitting here if we can't sleep. Babel's instructions say the supply center is by far the safest place to be. The other crews will be heading to the same center from their landing sites. I want to get us to a secure location as soon as possible. But let's get things straight: all we have is each other. Babel's up there plotting. The Adamites will have their own plans. Starting right now, we depend on each other. We fight for each other. Everyone got that?"

There are nods all around, but no one gets to their feet. Jaime pinches his eyes shut in pain. His perfect hair is slicked back with water. Azima gently rubs his shoulder like that will help. Only Anton looks up, his expression slanted and dark in spite of the firelight.

"We need to get all our shit out on the table now," he says. "I don't want grudges."

Wind slashes through the valley. Our circle grows cold with his words.

"I killed Bilal," he says.

There's only shame in his voice, but blood still pulses in my neck and through my arms and up my throat. I don't remember moving, but Morning has me by one arm. Azima's up too, holding me by the other. I'm dragging the two of them slowly forward.

Anton stares back, eyes dead stone, face colorless.

"I didn't want to kill him. He was in the room. Waiting

there. They didn't even tell me. He did, though. He said they were going to let him go to Eden if he killed me. Babel wanted us to prove ourselves, one last time." Tears streak down Anton's face, pooling along the rim of his nyxian mask. "I wanted him to at least fight me. Just fight me. I shouted at him. I pushed him. He just sat there. Refused to do it. He stepped to the side and told me to go. I didn't know what else to do. I . . . I went. The room vacuumed after. . . ."

I sink to my knees. My whole body trembles. Azima loosens her grip, but Morning holds on, and thank God she does, because I almost collapse into the flames. I want to rage. I want to hate. But Anton? The broken boy who was forced to kill my friend? He's a sword in the hands of Bilal's true killers. He's nothing. I remember Isadora's final look. The hatred that burned its way from her pod to mine. I realize she must think that I killed him.

But I didn't. And Anton didn't really kill Bilal.

It was Babel. It always comes back to Babel.

"Roathy," I say. "They tried to make me kill Roathy."

"Tried?" Morning asks.

"I used nyxia to seal him in the room and launched."

Anton's eyes snap up. "God help me. Why didn't I think of that?"

I don't have any answers. All I can do is look away. Morning's hand tightens on my shoulder. I hear Azima hiss a string of curses. Everyone looks at Jaime next. The bloody knuckles and the gut wound are their own answers to the question, but he still says the name.

"Brett. I killed Brett."

I always thought something about Jaime was wrong, that

he was Babel's favorite for some reason. I started to realize that was a lie on *Genesis 11*. The photograph of his family, the way Jaime acted toward me. I couldn't keep seeing him as wrong. Babel is just confirming that truth. He wasn't spared. No one was. The Adamites think Babel is sending a group of innocent children. They couldn't be more wrong.

Anton stands. I want to hate him, but it feels useless. How can I honor Bilal through hate? The boy who refused to kill for what he wanted. The boy who was better than us, than all of this.

"Remember him," I whisper. "Be better than they want you to be. Don't let them win."

He gives a nod as he wipes the dirt and the tears from his face. He glances over at Morning. "The other fight," he says, like he's realizing it for the first time. "Loche and Alex."

"Alex would have won," Morning says.

Anton shakes his head sadly. "You don't know that."

There's silence for a few seconds. Grief takes over Anton again. I remember how inseparable they were aboard the ship. I have no comfort to offer. Not with my best friend already confirmed dead. Anton lowers his eyes.

"It won't end there," I say. "They're going to try to kill us, too."

"They still need us," Morning replies. "But yeah, after we hit their mining quotas, I'm assuming they'll try to get rid of us. We can use that knowledge against them. For now we keep up appearances, fathom? We mine nyxia, we earn our keep, and we *always* remember who Babel really is. On *Genesis 12* my team had a saying: shoulder to shoulder."

"Shoulder to shoulder," Anton repeats.

"No gaps in the line," Morning explains. "We stand together or not at all."

The group nods their approval. I can't help asking, "You have a plan?"

"A couple. Let's get moving."

I walk over and offer a hand to Jaime. He looks at it for a second, then takes it. A bloody peace offering. A reminder that we're not that different. Azima and I take turns helping him walk. If the wound was any deeper, he'd probably be dead right now.

Morning leads us into wilderness. At first she walks up front. But a few minutes in, she falls back so that she's walking with me. She wears her hair in a dark braid over one shoulder. I can tell her mind is racing: the creased forehead, the restless hands, the clenched jaw.

She's so tough, but the weight of all of this is threatening to bury her.

We walk together, shoulders touching, like we're walking home from school on a normal day. But that's not reality. Reality is a new world. Reality is two moons hanging in the sky, bright and beckoning. Reality is what we're leaving behind as we move through an empty forest and out into a world that feels full of ghosts.

CHAPTER 2

A NEW WORLD

Emmett Atwater

As we walk, Morning slips each of us a food ration and a new gadget from Babel. She wasn't supposed to give them to us until we reached our first supply station, but she's smart enough to see that we need them. Too much time alone with our thoughts could be a bad thing right now. It helps that the scouters are a choice piece of tech.

Black nanoplastic suctions to the skin just above our nyxian language converters. The piece extends over a cheekbone and in front of one eye, ending in a tinted, transparent rectangle. I've only ever seen stuff like this in old anime shows. But there's nothing old about the scouters. A thought from my brain cycles the screen through different settings: night vision, satellite maps, even a point-and-click database for identifying random objects in the environment around us.

Our first taste of something alien comes from the surrounding forest. Azima points out that every tree has a slight lean to it. We realize it's because every single leaf is reaching out, curling in the air, grasping for the nearest moon.

"That happened to mi abuelita's houseplant," Morning says. "But with sunlight."

It gives the trees an imbalanced look, like they're being blown off course by a permanent western wind. Our surroundings have been so quiet that the first snap of branches sounds like a gunshot. Morning signals for our formation to tighten as the distant sounds draw closer. Her eyes look dark and serious above her nyxian mask. A huge section of the forest on our right fills with shadowed movement.

"Weapons out," Morning commands. "Be ready for anything."

Manipulations fracture the air. I pull my nyxian knuckles on. It takes about thirty seconds for the shaking branches to close on our location. I'm expecting something straight Jurassic, but the movement's coming from above.

We catch glimpses of flocking, winged creatures. Their swinging limbs aren't birdlike, though. They're more like feathered monkeys, sharp-clawed and strangely limber.

My scouter lands on one of them, and the word *clipper* pings into the corner of my vision. A thought will bring up a prepared description of them, but I'm a little busy staring as an entire pack swings overhead. Morning's the first to snap into motion.

"Let's keep moving."

"Are you sure they're not a threat?" Jaime asks through gritted teeth.

I glance over. Morning's eyes are unfocused. She's clearly reading the description I decided to skip. "It says they like shiny objects, but thankfully, they don't eat meat."

As one we start to move. We keep our formation tight

as the clippers swing overhead, clearly curious but keeping their distance too. I watch as Morning fishes something out of one pocket. She holds up a quarter, pinched between her thumb and forefinger.

"Should I give them my lucky coin?"

Anton smirks. "Didn't you read the sign back there? It said no feeding the ducks."

Morning waves the coin. "But I always ignore those signs."

Before I can even make fun of her for *having* a lucky coin, one of the clippers comes sweeping down. I know how quick Morning is—her reactions were godlike in our duels—but the creature's even faster. She stumbles back empty-handed as the thing bounds off with its prize. Half the pack gives chase, but the rest sticks to following us.

"Great," Anton says. "Now the other ducks are hungry."

A few of the clippers grow bolder. They swing into plain sight, baring filed teeth and beating chests and flashing bright wings. We're never in actual danger, but Azima has to hide her bracelet, and one clipper makes a swipe for Anton's watch. We're actually enjoying the distraction when one of the lead clippers lets out a hiss. The rest of the pack pauses, all dangling from branches, waiting for an order.

We've reached the edge of the forest, I realize.

An empty plain waits ahead. And as one the clippers start to vanish. We watch them move back through the forest. Their departure is so quiet I almost feel like we imagined them.

"Right," Anton whispers. "That's not scary as hell."

We all pause on the threshold. The waiting landscape

looks just like what we saw in the mining simulations. An oppressive wall of mist in every direction. Grass-knobbed hillsides rising like graves. Little creeks darting this way and that, snake-tonguing through it all.

Morning nods. "Well, we can't go over it. . . ."

Azima looks up excitedly, like she always does when she's in on a joke.

"Can't go under it!" she exclaims.

"Have to go through it," Jaime finishes.

I smack his shoulder. "You skipped a part."

He shrugs. "The last part is the only part that matters."

Anton stares at us all like idiots. "What is this? What are you talking about?"

"Going on a Bear Hunt," Morning answers. "You never read that book?"

Anton shakes his head. "We had more knives than books."

Morning rolls her eyes. "Great. We'll let the one with the knives go first."

"With pleasure," Anton replies.

He starts into the mist and we follow. The deeper we go, the more otherworldly Eden becomes. Even on the rare trip to Lake Michigan, I've never seen a place so empty of anything human. The grass crunches stiffly beneath our feet. Every now and again, ash from our heavier steps puffs out like smoke. The hills boast only a few plants, and all of them have the same skyward reach as the forest, like hands folded in prayer to the distant moons.

It looks like the moons have shifted in the sky, like they're on the verge of collision. I watch them for a while before realizing that quiet has snaked its way back through the group. I glance back and find Morning trailing the group silently.

"Hey, you want in on a little bet?" I ask. "Just to keep things interesting."

She cocks her head curiously. "What's the bet?"

"Our first alien sighting."

Anton laughs from up front. "Alien sighting? We're the aliens."

Morning notices what I notice. No one in the group has their head bowed now. Even Azima and Jaime are glancing over, wondering about the Adamites and when we'll see them and what they'll be like. It won't erase what Babel did to us, but it's a step in the right direction.

She nods at me. "I'll take that bet. But you remember I don't lose, right?"

"She really doesn't," Anton says grumpily.

I look around, trying to involve everyone. "Any takers?"

Everyone's in. Azima goes long shot, guessing it will be a full week before we see an Adamite. Anton throws his dart down on three days, and Jaime snags the hour window after his. Everyone laughs when I take the hour right before Anton's choice, squeezing the timing of his guess airtight. The Russian laughs loudest. "You're a pair of pisspots."

Morning goes last. "A day and a half from now," she says. "Early. A few hours after dawn."

The way she says the words makes them sound like prophecy. Anton reaches over and taps her scouter. "You have a captain setting, don't you? Some kind of radar for Adamites?"

"I don't cheat. I just win."

Anton shakes his head. My mind flashes back to Morning's score, nearly double what Longwei posted aboard *Genesis 11*. All we knew about their crew in the beginning was what we saw on those scoreboards. It's easy sometimes to forget that they came through space on an entirely different spaceship, manned by different astronauts, with different highs and lows. Did Morning ever get put into the med unit like me? Did Anton ever feel like an outcast? How did they become such a tight-knit family? It all has me curious.

"You didn't really win every competition," I say. "That's not possible."

Morning throws me a raised eyebrow. "I lost a handful of times in the Rabbit Room. Omar beat me twice in the pit. Oh, and one time this *punk* tackled me off a boat and into the water."

Azima glances back. "Emmett's leap! That was *amazing*."

Morning winks. "Doesn't make him less of a punk."

We keep walking. Whatever spooked the clippers hasn't made an appearance. Our maps show we're halfway across a basin that's marked by crooked creeks. I'm still not sure I could sleep, but Morning's plan is working. I'm getting tired, body-worn. If I can reach a point of complete physical exhaustion, maybe my body will turn my brain off for me.

I want to file the whole day under *N* for *Never Again*.

Anton clears his throat. "Azima, I hope you won't think me forward, but you have a great deal of distracting black marks on your . . . suit."

Azima glances back, cursing. "It's from my landing. One of the tanks busted."

Anton's mask hides his grin, but I can still hear it in his voice.

"Just let me know if you need my assistance."

She strides off to the nearest creek and turns back to throw a rude gesture at Anton before leaning down to wash the grime away. We all hear the faint, agitated moan. Before I can figure out what it is or where it's coming from, everything around Azima distorts.

The air looks like a corrupted file, a ring of broken pixels. The water splashes upward and four birds take flight. They're sleek things, no bigger than hawks, and their wings shiver black to white and back again. They were cloaking, I realize. Floating invisibly on the water.

Azima looks back, eyes wide and bright above her nyxian mask.

We all start to laugh at her, but the laughter dies when a grating shriek sounds above us. Our eyes swing up to the birds. Their formation breaks. But before they can scatter, *it* comes spiraling out of the mist. A pair of massive black wings snaps wide. A grotesquely human-looking body contorts, and the creature somehow snatches all four fleeing birds midflight. My scouter throws the name *eradakan* into the corner of my vision.

Wingbeats stir the hip-high grass. The eradakan hovers above, opening a gigantic beak and letting loose another deep-throated screech. I shiver as it looks down at us with all four of its eyes. Two set into an arrow-shaped head and two center-set in the rippling muscles of its chest. Eyes wide, the creature slams the first bird down its gullet and we hear the bones crunch.

"Let's go," Morning hisses. "Nyxia at the ready. Azima with Jaime."